J.A. KERLEY

THE
DEATH FILE

**KILLER
READS**

A division of HarperCollins*Publishers*
www.harpercollins.co.uk

Killerreads
an imprint of HarperCollins*Publishers* Ltd
1 London Bridge Street
London SE1 9GF

www.harpercollins.co.uk

This paperback edition 2017

First published in Great Britain in ebook format
by HarperCollins*Publishers* 2017

A catalogue record for this book
is available from the British Library

ISBN: 978-0-00-826376-8

To Virginia, who loved her beer and baseball...

1

Dr Leslie Meridien watched a vulture appear from the failing glow of a twilight sky to land atop a towering saguaro cactus fifty feet from her second-story window. The predator stared into her brightly lit home office, detecting the motion of Meridien's hands lifting a glass of Chardonnay and assessing their potential as prey.

After a minute the bird renewed its journey unsated, the black of the vulture consumed by the black of the sky. Meridien sat at her oaken desk dressed in a fifteen-year-old gray college sweatshirt – Harvard, her Alma Mater – and a pair of navy shorts, a workout on the exercise bike just over, her shoulder-length brown hair damp from the shower.

A psychological therapist and counselor, Meridien was transcribing notes from the day's sessions into her cloud account, currently recalling her last session with Adam Kubiac, ten days back. He'd not shown for today's scheduled session. Or last week's.

Meridien wasn't surprised. Adam had likely dealt with much in the past two weeks, given his father's sudden death. How had Adam taken the news? With sadness or glee? By weeping or partying? It could have gone either way. The father, Eli Kubiac, was a human mess, misdirected, often clueless in his relationship with his son. A self-made multimillionaire, Eli Kubiac loved being the macho, driven businessman; a man for whom traits such as compassion and sensitivity were suspect, somehow unmanly. And as was often the story in such individuals, Eli Kubiac had a dark side: he'd died on the floor in a motel in Scottsdale, nothing more in the news reports. There was probably a sad story there.

Meridien hoped Adam Kubiac found understanding. And, perhaps against all odds, maturity.

She leaned back and stared into the blank whiteness of her ceiling, a sharp contrast to the dark moods Kubiac often sank into during his private sessions, even carrying his private personal anger into group work, the reason she had removed him from group after several sessions. Adam could be charming and personable – though still emotionally closer to twelve years of age than nearing eighteen – but when his dark moods hit, or his bouts of insecurity-driven megalomania, he was hard to handle, even for Meridien.

Meridien jumped at the sound of a car door slamming. She ran to the front bedroom and looked out the window: a battered blue vehicle at the far side of her drive, the door slamming. But how? Hadn't she closed the gate at the end of the drive? She watched a rail-thin body leap from the passenger seat.

"I s-see you in the window, Dr Meridien," yelled a voice from below. "I w-want to talk!"

She blew out a breath and shook her head. Adam Kubiac. He had reverted to the stutter that plagued him when under stress. It had been worse when they started; perhaps the only true headway made.

Meridien walked down the wide stairs and crossed the open-concept great room, its walls of bright wood hung with Native American rugs and paintings, and opened the front door to see the Phoenix-centered desert valley, a 30-mile long plain holding nearly four and a half million people, tens of thousands of lights and looking like a galaxy blazing in the center of the desert.

In the foreground, centering the small porch, was Adam

Kubiac. Skinny to the point of gaunt, Kubiac was attractive in a puppyish fashion: large dark eyes, high cheekbones, full lips now framed in a pout. He looked different; the usual battered jeans and black tee now a short brown blazer over a blue work shirt and rolled-cuff black jeans over tan suede kicks. Was that skinny piece of fabric a *tie*? Meridien couldn't resolve the fashion with Kubiac: He looked like a kid trick-or-treating as a hipster.

Beside Kubiac stood a petite and gorgeous young woman dressed in a purple jumpsuit, her curling walnut-brown hair in a fluffy ponytail and her searching eyes huge behind outsize round glasses with red frames. She looked in her late teens or early twenties.

"Hello, there," Meridien said, holding out her hand.

The woman just stared, studying Meridien like cataloging a new species.

"Come inside, then," Meridien said, putting on false bonhomie. "Why don't you two have a seat? Would you like—?"

"You knew, d-didn't you?" Kubiac blurted, his voice thick with sarcasm.

"Knew what, Adam?"

"That my scumbucket male parent fuh-fucked me in his will."

"Pardon me, Adam? What are you talkin—?"

"I just c-came from the luh-lawyer's office. You were r-ratting me out all along. Telling the asswipe what I really thought about him. That's why he did it."

"Did *what*, Adam?"

"LEFT ME SHIT!"

Meridien felt her mouth drop open. "What? … How …?"

"HOW? Here's how … fucking papa dear had $20,000,000. I get $1 when I t-t-turn eighteen. ONE DOLLAR, Meridien … That's FUCKING IT! The rest goes to a bunch of foundations and charities and WORTHLESS SHIT. I put up with the bastard and his insults and his whores … IT'S M-MY MONEY!"

"Here's the truth, Adam," Meridien said, keeping her voice

3

calm. "I never spoke to your father about our sessions. Not a word. I told you about Doctor–Pati…"

"Doctor–patient p-privilege?" Kubiac sneered, his eyes pinpoints of fury. "DON'T LIE TO ME. I KNOW WHAT YOU DID!"

Meridien pointed to the door. "You have to leave, Adam. I'll be happy to talk to you, but not when you're angry."

"WE'RE DONE! I want EVERYTHING BACK!" Kubiac shrieked. "Everything I T-TOLD YOU!" He was flying out of control and making little sense; Meridien had seen it a dozen times before.

"Your records are confidential, Adam. Safe."

"I WANT MY RECORDS, B-BITCH! GO G-G-GET THEM!"

"I don't keep records here, Adam. Part of my precautions."

"I know where you store them," Kubiac grinned. "I can get them if I want." He jiggled his fingers in the air as if on a keyboard.

Meridien shook her head. "No way, Adam. The only person who can access your records is me."

Without a sound the woman crossed the room and tapped the back of Meridien's head. "They're still in here, Adam," she said. "Your records."

Meridien spun and slapped the hand away.

"Get the hell out of my house."

The woman pirouetted like a ballerina, striding to the door without a backward glance. When Kubiac followed, Meridien let out a breath. Whatever the reason for the bizarre visit, her visitors were leaving.

The pair stepped into the night. When the car screeched away, Meridien checked the gate system and saw that everything seemed normal. She must have forgotten to set the …

Wait. The gate, like the alarm system, was computer operated. Adam Kubiac was a computer genius. Meridien hurriedly chain-locked the door, set the deadbolt and paced for twenty minutes thinking about the discordant information swirling in her head.

Something was terribly wrong … or not. True, she had actually seen the will leaving Adam one dollar – the father showing it to her, telling her it was a way to force his son into line. "*To make Adam behave like an adult*," Elijah Kubiac had said. But he'd also intimated that the will was false, a dummy, a ploy for him to use only as a last resort.

My god … had that been the actual will? Had Eli Kubiac left his only child one solitary dollar? Or …

Jesus, what a quandary. Where to start?

She poured another glass of wine and returned to her office, pen in one hand, phone in the other, dialing a friend she hadn't seen in far too long.

"Leslie!" Dr Angela Bowers said. "So good to hear from you."

"I'm not calling you too late, am I, Ange? I just remembered that it's three hours later in Miami."

"You're fine. My first class tomorrow isn't until eleven so I'm binge-watching old *Seinfelds*. What's up?"

"I just had a disturbing contact with a patient. Or former patient, I guess."

"One of your brilliant young minds?"

"At the age of sixteen he devised a computer algorithm that sped up server traffic by a few nanoseconds. It seems that's a lot in the computer world. It made him a $100,000. He was about to start his first year at Caltech."

"Whoa. Not bad."

"His college career lasted two months. He quit, citing boredom. It's how we met: a week later his father all but dragged the kid to my office, the father referring to his son as *failure* and *screw-up* during the registration process. At one point he slapped the back of his kid's head."

"Jesus! The father's story?" Bowers asked.

"Wealthy, the self-made kind. Made twenty-something million selling cars."

"No way."

"He owned five dealerships in LA, one in San Diego, two in Scottsdale. He retired to Scottsdale when the son was twelve. The father was a mess, a heavy drinker who went through a series of women, kept some in a condo in Sedona, bringing others home for drugs and sex while his son was in the house, that type of thing."

"Not a candidate for father of the year."

"I actually think the man loved his son – he was, after all, of his flesh – but was horribly misguided and heavy-handed in his efforts to gain control … that's where things get murky."

"You said *was*. Is the father deceased?"

"Two weeks ago," Meridien sighed. "Something strange happened tonight, Ange. I'd like to run my thoughts by you. And do you still work with that medical ethicist?"

"John Warbley? Sure, his office is one floor down."

"Could you get his input on this ASAP? I could really use some guidance here …"

The conversation ended minutes later. Meridien typed up the notes from Kubiac's visit, summarized her conversation with Bowers and dialed her cloud account, inputting her password, surprised by the response on her screen.

Account in use. Please try later.

What did that mean? Rolling her eyes – she'd been sending her files to the account for four years without a hitch – Meridien quit the program, waited six minutes and tried again. The files went through like always. Worn from her day – the last two hours of it at least – Meridien finished her wine, undressed, and went to bed.

* * *

Teet … teet … teet …

It was 3.43 in the morning. Meridien knew because her clock was on the table beside the bed. Something had awakened her, but what?

Teet … teet …

There, a small sound from downstairs. It sounded like the timer on the stove.

Teet …

Somehow she'd set the timer … but how? The last time she'd been near the stove was yesterday morning.

Teet … teet …

Meridien pulled on her robe and followed the sound to the kitchen. She punched the timer off, confused. How had she set it?

A sound at her back. Meridien spun to see a shaven-headed man standing in the doorway, Hispanic, his neck and face coated with tattoos, his eyes as lifeless as chunks of coal. For some reason he wore clear plastic overalls and blue paper booties.

"What are you doing here?" Meridien whispered, her heart trapped in her throat.

The man produced a gleaming knife held in latex-gloved fingers.

"Earning a living, *chica*. Nothing personal."

2

The white and blue City of Phoenix PD cruiser blew south on Highway 10 at 80 mph, the flashing lights and piercing siren pushing traffic aside like a dog scattering chickens from a path, until a semi-truck moved aside to reveal an ancient gray van wobbling down the center lane at 30 mph, its roof piled high with a couch, three chairs, a kitchen table and, improbably – or perhaps exactly right – a kitchen sink, all lashed together by clothesline with various lamps and doodads crammed into the mix. The back doors of the van held a large hand-painted picture of Christ.

"JESUS!" deputy investigator Tasha Novarro screamed, cranking the wheel and sending the cruiser into a tire-screeching sideways skid, the rear of the vehicle aiming dead-center at Jesus's bearded chin until Novarro goosed the gas and yanked the wheel hard right, the cruiser's tires catching concrete as it straightened out and passed the van on the driver's side, Novarro's adrenalin-charged mind photographing the driver: Hispanic, wizened though likely in his forties, a woman beside him in the van, two infants on her lap.

The pair had looked at Novarro with surprise: *Qué estás haciendo aquí? – What are you doing here?*

Novarro exhaled a breath and stared into the rear-view. *A tough life*, she thought. Traveling with the crops. Moving north with the harvest, stoop labor, picking beans or grapes or tomatoes or perching on a flimsy ladder to pluck oranges or grapefruit from the tops of trees. Not much had changed since Steinbeck. She shook her head in sadness, sighed and blasted down the exit to Baseline Road, tacking her way south, Phoenix's South Mountain Park off her left shoulder, the craggy peaks rippling in the morning heat.

Novarro continued through several blocks of small houses with battered vehicles in the drives and angled uphill, passing a small ranch long past its prime, the split-rail fence tumbled, stalls once holding horses now storing a rusted tractor and a faded motorboat.

The road climbed a hundred feet in elevation. The address was in a dozen-home enclave sharing ten acres of north-facing mountainside abutting the park. Novarro pulled through an open wrought-iron gate set in high rock walls to see the kind of home she figured she'd buy someday, that day being the one right after she won the lottery: double-story hacienda-style with adobe walls, a tile roof, and acres of glass, a valley view from the front, the park in the rear. The front yard was landscaped with agaves and barrel cacti, bee brush and bursage, a line of white thorn acacias flanking the south side of the structure. Three City of Phoenix cruisers plus vans from forensics and county medical examiner jammed the circular drive.

A fourth vehicle caught her eye: an SUV from the Maricopa County Sheriff's Office. Novarro heard herself groan.

She passed the ornate wooden door, open, nodding at the pair of forensics techs checking the knob for latents. The room was large and sun-bright and through a side window she saw cops checking for footprints in the sand and pebbles.

"Back here, Tasha."

Novarro turned to see Agustín Sanches, a tech from the

coroner's department, enter from a room to the rear. Sanches was a friend, late thirties, moderate height, his cooking hobby displayed in a touch of pudge at his belt. His naturally black hair was tinted with just enough red that it could be noted under sunlight. He was one of the very few openly gay people in the department.

"Bad, Augie?" Novarro asked, meaning level of violence.

"Not butchery, but certainly not pleasant."

Sanches handed her paper booties and she followed him to a marble-tiled solarium off the living area where a woman's body sprawled on the floor, looking like she was running, upper leg extended, lower one bent back. She wore a threadbare sweatshirt and blue runner's shorts. The body lay in a dark pool of dried blood, and Novarro gingerly circled it until she discovered the neck cut from ear to ear. Novarro winced: she could see into the windpipe. Drawers had been pulled from cabinets and emptied on the floor, a jewelry box there as well. Flies buzzed throughout the room.

"Dr Leslie Meridien," Sanches said quietly. "Forty-four, psychologist. Unmarried. This is her home and office."

Novarro batted away a fly and continued to circle the body, leaning close while jotting in a notepad. She pulled the victim's sleeve up two inches, frowned, and made another notation.

"Blood's dry, Augie. No rigor. Got a TOD estimate?"

"I'm a tech, Tash, not my place to—"

"C'mon … give."

"She's been dead two days, give or take."

That made the death on Friday night or Saturday. "How'd she get discovered?"

"It's cleaning day and the Mexican housekeeper let herself in like always," a different voice answered. "Felicia Juarez ain't having a good Monday."

Novarro looked up to see Sergeant Merle Castle in the doorway, thirty-five, close-cropped brown hair and dark eyes with lashes so thick they could have been ads for Maybelline. Six feet and then some, with iron-pumper biceps crowding the short sleeves of the beige uniform shirt of the Maricopa County Sheriff's Office and ankle-high boots polished to a mirror gloss. Beside him was Burton Claypool, an officer with the Phoenix PD, and buddy of Castle.

"Little out of your new jurisdiction, Sergeant Castle?" Novarro said. "If I remember correctly, you left the Phoenix PD two months back."

A smile. "I was on Baseline Road when the call came through, got here five minutes before PPD. It's all Maricopa County, right?"

"That means you'll take the case and the paperwork?"

"Funny as always, Tasha." Castle clapped Claypool on his back. "Plus I wanted to say howdy to my old buddies."

"*Gracias* for the assist, Merle, but the City of Phoenix PD is here now." Novarro shifted her eyes to Claypool. "Where's Ms Juarez now, Officer?"

Burton Claypool was twenty-seven, medium height, but with a chest and shoulders that seemed to expand an inch a month. He'd started out with a normal physique eighteen months ago, but like several younger male recruits in the South Mountain Precinct, Claypool consciously or subconsciously emulated Castle: his cockiness, his Western swagger, and his physique, not cartoonish, but impressive.

"Juarez got freaked out by the body, Detective," Claypool said, standing straighter. "I got the name of one of her *niños* and he came by and got her."

Niño meant child, a youngster, generally. "How old was the kid? Novarro asked.

Claypool frowned. "I dunno. Thirty or so."

Another something Claypool had subconsciously or otherwise taken from Castle: an Anglocentric worldview. Novarro saw Sanches study the Claypool-Castle duo, roll his eyes, and return to cataloguing his findings.

"You couldn't have someone drive the poor woman home, Officer Claypool?"

"She lives in Gilbert, a half hour there and back. We're short on manpower, Detective."

She pulled out her notebook and began writing her initial thoughts.

"Want my take?" said a voice at her shoulder: Castle.

"Thanks for stopping by, Merle, but I've got it from here."

A grin. "So when everyone's gone, we're back to first names, Tash?"

A waggle-finger wave. "So long, Sergeant Castle. Have a nice day."

"Some assholes broke in and got surprised by the owner," Castle said anyway. "It's a shithole neighborhood. Put a big expensive house on the hillside and every low-life that drives by starts salivating at what's inside: TVs, computers, jewelry, cash."

"It's a mixed neighborhood, Sergeant. Rich, poor, everything in between."

Castle nodded toward the body. "If that lady lived in Scottsdale she'd be alive right now."

"You were here first … what was the entry point?"

"No break-in that anyone found yet. A door got left unlocked. People get careless."

Novarro crossed the room. She'd seen a sign out front advising of a security system, which meant a control panel. Novarro found it in the closet nearest the door. The green power supply light was on.

"Was the system armed when you arrived, Sergeant?"

"Turned off by Sanchez. She has a card key."

"What else appears missing?"

"There's an empty space on the vic's desk where a computer was. Desk drawers open, emptied."

Novarro pointed across the room. "Yet right there sits a Sony

Bravia … what? Fifty-inch flat-screen TV? About a grand, right?"

Castle shrugged. "The perp or perps killed the vic and started bagging up shit, but got spooked by something. A cop siren maybe, heading to some other problem in your, uh …" a hint of grin, "*mixed* neighborhood."

"Must have been a real scare, Sergeant Castle," Novarro said, leaning against the wall and giving Castle an indulgent look. "The doc's wearing a Movado watch, five-six hundred bills or so. Would have taken two seconds to pop off and pocket."

Castle jammed his hands into his pant pockets and scanned the ceiling for several seconds. "OK, so fuck my idea. What's yours, Three-Point?"

The name froze Novarro, but only for a split second. She studied the body on the floor before walking to the sliding glass door and tugging with a gloved finger. "There's an old Tohono O'odham Indian saying, Merle," she said. "'*O'nota'y'tanga olemano.*'"

Castle rolled his eyes. "Meaning?"

Novarro stared at a black vulture circling against a blue sky. Somehow the bastards always knew.

"I'll get there when I get there."

3

The nameplate on my door said, *Carson Ryder, Investigative Consultant, Senior Status.* The title was an invention of my boss at the Florida Center for Law Enforcement. Being a "consultant" got me out of the stultifying barrage of administrative meetings and other make-work tasks associated with any bureaucracy, even one headed by the bureaucrat-averse Roy McDermott. "Senior status" pretty much allowed me to do whatever I wished, as long as the end result was a better, safer Florida.

On my first day, Roy had said, "I don't really care what my people do, Carson. All I ask is that it stay within legal bounds and lets me stamp 'Case Closed' on a shitload of files."

So far, I hadn't let him down.

Outside my twenty-third story window lay the jagged and glittering skyline of Miami, the gemlike turquoise blue of Biscayne Bay in the distance. I was unable to appreciate the beauty, sitting at my desk and filling out reports, grumbling that for all my status bought me, I still had to do paperwork just like a beat cop in Mobile, Alabama, which is how I started.

My phone rang – mobile, not landline – telling me I probably knew the caller, which I did: Vince Delmara, a top homicide detective with the Miami-Dade County PD. We had been friends since my first case for the FCLE, almost three years ago. Vince was old-school, the best aspects at least, believing that experience, hunches, and shoe leather were what solved cases.

And sometimes just plain dumb luck.

"Question, Carson …" Vince said, jumping right in. "You still seeing that shrink in Miami Beach … Dr Angela Bowers?"

I threw my pencil to the desk and leaned back. "What you talking about, Vince?"

"You see a lot of crazy bullshit," Vince said sotto voce, like sharing a secret. "It's all right to visit a therapist. Anyway, I ain't gonna tell no one."

"Right now, I'm thinking I'm not the one needs a shrink, bud."

A sigh. "You're really not seeing a psychologist, are you, Carson?"

"I think I scare them. You got a point here, Vince?"

"I got a problem. You busy, or can you meet up?"

Five minutes later I slipped on a blue linen sport jacket to cover the shoulder rig, dusted eraser rubber from my blue jeans, and headed out, hoping paperwork faeries slipped in to finish my drudgery.

The offices of the Florida Center for Law Enforcement were on floors twenty-two and twenty-three of Miami's towering downtown Clark Center, the upper location for administrators and top investigators, the lower floor for mid-echelon investigators and support staff. On the way to the elevator I stuck my head into a small office being painted and prepped by a maintenance staffer: dropcloths on half the floor, a ladder, a couple cans of paint.

A painter was crouched in a corner and painting the floor molding.

"The guy who was here …?" I said.

The painter frowned. "He left. Said I was whistling out of tune."

I continued to a conference room and looked through the glass window to see fellow investigator, Lonnie Canseco, meeting with a pair of forensics accountants from the Tallahassee office. Cold: Not what I was looking for. Onward to a smaller conference room, this one with an FCLE operations manual on the round table, the empty pushed-back chair hung with a purple blazer, size 44 long.

Getting warmer.

I jogged back to the painting-in-progress office, checked for a gray canvas bag beside the desk. Not there, which meant I was warmer still. I took the back staircase to the floor below and pushed through a metal door, entering another door to the rear and smelling sweat and body heat. Angling past a partition I looked across a white-tiled expanse to see the black expanse of Harry Nautilus, pulling on his pants beside a naked white guy.

Hot. I turned to the nude guy, Larry Vincente. "How long was it, Larry?"

Vincente grinned from earlobe to earlobe. "Almost nine."

I shot a thumbs-up as Vincente shut off the shower nozzle and stepped to a rack to grab a towel. Like most pool investigators Vincente spent about a dozen hours a day working cases and the FCLE's small gym was a place to grab a quick, stress-reducing workout: a half-dozen strength machines, plus stationary bikes and treadmills. Vincente tried to get in six treadmill miles a day, but today had managed nearly nine – either a slow day or a fast run.

"Let's boogie, amigo," I said to Harry, now dressed and cramming sweaty shorts and tee into the gray gym bag. "It's time to meet Vince Delmara."

Harry splashed on a palmful of 4711 cologne, light and floral and antithetical to the wet heat of a South Florida summer. "Delmara? The Miami detective who's afraid of the sun."

I made a biting gesture. "It's the vampire in him."

"Can't wait."

*   *   *

16

Ten minutes later we were racing toward Coral Gables in my moss-green Range Rover Defender. Fully equipped for a safari, it rode hard, ate gas, had a manual transmission prone to sticking, and the AC wasn't quite up to the Miami heat, but if a case ever took me to the African veldt, I was ready.

"You say this thing belonged to a drug lord?" Harry yelled above the siren as we blew down I-95.

"Confiscated. I found it in the motor pool."

"When you gonna paint it with a roller?"

Harry was referring to my former ride back in Mobile, a battered pickup I'd repainted gray with ship paint and a roller. He knew because three years ago he was my partner at the Mobile, Alabama, PD; the man who'd convinced me to join the force when I was living on my mother's slim inheritance and wondering what to do with a psychology degree gained by interviewing every imprisoned maniac in the South.

We'd been the Harry and Carson Show for over a decade and last year a truly odd quirk of Fate had brought us together again, him on a case from Mobile, me on one in Florida. The cases converged and became one. After we'd closed it, Roy offered Harry a position with the FCLE. Harry finished out his time with the Mobile PD and had made the move just two weeks ago.

"I'm keeping the green," I said. "It's such a cheerful color."

Coral Gables is about six miles from downtown and we made the trip in five minutes. We pulled into the palm-canopied drive, seeing two MDPD cruisers plus a command vehicle, and vans from the ME's office and scene techs.

"Here we go, Cars," Harry said. "My first Miami crime scene."

We strung our IDs around our necks and entered the home, a celebration of pastels: yellows, blues, corals; an uplifting color scheme and *très* Miami. Vince Delmara, whose spirits didn't appear lifted, was conversing with a scene tech on the corner, the three-inch bill of Vince's black fedora projecting past his nose, but not by much. Vince wore a cobalt suit and white shirt, his only concession to color a lavender silk tie. Harry and I went over for introductions.

They shook hands as Vince's major-league beak probed the air around Harry. "Jeee-sus, something smells great."

"I shaved and showered before we left HQ," Harry said.

"You set a high bar," Vince said. "I try to remember to wash my hands after pissing."

Vince led us into the house, a flurry of activity, scene techs dusting for latents, vacuuming the carpet, studying doors and windows for signs of entry.

"Who's the vic?" I asked as we followed Vince to the side of the house. A young tech, Darla Brady, followed with a plastic evidence bag in her hand.

"Bowers, Angela. Psychologist. All we know."

"Cause?" I asked.

"A slashed throat. She bled out in seconds." He paused. "It looks like a single cut, Carson. Through the carotid and jugular on both sides. No hesitation."

A tingle of ice ran down my spine. We saw a lot of knife wounds, most ragged horrors that indicated frenzied slashing. This seemed a professional-style hit: the victim held tight while a razor-sharp blade did its ghastly work. No hesitation, no qualms, nothing but a single and probably practiced move.

We entered the room and I saw a woman in her early fifties, her face a rictus of fear, a dark echo of her final moments. A lake of blood pooled beneath her lifeless body. Harry knelt beside the sprawled form.

"Like Vince said, one deep cut from ear to ear."

"Take a look at her face, Carson," Vince asked. "Look familiar?"

"Vince, she's not my shrink. Or anything else."

"You're sure you never saw her before?"

"I wish I wasn't seeing her now."

"Bring it, Brady," Vince said, waggling his fingers in the *gimme* motion. The tech jogged over with the evidence bag and I saw a

5 x 7 index card inside.

"We found this in the vic's top-right desk drawer," Vince said. "On top of everything else there. Position tell you anything?"

"She kept the card within reach. Says it's probably important."

"Show the card, Brady."

The tech held it out to me at eye level. Printed on the card in heavy black marker was my name. After it were three question marks. I held it up to Harry.

CARSON RYDER???

"Why am I not surprised?" he said.

We returned to the department to stare at a copy of the card found in Dr Bowers's desk drawer. I'd tacked it to a bulletin board in a conference room.

"To me," I said, "a single question mark suggests a question about an unknown, like 'Who is this guy?' Multiple question marks seem to suggest a weighing process, like, 'Is he the one?' or 'Should I contact him?'"

Harry pondered the ceiling. "I'd like to hear you try that one on a witness stand, but I like it. Of course, the woman might have simply had a jones for question marks."

"We'll find out soon enough, I expect. Vince will put nails in the killer's coffin. He's an ace."

Harry frowned. "You're not going to take a case that, uh, has your name written all over it?"

"Doesn't matter what I want," I sighed. "I'm excluded."

"Peripheral involvement," Harry said, seeing the problem: I was a facet of the case.

I nodded. "No way I could be the lead investigator on the Bowers case."

Harry stood and went to the window, studying the Miami skyline. "OK, say Vince Delmara led the investigation. If you had thoughts on the case, could you present them to Vince?"

I nodded. "It'd be nuts not to be able to drizzle ideas to Vince. I'm simply restricted from any major role."

"And you want to follow this thing. From up close?"

"A dead woman I never met had my name in her desk. I'd like to know why."

He turned from the window. "So what happens if I take the Bowers case as lead? My very first FCLE case. You could follow me around like a little doggie and drizzle all over the place."

I gave it a half-minute of consideration. "That actually makes sense. And doesn't break a single rule."

"Maybe not, Carson. But let's try it anyway."

4

Detective Tasha Novarro pulled into the lot of a three-story redbrick building in an industrial park where Phoenix abutted Tempe. Emblazoned across the top story was a chrome-bright sign proclaiming DataSĀF. Beside it was an amoeba shape with squiggly lines running horizontally through it, probably representing a cloud. Novarro had combed through Meridien's financial records, finding receipts from DataSĀF and figured Meridien, like many concerned with security or just fast and easy data storage, sent her files to a data-storage firm.

There was private security in the lobby and Novarro flashed the brass pass. "Where you headed?" the rent-a-cop asked, an older guy in a uniform the color of a toad.

"I thought I was there," Novarro said. "DataSĀF. That's how you say it, right?"

"There's three divisions: MediFile, BusiniFile and JurisFile."

"The head office."

The security guy grinned and lowered his voice. "Actually, it's all DataSĀF upstairs. It started as three divisions but they're under the same umbrella these days. I think they think it looks impressive."

Novarro scanned the open atrium, glass everywhere, five-foot-diameter concrete planters holding small trees. At the far end an immense globe made of hundreds of squiggling rays of multi-colored glass hung from the ceiling. Novarro recognized the artist's work – she had seen it at the Desert Botanical Gardens a few years back – and remembered his name as Dale Chihuly. She figured it was an expensive piece of glassware.

"Helluva big building," she said. "How many people work here?"

"About thirty."

Novarro raised an eyebrow. "Must have a lot of empty offices."

The security guy grinned. "What they got are computer servers, three full floors of the things lined up like black refrigerators with blinking lights. They call it the cloud but it's made out of machines. It's spooky."

Novarro thanked the guy, picked up a visitor pass, and walked to the elevator. Phoenix PD had switched its files to the cloud – calling it "offsite storage" in official parlance – a year back. Whenever Novarro wanted a report or information she sat at her computer and *bang!* there it was. Sure beat riffling through clunky filing cabinets. *Good for you, Cloud,* she thought, momentarily wondering if it was cumulus or cirrus.

The elevator arrived and Novarro stood in the lobby of DataSĀF; hues of pinks and grays with a receptionist arena at the far end. A young woman with a severe look and hair sat within the granite-topped semicircle holding a clipboard. She wore a phone headset and was feverishly inputting data into a computer. "There's a sign-in sheet," the woman said, not looking up.

"I'm the heat," Novarro said, holding up the badge. "I need to talk to someone about accessing a client account."

The woman didn't blink. "Take a seat and I'll tell someone you're out here."

The chairs were designed to afford hipness before comfort and Novarro found sitting in one of the wobbly rail-and-canvas monstrosities was like trying to stand in a hammock. She leaned against the wall and read DataSĀF's annual report, the only reading material in the room. It seemed DataSĀF was the largest cloud-based business data storage firm in the Southwest. They were growing at an average of 16 percent a year. They stored about a zillion wiga-diga-gigabytes or something like that. Their motto was "Putting Security Above All."

Novarro fought the yawn and tossed the report back on a low table.

After ten minutes she returned to the receptionist, who seemed to have moved nothing but her fingers during that time.

"Excuse me," Novarro said. "I need to—"

"Someone will be out momentarily," the young woman said, not looking up from her keyboarding. "We're quite busy here."

Five more minutes passed. Novarro re-approached the recepti-robot. "Excuse me … could you direct me to the ladies' room?"

"Down the hall to the left," the woman said. "But it's not a *ladies'* room. It's unisex."

"Wonderful," Novarro smiled as she turned for the door, "that means I can use my penis if I want."

A perplexed receptionist staring at her back, Novarro went left, passing the bathroom and finding the hall opened into a dozen cubicles with tech types perched over keyboards. The décor was stark and soulless: gray walls, white floor, macro photos of color-enhanced computer chips on the wall, artsy in a way that could only appeal to computer geeks.

She saw several young men and women pow-wowing at a long table in a glass-walled meeting room. Standing at the end of the table was a tall and slender man wearing khakis and a pink shirt with wide red suspenders, his sockless feet tucked into what appeared to be suede loafers with running-shoe soles. He appeared in his late thirties, which made him the elder of the tribe. His head was shaved above with a short neat beard below, a contemporary look Novarro thought made men look like their hair had slipped. She pushed open the glass door and leaned into the room.

Mr Shiny-head frowned at her. "Excuse me," he said, his voice a mix of question and irritation, "but who the hell are you?"

Novarro fully entered the room, beamed, and held up the shield. "I need to talk to someone somewhere about an account with whoever."

The man blew out a breath, like Novarro had made him forget something important he was about to say.

"Talk to our-our office manager. Turn right and head down to—"

"You're important, right," Novarro interrupted.

A raised eyebrow. He still had those. "I'm Kenneth Larkin. The CEO." He said each letter like it was an individual word.

Novarro kept the smile but did a come-hither with her index finger. "Then you're just the guy to walk me back and introduce me around."

Larkin turned to the assembled intelligentsia with rolled eyes and exasperation in his voice. "Excuse me, folks. Back in a minute."

He led Novarro to an office around the corner, the nameplate reading *Candace Klebbin – Director, Administrative Services.* A woman at a desk looked up, in her early forties or thereabouts, solid but not overweight, her face handsome in a raw and Western way, with piercing violet eyes, square jaw, high and angular cheekbones. She wore a businesslike dark blue pantsuit, almost masculine in cut.

"Candace can get you started," Larkin said, spinning back toward the meeting room where Novarro figured there was currently a self-importance deficit.

"I need to look at files belonging to a late client of yours," Novarro said.

"You have an instrument?" Klebbin asked.

It was one of the few times Novarro had heard a non-legal

type refer to a court order as "instrument," meaning an instrument of the law. She pulled the writ from the inside pocket of her gray jacket. "It's right here."

Klebbin gave it a cursory glance. "The legal folks need to take a look. It's mandat—"

"Pardon my abruptness," Novarro interrupted. "I know this is an important office, and everyone's busy boxing up data or whatever, but I'm kind of in a rush and already got chilled in the lobby for a half hour."

Klebbin absorbed the information and shook her head. "Sometimes they're so busy being busy nothing gets done. Let me see if I can't speed things up." She picked up her desk phone and dialed, cupping her hand over the phone as it rang. "Arthur Lazelle." She winked. "A law degree from Loyola and I don't think he's ever set foot in a courtroo— Hello, Art? It's Candace. There's a Phoenix detective in my office with a CO allowing her to access— I know it's your workout time, Art, but ..." She listened and rolled her eyes. "Be that as it may, Arthur, the detective seems a personal friend of Kenneth's and he said to – OK, see you in a few."

"Thanks," Novarro said. "I hope that doesn't get you in trouble."

"No problem," Klebbin smiled. "I don't expect to be here much longer."

Three minutes later a wet-haired man in his early thirties bounded into the room. He wore a blue workout suit and a toothy smile. "Sorry, detective," he said, "we have a corporate gym and I like to get in some CrossFit and take a steam." The eyes scanned Novarro. "You look like you work out. Got a routine?"

"I like to run the trails at South Mountain Park. I bike some. A little tennis." Not a trendy or branded workout.

"Sounds, uh, fun," Lazelle said, suddenly disinterested. "What can I do for you?"

She handed him the writ. "We need to access the records of Dr Leslie Meridien, recently deceased via murder."

The lawyer read for several seconds. "The writ only covers—"

Novarro nodded. "Names of patients, dates of appointments. No interviews or session files can be viewed. I just need a copy of the aforementioned."

"No prob," he said. "Let's go see Chaz. He'll pull up everything you need."

Novarro's hallway pilgrimage continued around another corner, the nameplate this time saying *Charles V. Hinton, Director, Tech Services.*

"Knock, knock, buddy," the lawyer called through the door.

"Busy here," said the body hunched over the computer, a major-league monitor before him. "Come back later."

"Got a Phoenix detective with me, bud," Lazelle said.

"I don't care if you—"

"She's a friend of Art's."

Chaz Hinton spun to Novarro, the lawyer, and Klebbin, who had followed. The head atop his body seemed too large for the narrow shoulders, the round pink face looking about thirteen, though Novarro thought he might have gone twenty-five. His skin was the color of lard, like he'd been in the sun once in his life and found it distressing. He was wearing an Armani suit with purple sandals.

The lawyer handed Hinton the writ.

"Mostly I need Dr Meridien's appointment lists," Novarro said. "Calendars, dates, times, addresses, that kind of thing."

"I can read," Hinton said.

He spun in his chair and began ticking on the keyboard. Novarro, Klebbin, and the attorney stepped back. The lawyer turned to Novarro for a bite of schmooze pie. "So you're a friend of Kenneth's?" The attorney flashed teeth so pearly white they had to be caps.

"Come on, dammit," Hinton said, keyboarding away in the

background.

Novarro smiled slyly at the attorney. "Ken and I go back a ways." *About ten minutes.*

"Come on," Hinton repeated, more stridently. As if pressure helped, he pounded harder on the keyboard. Novarro wondered if the guy was always this stressy.

"Come on," Hinton almost screamed. "WORK!"

"Chaz?" the lawyer said, walking to Hinton's side. "Is something wrong?"

Hinton balled his fists and stared at the screen. 'IT CAN'T BE," he said, a fist slamming the desk. "IT CAN'T FUCKING BE!"

The door opened and the CEO strode inside. "What the hell's going on, Chaz … I'm trying to have a meeting down the—"

"Someone got inside," Hinton whispered.

Novarro had never seen a human being turn that white that fast.

"No way," Larkin said, looking like he might tip over.

"Dr Leslie Meridien, client A-4329-09. We've stored her data for forty-seven months." He pulled close a printed page. "The client printout from last week documents 2.5 megs of data in storage. But there's nothing there."

"The backups, Chaz," Candace Klebbin suggested. "It'll be safe there, right?"

"I JUST CHECKED THE FUCKING BACKUPS, YOU IDIOT!" Hinton railed at Klebbin. "DO YOU THINK I'M STUPID?"

"Chaz …" Larkin rasped. "Talk to me."

Hinton swallowed like it hurt and turned to his boss. "A-4329-09 is gone, Kenneth … every last byte."

Larkin put his hands on the edge of the desk and leaned close to the screen, incredulous. "You've done the restore protocols?" His voice was trembling.

"There's nothing to restore. It's like the data never existed. Even the shell that held them is gone."

The CEO, lawyer, and tech director stared at the dark screen with open mouths and mute terror.

Novarro shot a glance at Klebbin.

"A good day to update my résumé," the office administrator said.

5

"Angela didn't practice any more, Detectives," Professor John Warbley said to Harry and me, his eyes sad. "She taught."

We were at the U of Miami. Warbley's office was three doors down from Angela Bowers's university digs. Harry had come to root through both Bowers's office and life, at least as her colleagues knew it. There was, unfortunately, nothing in her office bearing my name or suggesting how it had come to be in her possession. We had already talked to seven colleagues over the course of the day, ending with John Warbley. A fit and trim man in his mid-fifties with graying hair, Warbley had been out of the department all day, but entered as we were leaving.

"Medical ethics?" Harry asked.

"It's a growing field, given the choices both patients and health-care professionals face on an increasing basis; end-of-life decisions, the pros and cons of assisted suicide, informed consent and so forth. As a psychologist, Angela was particularly interested in doctor–patient confidentiality and its ramifications." He swallowed hard and turned away. "Jesus, I can't believe she's …"

"We'll be gone soon enough, Professor Warbley," Harry said, his big hand on the distraught man's shoulder. "We need to know a bit more about Dr Bowers."

"Who would do such a thing?" Warbley said plaintively. "Why?"

"That's what we're here to figure out. When did you last speak with Dr Bowers?"

"Yesterday afternoon. She took me to lunch to discuss a topic that, I take it, was a concern to a friend of Angela's."

"The topic?" Harry asked.

"My field. A question about medical ethics."

"It didn't pertain to Dr Bowers? Not personal?"

"It only affected an old friend and former college roommate, a psychologist in Arizona."

Two thousand miles away, I thought, *not pertinent.*

"Did Dr Bowers seem worried about anything, Doctor?" Harry asked. "No boyfriend or significant-other problems?"

A sad head-shake. "Nada. And I'd have been among the first to know. Angela and I were close friends."

We started to leave, but I had one more question, more for my own edification, since I'd been in tangles where ethics and justice were in conflict and had even lectured on the subject at a couple of symposia.

"What was the ethical question Dr Bowers was asked about?" I said. "In a broad sense."

"It regarded concerns about doctor–patient confidentiality, among other legalistic permutations. The whole confidentiality topic is fraught with implications; a thorny road."

"Because psychologists and psychiatrists hear the most intimate aspects of patients' lives, right?" I said. "Dreams, wishes, fantasies, desires. Even the desire to harm or kill someone."

He nodded. "For instance, what if, in the course of privileged and confidential conversations, a psychologist comes to suspect someone may – only *may* – have committed a serious crime? And that this crime may be being perpetrated on one of the psychologist's patients. There is no proof, only suspicion. To reveal suspicions of this crime to the authorities likely violates doctor–patient privilege. To make matters even more difficult, it's quite possible there may have been no criminal act whatsoever. Events are proceeding exactly as they are supposed to proceed. What is the psychologist's legal obligation? Moral obligation? What if they diverge? And who decides what is right?"

"Thorny questions, indeed," I said, wondering if Warbley was using his conversation with Bowers as the example.

"Consider that there's also money involved," Warbley said.

"And suddenly thornier," I added.

We packaged a few pieces of Bowers's life for further investigation: a calendar, appointment book and such, then interviewed several of the doctor's colleagues. We drove to Bowers's home while mulling the bottom line thus far: Dr Bowers was uniformly respected as a psychologist, an instructor, and a person, selfless in the giving of her time and intellectual prowess to various causes. "Who would harm such a person?" was the one question on every lip.

Bowers had lived in an apartment complex in Wingate, expensive and catering to professionals. The super had a bypass to the electronic locking system. We passed through the living room to her office, stepping delicately around the dried blood on the floor. Her workspace was in muted gray and green tones, indirect lighting, two plush chairs and a long wide couch which made me wonder if she didn't see the occasional patient.

While I leafed through the deceased's desk – the one my name had been in – Harry tried the files.

"Locked," he said. "See anything like keys in the desk, Cars?"

I was going through the top center drawer, the usual pens and pencils and batteries and spare change and paper clips. A small key ring was in back, several small silver keys attached. "Try these," I said, tossing them over.

"Bingo," he said, opening the first of three cabinets, pulling the drawer and looking inside. "Six years ago," he said. "Typewritten transcriptions of therapy sessions, judging by the language. Fits

31

with the time she started working at the U and gave up private practice. I guess she …"

Harry froze, his eyes staring into the cabinet.

"What's wrong?"

Wordlessly, Harry fished a simple Manila file folder from the drawer and held it up. The subject tab said "Carson Ryder." He handed it to me, and I found a dozen or so photocopied photos and clippings inside.

"She didn't just have my name on an index card," I said, flipping through clipped newspaper reports, "Bowers kept a file on me, cases that made the papers. Check this out." I held up a photo that had been in the *Mobile Press-Register* a few years before: Harry and me receiving Officers of the Year awards from the Mayor of Mobile, Alabama.

"Any idea why Bowers kept a file on a detective with the FCLE?" Harry asked.

"Absolutely none," I said.

He leaned in to scrutinize the photo. "You need a haircut," he decided. "But I look pretty damn fine."

We returned to HQ to continue adding to the file on Dr Angela Bowers, riding up in the elevator with my boss, Roy McDermott, the head of the FCLE's investigative services division and de facto agency head honcho. Roy's square body was packed into a crisp blue suit, telling me he'd just returned from Tallahassee, where he was a *force majeure* in securing funds for the agency. Roy knew the names and predilections of every politico in the state down to their favorite foods and sports teams, traveling to the state capitol during budget sessions to give impassioned speeches too convoluted to follow, all with the same bottom line: *The FCLE gets results, so keep the funding flowing, folks.*

We did, they did, and thus the department – basically a state-sized FBI – was one of the best-funded agencies in the state. We loved Roy for getting us everything we needed, and he loved us back for working our collective asses off.

"Hey, guys," Roy said, yanking off his tie and jamming it in his suit pocket, the slender end dangling out like fifteen inches of flattened, redstripe snake, "did I read the daily reports right … a murdered psychologist had Carson's name in her desk?"

"We're working on finding out why," I said, not mentioning the latest wrinkle.

Roy raised an eyebrow. "Detective *Nautilus* is working on finding out why, right?"

"Exactly," Harry said. "Carson was just along for the ride."

"If you're gonna ride at all, Carson, ride in back," Roy said, patting down the hay-bright cowlick that immediately bounded back in defiance. "And am I correct in my assessment – sent to you last month – that you're getting a big backlog of vacation time?"

I was never big on vacation unless I had someone to enjoy it with. In the past this was a girlfriend or suitable feminine companionship, but I'd taken up full-time with Vivian Morningstar, whose hospital schedule currently precluded vacation and who would not be overly happy if I ran off with even a temporary vacation companion.

"I, uh – yep, Roy. I'll vacation, uh … soon."

"Didn't you claim a heavy caseload and say you'd take some time off when Nautilus came on board?"

"I, uh may have said …"

"Is this not Nautilus standing beside you, Carson?"

"It seems so," I admitted. "But Harry's new and needs—"

Roy turned to Harry. "Can you function without Ryder, Detective Nautilus?"

Harry, blast him, gave it two beats and a grin. "Sometimes better."

Roy clapped a huge red hand on my shoulder and pulled me close, half hug, half threat. "There you go, Carson, you're covered, even more when Gershwin gets back next week. Take some time off. Recharge the batteries." He paused, thought. "Y'know, that's an order."

And then the elevator door opened and the whirlwind of Roy McDermott blew out, pulling his pocket recorder as he turned the corner to his office, bellowing, "Memo to self, make sure Ryder starts taking his freaking vacation time!"

"Damn," Harry said, staring at the corner Roy had vanished around. "He always like that?"

"Not generally," I said. "Looks like he remembered his Prozac this morning."

6

Jeffrey Cottrell's desk was shaking so hard one of the drawers rolled open. His nameplate – T. JEFFERSON COTTRELL, ESQ. – tumbled to the blue pile carpet, followed by a ceramic mug loaded with pens and pencils. Cottrell's eyes were on the closet door across the room, opened wide and mirrored on the inside so he could enjoy the reflection, his jeans down to the tops of his hand-tooled cowboy boots, a woman on the desk with her red dress hiked to her waist, ankles locked around his buttocks.

"Oh yesssss …" the woman hissed as Cottrell's hands raked her side-drooping breasts.

He shot a glance at his watch. *Shit, lost track of time.* He increased his rhythm, pushing to the finish, pinching the engorged nipples.

"Easy, Jeffrey," the woman said. "You're hurting …"

Cottrell grabbed broad hips and pulled the woman tight as his orgasm arrived in a frenzy of grunts and spasms.

"Urrrr … UHHH."

And then he was backing away on unsteady legs and reaching for his pants.

"Jesus, Jeffy," the woman said, pulling down her skirt with one hand and pushing back a stack of disheveled brass-blonde ur with the other. "You're a crazy man. But fun. Got any more of that Cuervo?"

"You gotta get gone," Cottrell said, tightening the concho belt around his Levi jeans. "I'm supposed to meet a client."

"At ten at night?"

"It's the law biz, hon." He slapped her ass. "Come on, get moving."

The woman shot him a dark glance, had a second thought, pecked his cheek with a kiss. "You gonna take me to Casa Adobo this Friday?"

"Yeah, sure. Use the back door, would you?"

A sigh and the woman slung her purse over her shoulder and was gone. Cottrell put the fallen items back on the desktop, pulled on his black sport coat and popped a breath mint, his mouth still tasting of tongue and tequila. He buttoned his pink Oxford shirt in the mirror, slipping the loosened bolo tie to his throat and finger-combing the long silver hair back over his ears. *It might start tonight*, he thought. Less than three weeks until the reading of the Kubiac will. It might not finish tonight, but it had to start soon.

Let's get this done, kid …

Cottrell sucked in his gut and threw faux punches at the mirror. *Forty-six and I still got it …* A bit of roll over the belt, but he'd been busy lately, and the fucking gym was a drag. He had to look into getting a personal trainer, some skank with a hard-body going on. Both of them could get a workout.

Cottrell heard the buzz of the bell in the entry and shot a look at his Rolex, a gift from Ramon Escheverría, a client he'd made good money from in the past, with more undoubtedly coming in the future. *El Gila …* a scary street name, but Escheverría liked Cottrell, a very good thing.

Eleven on the nose; the kid's on time at least.

Cottrell went to the door and saw Adam Kubiac, a lithe young woman at his side. His eyes expressed several seconds of visible surprise at seeing Kubiac was accompanied, and he extended a lamp-tanned hand to him. "I haven't had a chance to call you again, Adam, but I want you to know you have my deepest condolences. Anything I can do to—"

Kubiac swept by with his hands jammed deep in his pockets. "Well, uh … sure," Cottrell said. "Step back into my office and let's get comfortable."

In addition to Cottrell's desk and chair, the room held a puffy brown leather sofa against a wall and two high-backed chairs facing the desk, also brown leather. "Have a seat, folks," Cottrell said, gesturing to the chairs. The woman took a chair, sitting and crossing long and slender legs. Kubiac fell into the sofa, arms crossed over his chest. Cottrell leaned back in his swiveling chair and regarded Kubiac with warm sincerity.

"Who's your friend, Adam?" Cottrell said, smiling politely at the gorgeous young woman while trying to avoid winking.

Kubiac ignored the question, arms tightly crossed as he glared fire at Cottrell.

"I think I know what you've come to discuss, Adam. But I have to be perfectly clear that nothing's going to change."

"You wrote the fucking thing, bitch," Kubiac spat. "Hashtag: fuckAdamKubiac."

Cottrell sighed. "I basically took dictation, Adam. The will reflects your father's wishes. I probably shouldn't have showed it to you, but … Hey, I wish I could change things."

Kubiac's eyes tightened to slits. "One freakin' dollar to me. Twenty million to charities and shit? WHAT THE FUCK WAS GOING ON?"

Cottrell tried to shape his face somewhere between empathy and inspirational. "Maybe the will was your old man's way of saying you've already got all you need, Adam: It's that amazing mind of yours. You can use it to make your own—"

"YOU'RE THE KUBIAC FAMILY LAWYER, RIGHT?" Kubiac screeched. "WHAT ABOUT ME!"

"Adam …" the woman said quietly. "We talked about this."

"He's one of them," Kubiac snarled as if Cottrell wasn't there. "A Neanderthal."

"I fought for you, Adam," Cottrell said. "I told your father: 'Think what you're doing, Eli. Don't punish Adam like this.' But your father … you know how Eli could get, Adam – *like you kid* – he was adamant. I figured I could change his mind with just a little time, but, uh, the sad circumstances and …"

"I'M NOT PAYING YOU A CENT, ASSHOLE!"

"Uh, actually, that's all been taken care of, Adam."

"What … did you steal a million bucks off the top?"

"Come on, Adam," Cottrell said, adding irritation to his voice. "Don't treat me like this. I've been on your side from the start. I think you got screwed royally, unfairly … there, I said it."

Come on, you screwy little bastard. You're supposed to be so goddamn smart … put it together …

"IT DIDN'T DO A LOT OF GOOD, DID IT?"

The girl left the chair to sit beside Kubiac, her arm around his shoulders as she spoke into his ear so softly that Cottrell could catch nothing. Kubiac stood and pushed the dark mop of hair from his blazing eyes.

"I'll be outside," he snapped at the lawyer. "Talk to her from now on."

"But Adam, you were the one who called me to—"

"Talk to HER!"

Kubiac glared at the lawyer and zipped his forefinger over his lips, *Done talking.* He strode through the door and slammed it shut. Cottrell winced. Seconds later heard a tapping at his floor-to-ceiling glass window and opened the blinds. Kubiac stood outside, his middle finger aloft in Cottrell's face.

Cottrell sighed and turned away, conscious of Kubiac's eyes burning into his back. He could have closed the blinds, but the goofy kid would probably have driven his fucking car through the window. He re-sat in his desk chair and looked at the woman.

"How much has Adam told you?"

The lovely woman offered a hint of smile. "Everything. He trusts me."

Cottrell nodded. "Then you know that when Adam turns eighteen he comes into his father's legacy." His eyes lifted to the woman's eyes and held. "I hope he starts to think about it."

The woman shot a glance at Kubiac, then returned her eyes to the lawyer. "He thinks about it a lot. I'm sorry if we took up your time, Mr Cottrell. Adam really wanted to come here."

"He needed to vent. He's angry."

"Very."

"I'm sorry," Cottrell said, standing and holding out a hand. "But I didn't get your name, Miss …"

The girl offered her hand over the desk. "Zoe Isbergen," she said. They glanced toward the window as Kubiac spit against it, thick and viscous.

"And your relationship with Adam, Miss Isbergen?" Cottrell said with a lift of his eyebrow.

A wisp of smile. "Complex."

7

It was eight minutes past midnight when Tasha Novarro pulled into the Dobbins Point Overlook in South Mountain Park, its sixteen thousand-plus desert acres and jagged peaks making it the largest municipal park in the continental US. The Overlook, far above the desert floor and up a winding grade, was always crowded during park hours, but the park had been closed since seven p.m. No problem for Novarro: South Mountain was under the jurisdiction of the Phoenix Police Department, the cop at the entrance long used to Novarro's nighttime visits and waving her through the gate.

The Dobbins Point Overlook was Novarro's own little parcel of Paradise, her sole company the spectral saguaros silhouetted in the light of a gibbous moon. Behind and above her, on the peak, stood a vast array of communications antennae with red lights blinking against the liquid sky.

When Novarro was young, she'd thought the lights themselves formed the communications, a version of the heliographs she'd read about in a book borrowed from the library, the lights flashing semaphoric messages to towers miles away. Only later did she learn that the structures communicated via invisible transmission of short-wave energy called microwaves and the lights were only there to ward off aircraft.

Novarro preferred her earlier interpretation.

She shut off her engine and stepped from the cruiser, looking north across a crucible of light: Phoenix the blazing nexus, Glendale to the west, Mesa to the east, Scottsdale northeast. Headlights shimmered down the geometric maze of streets as a jet dropped from below the moon to land at Sky Harbor International Airport, five miles distant and one of the few airports located in the heart of a major metropolis.

A woman killed, Novarro thought, staring into the vortex of light. She'd spent the last three days interviewing friends, neighbors, and business associates of Leslie Meridien, PhD. A pleasant and outgoing woman, by all reports, no apparent enemies.

No one had an answer, no one understood.

"*Leslie was more than a psychologist,*" a friend had wept. "*She was a force for good.*"

The killing had been brutal but efficient. Efficient murders were not the norm, Novarro knew from seven years in uniform and eight months in Homicide. The vast majority of killings were messy affairs, anger- or turf-driven, with slashing blades or emptied bullet clips, ball bats or shotgun blasts, people killed for being in the wrong bed or on the wrong corner.

Meridien's murder was different. It was dispassionate, ice cold. And all of the victim's patient files were gone, taken in a manner that baffled high-level computer types.

Merle Castle put it in a box he knew: breaking and entering, probably committed by Hispanics. But a television and watch had been left behind … *Overlooked?* Not by anyone professional enough to kill so efficiently. It was a wrong note, hell, a wrong chord.

Novarro paced the desolate parking lot for a full hour and came to two conclusions: One, that a highly competent professional had broken into Meridien's cloud account and erased it, and – given high competence as a standard – two, a similar professionalism was likely employed in Meridien's murder and what she believed was a staged robbery.

There were fierce and desperate people in the valley who would kill for a week's worth of heroin, pulling a trigger and running. Move up a level and several thousand dollars bought a backseat strangling and a body dumped in the desert.

This was a higher level still.

Her mind reeling with questions, Novarro returned to her vehicle and descended the mountain, angling down Central Avenue and aiming for her downtown home.

Novarro had owned a house in midtown for eight months, making the down payment two days after getting her detective's shield and the raise accompanying the new badge. The neighborhood was sketchy, but only four blocks from the Roosevelt Historic District, its gentrification effects moving like a slow-motion tsunami toward Novarro's block.

It was the first home ownership in Tasha Novarro's family. She'd grown up in a double-wide trailer at the edge of the Salt River Pima-Maricopa Indian Community between Mesa and Scottsdale, her mother there mostly, her father never. Though it was Novarro, her younger brother, and mother, rarely were there just the three of them in residence; a ragged procession of relatives constantly passing through the house, sometimes for hours, sometimes months. The fragile emotional conditions at the house led Novarro's Aunt Chyla to proclaim the domicile "a boxed set of thunderstorms."

Novarro sought refuge in school, her dedication to study leading to a pre-law scholarship at Arizona State University. Her contribution would have been forty-five hundred dollars saved from working nights and weekends at a Ranch Market in northeast Phoenix, but one of her distant cousins – a handsome thirty-year-old charmer needing a place to stay following a forgery stint in prison – boogied off to points unknown after two months, taking her virginity and checkbook and emptying her account before he disappeared.

Left with only grades and ambition she went to the police academy because it was an arm of the law and was free.

And maybe, someday …

Novarro swung around the corner and onto her street, driving to midblock and pulling into her driveway. It was a small house and the windows were grated out of necessity, but she'd spent almost a thousand dollars and dozens of hours landscaping the yard, hard brown dirt and sand when she'd purchased it, beaten down by three large dogs. Now the driveway was bordered with bright flowers, a desert willow embellishing one corner of the boxy structure, a palo verde the other. The backyard held a lime tree that had somehow survived the canine onslaught. It wasn't much, but everyone said it was the prettiest house on the street.

Novarro was ten steps from her front door when she noticed a centimeter-wide band of light leaking out. Ajar. A sizzle of electricity ran down her spine and she fell into a crouch, slipping her weapon from her rear waistband and creeping to the door. She put her ear to the crack, nothing. Novarro nudged the door open with her foot and peeked past the frame, smelling the sweet scent of marijuana.

"POLICE!" she yelled. "The house is surrounded. Put your hands on your head and walk to the front."

A sound from somewhere in the rear.

"NOW!" she yelled. "OR YOU'RE DEAD!"

Seconds later a slender Native American male stepped from the hall with his hands atop a head of long black hair in a rubber-banded ponytail. He was boyishly handsome, like a man not fully formed, the face poised between pretty child and handsome adult. He wore a bead-embellished leather jacket over a white tee and blue jeans, a black concho belt around his waist, his feet in red trail runners. He stepped into the living room and pirouetted, stopping with a stumble into the wall and a broad grin aimed at

43

Novarro.

"Jesus, Tash," he said. "You're such a drama queen."

The muzzle dropped. It was Ben, her twenty-one-year-old brother. She'd given him a key months ago, regretted it a week later, but now it was his. If she asked for the key back or changed the lock, she'd be …

An Indian Giver.

Novarro blew out a breath. "I didn't see your car outside, Ben."

"A buddy dropped me off. We were out doin' a li'l partying."

Novarro heard the slur of pot and alcohol in her brother's voice and she gave him narrowed eyes. "Your car's at home, I hope?"

The last time this happened he'd forgotten where he'd parked.

"Fuckin' bank came an' got it yesterday, the bast—" He belched into his palm, "—ards." He looked up. "'S'cuse me."

Novarro had a mental picture of the repo man hooking up the 2001 Corolla and driving away. Six months back she'd lent – OK, given – Ben the price of the down payment plus two months of installments.

"You got behind on payments," she sighed.

"The insur'nce was *killing* me, Tash."

"Think your driving record has anything to do with it?"

"I, uh, gotta take a whizzer." As usual when Ben didn't like the direction of a conversation, he fled.

It was five minutes until the toilet flushed, reminding Novarro of the time the family's commode had been leaking for a week until a nine-year-old Ben removed the tank top, stared at the mechanism as he flushed several times, then, using a bent bobby pin, fixed the toilet in thirty seconds.

"How are things at your job?" Novarro asked. "They still got you on thermostats?"

"I got tired of tinkering with little shit." He winked. "So I disappeared in a puff of smoke."

Novarro felt her heart drop. "Disappeared?"

"I'm the Coyote, Tasha," Ben grinned crookedly, invoking the mythological, shape-shifting Trickster in many Native American cultures, reckless, self-involved, with a sense of humor both clownish and cruel. "I have the magic in me."

Novarro shook her head. He'd quit or been fired. Her voice pushed toward anger, but she fought it. "You have too much liquor in you," she said quietly.

"Me Indian," Ben said in a cartoon voice, a distorted smile on his face. "Me like-um firewater. It make-um me big happy."

"Don't start that crap, Ben. It's demea—"

"FYA-WATAH!" he whooped, jumping from the couch and beginning a stumbling circular dance, hand patting his mouth. "Owoo-woo-woo … Owoo-woo-woo … Owoo–woo …" He paused as if taken by a sudden thought. "Me need-um a drum track here, Tash," he slurred, moving his hands up and down like drumming. "You got-um any tom-toms?"

"I got aspirin," she said. "Coffee."

Her brother scowled at his choices. "Coyote need-um more firewater." His hand flashed beneath his jacket and found a pint bottle of red liquid; his favorite grain alcohol into which he'd poured several bags of strawberry Kool-Aid. At 190proof, it was just shy of pure ethanol. Before Novarro could cross the floor it was in his mouth.

"Give me that shit," she said, grabbing his arm. Ben spun, his hand pushing Novarro away as his lips sucked greedily at the bottle.

"I said give … me … that." Novarro wrenched the spirits from her brother's hand and held it beyond his reach as he grabbed wildly at the pint.

"ME NEED-UM FIREWATER!" he railed.

Novarro retreated across the floor. "You *need* to go to bed."

He raised an unsteady hand, fingers opening and closing. "Gimme, gimme, Tash. Need-um bad."

"No fucking way, Ben."

"*IT'S MIIIINE!*" he screamed, kicking over an end table and lamp. The action seemed to surprise him and he stared at the fallen furniture.

Novarro's eyes tightened to pinpoints. "Get out, Benjamin."

He turned to her. "Hunh?"

"There's the door," Novarro said, finger jabbing toward the entrance. "Get out of my house."

It took several beats for her words to make sense. Her brother tipped forward but caught himself with hands to knees. "You can't throw me out, Tash," he said, taking a stutter-step sideways. "Me drunk Indian."

"Go sleep in the goddamn alley, Geronimo. Or crawl into a trash can."

"Don't be mean, Tash," her brother said in a voice closer to twelve than twenty-one. He bent to retrieve the toppled lamp but momentum carried him to the floor. He tried to push himself up, but his arms buckled and his nose slammed the carpet.

"I'm all fut up," he wailed, face-down, fingers clawing at the rug like trying to get a grip on a spinning world. "I'M ALL FUT UP!"

"Shhhh, Ben," Novarro said gently, slipping her hands beneath his shoulders. "Come on, let's get you to the couch."

She wrestled her brother to the couch and got a wastebasket from the bathroom. She pulled the area rug several feet from the couch and set the wastebasket beside him as a vomit pail. He'd miss it, of course. He always did.

She sat in the chair across the room and stared at her brother, his eyes rolled back as he neared sleep. Fixing the toilet was just the start, the harbinger of an innate ability with mechanical systems that led to a job in an uncle's garage at thirteen. His skills flourished in a high school geared to technical pursuits and he'd received a scholarship in mechanical engineering at Arizona State.

He'd dropped out one semester into the program, claiming to be bored, but Novarro suspected Ben had the same problem afflicting so many lower-class kids in college: Fear that he didn't belong in that world, that he was insufficient, miscast, hearing whispers only spoken in the mind …

How did that one ever get in?

Despite entreaties from his university counselor and two professors – one who took Ben under her wing like a relative – her brother went to work for a company that installed industrial HVAC systems, actually a decent job, his natural abilities impressing higher-ups from day one. But from the moment he'd quit school, the drinking and pot smoking ramped up. He fell in with a loose crew of ambition-free young men content to hang out near the res and do odd jobs, selling loose joints to needy tourists the most profitable.

Three months later the accumulating hangovers and stink of liquor on Ben's sweat and breath ended with a pronouncement from his supervisor.

"We really like you, kid; you got an incredible gift. But you also got a problem. Get it fixed and we can …"

A succession of mechanically oriented jobs followed, diminishing in complexity, the most recent reconditioning used hot-water heaters for twelve bucks an hour, a task he claimed – usually drunkenly – that a trained chimp could learn in a day.

Novarro watched her brother until his snoring became regular and unlabored. She bent and kissed his forehead and snuggled a comforter beneath his chin. Sighing, she picked up the half-full bottle and took it to the kitchen sink and turned on the tap. When she started to tip the flask over the drain, her hand froze and she stepped back.

Something on the far side of the planet whispered *Coyote*.

Novarro retreated to the kitchen table and sat with the blood-red liquid between her and the vase of fresh flowers purchased the previous day, their soft perfume scenting the air.

"Woo-woo," she whispered. She tipped back the bottle and drank with surprising naturalness.

Fifteen minutes later she was weeping like a baby.

8

Rather than drive from Miami to Upper Matecumbe Key, I went to the Coral Gables home of Dr Vivian Morningstar. Viv was my longest-ever significant other (the term always seemed ridiculous … other *what?*), our relationship entering its second year. I'd met her in the last months of her previous employment as a pathologist with the state forensics lab, but shortly thereafter Vivian had an epiphany: She needed to work with the living. Specializing in trauma medicine, she was completing her internship at Miami-Dade General, which involved long hours at the hospital and often sleeping there.

Harry was staying at the Palace, a former hotel owned by a scumball the FCLE had busted for human trafficking. All his other confiscated properties had been sold, but Roy convinced the accountants to retain the Palace as lodging for visiting agents and consultants to stay and as a safe house for the occasional snitch wanting to stay alive.

It was just past one a.m. when my phone rang: Vince Delmara.

"What are you doing to me?" he said.

"I'm not tracking," I said, wondering if I was dreaming. "But then it's two minutes after—"

"I'm in a front yard in Coral Terrace, Carson. I'm looking at a body that has your and Nautilus's cards in his shirt pocket. They're next to a U of Miami ID. You know a Professor John Warbley?"

My phone went off less than a minute after I hung up: Harry. Called by Vince, he was on his way to Viv's to grab me up.

We arrived at a single-story ranch-style house, two jacarandas up front, a bank of azaleas to the side, plus some big overhanging tree I couldn't identify. The ME and forensics vans were in place, plus three cruisers and Vince Delmara's black unmarked. The uniforms were working crowd control, horrified neighbors looking on as emergency lights bathed the night in pulses of white and blue and red.

We pulled in behind a massive step van, one of the forensic department's mobile labs and headed into the crowd, looking for Vince.

"There he is," Harry said, pointing to the right. We jogged over and brushed aside overhanging limbs to see the face of a man we had spoken with scant hours ago. Warbley stared into the sky with lifeless eyes, one reddened with blood seeping from burst veins, the grass beneath his head glistening with scarlet.

"Any idea what happened?" Harry asked.

"The rear of his skull is bashed in," Vince said. "Something big and heavy, ball bat, hammer, rock."

I saw Harry wince; he'd been struck from behind some years ago, sparking a long hospital stay and convalescence.

"Warbley worked with Angela Bowers at the U," I said. "His specialty is medical ethics. We talked to him today."

"Jesus," Vince said. "Think there's a tie with Bowers?"

"If not, it's a strange coincidence." But we'd seen strange coincidences before. Fate sometimes likes to play with you.

"Wallet around?" Harry asked.

"Nope. I got a tan line indicating he wears a watch most of the time. It's not there. No phone, either, if he was carrying one."

Classic robbery signs. And like a lot of cops I knew there was a statistical probability that hours after interviewing Warbley, he would fall victim to an unrelated attack. But the hollow in my gut told me my belly wasn't believing those odds, not just yet.

"Who found him?" Harry asked.

"Penn and Ortega," Vince said, nodding toward one of the MDPD cruisers. "Standard patrol, Penn driving, Ortega flashing the spotlight over the houses, yards. Then they see the bottom of shoes." Vince checked his watch. "That was at 11.56."

"And this is his home?"

"No," Vince said, nodding down the street. "He's four doors down."

We looked across the yards and saw a similar house, but lacking the heavy growth.

"Opportunistic," I said. "It's a perfect ambush point."

"No call, no reports of anyone in the area?" Harry asked Vince. "Creepers, peepers, people out of place?"

"Not that I've heard so far."

Harry got to his hands and knees and leaned his nose over Warbley's open mouth, sniffing delicately, his bulldozer-blade mustache almost brushing the victim's lips. "Scotch," Harry said, standing and dusting his hands. "And he's wearing a pair of Rockport walkers."

I caught the glint of an object on Warbley's belt and leaned down to inspect it. "A pedometer," I said. "Combine that with the walking kicks and whisky breath …"

"There's a neighborhood-type bar about four blocks over," Vince said. "The Lucent. It's the kind of place you find academic sorts: craft beers and single malts, a couple bookshelves with everything from Aristotle to Zen koans. A jukebox that plays the latest from Mozart."

"You keep a catalog of all the bars, Vince?" Harry asked.

"I live about a mile north of here," Vince said. "It's on my radar."

Vince put his uniforms and pair of detectives on interviewing the onlookers while Harry and I booked to the bar. Vince and his folks would take Warbley's house.

We rounded the corner to The Lucent two minutes later, a corner bar with a side courtyard. The hardwood sign over the door was handcrafted artistic, the smooth name in scarlet in reverse-relief.

"Damn," Harry muttered, trying the door and finding it locked. "Closed."

Closing time was likely two a.m., ten minutes ago, but a light was on and tapping the window with badges brought a face to the embossed and decorative door, one Larry Milsapp. Milsapp was pudgy, in his sixties and sported a waxed and pointed mustache that would have sparked envy in Salvador Dali. Milsapp wore khakis and threadbare blue dress shirt under a white and damp-spotted apron. In the corner of the bar I saw a mop bucket; cleaning up.

"John Warbley?" Milsapp said in response to my question, his eyes sighting between the twin antennae. "John was in here earlier. I guess from maybe nine until eleven or thereabouts." He frowned. "What's this about, if I may ask?"

It was technically Harry's case, which meant he pulled the ugly duty. He leveled his eyes into Milsapp's eyes. "Mr Milsapp, I'm sorry to say Professor Warbley was killed earlier this evening, likely on his return home."

If the bar hadn't been in front of him, Milsapp would have gone down. He grabbed it for support, wavered, but Harry had an arm under Milsapp's shoulder and guided the man to a chair, where he buried his face in his hands.

"Oh …" he said, trying to find a place to put his hands so they'd stop shaking. "Oh, oh, oh …"

Harry pulled two tumblers from the glassware rack, poured a treble shot of Pappy Van Winkle in one, spritzed soda water in the other and handed them to Milsapp.

"I, I, I …" Milsapp said. His wiring was shorting from sudden overload.

"First a deep breath," Harry said.

Milsapp sucked in air.

"Now the booze."

Milsapp downed half the bourbon, then half the soda. He closed his eyes and waited until the blast hit, then nodded thanks.

"Take your time, sir," Harry said. "Then we need to ask about Professor Warbley."

Milsapp polished off the bourbon. "John was part of the soul of this place," Milsapp said, shaking his head. "The conscience, maybe. John never knew an enemy, only friends. This place will never be the same."

"Was he married?"

"Married to his classes, his studies, his books. Married to the concept that reason, correctly constructed and passionately argued, would always win out."

"Anyone in here earlier seem especially interested in Professor Warbley?" I asked.

A sad head-shake. "It was a small crowd, the usual regulars, most have been coming here for years. People came and went, maybe forty over the course of the eveni …" He paused and narrowed an eye.

"What is it, Mr Milsapp?" Harry asked.

"There *was* someone else. A man came in, looked the place over for a few seconds, then turned and left. I got the impression he was looking for someone who wasn't here. Or maybe he saw that it wasn't his kind of place."

"How's that, sir?"

Milsapp studied a memory and frowned as it gained focus. "He was hardlooking, dangerous looking. Latin, I'm sure. Big shoulders, small waisted. Wore one of those knit caps. Though he had a jacket with the collar popped up, I saw tattoos on his neck. He looked like one of those guys in prison documentaries who lift weights all day. You don't think—?"

"We don't think anything yet, sir. We're just gathering data." Harry scanned the ceiling, the rafters. "Speaking of that, do you have any security cameras?"

"Never had any need."

We asked a few more questions and went to Warbley's house to find Vince sitting on the couch and making notes as techs worked beneath porta-lamps out front. He gave us *what'd you find?* eyes.

"He'd been at The Lucent," Harry said. "Left around eleven. Fits the timeline for an ambush."

"He have much to drink?" Vince asked.

Harry nodded. "The owner said Warbley liked single malt. Had four in two hours. Not smashed but happy."

"Not much to go on here," Vince said, grunting up from the couch. His eyes looked tired, but then it was past two in the morning. "It's like the standard-issue intellectual's digs: Lots of books, an office where he graded papers, a stack of student essays on John Stuart Mill, a briefcase with more papers. Nothing out of place, tossed … I doubt the perp was ever inside."

"Find a wallet?" Harry asked. "Phone?"

"Nada. There's a bowl in a drawer by the door, got loose bills, coins, keys, an old uncharged flip phone, but a new charger hooked in a plug. I'll bet it's where Warbley tossed the wallet when he came in and charged his phone."

"You're thinking robbery?" I asked.

Vince nodded toward the outside. "You've seen the street. Dark. Some broke junkie's driving around and coming down hard, maybe looking for houses to creep until he sees an older guy trotting in the shadows. Or maybe he saw Warbley exit the bar a little wobbly and thinks he'll be an easy target. The junkie pulls over, grabs the steel pipe or cut-down ball bat beneath the seat and tiptoes down the lawns while Warbley trots the sidewalk. As he walks by the darkest yard *bang* … he gets pulled into the shadows and stripped of anything worth a nickel." He looked at us expectantly. "You guys get anything besides Warbley sipping at The Lucent tonight? Something we can follow?"

"Maybe," Harry said. "If I understand how things work, Vince, you can do a few things for us, the FCLE, while we lead?"

Vince nodded. "I've got more manpower, you've got more specialists."

"I'd be wondering if there are any security cameras in the area that might have caught shots of a tattooed mutha in a dark skullcap, bodybuilder type, Latin maybe …"

Harry finished the brief description and Vince went to put people on it ASAP. Harry and I waited until the big white box took Professor John Warbley on the grim ride to the morgue. When there was nothing to do but watch techs pick through the grass, we headed toward the car.

"Carson, Harry!" Vince yelled. We turned to see Vince waving us back. "Ortega just interviewed a woman lives four doors down. You should hear what she's got to say."

We followed Vince to a tall and slim woman at the edge of the crime scene tape. She was elderly, gray-haired, but unbent by her years, alert and studying every aspect of the controlled tumult around her. Ortega, a big burly guy with a mustache to rival Harry's, was beside her.

"These men are with the FCLE, Ms Sabitch," Ortega said. "Could you repeat your observations, please."

She looked at us and nodded. "No big deal. I like to look outside at my birds, got a dozen houses in the trees. I sit in my living room and drink coffee and read magazines and watch the birds. I'm eighty-seven, it's what I do best. Some people may think I'm a nosy old biddy but they can take a—"

"What'd you see or hear, ma'am?" Harry said, stepping in.

"Just a car going down the street. Twice. It slowed down as it went by Mr Warbley's house, like checking for an address."

"What time was this, Ms Sabitch?"

"Earlier, around seven thirty. The guy inside was Mexican or Cuban or something like that. Not real old, like in his thirties. He had on one of those tight hats they all love so much. I saw his hands on the steering wheel, tattoos all over them."

Harry's eyes scanned the distance from the house to the street, fifty or sixty feet. "You have very good eyesight, ma'am."

"No. I have very good binoculars. I watch birds, remember?"

"Do you know the make or model of the car?"

"Some big shiny thing, red. Not like those boxes, SUVs? This looked low to the ground, like a prowling cat. It even made a purring sound."

We turned. Vince was standing at the edge of the conversation, listening. We now had two sightings of a tattooed and probably Latin male, one possibly scouting the neighborhood, the other in a bar at the same time as John Warbley. Vince turned and yelled some names, adding to the crew checking for potential surveillance in the area.

It was closing in on 3.30 a.m. and there was no more sleep tonight. Harry and I went to HQ and bagged out on our couches for a bit, anything resembling rest would keep us moving through what promised to be a long day.

I arose at 8.00, ran through the shower downstairs, put on one of the three changes of clothes I keep in my office, the suit option, since I had a 9.15 deposition at the DA's office, about fifteen minutes of looking serious and professional.

I returned 45 minutes later to find Harry in my office, rolled back in my seat and staring at my video monitor.

"I hid all my porn vids," I said, stripping off the formal look to change into jeans, blue tee, and a tan linen sport coat. "For ten bucks I'll tell you where they are."

"Your man Vince does good work," he said.

"He's in the vids?" I said, buckling my belt.

Harry walked to the player and loaded a disk. "If you're heading

56

to Warbley's place from the nearest major highway, there's one good route, the way a GPS would go. Detective Delmara had his men check for CCTVs along that three-mile route, found three. One's at one of those personal storage locations, but it doesn't reach the street, another's at a restaurant, nothing there. Then there was this from a restaurant three blocks down; had a couple robberies so they put in surveillance that overlooks the parking lot and some of the street. This was the nearest thing they found."

Harry pressed Play and we watched a grainy shot of a Camaro slowing for the corner stoplight and stopping for a three-count until the light changed. The windows were smoked and the driver was hunched down: Nada to work with.

"Sure looks like a cat," Harry said. "A big red prowling cat."

"It affirms Sabitch's story," I said. "But that's about all.

"One more snippet," Harry said. "This is from a c-store about four miles from Warbley's home."

"Four miles?"

"Like I said, your man Vince does good work. Casts a wide net. Check it out."

We watched a scene from an exterior cam at the c-store, probably there to record drive-offs. I saw a man filling the tank of a Camaro Z/28. He was dressed in black with flash at the beltline, definitely a shiny buckle. Topping his round dome was a black skullcap. He was shoulder heavy, a chunk of muscle, and he was moving fast, like he had an appointment somewhere.

"What time?" I asked.

Harry froze the playback. "Fifteen minutes before midnight. So here's the time frame: Warbley's in the bar from nine until eleven. If this is the perp, it wasn't opportunistic, because he'd scoped out Warbley's presence in the bar. He follows the prof, or is already waiting in the dark near Warbley's house, made easier because he's dressed in full black. He kills him with a single blow, yanks wallet and cell, and walks calmly to his vehicle, stashed around the corner."

"Putting him in at the gas pump in just that time frame," I said. It was all conjecture, but it was all we had and there had been times when we'd started with less.

"I can't make out a plate," I said, squinting at the monitor. "Mr Black pay in credit?"

"Nope. But there's one last scene, Carson."

Harry advanced to a shot from an interior camera; the door swinging open and our suspect entering while pulling his wallet, showing the tats on his hands. He seemed cautious, keeping his head down like knowing the camera was there.

"Awfully camera-shy, you think? All I see is the freaking hat."

"Wait for it ..." Harry said.

A horn blasted in the fueling lot, loud and strident, and for a split second Mister Black's head lifted and spun to the commotion. Harry pushed pause, framing a full-face shot, moderately blurred, but with enough definition to know the man was hard-eyed and looked Hispanic. I could make out tats on his face and neck.

"Say cheese," Harry grinned.

"Vince and his people have any idea who this guy is?"

"They're showing a still around MDPD, especially the gang units. But they're coming up blank."

I sat on the couch and pulled on black running shoes, staring at the half-focused face frozen on the monitor. I saw another face in my head: a short cheerful guy in his late fifties who thought it was forever 1975.

"You think Dabney Brewster's still running the facial-recognition project at Quantico?" I said.

9

Harry lifted my phone and called the FBI in Quantico, Virginia, putting the phone on speaker. When he asked to speak to Dabney Brewster, the voice on the other end sounded uncertain. "I'm not sure if we have a—"

"Try R&D," Harry said. "Research and Development."

"Got him," the voice said, taking Harry's name. "Here we go. Hang on while I connect you."

Harry covered the phone and spoke to me. "The Dabster's still there. Second piece of luck."

He picked up seconds later, a rich southern voice vibrating the lines. "Harry-freaking-Nautilus ... talk about a voice from the past. How're things in good ol' Mobile?"

Dabney Brewster was an old-school hipster computer geek from Mobile who sometimes consulted on our computer-crime cases back in the day. His spare-time hobby had been computer-generated art, portraiture, using pieces of photographed actual faces to construct odd and funny montages of invented faces. He'd created a library of facial features, building algorithms to define certain characteristics so he could catalog them. His work caught the attention of the FBI and he was suddenly in Quantico and at the forefront of facial-recognition software development.

"I retired from the MPD, Dab," Harry said. "I'm in Florida with the FCLE."

"No shit? I heard Carson's there."

"He's sitting across from me and grinning."

"Hey Dabs," I yelled.

"Muthaaafuck … The Harry and Carson Show is back on stage."

"Why we're calling, Dabs … we got a potential bad guy on CCTV vid, and would really like to know if he's in FBI files. Local mug shots are coming up blank. You make any headway since Tampa?"

I was referring to an early experiment in which facial-recognition equipment was installed in Tampa's Ybor City district, a miserable failure scrapped two years later and still the butt of jokes. Another experiment at Boston's Logan Airport had also ended poorly. But both were before Dabney got called to Quantico.

"Refining algorithms takes a long time. There are problems, but we've come a far piece lately."

"How far?"

"Given a fairly clear face – individualized features and not many deep shadows – we can feed it into a photo database of known criminals and get solid hits. We're above a 90 percent recognition factor."

"Got any time to slip us into the mix?"

"Maybe …" he said, a grin in his voice. "If you send me some love."

It was Dabney's quirk that before taking any outside job, he wanted a "love token," a meaningless gift that he found amusing. Our past tokens had included an Elvis Presley Pez dispenser, a harmonica that had once passed through a room where John Lee Hooker was dining, and a bag of novelty clam shells that, when dropped into water, opened to disburse little paper flowers.

"Get us in fast, Dabs," I yelled. "And we'll love you like Gertrude loved Alice B."

"I dunno what that means, but I'm on it."

We e-mailed Dabney the video and hit the street, hoping to find anyone who could tell us more about the killings of either Angela Bowers or John Warbley, now looking more and more like highly calculated – and connected – murders.

*　*　*

Adam Kubiac was an early riser. He liked the quiet of sitting alone on the balcony of Zoe Isbergen's apartment as Zoe slept and the sun rose in the east. He often used the time to game against players on the other side of the planet. But this morning he wasn't thinking about gaming, he was pacing the small balcony, four steps down, four steps back. Then repeat and repeat and repeat. Mumbling to himself.

He hadn't been able to sleep, too angry at his father and his father's stinking lawyer. Bastards! They had both conspired to keep his money from him. His money. His old man may have made it selling cars, but he owed Adam for putting up with years of bullshit. The drinking and drugging when he thought Adam wouldn't *notice.* Or the times he just didn't care. The women Adam would find in their home, *his* home. The times the local cops would bring his father home, half drunk, and he'd start pretending to himself and Adam that he was a real father.

"*Y'know what, Adam, we doan see enough of each other, do we, son? What say we head up to Aspen this weekend? You ever skied? I'll teach you to ski. You'll love it. An' wait till you get a load of the ski bunnies in the lodge, make your eyes pop out ...*"

Soon after, the liquor-reeking bastard would begin snoring, and then awaken the next morning with no memory of the conversation. He'd start right back in on digging at Adam for a host of supposed infractions: laziness, immaturity, disobedience, insolence, swearing, or any of a dozen other bullshit things. The old man had been a *bitch.*

61

But now he was gone, and Adam should have gotten over twenty million bucks on his upcoming birthday.

Instead, he would receive one dollar. One fucking dollar.

He screamed and kicked one of the cheap lawn chairs on the balcony, causing it to fold and fall to the floor. Seconds later the glass door slid open and Zoe's head poked out. He knew she didn't come all the way out because she slept naked.

"Jesus, Adam, what's going on?"

"I'm thinking. That's all."

Her eyes found the tumbled chair. "You're thinking about Cottrell, right? And your father?"

"Damn right, the scumbags, both of them. Hashtag: SCREWADAM!"

"Relax, Adam. Calm down."

"I don't *want to* calm down. I want my $20,000,000."

"I'll tell you what, I'll get dressed and we'll go to that little coffee shop down the street. Get a couple of muffins. Watch the robots going to work. You like that, right?"

He thought a moment. "I guess. Hurry up."

She pulled her head back inside and disappeared. Adam set the chair upright, hearing Zoe bustling around inside. He and Zoe had only been together about two weeks but it seemed a lot longer; they got along so good.

It had been that way from the beginning, when she'd noticed him at his favorite tacqueria on Indian School Road. He'd been sitting in a booth in the rear, playing *Clash of Clans* against some chick in Finland. She'd been pretty good but Adam had won easily. He'd returned to his beef *torta* and Cola when Zoe had just walked up and slid into the booth opposite him.

She'd said, "Whatcha doing?" like she'd known him for years.

"Do I know you?" he'd said.

"No," she had said. "But that's not set in stone, right?" Her shy smile seemed as wide as her face.

"S-set in stone?" *Don't fucking stutter! Whatever you do, don't*

62

stutter. Relax, Adam, he'd heard Dr Meridien say in his head. *Think first, then speak.*

The woman clarified: "Not set in stone means, 'Doesn't have to stay that way.'" She was still smiling, but like she was happy, not making fun of him.

"Oh, sure. No, I guess not."

"I was at that table over there." Nodding her head toward the corner. "You looked like you were having fun, laughing while you played with your phone."

"I was gaming against someone in Finland. She was good, but I won. I almost always win."

"I don't know anything about gaming. I've always wanted to learn, but there's no one I know that can teach me."

Adam's heart had leapt to his throat, and he heard himself say: "I can teach you. I'd be happy to teach you."

"Would you? You're not just saying that? That would be too cool."

He had affected nonchalance, almost yawning. "Yeah. It's pretty easy once you get the hang of it. It just takes some time to learn. We can start now, if you want."

She had slid out of the booth and slid back in on his side. *Close enough that they were touching!*

"OK, then," she had said tapping the phone in his hand. "Show me how this game stuff works."

The sliding door reopened. Zoe stepped out wearing black tights, ankle-high black boots with two-inch heels, and a crimson top that left her right shoulder bare.

"Let's go get coffee," she said.

"Let's take my car," Adam said.

"But it's just four blocks. We always walk."

"Let's go to that coffee shop over by Scottsdale, Higher Grounds?"

"Why there?"

"We'll be in the area."

63

Looking quizzical but saying nothing, Zoe followed Adam to his white 2011 Subaru Outback, a dent in the front right wheel panel, another in the hatchback. It needed a wash.

They got in and Adam started driving. He drove a few blocks to Van Buren and headed west to Highway 17, where he went north several miles, then turned east on the Pima Highway.

"Where are we going, Adam," Zoe asked, after fifteen minutes of watching Phoenix go past.

"It doesn't concern you, Zoe."

She went back to looking out the window. Adam drove for another ten minutes, then took an off-ramp into a residential neighborhood of tidy middle-class homes. He zigged and zagged a few times, finally pulling under a stone arch. Beside the arch a sign proclaimed, "Eastwood Memorial Gardens."

"Adam …?"

"Shhh."

He drove what seemed a memorized route, left then right and another right, past a fountain spraying water twenty feet into the air. He pulled off to the side of the slender asphalt road, parked. He looked all directions. They seemed the only living people in the cemetery.

"We're all alone," Adam said. "Good." He got out and Zoe started to follow.

"No, Zo. You have to stay here. This is for me and me alone."

She nodded, somehow knowing, and pulled the door shut.

The gravestones were all set at ground level, simple. Elijah Kubiac, perhaps planning on living to be one hundred, had died without making funeral and burial plans. Adam had left that up to some whispery asshole at a funeral home, after picking out the cheapest coffin possible. He'd first thought about cremation, but the idea of the old bastard slowly rotting away underground sounded better. He'd picked Eastwood as the cemetery simply because he'd driven by several times and remembered the name.

He continued past two large palo verde trees and turned down a row of black granite headstones, some with small bouquets of flowers stuck into the ground beside them. He stopped. Looked down at a headstone. Stared for a long minute.

Then pulled out his penis and began urinating.

The dark headstone below, its engraving quickly filling with urine, proclaimed simply, *Elijah T Kubiac, 1959–2017.*

Adam zipped up and walked away, whistling.

* * *

Tasha Novarro had awakened at eight in the morning; Mountain Time, creeping softly into the living room to find her brother snoring gently, the covers kicked off. As predicted, he'd missed the bucket.

After cleaning the floor and spraying the room with half a can of air freshener, Novarro went to work, returning to Dr Meridien's house and office and spending fifteen minutes searching closets and drawers until finding what she'd hoped for: Two albums of printed photos. Meridien was a chronicler: the back of each picture noted with date and place and others in the setting.

"*Sedona, August 24 2007, me and Taylor Combs and Lanie Buchwald. Hot day, 89. Just finished Pink Jeep tour. Now lunch at Taco Rancho!*"

They were standard travel shots. But eight of forty-seven photos of Meridien showed her wearing the same brooch, a stylized owl's head of silver half-orbs of turquoise forming the eyes and obviously a favored piece. Novarro also noted other pieces of jewelry and accessories in the photos. She marked them with corners of sticky notes and took the shots to tech services.

Twenty minutes later a tech handed Novarro close-ups of three different earring styles, two necklaces, a silver-and-turquoise bracelet, and two angles of the owl adornment.

"Nice brooch," the tech said. "Looks expensive."

Novarro started driving from pawnshop to pawnshop across the Phoenix basin, hoping killer or killers – perhaps aching for dope – had tried to sell the jewelry for fast cash: a long shot. Novarro wished she had a partner to handle half the work, but dual detective teams had been cut back with the economic downturn, now only assembled when entering a dangerous situation. Even that was discouraged, the suggestion being to take along a uniform when danger loomed.

When she was on the seventh pawnshop, her phone rang. The screen said CASTLE. She sighed and answered while bending low to inspect a jewelry case. In every shop it was the same, row after row of pawned wedding rings, probably not a good social indicator. "I'm kinda busy at the moment, Merle," she said, knowing to hold the phone two inches from her ear, Castle incapable of talking softly.

"Doing what?" Castle bayed.

"The pawnshop rounds. Meridien had a favorite piece of jewelry, a silver owl. Plus I've got shots of other pieces."

"Any luck?"

"Think, Merle. If I had luck I'd no longer be going from pawnshop to pawnshop."

"The shops all smell the exact same, right, Tash? Like your grammaw's attic. And in the Hispanic shops no one speaks English the moment you step inside."

Castle was right. A clerk who minutes before would have been arguing the price in perfect, unaccented English was suddenly all wide-eyed puzzlement and "*No inglés.*"

"What do you want, Merle?"

"Let's go eat somewhere tonight. It's been months."

Novarro sighed. "We're done, Merle. If we'd been jigsaw puzzles no edges would match."

"I thought we fit together real good," Castle chuckled. "Especially at night."

"Come on, Merle. Grow up."

Silence. Castle veered a different direction. "You're right, Tash, it was my fault. I was, uh …" he searched for a word.

"You were yourself, Merle. It's OK. You seem happy with it."

"C'mon, Tash. I think we can —"

Novarro clicked the phone off and pondered faxing Castle a single sheet of paper with the word *NO!* running from edge to edge.

10

After sending the material to Dabney, Harry and I headed to the U. Nothing of interest had been found at Warbley's home, but we hadn't been to his office since his death.

Warbley's office knew he had died and expressed it by emitting an aura of stillness and a scent as dank as if it had been weeks without habitation. Whatever life-force vibes Warbley's presence added had gone elsewhere, and the space was now just space. I took the filing cabinets, not knowing what I was looking for, if anything. Harry sat and found Warbley's desk locked but seven seconds with two bent paper clips popped the simple mechanism. He scraped around for a few minutes, putting the standard trappings atop the desk and looking morosely through nothing of merit.

"I don't think we're going to find anything in the papers and trinkets," he said, finally swiping it all back into the drawer with his forearm. "I think we're going to find it in you."

"Me?"

"Why was your name in Bowers's desk? Why did she follow it with question marks?"

"I don't know. We'd never met. Maybe she had a stalker, saw my name in the news. Wondered if she should call."

"I'd think if Doc Bowers had a stalker she'd call, not dither about it or keep files on individual cops."

"Yeah." Harry was right as always.

"You're sure you two never crossed paths? Met at a psychology function or whatever."

I shook my head. "I really haven't done a lot of that since coming to Florida. Just a few. And they weren't about psych stuff, per se, mainly groups of law-enforcement types there to hear about how the dark people think … or as much as I can tell them."

"Nothing at the U?" Harry said. "Where she might have wandered in and sat in back?"

I searched my memory. "Come to think of it, one of the venues was … let's get back to the office, pronto."

Harry looking quizzical but not saying a word, we sped back to the FCLE's offices. We elevatored up and I almost ran to my office. I sat in my chair, spun it to my file cabinet and started riffling through folders.

"What?" Harry said.

"I'm looking for my LAME file. It's in here somewhere."

The file had been named years ago, in Mobile, when Harry discovered I was keeping a folder noting my various appearances. He'd laughingly dubbed it my LAME file, for *Look At Me Everyone*. I pulled material from the folder and spread it out on my desk, mostly programs for various law enforcement seminars and symposia.

Harry leaned forward, elbows on his knees. "What are you looking for?"

I pressed my fingers against my eyelids. "I see it in my head … a darkened hall, me at the podium. A hundred or so people in the audience. I'm showing a video of Randall Jay Caudill howling about his rights from inside his cell. The vid ends and a hand goes up in the audience and a woman asks a question."

I squeezed my eyes tighter and replayed the memory. A woman's voice, pleasant, engaged, says something like, "*Did I not hear that the case against Caudill was made with information garnered inadvertently while he was under anesthesia?*"

I nod. "*Caudill was at his dentist's office undergoing root canal. While sedated, he said things that led the dentist to connect Caudill's ramblings to a case widely publicized in the Tampa-St Petersburg area. The dentist called the authorities.*"

The woman: "*I assume Mr Caudill's lawyer invoked doctor–patient privilege, did he not?*"

"*Yes, ma'am,*" I say. "*About every thirty-three seconds.*"

Laughter from the mostly cop audience.

"*It didn't hold sway?*" she asks.

I say something like, "*A dentist has a duty to respect a patient's right to confidentiality and self-determination, especially in regards to medical records. But in this case the court ruled that the dentist was not bound to remain silent about what seemed solid indicators of a patient's involvement in four murders.*"

"*Thank you, Detective Ryder.*"

"*My pleasure, ma'am. Do you happen to be a dentist with someone to turn in?*"

Laughter.

"*I'm a psychologist,*" she says. "*If you ever find my hand in your mouth, Detective, I'm probably searching for your ID.*"

Howls. Applause. I'm laughing louder than anyone.

The memory left and Harry watched me scrabble through programs and brochures with titles like *Southwestern Law Enforcement Convention; the Police Chiefs Association of Florida; the National Sheriff's Convention; the Criminal Justice Review Board* ... I'd even given a couple of speeches at ACLU gatherings, and since the audience expected a goose-stepping J. Edgar Hoover imitation, I was better regarded after I finished than before I started.

I came to a program guide for the *Southwestern Convocation of Judicial Issues,* billed as *"Top Minds in Criminal Justice Discussing Pressing Issues in Law Enforcement."* I unfolded the page and saw my photo, small enough to fit on my thumbnail. My topic had been, "Determining Insanity: Who Holds the Gavel?"

I was reading from the brochure and punching numbers into my phone.

"Who you calling, Cars?" Harry asked.

"The University of Florida, Criminal Justice Department."

I punched the phone on speaker so Harry could hear, and it was answered in two rings.

"Alexandro Salazar."

"Mr Salazar, I'm Detective Carson Ryder with the—"

"FCLE ... of course. You spoke at the event the department sponsored last spring. Great talk, scary in places. I'd love to have you back for next year's meeting. All of us would."

"I'll weld the date to my calendar today if you can do me a favor, Mr Salazar. Do you still have the list of attendees?"

"Of course. We use it for our mailings."

"Could you see if there's a Dr Angela Bowers on the list, a psychologist."

"Lemme pull the file. I remember there were several psychologists in attendance." I heard the ticking of a keyboard. "OK, here's the file ... scrolling. Yep, there it is, Dr Angela Bowers. Do you need her address?"

"Not necessary," I said, shooting Harry a glance. "I believe I have it."

It was past three and Novarro was on her twenty-third pawnshop, a grubby joint on the edge of Mesa that – true to Castle's description – smelled like an elderly person's attic. She'd shown the proprietor the jewelry photos and received a sad head-shake in return.

Her phone rang, Castle again. "Merle, give me a break,

would—"

"Hi Tash. Better start thinking what you want for supper tonight."

"Supper? You can't keep beating this horse, Merle."

"At Donovan's. My treat. I made reservations for eight."

"Eight people?"

"Eight o'clock. For two. For me and you. Hey … I'm a poet."

Novarro frowned. Donovan's was arguably the best steakhouse in a metro area with a dozen phenomenal steakhouses. Had Castle been drinking?

"We're not going to dinner tonight, Merle. Or any night, for that matter."

"Of course, we are, Tash. It'll be like the good old days."

"Good is a relative term. Besides, what makes you think—"

"I have something in my hands you've been looking for."

Novarro frowned. She'd left a pair of panties at his place. But that had been months ago. Had he just now found them? Given the way Castle cleaned—

"I'd forgotten how much I hate your childish games, Merle."

A pause. "It's something relative to the Meridien case, Tash. Something big … Muy im-por-*tan*-te."

Meridien? Novarro sat up straighter. "What did you find, Merle?"

"I'll pass it over after dinner. Trust me, you'll be amazed."

Novarro felt her heart speed up. *Castle has something … a lead?* It would have to be good, more than a way to lure her to dinner. Even the sensitivity-challenged Merle Castle would know a cheap trick would be a major mistake. Donovan's was a wonderful restaurant: red leather, dark wood, crackling hearth. Monumental cocktails. Brick-sized slabs of succulent aged beef …

"Where you at, Merle?"

"Home changing into my Donovan's clothes. Got to wear the elastic belt to make room for all that meat."

"OK, then," she said. "We'll meet at eight for dinner and your revelation."

"Great, Tash. You won't be disap—"

"But at La Azteca, instead."

It took several seconds for her words to register. "That cheap-ass taco joint on Van Buren? Christ, Tasha, I'm offering you a free meal at—"

"One, La Azteca is halfway between my place and yours. Two, it's cheap, like you said. Dinner for two at Donovan's is gonna set you back about a hundred and a half. Dinner for two at La Azteca will be about twenty-five bucks. And since I'm paying for my half, you'll do even better."

"C'mon, Tash." He sounded like a little kid pleading for a second cookie.

"It's the only way it's gonna happen, Merle. I'm starving, so let's make it 6.30. See you there."

Harry and I ended the day staring out my window as twilight settled over the strident skyline of Miami, the sky looking like the fading sun had been filtered through roses. Lights were appearing in the tall buildings and high-rises, random squares of illumination like spectral crossword puzzles blooming in the near-night.

"It has to be the convocation," I said, staring between my desk-resting feet to see Harry on the couch. "Something happened to make Bowers remember me."

"More than remember, Cars. Whatever you said, you must have made a big-ass impression, since Bowers started gathering information on you."

"But why?"

"I'd bet a week's pay she thought of you as a potential resource. Someone to turn to when a situation jumped from theoretical to real ... got hairy and scary. Warbley could provide the academic reasoning. Maybe she wanted the cop reasoning."

"But what could be the situation? What would it deal with?"

"What you handle, Cars: The broken people. I think the lady had a conflict that got her killed. What was it?"

Thus we ended the day at the crossroads of Death and Question, a place where Harry and I had spent enough time that we could probably get mail delivery there.

11

Merle Castle was in the lot and sitting on the hood of his huge black pickup when Novarro rolled in. He jumped down and followed her into the restaurant like it was a punishment. They passed the grill on the way to the order counter, a squat Hispanic cook flipping fajitas and chicken breasts beside a mountain of blackening jalapeños.

Castle sighed. "Melt-your-tongue peppers when we could be having melt-on-your-tongue filets."

"Quit pissing and moaning, Merle. Order up."

They placed orders with a smiling clerk named Juanita and took drinks to a table in the farthest of two brightly lit dining areas. The walls were yellow, with cartoon murals of diners at tables. Criss-crossing rows of plastic pennants were strung from the ceiling, touting Corona and Tecate beers. The tablecloths were woven Mexican rugs protected by clear plastic sheets.

The pair took a front table by a window looking onto Van Buren Avenue. Traffic was steady but light, the evening rush well past. Novarro took a sip from a blood-purple sangria loaded with berries and slices of orange and lime and shot a glance at the taped-shut box beside Castle's garish, hand-tooled Tony Lamas.

"Hunh-uh," he grinned, sucking from a Budweiser. "That's for dessert."

When their number was called they picked up their food: a beef *torta* for Castle; *Camarones a la Diablo* for Novarro. Castle went directly back to the table; Novarro to the condiments bar to load up on roasted *jalapeños*, spicy *salsa roja*, and *pico de gallo*. When she set her tray on the table, Castle grinned at the mound of zingy peppers.

"That's my girl … same cast-iron stomach."

Novarro tapped the purse at her waist. "Don't forget that I'm carrying a gun, Merle."

Puzzlement. "What?"

"If you ever call me 'my girl' again, I'll shoot you in the nuts."

He grinned and held up his hands. "Sorry, Tash, figure of speech."

Talk was sparse. Novarro squeezing the spicy shrimp from their shells with her fingertips as her lips sucked out the meat, loading a fork with rice as a chaser, taking a bite of flour tortilla, then repeating; Castle bit doleful hunks from his *torta* and chased them with beer.

They finished, Novarro dabbing away sweat beneath her eyes: the effect of a dozen *jalapeños* and the *salsa roja*. She nudged the box beneath Castle with her toe. "I'm ready for dessert, Merle."

"Bus the table and we'll begin."

Novarro frowned, but put the plates and sauce tubs and mounds of used napkins on the trays and took everything to the trash. When she returned the box was atop the table. Castle produced a black commando knife from his boot and sliced effortlessly through tape holding the top shut.

"Have a seat, Tash. And get ready."

She was pulling her chair to the table when Castle began emptying the box of items in MCSD evidence bags and setting them before her. One by one Novarro studied a shattered Toshiba laptop. A small and simple desk calendar. A pair of silver candlesticks. A silver gravy tureen. Next came jewelry: Over three dozen bags holding rings and earrings and bracelets and a pair of watches.

The clincher was in the last bag: Meridien's turquoise-and-silver owl brooch. "This is incredible, Merle," Novarro whispered, turning the brooch over in her hands. "Did you bust a fence?"

Castle sucked from his second Bud. "That would have been great, right? Squeeze the guy until he ratted out where he got it. There's luck here, Tash, but not quite that much. The stash was found in Queen Creek, not far from the West Sundance and Wild Horse Roads intersection. There's a fissured outcropping about a quarter mile away. This stuff was in a twenty-quart garbage bag and buried under about six inches of sand and rock."

"How'd it get unburied?"

Castle reached to the sack for a final evidence-bagged withdrawal: a few ragged strips of blue cloth crusted with rusty brown. He set it on the table, a grisly addition. "A shredded bandana," he said. "And, yep, that's blood. Let's see how long it takes you to figure it out, Tash." He looked at his watch.

A movie began playing in Novarro's head: a knife slashes through three-quarters of Dr Leslie Meridien's throat, blood spraying out, down, everywhere. She falls. Her killer studies the bloody knife – the path saying a five-inch blade at least, perhaps two inches at widest point – then pulls a blue bandana from pocket or head and wipes it clean. The blood-soaked bandana goes into the bag with the booty …

Later: the stolen goods in a vehicle passing through Queen Creek when someone or someones jogs several hundred feet to an outcropping, digs a fast hole in the middle of nowhere and buries the bag.

Then … the sun rises and the wet blood heats up and begins to smell. The odor sifts upward through the sandy soil until it hits the air.

"An animal dug it up," Novarro said.

Castle lifted the watch to his eyes. "Two minutes and seven

seconds. Yep. Coyote tracks all around the opening pit; the bandana dug out and gnawed on the spot."

"Who found the trove?"

"Two kids: brothers, eleven and thirteen who live a half mile away. A big cleft in the outcropping was their clubhouse, and there's your luck. If the banditos had scoped out the site in daylight they would have seen empty Coke cans and sandwich bags and, though the kids hid them behind a big rock, a couple of nudie magazines. The bad guys would have scurried elsewhere and you'd be searching pawn shops until doomsday."

Novarro scanned the tabletop of stolen items. "Three thousand bucks' worth of goods, at least," she said. "And it was buried in the freaking desert. It doesn't make sense."

Castle cracked his knuckles and nodded. "It should have gone straight to a fence. You were right, Tash. The robbery was fake, a diversion. Killing the lady was meant to look like a break-in gone bad."

Novarro nodded slowly. "It's the only thing that makes sense. Then only barely."

"Not my problem." Castle pulled some papers from the bottom of the box. "Here you go."

"What's this?"

"Chain-of-custody paperwork. MCSD is transferring the evidence to Phoenix PD. You've got the case to clear … we sure as hell don't need the evidence. You can put them in PPD bags when you're done looking."

Novarro signed her name in several places, assuring the transfer had gone by the book. She gave Castle her first real smile of the evening.

"Thanks, Merle."

Castle stood, pressed his Stetson on, hitched up his pants. "You nailed it from the git-go. Score a big one for you, Three-Points."

Novarro's eyes flashed. "Stop calling me that."

Castle ignored her words, tipped his hat and turned for the door. "Nice having supper with you again, Tash. But next time …" He paused, a sudden and pained look on his face.

"Next time what, Merle?"

"Let's for Chrissakes *please* go to Donovan's." He winced, bent with his knees outward and released a lengthy and pitch-rising trill of flatulation. "One more time here would about near kill me."

An hour later, Novarro sat on her couch, legs tucked beneath her, the only light a low cone of amber from the lamp on the end table, its shade still askew from Ben's kicking it to the floor. That he was out there in the night and likely doing things destructive to his future (did he still have one?) only occasionally intruded on her thoughts, pressed back by the task at hand: trying to discern if there was anything helpful on the paper desktop calendar buried with the remainder of Meridien's property.

Except for one thing, that was: Meridien's desktop computer, still missing and not buried with the other items. Assumption: Whoever took it either wanted to analyze its innards, or make sure it was shattered into a thousand unusable pieces, its secrets dead forever.

Novarro flipped through the calendar again, her hands sweating within the latex gloves. The calendar seemed a scheduling notepad for Meridien, a place to jot down appointments before transferring them to the cloud, and Novarro pictured the psychologist with phone tucked to her cheek – and owl brooch on her blouse – as she penciled the time across the calendar page. Unfortunately, Meridien's protectiveness of her patients' anonymity extended to her notations, all simply single or double initials followed by a time: *C, 9.30 a.m.; DA, 11.45 p.m.; TM, 1.30 p.m.; BN, 3.15 p.m…* She turned to a previous month, saw more of the same, and continued flipping to the first month, finding the pattern held: *AS, 9.15 a.m.; WP, 11.30 p.m., DA, 1.30 p.m.;*

BN, 4.15 p.m. There were a few sessions marked only with 'Group,' followed by initials: In June she saw *Group, 7.15, AS, BN, WP*; the same in July, only *Group AS, WP, CL, DD.* And pretty much the same for all other months, meaning nothing to be gleaned from the calendar.

Novarro sighed and started to return the dozen spiral-bound sheets to the evidence bag when she saw a scribble on the blank rear of the calendar: a name inked in ballpoint and followed by a question mark. Dr Meridien, for all her other attributes, had lousy penmanship. She squinted at what looked like

Carson Rider?

Novarro stared, feeling a scant awakening of her heart, like an injection of double mocha latte. Was it the name of a patient? Someone suggested as a date? Meridien's car mechanic? Novarro reopened the calendar and felt her mocha flush fade as she paged through the months. Not a single *CR* noted in the cryptic sketchings. It was like she perhaps got the name while on the phone – supporting a recommendation – and hastily flipped the calendar over to write it down.

She put the calendar back in the bag, zipped it shut, removed the damnable rubber gloves, walked to the kitchen sink to wash her damp hands beneath the tepid Phoenix tap water. She dried her hands and opened a cabinet to get a drinking glass. In the rear of the cabinet, behind mugs and glassware, was a 750 ml bottle of Cazadores Blanco tequila left over from her house-warming party. *Ben must not have noticed it,* she thought. *Or it'd be long gone.*

She fished the bottle through clinking glassware to find two-thirds of the premium brand sloshing in the glass. She looked at the clock: 9.42. There'd been a pair of sangrias at supper with Castle – delicious, just enough kick to relax her a bit – but she hadn't had a pop while inspecting Meridien's unearthed booty.

Novarro turned and shot a glance at the box of evidence on the low table in the living room couch … it could wait until the morning.

Novarro slipped on flip-flops and went to her backyard. To the south a jetliner descended toward Sky Harbor, its engine wailing as it fell from the stars. Dogs barked in the distance. Novarro crossed to her precious lime tree and in the dim city light gathered eight plump specimens and returned to squeeze a half-cup of pungent juice. She poured it into a pitcher, added a hearty dollop of tequila, splashed in a few ounces of orange juice from the fridge and finished by stirring in a couple tablespoons of demerara sugar. She took a sip, added a shade more sugar, and poured a glass over ice.

Novarro returned to the living room, put on *Music from a Painted Cave* by Robert Mirabel and Rare Tribal Mob and relaxed on the couch, toe tapping to the music as she sipped at her tequila concoction. But after a few minutes her eyes fell on the box of evidence like it was a ringing phone and she sat forward, pulling on latex gloves.

12

Though it was late, I drove home to Matecumbe, needing the hour-plus ride to clear my head. And I wanted to see Mr Mix-up, the huge canine constructed of mismatched parts that I'd saved from the needle years ago. My secluded tract of land bordered a wildlife sanctuary which Mix-up wandered cheerfully when I wasn't at home, coming inside through a doggie door, his meals dispatched twice a day via a contraption that cost almost three hundred dollars.

He was also a welcome visitor at the home of my nearest neighbor, Dubois Burnside, a former funeral home operator in Atlanta; so welcome, in fact, that Dubois had commissioned a special bed for Mix-up's resting pleasure, about eight hundred dollars' worth of plush comfort. I should be so lucky.

As if knowing I was coming, Mix-up was just inside the gate by the road, waiting for me to enter. I opened the door and he bounded inside, dark-mudded feet telling me he'd been playing in the mangroves. Mix-up licking my hand on the shift knob, we drove several hundred feet to park beneath my stilt-standing house.

Inside I mixed a bourbon and soda and retreated to the deck to sit in an Adirondack chair and stare over the small moonlight-laden cove that opened into the wide and shallow waters surrounding the Keys. Somewhere a big fish jumped, splashed. A couple miles out I saw the lights of a ship moving east toward the Atlantic. Mix-up lay beside me and my fingers scratched his ears in time to the dappling of waves upon the strand.

I used the quiet time to consider the Bowers case. It was becoming clear that a colleague had called her with a question or conflict regarding ethics. If Warbley had been using Bowers's friend's query as his example – which I was beginning to suspect more and more – it seemed her friend had been suspicious of something or someone, perhaps suspecting some form of deception. She had taken the problem to John Warbley. Both were possessors of a shared piece of information, and both were now dead.

My major conjecture was that a patient had revealed homicidal tendencies or even a tacit admission to murder. Was the deception a masking of the fact while a patient? The premises, especially the first, would be a tightrope walk for a shrink, the doctor–patient privileged-information contract suspended with suspicion a major crime had been committed.

Had Bowers been contemplating a trip or call to authorities? It explained my name being uppermost in the doc's desk. Her collection of material preparation for the day she needed the opinion of someone in law enforcement. Perhaps someone experienced with broken minds.

I momentarily cursed the fact that the phone company legal office was only reachable during business hours and we had to wait until tomorrow to get Bowers's phone records, but it was short-lived as the blast of bourbon damped my adrenalin and weighted my eyelids and my dog and I tottered off to bed.

I climbed from the sheets about the time the sun was climbing from the water, though far less colorfully, a process comprising groaning, stretching, and lamenting the lack of Vivian Morningstar's lovely visage on the pillow beside mine. It seemed like a month since I'd seen her. Ten minutes later I was freestyling slowly across the cove, pulling laps to loosen up. Five minutes after that I angled out into open water for twenty minutes of foaming-wake workout.

A shower followed, with a breakfast of 30-weight coffee and a *grittito*, my own concoction of leftover cheese grits rolled in a flour tortilla and – when Vivian wasn't around – drenched in sausage gravy.

I was at HQ a bit past nine, having to pass Roy's office. "You got that vacation lined up yet, Carson?" he bayed, a phone in each hand and his hair looking like it was re-enacting the Haymarket Riots.

"I'm close, Roy," I said, picking up speed. "I've got three getaway venues in mind."

Hither, Yon, and somewhere in-between.

Harry had texted that he was out talking to the clerk at the c-store where our man in the red muscle car had filled his tank, just to see if the guy could add to our info store. Harry showed up at 9.45, sighed and set his briefcase on the floor, shaking his head: *nothing new.*

"The subpoena for Bowers's phone records should be ready soon," I said. "We can head over there now and wait for—"

My phone rang. Bobby Erikson, the ex-cop who ran the phones, spoke over my intercom. "*There's a Dabney Brewster on line three, Carson.*"

"Got it, Bobby. Thanks."

I shot Harry a glance, feeling my heart ramp up. Thus far there'd been nothing from the mug books at MDPD, which seemed odd … the guy in the c-store had gangsta written all over him, almost literally.

I spoke toward the phone's receiver. "We're both right here, brother Brewster."

"Got me some love?" he trilled, a good sign. I'd passed one of those weird vintage-junkiness shops in Tampa and saw exactly what we needed in the window.

"A stuffed alligator circa 1970," I said. "Eighteen inches long and ridden by a troll doll dressed in a hula skirt. Unfortunately, there's a bit of mold on the belly …"

"Mold adds to the charm, Carson," Dabney trilled. "Glorious kitsch! Beautiful."

"I'll mail it today, Dabs. Got us some love in return?"

"Maybe, baby. I ran your video through the most advanced program we have, still experimental, but right 93 percent of the time. Given the blurring of the video, I'd guess this is maybe 80 percent. I've got a name and some info, but I don't have your new e-mail addy."

I gave it to him and heard the clicking of keys. "On its way. Should be there in a just a—"

Bing. I heard my e-mail alert. Harry moved to my back as I opened the file to see a mug shot of a guy who looked Hispanic, tatted on a neck that looked thick as a phone pole. His glittering eyes nonetheless looked as dead as the eyes of a cobra. I noted the 6'3" marking a bit shy of the crown of his head.

"The program IDs him as Ramon Escheverría," Dabney said. "But his friends call him El Gila."

"The healer?" Harry asked.

"Hee-la, like in Gila monster. Seems he got into a fight in prison – first time in, just nineteen years old – Escheverría was getting the worst of it until he clamped his teeth down on his assailant's neck and hit the carotid. Blood's squirting everywhere, in his eyes, down his throat, but …"

"Escheverría hung on," I said, recalling the myth about the Gila monster: When it bit, it didn't release its jaws until the sun went down.

"If you guys are going after this bastard, go together. And take a flame-thrower."

"What's his story," Harry said.

"The info is sparse. Problem is that no snitch will inform on him because he scares them shitless. Mention his name and CIs go mute. What there is suggests Escheverría's primary occupation seems to be a kind of high-level enforcer. No gang affiliation; he'll work for whoever's got money. It's assumed he also does contract murder, but never proven. Probably because he keeps a low profile. It's get in, do the job, get out, and leave no evidence behind. He's supposed to be wicked smart. And totally cold."

"Wicked smart? He's been busted."

"Squeezes out on plea bargain or a witness shows up with an impaired memory. Probably owns a sleazy lawyer or two."

"How you know all this stuff, Dabs?"

"He's in the database here. The Bureau was looking into a killing of one of their informants a couple years back. It was in LA. They were looking at several potential hit men, Ramon among them. This is what they amassed, mainly from sources familiar with ol' El Gila. But then …"

I was familiar with the story. "Right. Half the Bureau's been switched to Homeland Security."

Harry had been checking the computer. "Miami-Dade PD has no files on Escheverría, Dabney."

A pause. "Probably because Escheverría's never been seen east of the Mississippi, Harry."

"What are you saying, Dabs?" I said.

"Escheverría's from the Southwest. All his busts or sightings were in Arizona, New Mexico, California, and Nevada. By the looks of things, those at the Bureau think El Gila's based somewhere around Phoenix."

Aided by flashing lights and the occasional blast of siren, we were at the phone company in twenty minutes. Bowers being deceased, all we needed to obtain her records was a subpoena, easier to obtain than a court order or warrant. We chilled our heels in the waiting room of the phone company's legal division for under fifteen minutes until the motorcycle dispatcher brought it by.

"I figured you'd get one," said Sonya Burroughs, a Rubenesque forty-something African-American lawyer with plump red lips and big brown eyes that kept drifting to Harry. "So I had the printout ready." She handed my partner a sheaf of computer printouts encompassing the last two years of Doctor Bowers's life, though we were mainly interested in the last couple of weeks.

"Would you happen to have an office we could use for a few minutes, Ms Burroughs?" Harry said.

"Of course, Detective Nautilus. And it's Sonya."

She led us down the hall with a motion-augmented high-heel perambulation that likely set off seismographs throughout South Florida. She flicked on the lights in a small meeting room and I was amazed the pictures were still hanging straight.

"I can get you some coffee," she purred, not at me.

"If it's not too much trouble," Harry said.

Double eye-blink. "Never."

The coffee arrived in a carafe that found its place in front of my partner. We poured mugs of decent brew and began poring over the pages.

"Local, local, local …" I said, looking for anything from the Southwest.

Minutes past until Harry smacked the table. "Bingo! An incoming call from Phoenix, Arizona. Made at 23.28 hours. That would be uh, 11.28 here in Miami. Phoenix is on Mountain Time, I think. But it's daylight savings, so—" he checked the clocks on his phone, "it was 9.28 there." He scanned the pages. "I've got a couple calls to LA, one to Dalton, Georgia, three to NYC, but this is the only Arizona connection."

"Read me the number."

Harry read, I dialed, the phone on speaker. Three rings and the answering machine clicked on. "You've reached the office of Dr Leslie Meridien," said a professional but smiling voice. "I can't get to the phone right now, but please leave a message and I'll get back to you."

"Hello, Doctor," I said, simultaneous with scribbling down her name. "This is Detective Carson Ryder with the Florida Center for Law Enforcement. Could you give me a call as soon as you get this? It's important."

I added my cell number and looked at Harry. "Now we wait. And hope Dr Meridien can answer some questions."

Harry sighed crossed the big arms. "I hate waiting."

Burroughs drifted past the door, smiling inside, and continued the bouncy-bounce down the carpet.

"At least for some things," Harry amended.

13

Novarro awakened to a motorcycle blasting down the street. Her eyes felt glued shut and her mouth tasted like boiled paper bags. She rubbed the mucilage from her eyes and turned to the clock, 8.56 a.m. She'd forgotten to set the alarm.

She was padding to the shower when something made her detour into the living room. Her heart jumped: Someone had gotten into the house and messed with the evidence, some bags open and empty, pieces of jewelry strewn across the tabletop, the owl brooch glistening from the floor.

Ben? Had Ben come in, seen the box, scrabbled through it? Novarro blinked her eyes and her heart raced … *and then …*

And then the disparate pictures loomed into view: the second drink, diluted by melted ice and needing another splash of tequila, then sitting and comparing the items with the descriptions supplied by the Maricopa County people, squinting at the descriptions, blurred …

Written by a chimpanzee, she recalled thinking.

A third refill.

Swallowing hard, Novarro went to the kitchen and opened the refrigerator. No pitcher. She opened the cabinet. The bottle was there, tipped on its side, empty. Two limes were on the floor.

Feeling a wave of nausea, she went into the living room and looked on the far end of the couch. There was the pitcher, as empty as the bottle, and also on its side.

It hadn't happened in years. But here it was again.

Beside the pitcher was one of the evidence bags. She'd opened them up, pulled out the pieces, did whatever, and left everything open and in disarray. The entire chain-of-custody could be ripped apart by a first-year law student: "*The evidence was improperly handled, Judge. Perhaps even tampered with on purpose. It's tainted and unusable, and I move to have it stricken from the case.*"

Novarro stared in horror: Had she kept her gloves on when she was doing whatever … cataloguing, comparing, making sense to herself as she fell deeper into drunkenness? A single print could compromise everything.

Feeling her pounding heart keeping time with the dull thud of the headache in her temples, Novarro pulled on latex gloves and began trying to regain order in the evidence and in her life.

A half hour later she hoped she had everything back in original position, the correct piece in the correctly numbered bag, her head moving between pieces, bags and printed-out listing a dozen times. It was time to take the pieces to the forensics lab and hope her prints weren't all over the things.

The City of Phoenix Forensics building – or simply "Crime Lab" to most – was a clean and functional-looking brick structure on West Washington Street, almost dead-center of the Highway 10 and 17 rectangular circumurban that delineated downtown. The building was under a mile from Novarro's home and she was pulling into the parking lot before the conditioner cooled her vehicle. The sweltering heat combined with her fear and the previous night's alcohol consumption and for a moment she felt she'd vomit into the parking lot, but fought it until the nausea subsided.

The lab was predominantly white inside, the tabletops black

with tan wooden drawers, the lighting recessed into the ceiling. Agustín Sanches was the first person she saw, standing beneath a fume hood and holding a beaker of a ruddy fluid, the blue lab jacket tight on his mildly chubby form. When Sanches looked up and saw Novarro, his dark eyes narrowed in scrutiny.

"Jeez, Tasha, you look like twice-boiled hell."

"Freakin' flu, Augie," she said, holding up a hand, "so stay back." She lifted the box to the tabletop while explaining its odd provenance.

Sanches nodded. "Castle called to say it was on its way. That he'd passed it over to you at dinner last night." Sanches raised an eyebrow at the final three words.

Sanches, a friend and confidant, knew that she and Castle had dated for a while before it exploded. Novarro shook her head. "Not like that, Augie. Drinks and eats and separate ways."

"Salvadore just finished a job," Sanches said, nodding toward the latents section. "I'll beg him to jump on this right away and to put a tech on it as well. Bet we'll have a read in a couple hours. Go home and grab some rest, girl."

Novarro faked a cough. "Good idea, Augie. You'll call when you have something, right?"

Sanches did the thumb-pinkie phone thingie. "The second we're done. Go, girlfriend! You're spreading germsies."

*　*　*

Adam Kubiac sat in the shade of an awning on the patio of the streetside coffee shop and Internet café. It was in downtown Phoenix and near Arizona State University, explaining the preponderance of young men and women on the street, chattering into or tapping at mobiles, shoulders slung with bookbags and backpacks. Bicycles and skateboards competed with motor vehicles on the narrow avenue. It was past noon and heat rippled from the pavement.

Adam didn't particularly care for the café, but it was close to where he and Zoe lived. Kubiac didn't want to live in his father's house – especially after Cottrell revealed what the bastard had done with the will – and had moved into Isbergen's apartment nine days ago, carrying little more than a backpack filled with e-gadgets and a garbage bag full of clothes. It was a cool apartment, though about the size of two rooms in the old bastard's place in Scottsdale, which had about fifteen. The fun was being with Zoe and having sex with her anytime and having dinners like they were married and everything.

Kubiac sipped a double mocha latte that had taken the moronic barista two tries to get right and played *World of Warcraft* with a gamer in Thailand, blowing the poor Thai to noodles while waiting for Zoe to get back from shopping for boots. Shopping was a chick thing and she'd probably look at every goddamn shoe store in twenty blocks before finally going back and *getting the ones I dearly loved Adam, aren't they too hot?* at the first store.

Zoe was smart, not one of *Us*, but he let her think so because she came with benefits. And she was in love with him. He'd read that women sought strong males for seed, a need driven by evolution's desire to constantly trade up, to build better humans. Zoe was no exception.

As he sipped and tapped he became aware of eyes on the back of his neck. He turned to see a girl – late teens, early twenties – sitting at the table behind him. About the regular height for a girl. A bit chunky, but not much. She seemed Hispanic in the dark and liquid eyes, black hair, and olive complexion, but something also looked Asian. Kubiac registered a long gray dress and round dark-framed glasses. Large sad eyes.

She was probably looking because she thought he was cute. Zoe had dressed him in a pale pink shirt with a vest that looked like it was made of sweepings from a fabric store, but colorful. His jeans were coal black and so tight they made his balls hurt when he crossed his legs. The shoes were red Vans. Sometimes Zoe pissed him off by dressing him like he was a fucking Ken doll. Adam Kubiac saw no reason to dress in anything beyond shorts and tee shirt. It was *comfortable.*

And no matter how he dressed, Zoe said he made her wet.

Kubiac gamed for another two minutes, feeling the eyes again. He snapped his head around and saw her leaning to see more of his face.

"Are you looking for something?" he said.

"No. I'm s-sorry. I …" The girl colored with embarrassment, swallowed hard and turned away. Kubiac went back to his competition but still felt the weight of eyes on him. When he spun to the girl her eyes were on her computer screen, but he was sure she'd been studying him. As if feeling *his* pressing eyes, the girl's eyes rose.

"What?" he demanded.

"N-nothing. I just …"

Kubiac stared at the screen and cursed. "You just made me lose my game," he said. "To a moron."

"I-I'm suh-suh-sorry."

"Why are you staring at me?"

The girl waited until a departing patron passed between them. "I … it was a m-m-mistake. I thought—"

"What did you think? Stop babbling."

The girl looked frightened but spoke after a deep breath. "You l-look like, um, someone I saw once in a place that was … I was just, s-skip it, it's just fuh-freaking r-ridiculous anyway…"

A stutterer, rare in females, Kubiac knew, having learned that from the treacherous bitch Meridien. He affected a glower, but inside he was making himself think calm thoughts so he wouldn't stutter as well. Meridien had told him stress was a trigger. Probably the only thing the traitor ever said that made sense.

"What are you talking about?" Kubiac demanded. "Where is it you think you saw me?"

"I, um, a-a-at Doctor Muh-Meridien's house. Her office."

Kubiac's eyes widened. "How? What did you see?"

"I made a m-mistake with time and got there early. She put me in the s-side room … the solarium. I saw a car drive up and duh-drop you off. Someone who looked like you, I m-m-mean."

"You're a *patient* of this Doctor Meridien?"

She shook her head. "Not, uh, any more."

"Why? Tell me."

"I turned eighteen and …" she swallowed hard and took a deep breath, "I got free and never wanted to see that buh-buh-buh-buh-buh …"

"Relax," Kubiac advised from experience. "Think of what you want to say, then talk."

The girl took a deep breath. "I never wanted to see that b-bitch again. I was sick of her t-telling me I was nuh-normal like everyone else. I'm n-not."

Kubiac sat motionless. No one else existed but him and the person at the nearby table. The barista in the window, the chattering patrons at other tables, the skateboarder grinding down the pavement, they were all little more than robots made of pimply flesh and useless ancient drives. Instinct-driven automata. Neanderthals.

"Why did you hate Doctor Meridien?" he said quietly, scooting his chair closer to the girl.

Her almond eyes looked down in shame. "It's kind of a secret thing. M-mine."

Kubiac put his elbows on the girl's table, leaning her way. "You were right. I was her patient. Meridien's. *Was.* I hated the bitch, too. She told me that exact same thing in those exact words: that I was a normal human being. You can tell me why you hate her."

The girl looked into Kubiac's eyes as if wondering whether to trust him with her secret. She made her decision: "I'm not normal," she said, the words coming out with soft force, clean and clear. "I'm not anything near normal. I *hate* the idea of being normal."

Kubiac stared. As if unburdening herself had drained her energy, the girl stood, began loading her laptop into the backpack.

"What are you doing?" he said.

"Going back to my apartment. I've b-bothered you enough. I'm suh-sorry."

"You're not bothering me. You were but you're not now."

"I-I have to gather some stuff together, papers. Stuff to send to a college recruiter."

"What college?"

"Stanford. I'm not sure if I really w-want ..."

"What do you plan to study?"

The girl shrugged. "C-chemistry. Muh-maybe some math."

"What's your name?" Kubiac asked.

The girl swallowed hard. "Catherine Maruyama." She said it syllable by syllable to avoid stumbling on her own name.

Kubiac thought a moment and nodded. "I've heard your name before. I was in a group with people who knew you. They said you were fun, not all messed up. One was a guy named Mashburn."

"*Cat Maruyama ...*" Darnell Mashburn sighed in Kubiac's memory. "*She's so cool.*"

"*You want to do her?*"

Protective anger from the twitching fool. "*No man. If I could I'd marry her. Everyone likes Cat because she's nice to everyone. She's smart and pretty and not so screwed up. She's perfect.*"

"*Yeah? Then why is she a patient here?*"

"*Cat's real shy. She sometimes has panic attacks. It was more like an anxiety thing with her.*"

"I was in a couple of Meridien's groups," Maruyama said, jolting Kubiac from his memories. "Did you like Darnell?"

"He was too jumpy for me, like he was gonna pop out of his skin."

Maruyama flinched like it hurt to hear harsh words about Mashburn, and Kubiac felt a twinge of regret. "Uh, but outside of that, Darnell was OK. I remember he said that you were smart and cool. He wanted to marry you."

Maruyama looked down in embarrassment. "He was j-just kidding. I liked Darnell. He was fun."

Kubiac crossed his arms and stared at Darnell Mashburn's ideal woman. "You don't look that Oriental."

"I, uh … my papa is half Japanese, my mom is Australian."

Kubiac took a deep breath. "Look, uh, Cat … can we, um, see each other again? Soon?"

Looking a mix of surprised, confused, and delighted, Catherine Maruyama pulled on the backpack, straddled a single-gear cruiser bike, and nodded demurely before pedaling away.

Fifteen minutes later, Kubiac was still recalling the chance encounter with another of Meridien's lab rats. He looked up to see Zoe Isbergen approaching, shopping bags in hand.

"Check these out," she said, spinning on her heels to display new boots.

"Cool," Kubiac said without inflection. They were brown boots, *so the fuck what?*

"I also got a blouse and two skirts," Zoe said. She winked. "And some lingerie I think you'll like"

Kubiac said, "I met another of Meridien's patients."

Zoe froze, eyes wide. "When? How?"

He relayed the circumstances: The surreptitious looks followed by the conversation. How they both hated Meridien.

"She just appeared?" Zoe frowned. "This Harakawa woman?"

"Maruyama. She lives in an apartment somewhere around here. I figure she comes here a lot."

"You never saw her at Meridien's?" Zoe said quietly, studying him.

"I'd heard of her from people in my groups. She was one

person everyone liked. Meridien kept people moving around, like we'd cure each other or whatever. I hated the groups. You were like, supposed to talk and shit. It was moronic."

Zoe kept pressing like it was a big deal. "Wait a minute, Adam. If you weren't in any of her groups, how did this Maruyama know you?"

"She got there early for one of Meridien's sessions, saw me leaving. I registered in her mind, Zoe. I'm not hard to remember."

"She's still—"

"She stopped going when she turned eighteen." Kubiac paused and smiled. "For the right reasons … Hashtag: hatemeridien."

"What else?" Zoe prodded, her eyes searching Kubiac.

"She's shy. Nervous. But she's obviously …" Kubiac pointed his finger at his temple. "—not a Neanderthal."

14

Novarro's phone rang: Augie Sanches. "Uh, Salvador's done, Tash. Latents raised."

Novarro swallowed hard. "Anything there?" she asked, trying to recall how she normally said the words.

"Bowers's prints, of course. On everything. It's just …"

"What?"

"Uh, whoops, my centrifuge just stopped," Sanches said, not very convincingly. "Gotta deal with it. See you soon."

Sweat prickled from Novarro's brow as she tucked the phone back into her pocket. Something was wrong with the evidence. She'd screwed up, probably had her prints over everything. When it was discovered she'd compromised evidence, the gold shield would vanish. Most likely, the house would follow.

The ten-minute trip to the lab was an hour long. Though she'd showered, Novarro could smell fear blooming from her body. Despite a dozen antacids her stomach churned and boiled. She forced a nonchalant, businesslike look to her face as she entered the lab, walking past several techs working at their tables before coming to Sanches.

"Yo, Augs, got in a little nap," she lied. "Starting to feel better.

Maybe it's just a 24-hour bug."

Sanches didn't seem to hear, concern written across his square brown face. He cleared his throat. "Listen, Tasha … you know Salvadore Aldondo in latents, right?"

"Not too well. I've mostly worked with Bristol or Hughes."

"Salvadore and I are, uh, friends. He called me while raising latents on the jewelry and pieces." His eyes searched hers. "Was there some kind of problem with the evidence, Tasha?"

She forced an uncomprehending frown to her face, not betraying the sound of her blood in her ears. *The last sound you hear before you lose your job will be your exploding heart.*

"How's that again, Augie?" she said.

"The only clear prints on the pieces were Meridien's, Tasha. Almost, that is."

"Almost?"

"There were, uh, someone else's partials on two pieces, the owl and a charm on a bracelet."

Only two pieces held her prints. Novarro considered her expressions carefully, then played them one by one: *confusion, recollection, dismay, exasperation.* "Aw fuck," she said after *exasperation.* "It's my goddamn prints on the baubles, right, Augie?"

He sighed. "All cops are in the database. The scanner matched on seven points on a thumb, ten on an index."

Before Sanches could say *What happened?* Novarro turned away and made her eyes blaze. "Goddamn Maricopa."

"Maricopa?"

She stared at her shoes and shook her head. "I went directly home and started checking the COC sheets to make sure all the listed items were in my possession and I picked up a couple bags …" she let it hang, knowing it would be better if Sanches made the connection.

"Oh no," he said. "They hadn't been closed tight."

"When the jewelry headed floor-ward my hand shot out in reflex." Novarro stuck her hand out at waist level to demonstrate.

"At the last second I thought to keep my hand flat, just a surface. Then I slipped them back in the bag and zipped it tight."

"You probably did this …" Sanches said, replicating her motion but snapping his fingers closed for a microsecond, "and never realized it. Just a touch and you've transferred prints."

"Shit," Novarro said, shaking her head. "I didn't know it was that easy."

Sanches gave her an indulgent look. "You didn't want to note lousy handling in the chain-of-custody paperwork, right? Lay the shit on Maricopa for not sealing the bags?"

Novarro did her best near-beatification face. "It was a simple mistake, Augs. We all make them."

Sanches tapped his foot for a moment, then put his hand on her shoulder and leaned close. "I'll explain to Salvadore what happened," he whispered. "Nothing was compromised. It'll take ten seconds and a piece of cotton and everything will be cool. Oh, any by the way, the only other prints on the jewelry were the victim's. Sorry."

Novarro managed to walk away without betraying the weakness in her knees, only feeling them soften when she exited the building and leaned against a wall for support, the world spinning with hangover, fear, sudden emotional release and now, guilt. In the past eight hours she'd gotten drunk, almost ruined the evidence, faked an illness, then laid the blame for the evidence mishap on someone else.

Nice job, Tasha, she thought as she walked slowly to her car. *You're falling apart faster than Ben.*

Novarro went to HQ, thankful the detective's room was almost empty, the only one there being Mike Fishbach, fifty-six with a recent hip replacement, and waiting out a couple months until retirement by doing paperwork and research for Captain Solero. He was leaning forward in his chair and tapping his computer keypad. Fishbach looked up and grinned like a crazed jack-o'-lantern.

"There she is, ladies and gennulmens," Fishbach announced in a circus impresario's voice, "Tasha Novarro, hero of song and fable. Keeper of the flame and my heart."

Novarro smiled. You couldn't feel shitty around Fish. "What you up to, Fish?"

"Livin' the dream, Tasha," Fishbach said, spinning his forefinger in the air. "Cap's got me assembling crime stats neighborhood by neighborhood."

"Better you than me."

"Ain't so bad now that all the files are online or wherever; I can call up reports pretty easy with the search engine."

"Did you just say 'search engine,' Fish?" Most of Fishbach's previous thoughts on computers turned the air blue.

A big-teeth grin. "I'm a regular computer geek, Tash. The next Bill Jobs."

Novarro entered her cubicle – spare, save for a photo of she and Ben a few years ago smiling for the camera with Camelback Mountain in the background – and sat at her desk, turning on the computer. She'd had the lab make a copy of the reverse of Meridien's calendar and pulled it from her briefcase.

Carson Rider

She googled the name, saw a page of hits, scanned down. A Carson T. Rider in Memphis, an accountant. Another Carson Rider who headed an advertising firm in Connecticut. It wasn't a popular name, obviously, the spellings shifting by the middle of the page. A Carson Rider in New York.

Fishbach's phone rang, the internal line. He kept the speakerphone on low. It was Captain Solero.

"Got a few extra minutes, Mike?"

"Shoot, Cap."

Novarro kept studying her monitor. There was a Carson Rider in Wichita, a dentist, a Carson Rider in Cleveland, something to

101

do with antiques …

"… *this detective in Miami,*" Captain Solero was saying to Fish, "… *looking for anything we can send on Ramon Escheverría.*"

"That hunk a shit?" Fishbach snorted. "What'd that psycho do in Miami?"

"*Showed up on CCTV near a crime scene. I guess there were reports of …*"

Novarro dropped her eyes farther down the page. Ridley Carson was a TV weatherman in Seattle. She stared at the screen … *what did any of this mean?* She should be out pounding the pavement and sweating the alcohol from her system.

"*Could you give the guy a call, Mike? Arrange to get him whatever we have on Escheverría?*"

Novarro's eyes tracked to the bottom of the page. There was a Carson Rider who sold insurance in Bloomington, Indiana …

"Sure, Cap … gimme the guy's name …"

It seemed Carson Rider was not as uncommon a name as it sounded. Novarro was about to write Meridien's scribble off as a tip on a handyman or rug cleaner and hit the streets where she might do some good.

"*Carson Ryder,*" the captain completed. "*R-Y-D-E-R.*"

15

"Detective Ryder, this is Detective Tasha Novarro with the Phoenix PD."

"*Thanks for getting back so quickly, we're looking for anything—*"

"Leslie Meridien, Detective Ryder. Does the name ring a bell?"

"*I'm sorry, I was calling about information on Ramon Eschev— Wait, sure … I've got a call into Dr Meridien.*"

"Why, may I ask?"

"*She recently spoke to a Dr Angela Bowers here in Miami. Dr Bowers was murdered two days later. The next day one of her close colleagues was killed. I was wondering what the two doctors talked about. I'm waiting for Dr Meridien to return my call.*"

A sustained pause.

"You're going to have a long wait, Detective Ryder …"

16

"We've begun our descent to Sky Harbor International in Phoenix, folks," the pilot said over the intercom. *"Where it's a sunny 94° at present; 7 percent humidity. Time of landing should be fifteen minutes ..."*

From three miles up, southern Arizona looked forbidding, at least the Sonoran Desert portion, vast and desolate stretches of gray and brown which now and then rumpled into sharp-peaked mountains. Towns were small collections of boxes arranged along straight roads that disappeared into the horizon.

I was on vacation. Roy didn't seem to mind the two-day notice. Gershwin had returned early and the investigative section was fully staffed. Harry would continue to work the Bowers and Warbley cases – with Gershwin on hand if he needed assistance – and I'd catch the sights in Phoenix, my first-ever trip to the Southwest.

The plane continued to descend for several minutes, then banked. I looked out the window, whispered, "Holy shit."

"What?" said the fortyish and suited guy beside me, a native Arizonan back from a sales trip to Miami.

"Is all that *Phoenix*?"

A laugh. "Phoenix, Mesa, Glendale, Scottsdale, Tempe, Sun

City, Peoria, Goodyear, Guadalupe, Fountain Hills and well over a dozen others, all jammed together in the Salt River Valley. It wasn't that long ago they were distinct cities and towns. But people kept coming and the cities grew until there was no land between them. The aggregate population is about four and a half million."

I hadn't had any time for checking out the Phoenix environs. Yesterday I'd cleared my fast jump-out with Roy, called the DA to bump a next-week meeting for another week, explained my impromptu trip to Viv, who grew so quiet I twice asked if she was still on the line. I next hauled Mix-Up to Dubois Burnside's for dog-sitting, then ran back home to jam clothes into a suitcase, the call from Detective Novarro tumbling through my head all the while.

I'd been gobsmacked to find Novarro had her own dead psychologist, she horrified to discover mine. We traded details for fifteen minutes, and that's when it hit me that Phoenix would be an ideal vacation venue.

I deplaned and picked up my suitcase, my carry-on backpack slung over my shoulder. My Glock had ridden beneath me in my suitcase. Turning from the luggage carousel, I saw a woman in jeans and a mocha jacket striding toward me, thirtyish and slender, dark of eye and hair – striking eyes, even from a distance – and a face more handsome than pretty.

"Detective Ryder," the woman said.

"You must be Detective Novarro. Thanks for meeting me."

"I'm interested in hearing more about your case. I figured I'd waylay you here and we can go somewhere to talk. Where are you staying?"

"Somewhere downtown, one of those vacation-rental homes on Airbnb. I figured it'd be central."

"Beats a motel. You familiar with the area?"

"Never been any closer than Boulder, Colorado."

"Your rental vehicle should have a map. How about we meet

for lunch? There are nice places not far from here. You like Mexican food?"

"The hotter the better."

She gave me directions to a restaurant less than a mile distant, and I watched Detective Novarro walk away. Though Harry enjoys seismic motion, I prefer poetic, and the fifty feet it took Ms Novarro to get to the door provided two sonnets and a villanelle.

Fifteen minutes later we were at Mariscosa Playa Hermosa on Garfield Street, Camarones Ranchero for me, a grilled fish filet for Novarro. It was two p.m. in Phoenix, which made it four p.m. in Miami, close enough for me to order a brew. Novarro ordered a *horchata*, that sweet Mexican favorite made of powdered rice, sugar, milk, vanilla, and dusted with cinnamon.

"All of Meridien's records disappeared?" I said after we'd launched into both the meal and a discussion of the cases. She'd taken me through the discovery of Meridien's body, her suspicions that it wasn't as seemed, and the clincher of the stolen goods found buried in the desert. She was now telling me about the vanished files.

"From what I gather, getting through all the firewalls that DataSĀF has in place would take super-high-level hacking abilities." She paused in thought. "Which reminds me that I need to make another visit to the place. Maybe they've learned something."

"I wouldn't mind going with you," I said, wondering if it would be possible to convince her to let me follow along if I promised to stay out of the way.

"We'll do it right after lunch," she said, unfazed. "No, it'll be the second thing we do."

The first thing was the smart thing and the right thing. After lunch Novarro took me to her headquarters and made sure her Chief of Detectives, a Captain Frank Solero, knew that I was in the mix.

"You're convinced the two cases are connected, Detective?" Solero asked as we sat in his office. He was in his late fifties, looking constructed of sinews and rawhide. His dark eyes held an electric intensity. Solero wore a tan suit with a blue shirt, his bolo tie centered with a five-pointed star in a circle. Brown cowboy-style boots. His voice was soft and held echoes of a Spanish-speaking youth.

I said: "I think Meridien called Bowers with a question or conflict regarding professional ethics which Bowers shared with Professor Warbley. They're all dead."

A raised eyebrow. "And Escheverría?"

"Unless the most current and sophisticated facial-recognition program at Quantico's computer lab is wrong, Escheverría was in a Miami convenience store three days ago … four miles from where Warbley was killed."

"You got the FBI to jump that fast?" Solero said, surprised.

"I had to buy a man an alligator."

A smile. "I won't ask. Have you read the materials on El Gila?"

"I plan to do that tonight. My partner in Miami has everything as well."

Solero sighed. "I can only hope that Escheverría stays in Miami forever, though I expect he'll resume being a thorn in our side. A very nasty and elusive thorn. Every time we try to draw close – like establishing surveillance – it's like he knows what we're doing, and he retreats under his rock or adjusts accordingly. It's frustrating." He looked to Novarro. "I expect Detective Ryder's revelations will create a shift in emphasis in your case, Detective Novarro?"

She nodded. "I'll be on the tracks of Escheverría. This could be the break we've needed."

Solero frowned. "Death follows him like smoke follows fire. Be very cautious."

"Caution is my middle name, Cap," Novarro said.

"Then that would be a new addition." He paused. "Could you

both wait outside for a few minutes?"

We waited outside his closed door, Novarro pacing as I leaned against the wall. After seven minutes he yelled, "You can come back in now."

Solero was at the window gazing into a rich blue sky, his hands clasped behind his back. He seemed to be making a decision. He turned, looking into my eyes. "I took the liberty of calling the FCLE, Detective Ryder. I spoke to a gentleman named Roy McDermott."

"Oh?" I said, keeping my voice noncommittal.

"He speaks very highly of you, Detective, though McDermott doubted you were on a true vacation."

"Roy has a dubious nature."

Solero kept his gaze straight into mine. "Mr McDermott, who seemed a very intelligent man, believed your experiences and special knowledge would make you an asset. Especially if the cases involve Escheverría, a true psychopath. Very canny, very stealthy, but as loco as they come. A sick man with no moral restraints."

"I've known many Ramon Escheverrías, Captain Solero. I've put a lot of them away. Or in the ground."

A nod. "I'm told you've made such people a study for years." The big boots brought him my way, stopping a yard from me, the electric eyes directing a band of current into mine. "I truly don't want you out on our fine streets freelancing, Detective Ryder. Going it on your own. Mr McDermott also warned me that such a thing was your nature."

"I was sort of hoping, that is, I thought I could maybe just follow along and—"

Solero said, "Hold up your right hand."

"Pardon me, sir?"

"It is within my power to deputize you. That might save us all many headaches."

17

I followed Novarro to her office to look at files, noting that twice in a minute she received a call on her mobile, checked the caller, winced and didn't answer. The detective's room was wide and bright and populated with only a few people, meeting in corners with coffee in hand, talking on phones. Familiar turf. A few curious eyes wandered my way, took a snapshot, and went back to work.

Novarro had a small desk in a six-foot-tall cubicle and I leaned against the side as she sat and pulled her keyboard close. I was about to comment on the sole framed photo on the desk, Novarro and a kid about ten years younger, smiling in front of a mountain, but her desk phone rang.

"Tasha," the speaker said, "Merle Castle's on line two."

I saw her shoulders slump. She stared at the phone, then punched the button.

"Merle, dammit, I …"

"*I been calling your cell,*" a male voice said on speaker, talking like there was interference on the line. "*You're not answering.*"

"Merle, I haven't got time for your—"

"*I'm in Estrella Park and looking at a DB. It's a seventeen-year-old kid. Looks like he fell from a cliff while hiking.*"

I heard an odd but familiar sound in the background. Was that a horse whinnying?

"It's your jurisdiction," Novarro said. "Why are you cal—?"

"*We pulled the wallet. I've got $63. A pair of credit cards …*"

"Merle, is there a reason—?"

"*An REI membership card …*"

"Merle …" Her voice edged on anger.

"*And a business card from one Leslie Meridien, psychologist. I doubt it means shit, since I'm seventy feet below a trail and there's no look of foul play, but I know how you get about these things.*"

Twenty minutes later we were in a Phoenix PD four-wheel-drive SUV and somewhere southwest of the city. The desert was raw and spare, with low trees and bushes, the tallest growth being the saguaro cacti, some thrusting three stories into the arid atmosphere. I'd thought they were endangered, but they seemed as ubiquitous as oaks were in Mobile, every direction you looked. I'd never been in a desert and it was as strange to me as the surface of the moon.

"Is it the dry season here?" I asked.

"It's the dry season most of the year. The valley averages seven inches of rainfall annually."

I shook my head. "I've been in Mobile when it's rained that much in two hours. How does anything grow here?"

"Nearly every plant has thorns or spikes or a tough exterior. It's all about grabbing water and protecting it."

I nodded and kept looking out the window, fascinated. Novarro jerked the wheel hard left and we bounced off the asphalt onto a slender gravel road. "Phoenix PD's jurisdiction ends here," she noted. "Maricopa County Sheriff's Department takes over."

A series of jagged peaks loomed ahead. We drove another couple minutes until I saw a grouping of vehicles at a trailhead: four or five cruisers, an SUV, an ambulance, medical and forensics vehicles, and a multi-stalled horse trailer pulled by a Dodge

Ram 350. We got out and stood in stultifying heat, as much reflected from the hard ground as beating down from above. Novarro seemed not to notice.

Four men on horseback came clopping down the trail. Three passed by shooting glances and nods at Novarro while a fourth – early mid-thirties, gym-rat build, brown uniform with a Stetson up top – stared squint-eyed at me like trying to guess my weight, then snapped the leash or whatever to aim the beast our way.

"You got here faster'n I figured, Tash."

"Where's the body, Officer Castle?"

The guy on the horse pulled up, craning his head toward the peaks. "On its way down. Should be here just about …"

I heard the sound of a chopper in the distance and turned to see the helo appear in the cleft between a pair of mountains, the body suspended below on a line, no need to pull it to the chopper. The chopper was hovering above a minute later and whipping dust into the air as a pair of techs set the corpse on a body board. I could tell he was young. A tech gave a thumb-up to the pilot and the basket retreated into the sky as the chopper roared off into a blazing yellow sun.

The Maricopa County Cowboy dismounted in what seemed an unnecessarily theatrical move, boot heels puffing dust from the ground. He looked at Novarro, then at me.

"Who's this, Three-Point?"

"I'm Carson Ryder," I said, capable of answering on my own. "With the Florida Center for Law Enforcement."

"You take a wrong turn somewhere?" His expression split the difference between curiosity and mockery. He made no effort to extend a hand, so mine remained at my side.

Novarro said: "Detective Ryder has a case in Miami that seems to be connected to the Meridien murder. And thus perhaps with this one."

"I doubt it, Tasha," Castle said.

"Got a reason?"

Castle gave a come-hither twitch of his head and Novarro and I followed him to the victim as the needless paramedics unbuckled the body from the basket and set it on the carry board. The vic was as limp as a rag doll, the neck obviously broken, as was a leg, turned at a 45-degree angle from the knee. The kid was slender, in decent physical condition, and wore a blue tee shirt – now half torn away – cotton cargo shorts, with one green Converse All Star on a white-socked foot, the other shoe beside the body, telling me it had come off in the fall.

Castle stared down at the body. "Everything says accident, Tash. He was coming down the trail at the 2.6 marker, a rugged section. He probably got a few feet off the trail to take a picture or check the view. He slipped on loose footing and took a sixty-foot tumble."

"The parents know?"

"We sent a sergeant and a chaplain to deliver the news. I guess the parents are waiting for the victim to go to the morgue."

"Your folks got shots of where he landed, right?" I said. "From different angles?"

The eyes turned to me, assaying. "You know you have no jurisdictional standing here, right, Floor-da?"

Novarro stepped in. "Captain Solero deputized him, Merle. He's a bona-fidey Arizona lawman."

Castle stared at me, absorbing the new information. He didn't appear cheered. But Novarro offered an encouraging smile and clapped her hands.

"So here we are, three professionals working toward a single purpose. Mr Shackleton died in Maricopa's jurisdiction, Dr Meridien in ours. It appears the victim died in your jurisdiction, but resides on ours. How about we continue working together, Merle … like we did with the evidence your folks unearthed? That worked out nice, right? And by the way, the cap sent your superiors a big thanks for conveying the Meridien evidence to PPD so quickly and professionally."

112

I wasn't quite sure of the specifics of what Novarro was talking about, but was pretty sure I was hearing a piece of diplomacy and back-patting. The guy shrugged the big shoulders.

"I doubt there'll be much investigation of an accident, but I'll copy you on whatever we get here." He paused and thought a moment. "Of course, you gotta start sending us everything you get on Meridien."

"It's a deal," Novarro nodded. "And do you have the GPS coords for the scene?"

A dubious look. "You going hiking?"

"Not today. But I'd like to see where he fell."

Cowboy Castle pulled an old-school Garmin from his belt and displayed a flagged coordinate which Novarro copied to her phone.

"Would you like to see where he landed?" the guy said.

Novarro nodded. "Yes."

Castle grinned. "Take along a good rope."

And then the guy was walking away, the horse clopping beside him. Just before leading the beast into the trailer he shot a two-beat backward glance, one beat on Novarro, the other on me.

I climbed into Novarro's vehicle and we were on our way back. "Is there a jurisdictional dispute with Meridien?" I asked. "Why Castle wanted to be copied on the findings?"

"Meridien is entirely within Phoenix PD's turf. Merle wants me to copy him just to pull my chain an' make me send him e-mail. I imagine he'll give it a smug smile just before hitting Delete."

Novarro drove another couple miles; what I now understood to be the taller buildings of the Phoenix Business District moving closer. My mind reviewed the interaction between Novarro and Castle, picking up on little things.

"You seem pretty familiar with Officer Castle," I said noncommittally, a fishing expedition.

"Until early this year Merle worked with Phoenix PD in uniformed patrol division, like me." Also noncommittal.

"He called you Three-Point," I said, adding bait. "You didn't seem overly pleased."

We pulled to a red light. She put her hands atop the steering wheel and sighed. "The Department's been shedding jobs, not adding them. Detective positions, too. But last year a guy retired, a position opened up, and Merle and I both applied."

"You got the job."

She nodded as we turned onto Dobbins Road. "Yep."

"You were three points ahead on the test," I theorized.

She shook her head. "Nope. Three points behind."

She saw my confusion and smiled; a pretty use of the teeth. "Merle memorized and memorized until he knew all the book answers. He spent all his time knowing the exact answers. We both scored high, but he scored three points higher."

I thought about it as we drove away. "Castle had the facts," I speculated. "But you had the magic." Harry and I had interviewed detective wannabes, looking for more than memorization; we sought intellect, imagination, and – number one – that indefinable power some call intuition, others just "the magic". No amount of book learning could replace the magic.

Novarro nodded. "The personal interviews were conducted by three old pros – two active, one retired – a combined total of thirty-seven years holding the gold. I booted Merle's butt." She thought a moment and chuckled.

"What?" I said.

"The retired dick pulled me over after the interview, nodded across the room at Merle, and whispered, 'There goes a guy born to hand out speeding tickets.'"

"Ouch," I laughed.

"Merle doesn't know he lacks imagination because he lacks the imagination to consider it. It doesn't make him a bad cop – he's actually quite decent – it just makes him a poor candidate for an investigative position. When he didn't get the position with Phoenix PD, he went to the Maricopa County Sheriff's Department. It was basically a trans-jurisdictional pout."

"Does Castle want to be a detective for Maricopa?"

"There's a lot more enforcement, particularly round-up and deportation of illegals. Merle gets to pal around with ICE agents, Homeland Security types, the various border patrols. It's macho and manly stuff. And every now and then, as a part-time member of the mounted patrol, he gets to ride his horsey. *O'itnaldo'a'ataha itnohnoha-pa.*"

"Which is?"

"Give a man a horse and he feels complete. Merle, at least."

"I get the feeling he'd feel even more complete if you paid him added attention …" I paused, thinking I probably shouldn't speculate on the private life of a woman I'd just met, did it anyway, adding: "Like you used to."

She shot me an eye. "My, you are good, aren't you? Merle and I dated. It lasted almost three months. The problem is that I know it ended; Merle hasn't got the word yet. Maybe his horse will tell him."

The victim and his parents lived in north Phoenix and Novarro pulled to the side to call them and find out if they were still at home. She blew out a long breath when the call was over.

"You find out your kid is dead, then the cops call and want to talk. I truly hate this shit."

I nodded, nothing coming in words. I'd been here too often.

When we arrived at the address we could see through diaphanous curtains to a man and woman clinging to one another in the front room. I heard a heavy sigh from Novarro. We knocked. The clinging couple were Shackleton's parents, Herbert and Deanna. They'd received the word. "We're just …" the mother said, waving her hands like fighting off wasps, "they say he'll soon be, be at … in the, the …" She couldn't form the word morgue.

"We're going to meet him there," the father said. He was holding it together, but barely.

"We hate to intrude like this, sir," Novarro said. "But do you know what Brad was doing up on the mountain?"

"Brad loved the outdoors. Even when it was over a 110 outside, he was out in the desert. It was his escape from pressure."

"Pressure?"

"He's attending college, a sophomore."

"At seventeen?"

"It caused … some issues, being so young. Self-doubt, insecurities."

Mrs Shackleton turned to us. "Brad's s-studying to be …" She realized she was in present tense and broke down again. Her husband wrapped her in his arms and spoke to us over his shoulder. "Brad was studying to become a surgeon. A neurosurgeon."

"Why was Brad seeing Dr Meridien? He had her business card in his wallet."

Shackleton swallowed hard; I admired his courage. "His age … he had doubt, insecurities. Dr Meridien was giving Bradley a sense of self-worth, of making him realize he may have been smart, but it didn't mean he was a mutant or something from another planet. He was a normal and very bright kid doing what he would have done anyway, just a couple of years earlier."

"May we take a look at Brad's room? It might help us gain some insights."

"You're detectives. You d-don't think Brad was, was …"

I shot a glance at Novarro, shaking her head. "It's just procedure, Mr Shackleton. We have to look at everything."

He wiped away tears and nodded. "Upstairs. To the right."

A bed, a desk, books. Multiple dozens of books, medical texts, mostly. There was a terrarium with a pair of anoles inside and perched on a branch, heads bobbing. I checked for any sort of diary or address book, nothing. I saw a laptop on the desk and set it aside.

Novarro went to the closet as if drawn by gravity, pushing aside the accordion-fold slats. She lowered to a squat and studied the shoes for several seconds, then picked up a pair and studied the lugged bottoms. I saw a brand name: Merrel. She set them back on the floor and stood, pushing through shirts on hangers, studying several front and back. She next went to the dresser, opening drawers and paying attention to the tee shirts. She reminded me of a hound dog with a wisp of a scent and sniffing for more.

Her final move was to stand in the center of the room and turn in a circle. She re-checked the closet, looking in the back, then went to the door we opened on entrance. She pushed it closed and made an affirmative grunt. There, hung on a peg on the back of the door, was a backpack with a hose hanging from the side. She ran her hand up the side, popped a pocket and looked inside. She studied the hose, nodded and pushed the door back in place.

"What were you looking for?" I said.

She sat on the end of the bed and held up two fingers. "There are two kinds of hikers, amateurs and the knowledgeable. Amateurs wear tennis shoes, cross-trainers or cheap-ass things that look like hiking shoes but are next to worthless. They wear whatever shirt and pants they've got on. Amateurs stick a bottle of Dasani in a pocket and that's their hydration."

"The knowledgeable?"

"They wear shoes selected for the trail conditions and often use what's called 'technical' clothing like non-cellulose shirts with wicking capability. At very least they carry a knife, a compass, a lighter. Water is vital, and more, they wear a hydration bladder, especially younger types."

I nodded to the open door, behind it the odd backpack. "That's a hydration bladder on the peg."

She nodded. "A hundred-ounce Camelbak. In the pockets were

117

a knife, compass, two lighters."

I nodded toward the closet. "Good hiking shoes, too, right?"

"First rate, and getting worn. He used them. He also had tech shirts, shorts and tees."

"You're saying Bradford Shackleton was knowledgeable."

She sighed. "He was also seventeen."

The Shackletons were moving slowly toward the front door when we went downstairs. "Brad's at the … the facility," the father said, his eyes a thousand miles distant. "We're going to, uh …"

"We're just leaving," Novarro said. "May we take Brad's laptop? We'll return it very soon."

"Whatever," Mr Shackleton said, eyes a thousand miles away, more pressing matters needing his attention.

"Please, one more question …"

"Sure," the father sighed.

"When Bradley went out into the desert, was he prepared … water, clothing, gear?"

"Always if he was going out for a couple of hours in the heat."

"But not every time?"

"If he was out and went near one of his favorite hiking places, he might take a quick hike. Just to release some energy, some … of the pressure. Uh, we've got to …"

The father was shaky, the horror setting in. I nodded and started away.

"No," Novarro said, watching the couple standing before a Windstar van like trying to remember how it all worked. "I'll drive. You folks sit in back. Detective Ryder will follow us to the … to Bradley."

The father swallowed hard and nodded his thanks, angling his wife to the rear of the van. I took the wheel of the PPD vehicle, pasted myself to the Windstar's rear bumper, and we made our sad pilgrimage to the place never spoken.

18

After delivering the Shackletons, Novarro and I stood on the street outside the morgue and watched the long shadows cast by a falling sun. After a few minutes of silence I turned to her.

"You didn't tell the parents about Meridien's death. I thought you might use it to see if they knew any others of her patients. Because they'd been through enough, right?"

"They were broken … and then I start asking if they met any of the son's fellow patients?"

"Yeah … not a good time to try and get names and memories."

"Tomorrow, maybe. Now I think we pay a little visit to one Ramon Escheverría. Rattle his cage. Let him know we know he visited Miami. We are sure, aren't we?"

"My guy at Quantico says chances are 90 percent or better."

"A politician tells you he's 90 percent sure a taxpayer-funded project is going to come in on budget, do you believe him?"

I laughed. It was all I had.

Novarro said: "What the hell, let's go brace El Gila. Something to do, right?"

"You actually know where he's at?"

"He seems to be staying in plain sight at the moment. According to my sources, he's been spending his days in a ratty little gym about fifteen blocks from here. Feel like a workout?"

"A gym?" I said.

"He's listed as an owner, a cover, obviously. He also keeps a crew there: three to four sycophants who run errands and likely tell him how great he is."

I nodded. Sociopaths generally loved praise, further bolstering their already hyper-inflated self-image and sense of invulnerability.

We wound down streets where the majority of the signs were in Spanish. I saw more tire shops than I thought possible. The worn sign on the outside of the yellow block building said *Ortega Gym – Boxing, Martial Arts. We Train Champions.* We pushed through the door to an oppressive reek of sweat and liniment. There were resistance-type machines lined up against a wall, but mostly it was old-school free weights, racks of them. A battered and sagging boxing ring was in one corner. A trio of Hispanic males sat around a table near the shadowed rear, hulking, tattooed blocks of meat drinking beer from bottles. On the far side of the room a guy with a chest like a bull was bench pressing about three hundred pounds.

We were inside for a half step before the guard dogs were up and moving our way. Novarro had the shield out and they didn't look pleased.

"What choo wan'?" one challenged, looming over Novarro while the others tried to burn us down with glares.

"Need me a little pow-wow with Ramon Escheverría."

"He ain't here."

Novarro leaned past the wall of meat and pointed to the guy doing the bench-press work. "Is that not him right there?" She smiled and waved. "How you doing, Ramon?"

"It's cool," Escheverría called; the barbell in the air, no spotter behind him. "Let them by."

The wall parted and we crossed the room. Escheverría looked

like one of the Spartans in the movie *300*, built of rippling plates of meat and gristle though, unlike the movie warriors, his were overlaid with tattoos … flaming skulls, knives, a grim reaper. Escheverría glistened with sweat that looked thick and oily. Beneath the art I saw scars and the pucker of a bullet hole in a ham-thick thigh. I could smell that he hadn't bathed today. Or maybe all month.

"Howdy, Ramon," Novarro said. "How was the weather in Miami?"

A split-second pause. "Mi-*uhh*," he grunted the weight aloft, "ami?"

Novarro tapped the barbell. "Workout's over, Ramon. We need to talk."

Escheverría set the barbell in the mount like it weighed ounces, sat up on the bench, retrieved a towel from the floor, wiped the sweat from his face. He snapped his fingers and one of the *cholos* hustled over with a water bottle, handed it to Escheverría, and retreated.

"Miami, Ramon," Novarro said. "You were there last week. Helluva drive. You do it straight through?"

A long drink of water followed by a shrug and head-shake. "I got no idea what you're talking about, pretty lady."

"That tank of gas you stopped for after the job?" Novarro reminded him as she popped her briefcase. "There was a security camera in the store. Take a look."

She handed him the 8 x 10 of his face in the c-store. He regarded it for several seconds and handed it back. "Nice looking dude. Ain't me, though."

She passed over a blow-up of him fueling the red Camaro. "Here's another. Check that big bright red Camaro. Oddly enough, that's what you drive, right Ramon?"

Mock perplexation. "What, you think that dude stole my ride?"

I stepped up. "Come on, Ramon. We know you were in Florida last week. Miami. It's all coming together."

"All coming together?" He said it like trying a sentence in a foreign language.

I leaned close enough to feel the heat rising from Escheverría's thick shoulders. "We're gonna put you there, Ramon. At the Bowers scene. And Warbley's. You'll be extradited to Florida. Not only do we have the death penalty, we like using it. Cleaning up the gene pool, right?"

He gave me a look like I was barely there and turned his attention back to Novarro. "And all of this because you got a guy looks a little like me on a picture? And you got a red car in another picture?"

"It's *your* red car, Ramon," Novarro said. "What were you doing in Miami?"

Escheverría stood and walked to the window, the reek of his body in his wake. He stared across the broad highway. When he turned there was a grin on his thin lips and mockery in his eyes.

"It's *Señor* Escheverría, pretty lady. And here's what Señor Escheverría requests you do. He respectfully requests that you visit the Chevrolet dealership on Scottsdale Boulevard. He wishes you to enquire if they had Mr Escheverría's fine red Camaro all of last week. And when you find out that they did, I expect you to come back and apologize to Mr Escheverría for whatever it is you think he did in Miami in his bright red car since, as you will discover, he was not in Miami ever." A wisp of smile across the dark eyes. "Are we completed here?"

The Chevrolet dealership was open until eight p.m. and we arrived with minutes to spare. The service manager was named Dave, according to his shirt pocket. Dave was a beefy guy in his late thirties with red hair and a smattering of freckles. We were in front of his counter as a half-dozen mechanics in the bays worked on both floorbound and elevated vehicles. The place smelled of heat, grease, and detergent.

"Yeah, a 2015 Camaro 2SS, Ramon Escheverría," Dave said,

reading a pink work order pulled from a drawer. "The address is in Phoenix. Got the 426 engine. A monster power car. Runs about fifty grand with all the add-ons."

"And you had it in when?"

Dave squinted at the form. "Monday through, uh, Friday, for its three-month checkup. Let's see … Mr Escheverría wanted it tuned, alignment checked, tires rotated."

"'Three-month checkup'?" I said.

Another service guy – Carlos, by his pocket – went to a locker behind Dave and lifted a set of keys from the hook, checking the name tag.

"Mr Escheverría really likes that car," Dave continued. "And the model. It's his fourth in eight years. He brings them in for regular checkups … like it's a kid or something."

"He kind of a scary guy?" Novarro asked.

A smile. "First time I saw him I wanted to hide in the can. But he loves his Camaros, so good for him." Dave looked down the list, said: "Oh yeah, in addition to the tune and so forth we also installed a new muffler."

"The muffler died after a year?" I said.

"I don't see a warranty repair, so I expect—"

"You talking about the red SS?" Carlos said, turning from the key locker.

Dave nodded. "Yeah."

"I did the install. It was kinda weird."

"Weird how?" I asked.

"I think it had a bullet hole in it."

"A 'bullet hole'?" Novarro said.

Carlos nodded and moved his pointed forefinger horizontally. "Right through the center. In one side, out the other."

"It's gotta be a set-up," I said as we pulled from the dealership. "Planned. And damned canny."

"How you figure?"

"Escheverría probably wanted to be seen with the car. It shows there was a guy that looked like him in Florida last week, but obviously wasn't."

"Wasn't? You're backing out on your 90 percent?"

"I'm talking lawyer-speak, Detective Novarro. Any second-year law student can now use the picture showing Escheverría was in Florida …" I let it hang.

"To prove he wasn't in Florida," she sighed.

"He was there; I'd bet my pension. In a car similar to his actual vehicle, which was demonstrably in a reputable, record-keeping shop. All he needed to do was lay on his belly and—" I stuck out my forefinger like a gun and twitched my thumb, "put a round through his muffler to make sure it stayed in the shop longer than an afternoon."

We headed back to HQ so I could pick up my rental and head back to my lodging.

"Wanna grab a drink?" I said, nodding to the side as we passed a row of bars. "Something wet after a dry day?"

I saw her consider it, but it ended with a shaken head. "*Gracias*, but I'm beat down. Plus I want to see that trail tomorrow, early. Where the kid fell. No need for you to go if you don't want to."

"I want to," I said. "When?"

"It's gonna be hot tomorrow, well into the nineties. We should set out early. I'm thinking sunrise, which is around six a.m. Which means I'll pick you up at five. Or do Floridians need more beauty sleep than Arizonans?"

"Not that it makes any difference," I said, "but I'm from Alabama. I'll see you at five."

She dropped me off beside the Avis Forerunner I'd barely used. My rental digs were on West Washington Street near downtown, a cute little adobe-esque bungalow with an arched overhang on the porch and an orange tile roof. The yard was smooth pebbles the size of grapes. Pressing from the earth were spike-quilled yuccas as tall as my shoulders, plus some weird blue-green multi-trunked tree that, had it been red, would have reminded me of a close-up of human capillaries.

Novarro's taillights retreating in the distance, I walked the concrete path to the door and went inside, suddenly cooler by fifteen degrees. I had often heard about the heat of the Southwest being a "dry heat" and thus more bearable. I'd been skeptical but it seemed true, 7–12 percent humidity far less wilting than the often seventy-plus humidity of Florida and South Alabama.

I passed through a small and neatly arrayed living room to the kitchen and realized I'd not had time to provision up. All that waited in my refrigerator was cold air. The pantry yielded a former renter's can of mushroom soup and a packet of Ramen noodles.

Supper, with a water chaser.

19

Novarro showed up one minute early. She hit the drive-through at an all-night Mex joint where we grabbed coffee and tortillas crammed with eggs, beans, and chorizo sausage. Like all cops, Novarro was an expert at eating while driving. I got to use both hands, filling the void left by last night's meagre meal.

Thirty minutes later we were at the trailhead, Novarro shouldering into a backpack while I slung two canteens. The eastern amber of promised sunlight cast long shadows from the saguaros, as individual as humans in their arrangements of arms and veins and craggy hollows. I couldn't stop staring into the landscape, stark and dramatic.

"Sunrise is my favorite time of day," she said, echoing my appreciation. "There's a sense of hope."

The path began level, ascending after a hundred yards, expertly planned, switchbacks reducing the grade wherever possible. As we climbed higher I noted green plants resembling jellyfish with head, or bell, jammed into the sand as the tentacles waved in the breeze.

"What are those?" I asked.

"Ocotillo, my favorite. Over there's a barrel cactus."

"What are the bushes with the tiny yellow flowers?"

"Creosote. And this is Mormon Tea. Over there's sage."

"That's a weird tree up there. I have one in my front yard."

"Palo verde. I have one in my yard as well. And a lime tree."

"Instant margaritas! What's that fuzzy thing down by that gulley?"

"A teddy-bear cholla, also called a jumping cholla. And out here they're called arroyos or washes instead of gullies."

"You've lived here all your life?" I asked, impressed by her knowledge and pausing to take a swig of water.

"I grew up on the Pima Indian reservation," she smiled. "We're supposed to know this stuff."

"I thought you looked Native American. But then I also wondered, the name and if you might, you know, the ending vowel and all …" I was babbling, what I did when suddenly uncertain of my position. Novarro seemed to find it amusing.

"You thought Mexican because of the name? My father was Pima on his mama's side, Mexican on the other. My mother was mostly Pima."

"I confess to knowing little about Native American tribes."

"The Pima are also the *Akimel O'odham*, the River People, historically regarded for their skills at irrigation. Making every drop count. They also wove a helluva basket."

"You much of a basket weaver?"

"Never tried it."

"Does the word 'Pima' mean anything?"

"I don't know."

I nodded. "Yep, I guess the meaning could get lost in antiquity."

"No, literally," she said. It may be from *pi añi mac,* which means "I don't know," a phrase often used in early encounters with the Europeans."

"Probably the safest thing to say."

"Didn't work."

We grunted upward for the next forty minutes, traversing

open stretches of trail followed by tight passages between house-sized boulders, the now-bright sky so blue it seemed luminescent. Novarro kept one eye on her footing and the other on the GPS coordinates as we clambered up a rocky staircase to find a wide outcropping overlooking a plunging gorge.

Keeping my walking stick firmly planted with each step, I followed Novarro to the edge of the outcropping and looked down a dizzying stretch of near-sheer rock. I looked up to see another ridge angling in the far side and figured I was looking into a box canyon. Novarro checked the coordinates.

"This is where Shackleton went over. He landed straight down there, to the left of the gray boulder."

"Jesus," I whispered, thinking you'd have several seconds between stumble and landing to know it was all over.

Novarro surveyed the scuffed ground in the vicinity, a hodge-podge of footwear tracks. As with many overlooks where people can rest or gaze, self-centered morons had carved their initials or love yearnings into the rock. Novarro went back to the edge of the outcropping for a final gaze, then rejoined me, leaning against the rock wall at our backs.

"Let's think the worst," she said. "Bradley Shackleton was murdered. How would it happen?"

"Thrown off the cliff seems the correct answer."

She crossed her arms and thought. "Possible. But that's a big risk. Look." She pointed across the valley to the adjoining ridge. I saw a trio of mountain bikers rolling down a trail.

"And over there," she said, pointing in the farther distance.

I saw a pair of riders on horseback, ant-sized. "It's not as isolated as it looks up here."

She nodded assent. "This stretch of trail probably sees three dozen hikers a day, plus another dozen mountain bikers and a half-dozen horseback riders. They tend to be here later, like when Shackleton was out. Unless the kid came here with people he knew and trusted and they pushed him off, it would be hard to drag a struggling man up here. He'd have to be incapacitated. Bound. Gagged."

"And carried," I said. "Someone's gonna notice something like that."

She returned to the outcropping and looked over, then pulled off the backpack. "Castle was joking when he said bring a rope, but we'll pick our way down. Just be careful."

I glanced over the edge. No trail, just rock outcroppings.

She pointed to the west. "We're going about two hundred yards up the trail where there's more of a slope."

I studied the jagged stairstepping of broken rock thinking *slope* was being hopeful.

We started down, me watching every place Novarro put her feet, trying to emulate her every step. I would have felt a lot better if there had been a railing.

"Just watch where you put your hands and your feet," she said. "Rattlers love to sun on warm rocks."

Great.

The descent to the bottom took ten careful minutes. I followed her up the canyon to below the vertical cliff where Shackleton had been found. "Here's where he must have landed. I've got bloodstains. Some on this rock over here as well. And here's boot tracks from the medic dropped down on a line from the chopper."

I looked up at the outcrop knifing into the air seven stories up. We were near the terminus of the box canyon, scrubby trees and spike-branched bushes in every direction, broken rock beneath our feet. I looked up and saw a vulture wheeling in the hot air.

"Where from here?" I asked.

"This canyon widens out to the west and ends after a couple miles. I want to walk some of it."

Pushing through thorny brush and ducking mesquite limbs, we continued down the canyon, Novarro checking the map every couple of minutes. She pointed out horse shoe prints belonging to Castle and company.

"It flattens out from here," she said after we'd gone a half mile, Novarro occasionally crouching to stare into the pebbles and sand.

"What are you looking for?" I asked.

"There's an old Indian saying, Detective Ryder: "*T'annai al talla m'oshona*.""

"Don't know that one."

"Close up, it's clear the rabbit is not a fox."

"I still don't get it."

"How about, I'll know it when I see it."

We kept walking, me studying the looming gray cliffs on three sides. I saw no footprints in the looser sections of sand, almost beach-like. "It's beautiful here," I said. "Why no hikers?"

"Off limits. This particular canyon's a habitat of pygmy owls. They're endangered."

We came to a sandy wash overhung with mesquite. "I think I see something," Novarro said. "Let's take a look."

It was easier to say than inspect. We had to butt-slide down rounded boulders and edge past clumps of prickly pear. Novarro took the lead, crossing a rocky wash and being careful where she put her feet. I stepped to where she stood, finding a wide impression on a stretch of loose brown sand.

"ATV tracks," she said. "Which means either the rangers have been back here recently or it's someone else." She opened the map and stared for a few long moments.

"Yes?" I said.

"Time to head back up."

We spent hard-breathing minutes pulling ourselves from ledge to ledge back up to the trail. We arrived at the trailhead as a group of middle-aged female hikers exited a van. They were all fit, wearing proper gear, and chattering like giddy magpies. Another half-dozen vehicles sat in the lot, arrivals after we had set out on the barely sunlit trail. It was not a good place to try and sneak someone up a mountain to toss him over.

Novarro drove to the park office, a rock and log structure. She spoke with a ranger in his thirties who'd been setting maps in a display rack. "This about the kid yesterday?" the guy said, shaking his head. "Horrible."

"You get much of that?" I asked. "People falling?"

"Mostly what we see are sprains and bruises. Dehydration. Cactus-spine punctures. But yes, every now and then someone takes a tumble."

"We went down in the canyon where the victim landed," Novarro said. She opened the topo map. "There's a sandy wash in this section; you know it?"

"Main drainage for the canyon. When there's water in there it drains into the Gila River."

"You can get an ATV most of the way in, right?" She tapped the map. "Until maybe here or so … the big pile of boulders."

The guy nodded. "The end of the road for anything with wheels."

"Has anyone taken an ATV back there recently? Plant or animal survey, checking fire conditions, anything like that?"

"Not in a month."

"Ever get people back there? Civilians?"

A shrug. "Not often. Most people don't know how to find the entrance. Plus it's posted as off limits. Now and then we'll get locals going back there to party, kids mainly."

From there we drove around the mountain, Novarro pulling off twice to consult the map and check her GPS coordinates. We pulled onto a road barely a road, just tire tracks in the hard earth. The tires kicked up stones which drummed the undercarriage. And then we were between two diminishing ridges, an opening perhaps a quarter mile wide and studded with boulders which had tumbled from the ridges eons ago.

"The opening of the canyon," she said. "Can you guess my

thinking on this?"

"Shackleton's incapacitated, brought here. An ATV takes him up the canyon. Wait ... how about the noise?" Every ATV I'd ever seen sounded like a chainsaw on steroids.

"You can get special mufflers. Super quiet. They're big with hunters who don't want to scare off game."

"Gotcha. Go on."

"Shackleton's driven up the canyon until the buggy can go no farther, just a quarter mile from the end. She paused. "The poor kid has to be busted up bad to look like he fell down a cliff. Maybe bashed with a heavy rock. He gets his neck broken."

"Ugliness," I said.

"But is it likely? Or am I putting way too much into a fall? Believing just because I need to believe in something, anything, that it really was just an accident?"

"There were the ATV tracks you pointed out."

I watched her expression fall to self-doubt. "Bored kids from one of the nearby ranches going back at night to drink beer and smoke weed." She sighed, putting the car in gear and driving away. "It's all bullshit ... it's stuff I'm making up because I need to believe something."

We wound our way back to Phoenix. I understood Novarro's sudden depression because I'd been there before: every road a dead end, every thought little more than speculation. We needed a solid lead, or at least an idea to advance the case.

I had exactly nothing.

20

We got to Phoenix PD a bit after eleven a.m., Novarro still in her funk as we crossed to her cubicle. I saw a pudgy fifty-something guy in the cube next door, kicked back in his chair with his feet on his desk and his keyboard in his hands. His tie was askew and his gray suit jacket was in a ball on his desk.

"Here she comes, ladies and gennulmens," the guy announced like a carnival barker, his eyes alight with mirth. "Tasha Novarrooo, queen of Phoenix and of my heart."

Novarro continued to the guy's doorway and gestured me over. "Detective Ryder, this is Mike Fishbach. If you can figure out what he does, you're a damn good detective."

The guy extended his hand and I took it. "And if you can discover if those Indian sayings Tasha's always spouting are real or made up on the spot, you're an even better detective."

I looked at Novarro, she was giving nothing away. Fishbach looked to her, concern in his eyes.

"You look worn, Tash. You OK?"

She shrugged. "There's something going on out there, Fish. But whenever I look at it, it disappears. There's nothing to hang on to."

Fishbach looked at me. "I had hip replacement a week back

and I'm supposed to stay home, but all I do there is drink beer and yell at the dog. So I come here and the cap gives me little projects." Fishbach turned to Novarro. "But he ran out of doodle work. Since I got shit to do, I looked at your reports. Tash. You're thinking El Gila is involved?"

"How well you know Escheverría, Mike?" Novarro said.

Fishbach retook his chair, tapping the desk with a sturdy finger. "I was working a homicide, oh, fifteen months back. Before you got here, Tash. A drug dealer got whacked. Not a street rat, a guy up the ladder. We figured a rival ordered the hit. A well-placed snitch of mine put the deed on good ol' Ramon: contract hit for a rival kingpin."

"And?"

"I made Escheverría a personal study. He's bad news squared. The hit had Escheverría all over it, well-planned and executed: The dealer lived in some fortified place in west Phoenix, pulling strings by phone, never went outside. He's got no life outside of running his business." Fishbach pause, winked. "Except … he loves *lucha libre*. Watches it all day long. Fucking bets on it, if you can believe that. It's completely fixed; a big story line. But the asshole gambles on it."

"Excuse me," I said, feeling lost. "*Lucha libre?*"

Novarro said: "Ever see those Latino wrestlers with the masks?"

I nodded, having seen them on television a time or two when surfing channels. "Masks, bright costumes, capes sometimes. Leaping all over the ring?"

"That's *lucha libre*, or free wrestling," Fishbach said. "The wrestlers are called *luchadores*. It's theatrical and colorful and about as big a part of Mexican culture as sombreros and mariachi bands. Anyway, the dealer is a *lucha libre* fanatic and his favorite *luchadore* is a guy named El Tigre, the Tiger. So one day the dealer hears huge news in the neighborhood … El Tigre is not only in Phoenix for a match, he's having lunch at the little Mexican restaurant two blocks down."

"Uh-oh," I said.

"The dealer figures what the hell, it's close by. He'll run over for a few minutes and get his picture taken with El Tigre, an autograph. What could go wrong?"

I smelled the bottom line. "How far did he get?"

"Halfway to the street. A shooter hiding behind a wall of tires at a *llantera* a hundred paces away put a 30-30 round through the dealer's temple. With a decent scope it would have been like shooting a sitting duck."

"El Tigre in on it?"

"Naw, El Tigre's a straight arrow, a big pussycat. It turns out that he was paid five grand to eat at the restaurant that day. The owner said he invited him for publicity purposes."

"The owner was in on it. Anything there?"

A sad shake of the big head. "No fucking way to prove it was anything but what he said. And anyway, if Escheverría wanted the owner to invite El Tigre to lunch, there's no way he'd ever refuse. Not if the owner valued his health and the health of his family."

"You're sure it was Escheverría?"

"He figures things out, how people work. It's like a sixth sense. He's freaking cold, but he's smart and always one step ahead. Oh, and the next week my snitch turned up dead. He'd been beaten so bad he didn't look like a person. That was maybe the scariest part."

"The killing of your snitch?"

"My snitch was two layers from Escheverría, insulated. But somehow Escheverría discovered he'd been ratted out. It was almost impossible, but it happened."

"Nothing tied Escheverría to the hit on the dealer?"

"A half-dozen fine and upstanding citizens swore on their mamas' graves that Mr Escheverría had been in a whorehouse with them the entire evening. We couldn't break anyone."

"Tough case, Fish," I sympathized.

"I'm not unhappy that Escheverría took out the dealer; he was a scumball. And when the assholes are killing themselves, they're not killing any real people." He sighed. "But that was my best snitch."

"Like you said, Mike," Novarro said. "Escheverría's screwing with us. And laughing."

"Yeah, but we're sure it was Escheverría in Miami," I said. "He obviously likes driving pretty red Camaros with great big engines, but if his particular pretty red Camaro was in the shop …"

"The one he drove to Miami was borrowed or stolen," Fishbach finished. "Maybe it's a thing with him. He gets a new red Camaro every two years. Loads 'em up with chrome and spinners and low-profile tires and that kiddie shit they love."

Novarro crossed her arms, leaning in the doorway of the cube and gave Fishbach a glittering smile.

"Did I hear you say you had a little free time, Fish?"

Novarro next made a call to the Shackletons. The father agreed to answer a couple of questions over the phone and she put it on speaker.

"Did Brad ever talk about other patients?" she asked. "Did you meet any?"

"*Brad spent some time in group therapy. Dr Meridien thought it good for some patients to spend time together … to relate their experiences. Bradley didn't talk about it much, but …*"

"Sir?"

I heard a finger snap. "*But I remember a name. Mashburn. Brad said he was a nice kid but that he'd gone … crazy. I take it Mashburn developed schizophrenia and fell into depression or whatever. Bradley was very affected by it.*"

"First name?"

"*Daryl? No, Darnell. That was it. Brad said he was fun at first. But then he got sicker and I'm not sure if Dr Meridien kept treating*" *him."*

"Any others?"

"He mentioned a girl a couple times. Cat. I think he called her a few times just to talk."

"Last name?"

"Not a clue. I'm sorry."

The phone directory showed a dozen Mashburns in the region; Novarro hitting on her eighth call. She got the number and made arrangements for us to visit the only other patient of Leslie Meridien's that she had identified.

"I spoke with Darnell Mashburn's aunt," Novarro said after hanging up. "She said Darnell's having a tough day."

"What's that mean?"

"Guess we'll see."

The Mashburn house was a two-story split-level in a modest neighborhood one street behind one of those suburban connectors filled with Outbacks, Friday's, Chipotles, Pizza Huts, and the like. The still air smelled like meat and grease. We parked and walked to the house. Mrs Alyce Mashburn was African American, in her early forties, pretty once, but heavy now, with eyes bagged and hair going gray. She wore a purple dress and kept her hands clasped together at her waist, probably to keep them from wringing.

"He sits up there and watches movies," she said after we'd provided a sparse outline of our purpose. "Old ones, new ones. Documentaries. Sometimes he talks to them. But it keeps him calm."

"Why was Darnell seeing Dr Meridien, if I may ask?"

"He had socialization issues. That was ... when things were better. Last year he developed SAD."

"Schizoaffective disorder," I nodded. "Schizophrenia combined with mood disorders."

"They said his IQ was above a hundred forty. He loved school, math, chemistry, everything. And then it all started to disappear. He wasn't with Dr Meridien much longer after that. She said it was more a brain chemistry thing and not what she dealt with. She recommended other doctors. I liked Dr Meridien; she was honest about Darnell's problem and called afterwards to make sure we were all right."

"May we see Darnell, please?"

She led us up the stairs to a closed door, knocking three taps with a short pause, one tap, long pause, and a final tap.

"WHAT!" a voice bellowed.

We stepped into the room. Darnell Mashburn was a spaghetti-thin seventeen-year-old who looked like he'd been plugged into a 220 volt outlet: sprigs of untamed hair in all directions, bulging eyes with the full white showing around the irises, flared nostrils, and hands in constant motion, like sculpting from invisible clay. He sat on his made bed wearing only a loincloth fashioned from two red washcloths front and back and held in place by a large rubber band, and a pair of blue flip-flops at least four sizes too large.

His eyes narrowed with a combination of anger and confusion and the hands sculpted faster. I studied the scope of Darnell Mashburn's world: bed, desk, chair, chest of drawers. In the corner was a large flat-screen TV, and DVD player. Beside his bed a TV tray held a paper plate with a half-eaten burger and some fries barely visible under a thick mound of ketchup.

"These folks would like to talk to you, Darnell," his aunt said. "It's about Dr Meridien. You liked her."

"She was MY BITCH!" Mashburn spat. "I FUCKED HER EVERY DAY FOR A YEAR! I MADE HER SUCK MY COCK!"

I wasn't surprised by the outburst: sexual scenarios were part of many damaged minds, often involving caregivers.

"Darnell ..." his aunt cautioned.

His eyes turned to Novarro and me and his nostrils flared. "I don't like how they smell, Auntie. Make them GO AWAY!"

Mashburn's aunt shot us a look. "Do you want me here or …?"

"We'll be fine," I said.

She blew out a breath and retreated, leaving us alone with Darnell.

"We don't want to take much of your time, Darnell. We just have a couple of questions about Dr Meridien and some of the people you might have met at her office."

Mashburn backpedaled on his bed and coiled against the wall. "I can't talk to you. You're TOO CLOSE."

Novarro looked at me and we stepped back several feet. "Now?" she asked.

Mashburn shook his head violently. We backed to the door, as far as we could go. He looked even more distressed. I said: "Be right back," jogging past a perplexed aunt and outside, returning a minute later with the tennis racket I'd seen in Novarro's back seat. I approached Mashburn slowly and put the handle of the racket in his reluctant hand, angling the stringed head in front of his face like he was behind a fence.

"It filters proximity," I explained to his questioning eyes. "It's a distance machine."

Mashburn's brilliant but afflicted mind stared through the strings, moved the mesh aside, frowned, brought it back into place between us. "OK," he nodded, satisfied. "What?"

"Did you know any other of Dr Meridien's patients, Darnell? Think hard."

Mashburn imitated a rapper, holding out thumb and pinkie and shaking his hand while grinning through the racket. "Yo yo yo, bro … the Shakster. Shaks man. We were groupies, brother. Brad's my best friend YOU ASSHOLE!"

"Brad Shackleton?" I asked.

"Yeah, buddy … The Shakster. SHAK-A-DOODLE DO!"

"When was the last time you talked to the Shakster?"

He thought a moment.

"Tomorrow."

"Did Brad ever have anyone angry with him, Darryl? Maybe threaten him?"

"Atom bomb. BOOOOOOM! Fuck atom bomb. Brad hated the atom bomb. The bomb blew itself up."

I shot Novarro a glance. It wasn't going well, or at least in any reality-based direction.

"Did you know any of Dr Meridien's other patients, Darnell?"

He stuck the racket between his thighs and moved his arms up and down like a robot. "There was a mechanical boy. He was funny. I liked him."

Darnell had fallen into the world of delusion. "What was the mechanical boy's name?"

"I don't know."

"You must have known—"

"I SAID I DON'T KNOW!"

"How about Cat?" Novarro said. "Did you know her?"

He froze and his eyes tightened on us. "How did you know about the Cat?"

The cat. Had his aunt been mistaken about it being a woman's name, or had Mashburn made a new connection in his mind-scape?

"We're friends," Novarro said.

"YOU'RE LYING YOU DIRTY BITCH."

"Tell me about the Cat."

"THE CAT WAS SWEET, THE CAT WAS KIND, THE CAT WOULD CLAW A MAN OUT OF HIS MIND!" He gave us a quivering smile. "The Cat made me crazy."

"Where does the Cat live?"

He pointed upward. "In the sky."

"She's dead?"

His eyes widened. His mouth fell open. "THE CAT IS NOT IS NOT IS NOT IS NOT!" he screamed, standing and swatting

140

at the air with the racket.

We retreated to the hall with Mashburn making bird sounds and beating his bedspread with the tennis racket.

"Want your racket back?" I said to Novarro.

"I don't have anyone to play tennis with."

Ms Mashburn met us at the bottom of the stairs. "It didn't go well, did it?" she said.

"Not very," I admitted. "He mentioned a Brad, which has to be Shackleton And a Cat. Have you ever—?"

"I don't know who they are. Or even *if* they are. Did he talk about the mechanical boy?"

"A bit."

"I'm not sure which are real and which aren't. The doctors are trying some new medications. It's all they seem to do. You can come back if you want, but I can never guarantee what you'll find from one hour to the next." She paused. "Or maybe it's down to minutes now."

21

Adam Kubiac was pulling on clean pants, trading them out for the ratty shorts he'd worn for two days. Isbergen had tried to get him into some of the hipster clothes she liked so much, but all that stuff itched.

Isbergen passed by the doorway. "Where are you going, Adam?"

Kubiac frowned. "I don't know, *Dad*. Where do you think I should go?"

"Dad?"

"Where are you *going*, Adam?" he said in a mocking voice. "Who are you *meeting*, Adam? Are you going to wear *those* pants, Adam? Hashtag: stopbeingdaddy."

"I'm sorry," Isbergen said. "I just didn't want you to forget we have a meeting tonight with Cottrell. It's important, and we have to talk about it first."

"Talk about what?"

Isbergen crossed her arms and leaned against the wall. "I have an idea. A super idea, Adam."

"We gonna cut the bastard's throat? Hashtag: great."

"No, Adam. We're going to get your money back."

Kubiac froze and stared. "What did you say, Zoe?"

"I've been thinking about Cottrell. What's going on in his

brain. We're going to get your inheritance, Adam. You deserve it, so we're going to get it."

"It can't happen." Then, in a whisper: "Can it?"

Isbergen crossed the room to Kubiac and wrapped her arms around his waist, whispering in his ear. "We can't get all of it, but I'm pretty sure we can get most of it. And that's a long way from where you are now. Here's a hashtag, Adam: hope."

"It's impossible." A long pause. "How?"

"We make an investment."

"In what?"

"Greed."

*　*　*

Novarro pulled into her parking spot at HQ, put the car in park. We stepped into searingly bright sunshine and walked toward the building, the wind a hot breath blowing from the south desert.

"More wasted time," Novarro moaned. "Christ … mechanical boys, girls in the sky. You think Mashburn's ever gonna get better?"

"I've seen it happen. Dosages get adjusted. New meds work better."

"Optimistic. I like that. I just don't believe it."

"Yeah," I sighed, back to reality. "Me neither."

I followed her to the detectives' floor. It was, as usual, almost empty and I took it that Solero believed in keeping his people on the street.

"Ladies and gennulmen …" Fishbach trumpeted as we approached.

"Not now, Fish," Novarro said. "I just left one madman."

Fishbach knocked and entered Novarro's cubicle simultaneously, waving a scrap of paper. "I got a hit down in Tucson, Tash. I like it."

"A girlfriend?"

"A red 2014 Camaro 2SS. I like it for Escheverría."

Novarro snatched the paper and looked at it, dubious. "How many red Camaros are in Arizona, Fish?"

"According to the license branch, a hundred or so."

"Why this Camaro, particularly?"

"Same basic model, the big-ass engine. Color's right. It's owned by one Thiago Benitez Carazo."

She gave him a look. "And?"

"The name struck a bell from when I was investigating Ramon. I did some cross-checking. The last time Escheverría was doing time, guess who his cellie was?"

"Carazo," Novarro said, suddenly fully engaged. "Tell me it's Carazo."

Fishbach just grinned.

"So it was Carazo," Novarro said. "Feed me the whole story, Fish."

"It was three years back. Crazy Ramon beat the hell outta some guy in an alley, shattered jaw, kneecap kicked backwards, teeth snapped off. Everyone knows the guy'd been slack on payments to his meth source and El Gila was making a statement."

"But …" I said.

"But everyone in the joint says the vic started the fight … including the vic. The judge isn't buying it. He tallies up some similar situations before Ramon learned self-control, and labels Escheverría a habitual offender. He pitches Escheverría in the can for six months, about all he can do. For five of those months Carazo was his roomie."

'You're thinking?"

"I'm thinking El Gila comes up with a job – two maybe, if what Ryder thinks is right – in Miami. He's a careful guy, a planner. He won't fly because there's too much documentation. He has to drive. But it's over 2,000 miles; he ain't gonna take a Prius, he wants what he likes. He knows his old cellie has the same thing – Escheverría probably bragging on his ride in the joint, why Carazo gets one just like it."

"Escheverría borrows his buddy's car."

"Probably rented it for a price Carazo couldn't resist. And because Ramon's a smart-ass sociopath, he parks his Camaro in the shop for the duration, knowing if he's spotted, it can actually be better insurance than not being seen. It's proof it can't be his car in Miami, therefore it can't be him."

"Got to give this asshole credit," Novarro said.

"Tucson's how far?" I said.

22

I drove so Novarro could work the on-board computer, tuning the dash-mounted monitor her way as she dug up all she could on Thiago Benitez Carazo, alternating it with various phone calls, feeding me info as I blew southeast down Highway 10 toward Tucson.

"Carazo's a shitbird," she said. "Got a pissant record going back to age fourteen. Petty thievery early on, a few possession busts, minor, then moved up into Grand Theft Auto, took two falls. I just spoke to his last parole officer, says he thinks Carazo manages an auto junkyard in the desert north of Tucson. A car thief managing auto parts tell you anything?"

"He's still moving metal," I said. "Maybe not whole cars, but I'd bet he's tied in with chop shops."

"Fish just sent an e-mail saying the Camaro 2SS or whatever is base priced around forty grand. If I can't afford one, how does a guy who oversees ten acres of rust afford one?"

"You said the auto graveyard is in north Tucson. That's closer, right?"

"We gotta stop in town first."

"Why's that?"

"*Ana'h'ahowa, ey'itawna o'dno,*" she said.

"Meaning?"

"Before you poop in another village, clear it with the Chief."

The Chief of Detectives in Tucson was Hulbert Stringer, a pleasant red-faced man in his early fifties. When Novarro outlined the reason for our visit, Stringer called in his Theft-crimes Lieutenant, a whippy woman in her late thirties with short brown hair and the great name of Hialeah Begay. Begay was familiar with Carazo, wrinkling her nose at the mention of his name.

"You got the shitbird assessment, right, Detective Novarro. Carazo's small potatoes. Not bottom level, but not a big player in anyone's game. I imagine he jacked a car a week back in the day, enough to keep a room and party supplies. Small dreams."

I'd known pros who knocked down a car or more a night: focused professionals.

Novarro said: "Still, Carazo sports some nifty wheels."

"Probably the major expenditure in his life. He knows cars, knows the underground parts market. We'll nail him one day soon."

"How'd a loser like Carazo end up celling with Escheverría? You folks know about him, right?"

Stringer leaned into the conversation. "Escheverría – can you believe that Gila monster story? – worked out of Tucson some years back. I'm happy he moved north, though I wish he would have kept going."

Begay's turn. "As for celling with Escheverría, Carazo's a natural-born slave. Not in a sexual sense, but bowing and scraping. I figure he was Escheverría's gopher, and proud of it. Carazo would have received protective services in return, which he would need in a custody situation, being neither smart nor strong."

"Understood," I said, having seen it often; an alliance between the strong and the weak. Hell, it was all over nature. Carazo was the plover that cleaned the crocodile's teeth, or perhaps the remora to Escheverría's shark.

We thanked the Tucson folks for their time and drove back north, passing more desert until we came to a sheet metal wall running beside the road for hundreds of feet, at the far end an entrance and the looming sign saying: *Oro Valley Car Parts: Buy-Sell-Trade. Open Weekend and Nites.*

We passed into the land that is every auto graveyard: rank after rank of vehicles of all colors, shapes, and degrees of deterioration, some looking showroom bright (though with a crushed trunk or side panels or the always depressing front-end crash damage with shattered windscreen) or rust brown. They were arrayed in a general attempt at order per year and model, but it wasn't the Dewey Decimal System.

A low concrete block building sat to the side, a flashing sign saying OFFICE. "Well, well," Novarro said, "check the wheels around the side."

I saw a bright red Mustang as sleek as a crouched cat. Novarro shot me a wink and we went inside. We knew Carazo from his mug shots, the skinny guy behind the counter and twiddling with a carburetor. A radio on the counter blasted Spanish-language rap at jet-engine level.

"Howdy, *hermano*," Novarro said, flashing the brass so fast it only registered as badge, then flicking off the radio. "We is the po-leece.'"

Carazo frowned and set the carb aside. "All our cars are good. Nothing stolen. And anyway, I am jus' the manager."

"There's really just one car we're interested in, Mr Manager."

He pointed through the window at hundreds of rusting hulks. "If you know which one, please, be my guest."

Novarro smiled. "We're interested in a 2014 Mustang 2SS, red, registered to one Thiago Benitez Carazo of apartment 3-C, 112 Skyway View Drive, Tucson, Arizona."

Tension and a narrowed eye. "That's mine. Why do you have interest in my *bebé* ?"

"We'd like to see it. That's all."

Something was turning in Carazo's mind, like remembering the way he was supposed to speak and act if cops came to look at the vehicle. And then Carazo was all smile and bonhomie as he led us to his wheels.

"Be my guest, *amigos*. I have nothing to hide."

"You lend this car out lately?" Novarro said.

Wide-eyed amazement. "Lend? No way, *señorita* ... she's my *bebé*."

"Like your baby hasn't been to Florida lately," I said. "A little sightseeing perhaps? A trip to Disney World?"

Carazo patted the trunk. "No way. The salt air might rust her sweet bootie." He paused and made a big deal out of looking into the air and scratching his chin. "You know, there was one loco thing a couple weeks back."

"Loco how?" I asked.

"Some thief stole her plate, man. I hadda pay good *dinero* to get a new one."

Novarro and I exchanged glances. Carazo had just explained why his license tag might have been recorded in Miami. It hadn't been, but he'd had a story ready. From what I knew of his sad record, he hadn't been the one inventing the story.

"Stolen?" Novarro said.

"Si," Carazo lamented, the picture of innocence. "Can you imagine? I wonder where the car the tag was put upon is today?"

Again, we'd been handed a dead end. There was only one play left: the Hail Mary, though I guess here it was the "Ave Maria". We had to push the bounds of the law a tad, simultaneously depending on Carazo's naiveté or stupidity. How gullible was he ... and how much was he afraid of going to prison? We'd know in a couple minutes. And I'd also learn how adept Novarro was at playing a role.

I asked Carazo where the bathroom was and he directed me to a stinking shoulder-wide cupboard that hadn't seen a mop in a month. I tore off a piece of toilet paper, stuck it in my mouth, pulled it out damp and shaped it into a small ball. Somehow the hand dryer worked and I gave it a full cycle of drying, then stepped back outside.

I walked back to the Mustang, peered in the rear window. "Still OK for me to check things out, Thiago?"

A flash of uncertainty. "Ain't nothing wrong in there, *señor*."

"Seeing's believing," I said.

The false grin returned. "Check it out, man. My *bebé* is the cleanest machine you ever seen."

I climbed in the front and made a cursory inspection, finding nothing. I went around and climbed into the tight rear seat, making a big deal out of feeling under seats, lifting the mats and so forth. When I knew his eyes were on me, I froze, picked at the floor, dropped something into a baggie. I backed out of the car, my face serious.

"What is that, man?" Carazo said, eyeing the bar. "What you got?"

I ignored him and motioned Novarro over. I showed her what was in the evidence bag in my hand. She turned a penetrating gaze on Carazo. I whispered in her ear and she nodded.

Carazo had lost the grin. "Come on, man … what is it?"

Novarro was Oscar-quality perfect, walking to Carazo with the assurance of the Angel of Death.

"Everything," she said.

"*What?*"

"Tell us everything, Thiago. It's the only way you'll keep driving the *bebé*."

"I dint do nuthing! What are you saying?"

My turn. I walked over wiggling the bag before Carazo's eyes, inside a gray-white object rattled back and forth, too fast to register focus. "A fucking tooth, Thiago. A human tooth in your car. Is your baby teething?"

"I don't know where it came from, man," he wailed. "I ain't done nuthin' wrong."

"A man died in Miami last week, Thiago. There was a witness saw the guy being driven away before his body was found. He was tied up."

Terror in Carazo's eyes. "I don't know what you're saying."

Novarro spun the guy to face her. "HE HAD FOUR TEETH BASHED OUT, THIAGO," she screamed into his terrified eyes. "WHY DID YOU KILL HIM?"

"I dint DO NUTHING! YOU GOTTA BELIEVE ME."

"WHY DID YOU MURDER HIM, THIAGO?"

"I wasn't in Florida." Carazo was near weeping. "I ain't never *been* to Florida."

I did the bag wave again, Carazo averting his glance like it was a voodoo doll. "A dead man's tooth under your car seat," I explained. "A witness who saw a soon-to-be dead man in the backseat of your car. Congratulations, Thiago, you've moved into death penalty territory."

He pressed his palms against his eyes. "No ... no ... no ... It wasn't me. My car was there, but it wasn't me. I never knew about any of this. I only let a man borrow my car."

"Tell us the story," Novarro said. "Everything."

Carazo's eyes were wet, his shoulders slumped, his face a study in misery. "I can ... tell what happened. And you will understand how it is I know nothing of Miami, of your events there. But you can never say where it came from. I will die. I will die terribly."

"What a fool," Novarro said on the way back to Phoenix.

"Fools are our best currency," I said. "And today was fool's gold."

"Please," she laughed, "spare me."

"We now know for sure Escheverría was in Miami. It wasn't a glitch in facial-recognition software."

"And if he was there, he was almost certainly the ink-necked guy in the bar Warbley left."

"Which gives us a 99.99 percent he killed Warbley. And if he murdered Warbley, he murdered Bowers."

"Which brings us back to Phoenix where we have two bodies: Meridien and Shackleton, doctor and patient. What in the hell is going on?"

We had no clue. But what we did have was a sense that an answer was now possible, though distant.

When we returned to her office I mulled the details over as Novarro did the paperwork, dutifully sending a copy to her ex-lover or whatever, Merle Castle, of whom, for some bizarre reason, I felt a tinge of jealousy.

23

T. Jefferson Cottrell had traded out the blazer for a suit, charcoal gray and lightly pinstriped. The cowboy boots had turned into lustrous black wing tips, only hours from the store and hurting like hell. The bolo tie had become muted blue silk. Cottrell studied himself in the door-back mirror.

Pretty fucking good … I look like a freaking funeral director. Or an honest lawyer.

Cottrell grinned and straightened the knot on his tie one final time then glanced at his watch. Three minutes until Kubiac walked through the door. The kid's *girlfriend* – Cottrell smiled as he considered the word – had called this morning, wanting a major pow-wow.

"What does Adam wish to discuss, Ms Isbergen?" Cottrell had asked.

"A concept," she had said, and Cottrell knew Kubiac was listening. "An interesting concept."

"In regard to what?" Cottrell replied, working to keep the sarcasm from his voice as he winked at his image in the mirror.

"Money," the woman said. "What else?"

He met the pair at the door five minutes later, the sun just an orange-tinged memory in the western sky. The air had cooled and a breeze seemed to follow Kubiac and the girl into the lawyer's office.

Again the kid sprawled on the couch as the woman took one of the two chairs before Cottrell's desk. He cleared his throat and solemnly took his place behind his desk.

Gotta happen today, kid … we're running out of time …

"I have to admit I was intrigued by this afternoon's call, Adam."

Kubiac nodded toward Isbergen. "She called. I didn't."

"But I must assume that since the only issue binding us is your father's will, that is in some way the subject. Thus the call must necessarily be representative of some facet of the process that—"

"Can't you just talk normal? Hashtag: speakenglish."

"If it seems overblown, I'm sorry. The legal profession, much like the computer-software profession, has – as you must know as a computer expert – its own vocabulary and . . ."

"How much?" Kubiac spat, his eyes narrowing at Cottrell.

"Adam!" the woman admonished.

Oh ho, the kid's pissed, but he knows the concept …

"This shit ain't gonna happen," Kubiac said, waving Cottrell away as if to make him disappear. But beneath the anger and bravado …

Fear. The little fucker's scared …

"There's nothing to worry about, Adam. We're safe here. Whatever we say in here is covered by lawyer–client privilege. It's like doctor–patient privilege, safe forever."

"Sure, I used to think that, too, shyster."

Cottrell wanted to use one of the hard wing tips to kick the sneer down Kubiac's throat. *Kid, you may have an IQ up in the clouds, but for everything else, you're dumb as a box of rocks …*

"It's true, Adam," Cottrell said quietly. "Whatever you want to discuss, you may talk freely."

Silence held the room for several seconds. Isbergen stood and walked to the window, *moving like a freaking panther,* Cottrell thought. *Here it comes …*

"Do you like money, Mr Cottrell?" Isbergen asked quietly, turning to the attorney. "What it does, what it brings you, the problems it solves?"

Cottrell smiled and nodded. "I think we all do, Miss Isbergen. Money is a good thing."

"How many people have seen the will, Mr Cottrell?"

"Pardon me?"

She walked to Cottrell's desk and stared levelly into his eyes. "I get the impression that the only eyes ever on that legacy are yours, Adam's, and those of one dead man. Am I right or wrong?"

"That is true, Miss Isbergen," Cottrell said evenly.

"How about your secretary or whatever?"

"It was, uh, a very simple document. I drafted it myself." A lie.

"Don't you file a copy with the probate court?"

Stay calm … frown … "I'm set to file it this week. I've been busy."

"But the second you file with the court," the girl said, snapping her delicate fingers, a surprisingly loud and crisp sound, "it means the world knows of Adam's father's … meanness."

"Yes. And then there's the official reading when Adam turns eighteen in a few days."

"And $20,000,000 gets flushed down the toilet."

"Not if you're one of the toilets that get a cut of the largesse. The Institute for Applied Entrepreneurism, the American Marketing Roundtable, The New Health Fund …" He looked at Adam. "You said your father showed you his will a few weeks back, Adam. I'm sorry, but he obviously wanted his money to go to those and other institutions."

"YOU LET HIM SCREW ME! YOU'RE SUPPOSED TO BE THE EXECUTIONER!"

"It's executor, Adam. And it only means I see that the terms of the will are followed."

155

"Adam," Isbergen said softly, "let me speak."

The spoiled little brat crossed his arms, grunted, studied the floor.

"It does seem sad, Mr Cottrell," Isbergen said. "You knew Adam's father. He was a friend of yours."

Cottrell's mind flashed with recollection. He'd been Elijah Kubiac's lawyer ever since Eli slapped around one of his bimbos, the greedy bitch planning to use it to extort money from the wealthy automotive dealer. Eli had made discreet inquiries about what lawyer could handle darker cases and found Cottrell. Three days later the woman was confronting a tattooed monster a whole lot scarier than a car salesman and she decided to drop all charges.

"I was Eli's legal counsel for years. And yes, a trusted friend."

Isbergen nodded. "Then you know how Adam's father could be."

Cottrell gave a sad smile. "The word is mercurial."

"The word is asshole," Kubiac snarled from the couch.

"And when it's discovered how Mr Kubiac treated Adam in his will," the woman continued, "Eli Kubiac won't come across very well, will he? His reputation will suffer."

"Eli will be judged harshly in the court of public opinion," Cottrell said. He paused. "It does seem a shame, a waste." *Sigh heavily ... make it good ...*

Isbergen smiled for the first time. It was a dazzling smile, wide and bright and model-perfect.

"I have an alternate idea, Mr Cottrell," she said. "One I think you'll find very interesting. All we ask is that you think about it overnight."

FINALLY! Halle-freaking-lujah! Lean in, look perplexed but intrigued. Damn, is that a hard-on down there?

"I'm all ears, Miss Isbergen. And please call me Jeff."

24

I arose early, the eastern sky a glowing mix of pink and orange. In the west, the sky was still cobalt and strung with stars. I put on running shoes, shorts, and a tee and took to the streets, the sign on a lamp post telling me I was in the Willo Historic District. I ran a block of large two-story dwellings, past yards that were arrangements of botany I'd never viewed until yesterday, but thanks to Novarro, I could peg a palo verde, a barrel cactus, an agave, native to the New World, and resembling but apart from the aloe, a former denizen of Africa.

I crossed to another block in the district, this one with smaller homes and a few multiple dwellings looking like condos. I passed beneath a tree hung with bright oranges, resisting the impulse to leap up and snatch one. Novarro had a lime tree in her backyard, which sounded like a good thing. Thinking about Novarro reminded me that I was an attached man, so to speak, and I stopped for a breather in the center of the block, pulling my cell to call Viv. It hit me that we were separated by two time zones plus another hour for daylight savings time, and though it was just past six a.m. here, it was nine in Miami.

I should have called earlier, Viv now at work, though I really didn't have much to say, having been here a day and a half. She probably wouldn't either, more hours of waiting for wounded bodies to enter the ER. Truth be told, spare conversations were happening more and more lately.

"*How was your day, Viv?*"

"*Busy. Crazed. Yours?*"

Shrug. "Yep, same here."

I dropped the phone back in my pocket and picked up the pace again. After a half hour traffic thickened and I beat feet to my digs. Last night I'd stopped at a supermarket, my larder now well-stocked with beer and edibles, including three kinds of salsa.

Breakfast was *frijoles refritos* with *queso fresco* and scrambled eggs cut in, the whole delicious mess lashed with a thick *salsa roja* and rolled in a twelve-inch flour tortilla. I was amazed at the variety of tortillas sold in the Southwest, from maize ones sized like saucers to flour versions fourteen inches across, some thin as dimes, others fat and puffy and a quarter-inch thick.

I nodded at Solero from across the room and made my way back to Novarro's cube. Fishbach wasn't in yet or was elsewhere in the building. She looked up from reading the newspaper and smiled, the teeth like pearls behind slender lips. I was about to say good morning when her phone rang.

"Hang on" she said, reaching for the handset. "Yes, this is Detective Novarro. Oh, howdy, Loot, I was gonna call you this morning and let you know what—"

She paused. Repeated the *What?* only louder. Then added a breathless *When?* and *Where?* Finally came *How?*

When she replaced the phone in the cradle she was ashen, her eyes staring at the floor.

"What?" I said.

"That was Lieutenant Stringer from Tucson. Thiago Carazo was found dead this morning. He was beaten to death at the auto yard. Probably with fists, personal. There was also torture involved. It would have been late last night or early this morning."

"Escheverría," I whispered.

"It was just us who knew we were there," I said, reeling. "You and me and Carazo. You didn't mention anything to the Tucson people, did you?"

"I was gonna call Stringer this a.m. and let him in on what we discovered. But I hadn't spoken to him yet."

"Did you mention anything to Fishbach?"

"I did. Since he put us on to Carazo's vehicle."

"Then four of us knew."

"Carazo freaked maybe, confessed to a supposed friend who figured to get on Escheverría's high side by snitching out the snitch."

"Excuse me, El Gila, but Thiago Carazo just whispered to me that he told the police something about a car? I thought I should mention it, just in case you found it important …"

It was possible and I nodded assent. "Where from here, Detective?"

The nose wrinkled. "I'm not ready to smell that place again, but we're off to Ortega's Gym."

This time the *cholo* gladiators remained seated, mean little smiles on their faces as we crossed the room. I had the odd feeling we were expected. To the side two women sat on a couch and looked like one had just told a joke, eyes alight as they stared our way. They were undeniably pretty, one verging on gorgeous. Whoever sold them make-up had a solid gig going.

I heard a toilet flush and Escheverría appeared from a side door. A second later Novarro was an inch from standing on his toes.

"Where were you last night, Ramon?"

The cold eyes glittered. "Why do we keep doing this, Detective Novarro?"

"Let me see your hands," she demanded.

Looking like innocence personified, Escheverría held out thick paws, unmarked save for the tats. It occurred to me that the last time I'd seem Escheverría he'd had on thick black weightlifting gloves with leather palms and leather across the knuckles, perfect for keeping the skin unblemished while beating a man to death.

The monster canted its head in mock confusion. "What are you looking for, if I may so bold as to ask?"

Novarro pushed his hands away. "Last night," she repeated. "Where?"

"In my bed, pretty lady."

"Alone?"

Escheverría turned to the gorgeous woman on the couch. "Conchita … where was I last night? All night?"

She pointed to her crotch. "Here."

Everyone in Escheverría's crew laughed. Novarro strode over and stared into the woman's eyes.

"You're saying you can account for Ramon's every minute last night?"

"*Si*." A grin. "He never left me."

"You can go to prison for lying," Novarro said, dark clouds roiling through her voice.

The woman laughed like it was the funniest moment in an already delightful day.

"He did it," Novarro said when we were on the littered sidewalk and retreating from the gym. "He and his crew whacked Carazo. Did you see them laughing at us?" We climbed into the SUV and drove off, Novarro scowling into the rear-view.

"I disagree," I said after several blocks of consideration. "If Carazo was killed for ratting, Escheverría did it personally."

We pulled to a red light and Novarro turned to me. "Why … when he's got three large blocks of dumb muscle at his command."

"No way a man nicknamed El Gila sends in a sub to whack a guy who ratted him out."

The light changed. She thought it out. "It would be a matter of honor."

I nodded. "Escheverría'd been betrayed, which demands personal attention. There's also the matter of the killing itself. I read the *cholos* as stupid, nasty, and amoral, but not sociopathic. Chances are they'd race to Tucson, shoot Carazo down where he stood, burn rubber back to Phoenix and have a beer to celebrate."

"Carazo was tortured. Which took time."

"With Escheverría enjoying every second," I added.

We arrived at Phoenix HQ and were heading back to Novarro's cube when my cell rang, the screen showing *HARRY*.

"I'll meet you inside." I leaned against the side of the building, sunwarmed, bright, and pressed the phone to my cheek as I figured times: 11.15 here, 2.15 in Miami. Harry would have just gotten back from lunch.

"Hey, bro. You at HQ?"

"Home, but heading to HQ soon. What's happening in Phoenix, Cars?"

"I got two more dead bodies; I have Escheverría playing us like fools; I have a crazy kid who sees flying girls and mechanical boys. It's a mess in every direction."

"You've been there before. How's that lady detective you're working with, Novolo?"

"Novarro. Tasha Novarro."

"Tasha Novarro sounds Russky-Spanish, like Boris Mendoza."

"Actually she's a Native American. Mostly at least. From the Salt River Pima-Maricopa community here. It's actually two tribes: the Pima or *Akimel Au-Authm*, or River People, and the Maricopa. Both tribes were wizards at irrigation and made swell baskets. The Pima are believed to be descendants of the *Hohokam,* or Those Who Have Gone. They lived in central Arizona over two thousand years ago and were known for—"

"Uh, Carson?"

"What?"

"This lady, Novarro. You enjoying her company?"

"Smart as a whip and an excellent detective. Plus she's intuitive. Yesterday she—"

"Is she pretty, Carson?"

"I, uh, haven't noticed."

"Which means she's pretty. And unmarried, I'll bet."

I frowned into the phone. "It's not like that, Harry. It's, we're ... we're partners on a case together. Just like you and me."

"I'm neither female nor pretty."

As usual when Harry took this hectoring tack, I began to feel irritated. "There a reason you're calling besides to tell me things I already suspected?"

"Yeah, I been doing some follow-up on the Bowers-Warbley killings, broadening a circle so to speak."

"Oh?"

"Remember the bar owner saying Professor Warbley was married to his work? He may have been married to his job but he was having a casual affair with a former graduate student, a thirty-two-year-old guy named Beaumont Malone; Mr Malone now teaching in the Philosophy Department. He's also married with a kid."

"How'd you get that?"

"I met Malone at a campus coffee shop last night where I assured him I had no interest in his relationships, only in recent conversations with John Warbley."

Harry was a genius at gaining trust fast, people somehow knowing he was being honest with them. "And?"

"Malone and Warbley met last week at a bar near campus, and Warbley was puzzling out an 'interesting ethical problem handed to him by a friend,' in his terminology. Oh ... and Malone said Warbley may have said, 'friend of a friend'. He couldn't recall."

"Bowers would be the friend, Meridien the friend of the

friend."

"Here's the gist of a brief conversation: the friend, or friend of, came into possession of a piece of information that seemed in direct conflict with what she thought was true. But she saw how the problem might have occurred, and if it happened that way, something illegal may have been transpiring. The only thing was, the situation also might have been exactly as intended. There was no way for the friend-of-friend to know which was which. I pressed Malone harder and he allowed that Warbley had gone into a bit more detail. The 'information' seemed to be in the form of a will. The friend-of-friend thought it was supposed to say one thing, but it said another thing. But that's also what it might have been supposed to say. Oh, and there was also something about a pissed-off father. Malone said it didn't make much sense to him, but Warbley was fascinated by whatever the conundrum was."

"That's about as clear as fog. Was there anything about doctor–patient privilege?"

"Yes. The 'friend' had acquired the knowledge through a relationship with a patient and—"

"Meridien. Bowers gave up seeing patients."

"Anyway, the doctor suspected something *might* be amiss, but couldn't do anything to verify her suspicion without going to authorities."

"So Meridien discovers something in her practice that causes her to suspect a crime has been or will be committed, and she's conflicted about going to the police."

"Seems likely. But Malone and Warbley had a theoretical conversation, like math: 'Doctor A sees patient B and suspects act C has occurred with a will' … They only spoke about it for ten minutes or so, then Malone had to run off to class. I'm happy he remembered this much."

"Thanks, Harry. I'll pass this along to Novarro."

"What tribe was she from again?"

"Pima or *Akimel Authm.* From the Maricopa-Pima community located down by the … What? Why?"

"Keep busy, brother."

25

Adam was in his room tapping away at his computer, his fingers a blur. Isbergen walked in, a bottle of Diet Pepsi in hand.

"Cottrell just called. He'd like to see us at one. It's when his secretary or whatever is at lunch. I don't think he wants anyone to see us at his office. It makes sense if he's going to go for our idea."

"How can you be so sure, Zoe?"

"Intuition."

"If this doesn't work I'm gonna have to get a fucking job at Google or some shit. Hashtag: screwed."

Isbergen kissed the top of Kubiac's head. "Don't gloom out on me, babe. I think you're gonna win."

Isbergen and Kubiac were at the lawyer's officer at a minute past one, Cottrell gesturing them inside after locking the front door. Isbergen took the chair and Kubiac, per usual, dropped to the couch.

Here we go, kid, Cottrell thought, offering a concerned visage. "Nothing good can come of you getting cut out of your father's will, Adam. Not good for Eli's lifelong reputation as an automotive leader; nor for you, lacking any inheritance and spending the rest of your life hating your father."

"It seems right," Kubiac snapped. "He hated me."

No, you little self-absorbed brat. He just couldn't understand you …

"I firmly believe that he didn't, Adam, but that's neither here nor there."

Cottrell stood and rocked on his heels, his eyes deep in thought, seemingly on the verge of a momentous decision. "It goes against everything I believe," he said, his voice somber. "But I have never been in a position where someone has been treated so unfairly before. I believe in the ultimate triumph of justice, but this is triumphantly unjust."

Did I just say that? Fucking Cicero!

Isbergen leaned forward. "Excuse me, Mr Cottrell, are you saying …?"

"It can be done," he said softly, a man not yet convinced. "I can effect changes in the will." He paused. "I can fix it so Adam receives everything."

Kubiac didn't appear to understand, his mouth drooped open and head cocked. The kid was a dolt who somehow understood computers.

"But … isn't this very, uh, risky for you?" Isbergen said. "Like way against the law?"

Glad you asked that, little lady …

"It imperils everything I've worked for," Cottrell said, his eyes filling with concern. "My license to practice law. My firm. My reputation. Even worse, I imperil my freedom. If caught I would end up in prison for changing Eli's will. And when I finally returned to society, I'd be a broken and penniless old man."

The sleepy-eyed kid looked wide awake now, Daddy's money a $20,000,000 dose of smelling salts. Cottrell's eyes shot to Isbergen's for a split second, then returned to Kubiac. "I will take care of you, Adam. That's my decision. What do you say?"

The kid looked lost for a moment. "Thank you?"

"You're welcome. But you also have to take care of me, right? So before I, um, revisit the will, I'll need you to sign a document."

Kubiac frowned. "What does it say?"

"First, it puts this firm in charge of all your upcoming legal work."

Puzzlement. "I don't have any legal work."

"Yes, you will, Adam: investments, counseling, trademark searches, your own will and other documents, incorporation papers for your new businesses, advice and counsel for …"

"For *what*?"

"Work and counsel for which you'll contract to this firm, first with an initial block of funds for, um, upcoming expenses – let's say a flat million – then with an annual outlay for the services of this firm. What's called a retainer."

"Annual outlay?" Kubiac said.

"Three hundred and fifty thousand dollars a year for fifteen years. A pittance, really, considering how much risk I engender."

"That's six and a quarter million dollars of my money," he whined. "Hashtag: Whatthefuck?"

Cottrell paused and blew out a breath. He stood, muttering, "I can't take this shit anymore." He grabbed a sheaf of papers from his desk and held it out to Kubiac. "Remember the will, Adam? Read it again, you spoiled little pissant. Here …where it says you get one fucking dollar. TAKE IT OR LEAVE IT, YOU UNGRATEFUL LITTLE SHIT!"

The pair returned to the apartment, Kubiac silent for the duration of the drive back.

"What is it, Adam?" Isbergen said, closing the door.

There was an empty can of Red Bull on the floor and Kubiac kicked it into a wall. "The bastard changes a few words and he gets like a third of my money. Hashtag: thief. You should have seen this coming, Zoe."

"I should have *what*?"

167

"Call me *Jeff*, Ms Isbergen," Kubiac said sarcastically. "He's your *buddy*, Zoe. You should have known he'd screw me."

Isbergen spun to Kubiac, her eyes blazing. "Yesterday you were getting nothing, today it's going to be millions. You give $1,350,000 to Cottrell this year and have $18,650,000 left. Money makes money. It'll make enough sitting on its ass to pay Cottrell's retainer and still have NINETEEN MILLION DOLLARS! And if you ever decide to use that amazing brain of yours to do something, you'll turn it into A FUCKING BILLION!"

"Jesus, Zoe, all right," Kubiac pouted, crossing his arms and sinking into the couch. "Everybody's yelling at me … Hashtag: kickAdam."

Isbergen's features relaxed and she sat beside Kubiac, stroking his tousled hair. "Be happy, Adam," she whispered. "All I want is for you to be happy."

Kubiac looked up and arched an eyebrow. "Are you saying it's Happy Adam Time?"

"Whenever you want it to be," Isbergen purred. "You know that."

Kubiac grinned like an eight-year-old about to receive a cookie and unzipped his fly.

26

Twenty minutes later Adam Kubiac was walking toward the cyber-café, his mind analyzing possibilities, his face alternating between anger and elation.

"Adam," a voice called to his back.

He turned. He'd walked a dozen feet past his destination, absorbed in his thoughts. He waved and walked back, a sheepish grin on his face.

"I was thinking, Cat. I got lost."

Catherine Maruyama smiled. "I'm glad you called. Have a s-seat."

Kubiac pulled out a chair, eager to be with Catherine Maruyama again. There was something about the woman that made him relax, like she understood what he was going through. He'd called her as soon as Isbergen had finished and was taking a shower, texting Zoe's phone that he had needed time alone with his thoughts.

"You look happy," Maruyama said. "The other d-day you looked sad. I felt so bad for you."

"I was worried the other day. I'm still worried now. But it's a different kind. Like everything has a chance. Like I have a chance."

"C-cool, Adam. Y-you want to talk about it?"

Kubiac started wriggling in his chair. "If I talk about … *it*, I have to talk about *him*. I don't want to talk about *him*."

"By him, do mean … y-your-your—" Her face twitched and she gulped air.

"Calm down," Kubiac said. "Take a breath, Cat."

"Your fa-father, Adam. Is that who you don't wuh-want to talk about?"

Kubiac's jaw dropped. "How did you know that?"

"J-just a g-gu-guess. I-I-I'm suh-sorry." Her hands waved help-lessly in the air. "I c-can' t-t-talk. Wuh-want to go t-t-to my place? I wuh-wuh want a drink of s-something. It mu-makes it easier t-to talk."

Catherine Maruyama's apartment was five blocks from the café, not far from the university. It was on the ground floor of a six-unit building of nondescript brown brick. Maruyama unlocked two deadbolts and Kubiac followed her inside.

"Why aren't you living at home?"

"This is my home, Adam. I became an emancipated minor when I was seventeen."

"What does that mean?"

"It means a court declared me an adult capable of taking care of myself."

Adam thought for a moment. "That's way cool, Cat. I wish I'd known you could do that. Why did you become a, a …?"

"Emancipated minor. Because it was necessary." She looked away. "I don't want to talk about it now, Adam."

"That's cool. I understand. I think."

Adam reclined on the sofa. The dressing of the room was spare but artsy, he noted, posters on the wall and a series of photographs of old buildings. Everything looked new. He saw a bookcase with tomes on history, physics, mathematics, philosophy. There were candles everywhere: Fat things with all sorts of colors, some with holes in them like Swiss cheese, some tall, some short. He liked

170

candles and had once told the bitch doctor he wished all the light bulbs in the world could be turned into candles.

"*Why?*" she had prodded. Meridien was always prodding.

"*Because then the only real light would come from screens,*" he had said. "*Like open windows.*"

"I h-have some b-beer," Maruyama said, looking more stable in the safety of her home. "I'm having some w-wine."

"A brew'd be cool."

Maruyama opened a bottle of Oak Creek Ale and handed it to Kubiac, then poured a tumbler of red wine, talking several sips before wandering the room with a lighter, igniting candles and a stick of incense.

"Are you better, Cat?"

She took another sip of the wine and sat on the couch. Kubiac was in a low chair, a round glass table between them, two candles blazing away on its surface. "I g-got too excited. Sometimes if I th-think a-a-about …"

"Stay calm. Relax."

She rolled her head on her neck, took a deep breath and blew it out. "I feel better now."

Kubiac pulled his chair closer to Maruyama. "How did you know I was talking about my father? It wasn't a guess. You *knew*."

Maruyama started pacing nervously, dabbing a tear from her face with her sleeve.

"Cat? Talk to me. What's wrong?"

"I h-hated my fa-fa-father. H-he controlled everything I d-did, all the t-t-time. D-do this, d-do that. Read t-this book, go to th-that class. D-dress th-this way, comb your hair t-that. He t-took me to the beauty salon and explained how to c-cut my h-hair."

Kubiac scowled. "My father took me to the barber when I was fourteen and did the same fucking thing. Fourteen."

"He u-used to m-m-make f-fun of my stu-stu … *linguistic* impairment. S-said I could stop it if I wuh-wanted."

171

Kubiac's eye narrowed. "If you had the personal willpower, right?"

"Al-almost those exact words. That stu-stuttering was a sign of wu-wuh-wuuuh—" the word seemed stuck.

"Weakness," Kubiac finished, suddenly understanding why he felt comfortable with Cat Maruyama. She'd been through the exact same shit he had. It was like they'd had the same father.

Maruyama nodded her thanks. "T-talk about wu-weakness; he divorced my mother so he could marry a woman h-half his age. It was wh-when Mom had cuh-cuh-cancer. He had a girl-friend, too. He kept her in a c-condo in Chandler and didn't care who knew."

"The fucker! Were you smarter than him?"

"H-he hated it. He once called me a fuh-fuh-fuh-fuuu…"

"Freak," Kubiac said from personal experience.

"I can't help who I a-am," Maruyama continued. She put out her hand and grasped Kubiac's. "B-but I'm not a *freak*, Adam … I'm an *improvement*. I'm not sure how to say it, but I think about history, about evolution … I'm making no sense again."

Kubiac went to the window, watching through the blinds as a dozen students passed by, the men showing off for the women, the women giggling, blushing, or rolling eyes. Some babbled into cell phones. One of the Neanderthal men saw Adam behind the blinds and shot the finger. Adam shook his head and turned back to Catherine Maruyama.

"The world used to belong to Neanderthals, Catherine. Stinking, grunting, primitive machines. Then Evolution said: 'Screw this shit' and upgraded. Think how one of those first upgrades felt in a crowd of Neanderthals. When the upgrade tried to communicate, all he got was grunts and stares, the Neanderthal brains too small to understand the improvement among them."

"I can't imagine."

"Yes, Cat," Kubiac said, "you can."

27

"Back to the ethics angle again," Novarro said, staring at her desktop and shaking her head.

"It's all covered in clouds," I said. "Meridien was having a problem with an ethical aspect of a patient relationship. She called Bowers who consulted with Warbley."

"But your partner, Harry ... he had no idea what it was about?"

I laughed without humor. I was getting good at it. "Only that Meridien may have been uncertain of what was happening and that it may have involved something illegal. Or, on the other hand, maybe not. Whatever it was, she thought it had ethical implications. She seemed split about reporting whatever it was to the authorities."

"You said *may have* twice."

I had a coffee cup in front of me and spun it in my fingers. "Would you be upset if I threw this against the wall?"

"It pisses off the cleaning staff."

"Sounds like you've done it be—"

"We'll not go there."

Her phone rang, the intercom. "There's an Alyce Mashburn on line one, Tasha. She says she's—"

"I know who she is. Put her on." Novarro turned on the

speaker so I could eavesdrop.

"I found something in Darnell's phone, Detective," Alyce Mashburn said. "I'm not sure if it means anything but …"

"I'm with Detective Ryder," Novarro said. "Are you home?"

We heard a distant howl and I figured it was Darnell.

"Where else?" his aunt sighed.

"On our way."

We were silent on the drive, both hoping whatever was on the phone, it would push the case into another realm: like having an idea of what was happening.

When we arrived the aunt showed us into the living room and we gathered around an iPhone in her hand as she flicked through photos. "I was cleaning his room and found it hidden between the mattress and box springs. Mostly selfies and people from his high school or friends or family. They go back before he … changed. But the last one wasn't anyone I knew. And I know you wanted to know about people he knew after he started up with Dr Meridien."

Novarro took the phone and went to the last shot. The photo was poorly focused, or the lens needed cleaning. The setting was somewhere in the desert, a pair of saguaros in the background. Ragged boulders. A steep peak. Novarro leaned close.

"That's a blue palo verde staring to bloom. This year it was mid-April."

"So roughly two months ago."

She nodded and reverse-tweezed to a close-up. In the middle foreground stood four young people. One was Darnell, the second was a slender male in jeans and a black ball cap, the third a plumpish dark-haired, Hispanic-looking kid in shorts and a Phoenix Suns shirt, and finally a dark-haired young woman in a yellow sundress and bearing a wide smile below her shades. Even with soft edges, there was a prettiness to her face.

"I'm sure that was taken in Meridien's backyard," Novarro

whispered. "South Mountain Park."

We leaned in and studied the second male in jeans and cap. Even with the lack of definition, we knew the face: The late Brad Shackleton.

"Can we talk to Darnell?" I asked his aunt. "About the photos?"

Another howl from above. "You can try," she said.

We went upstairs and knocked. "Darnell? It's Detectives Novarro and Ryder," she said. "May we come in?"

"NO!"

"We have some pictures of you," I said. "Cool photos."

It hooked him. He said: "OK."

We entered, Novarro and me up front, Alyce Mashburn in the rear. It was as if Darnell Mashburn hadn't moved or changed clothes since our last meeting. He reached to the floor beside the bed and grabbed the racket he'd kept within easy reach.

"I don't think you'll need a distance machine, Darnell," I said quietly. "Once you've used the power, it stays used. Try it."

He looked at me through the webbing, then cautiously peered outside the frame. Whatever he saw agreed with his tormented mind. "All right," he said.

"May we show you a picture?" I said.

A frown. "That's *my* phone. Where did you GET MY PHONE?" I fought the wince. His agitation was starting.

"You gave it to us the other day, Darnell," Novarro said quickly. "Don't you remember? You said you wanted us to make sure it was safe for you to use. That the dark things had been removed."

The frown softened as Mashburn pondered the information. *Nice*, I thought.

"I remember," he said.

"It's clean," Novarro said, handing Darnell the phone and taking a chance he wouldn't throw it through the window. "It likes you a lot. It said your name."

Personalizing the device; making it his again. Novarro was beginning to amaze me.

Mashburn brightened. "I taught it to do that."

"The last picture you took, Darnell," Novarro prompted. "The beautiful one. Where was that? Everyone looks so happy."

Mashburn turned the screen to his eyes. His mouth fell open and he stared as if entranced. "My chick-chick-chickies."

Novarro nodded. "Oh, your peeps. Your people."

Darnell grinned. "We were like a secret club. Dr Meridien's secret club. Our group session. WE WERE SPECIAL."

"Who's this good-looking guy here?" Novarro said, an elegant forefinger tapping Shackleton's chest.

"That's my gangsta Brad-Brad-Bradleeee …"

She moved her finger to the other male. "And him?"

"That's my boy, Leo. He's the lion lion."

"Leo the lion?"

Mashburn did a lion's roar and laughed. "Leo made things appear. He had magic." His face screwed up in anger. "I USED TO HAVE FRIENDS."

"Easy, Baby," his aunt said quietly.

"Tell me about Leo, Darnell," Novarro asked. "Did he have a last name?"

"He was living inside the red rocks. That was his name." Mashburn's hands balled into fists. "Don't make me hit you."

"Shhhh," his aunt said. "We'll have none of that today. Tell these good people about Leo, Darnell."

"He drew me into his world."

It was the clearest statement he'd made. "'His world'?" Novarro asked.

"He lived in the stars. He drew me into the stars."

"Do you mean he—"

"I live in the stars whenever I want." He snuck a sly glance at his aunt and whispered: "I live in the stars whenever she goes away. Leo draws me there."

"You mean like up in the sky?"

"STOP TALKING. YOU HAVE TO GO!"

"Very soon, Darnell. And we thank you for being so nice to us today."

A sideways grin. "You're a wet comb."

Novarro looked perplexed. I stepped close. "He's saying you're welcome."

She nodded and tapped the third figure in the photo. "Who's the lovely woman, Darnell? Does she have a name?"

He turned away.

"Darnell?" his aunt said. "Remember your manners and please answer the nice lady's question."

"She's the Cat. She broke my eyes."

"You said the Cat flew away."

He pointed out the window. "She flew into the red sun."

"That was your group … with Dr Meridien?"

He studied the photo and his hands moved faster. The memories were agitating him. "Almost. All. Almost. All."

"Who's taking the picture, Darnell?"

He started pinching his thigh. His aunt gently moved his hand to hers and held it tight. "Darnell?" she prodded. "Who's not there?"

"I can't tell. The boy was hiding."

"Hiding from who?"

He yanked his hand from his aunt and pointed at us both like a pair of pistols. "A BIG BLUE SISSY!"

"You said *he*, right, Darnell? The one hiding from, uh, a big blue sissy? Do you remember his name?"

"I WON'T TELL WON'T TELL WON'T TELL …"

He glared between Novarro and I as she recalled parts of the previous meeting with him. "Wait, Darnell," she said, "the hiding boy, the one not there. Was he the what … the robot boy, the mechanical boy?"

Darnell Mashburn's eyes widened. His fingers went into his

ears and he fell back on his bed with eyes closed tight, done listening for the day.

There was nothing to be done but thank Alyce Mashburn for her call and climb back into the vehicle. It was getting late in a day where the man who'd lent his car to Escheverría had been found dead, we'd gotten more enigmatic information from the Bowers-Warbley cases, and a kid who might have some answers was ranting about red suns, mechanical boys, and a blue sissy.

"What next?" I sighed as Novarro pulled away and I sunk into my own depression.

"I've been wanting to go to DataSĀF again. Let's run in and see if there are any revelations about the missing files."

We drove for fifteen minutes, parking in a small employee lot holding a collection of expensive sporting wheels: Beamers, Mercs, Porsches.

"Whatever they do here," I said, scanning the high-ticket metal, "it seems to make money."

"They do filing. They just do it on big computers and for a bunch of places at the same time. It's a cloud or in the cloud or whatever."

We walked to the security checkpoint. The guard smiled recognition at Novarro. "You're back."

"Couple more questions for the Ken doll."

The guy smiled. "Ah, yes … Mr Larkin."

"He in, you know?" Novarro eyed the sign-in sheet.

"Mr Larkin doesn't sign in since he's, uh …"

"Too important." Novarro finished.

"He should be up there." A wink. "Don't tell him I said so."

Temporary visitor badges slung from our necks, we took the elevator to the second-floor lobby of DataSĀF. I saw a pretty but vacant-eyed woman at a round reception structure at the far end of the room and followed Novarro.

"Excuse me," she said to the receptionist, "could I talk to Mr Larkin, please."

The women looked through us. "He's not in right now."

Novarro met the frown with a dazzling smile. "I'll just sit over here and clean my gun until he arrives."

Novarro sat cross-legged on the floor and pulled out her pistol, ejecting the clip and pretending to buff everything with a tissue. The woman's eyes widened and she was suddenly on the phone. Novarro looked down the hall, smiled, jumped to her feet, and put away the weapon. "Here comes the big boss, Carson. No wait, the C-E-O. I think it stands for Compulsive Egotistical, uh … Osshole."

The glass door flew open, Larkin striding to us. "What are you doing?"

Novarro slipped her weapon away. "I wanted to see if anything had been discovered about how Dr Meriden's account was hacked."

Pursed lips, nose in the air. "We don't know that it was hacked. That's an assumption you shouldn't make."

"Four years of data disappeared," Novarro recounted. "Patient files, appointments …"

Larkin crossed his arms, toe tapping like a nervous metronome. "We're looking at it as an anomaly. Maybe an internal problem."

An arched eyebrow from my partner. "Someone pressed the wrong button?"

"It would be more extensive than that. But yes, in a way."

"That happen a lot, you think?" Novarro was needling the guy, figuring he'd spill more if irritated. I stayed two steps back; this was her show.

"It's virtually impossible to get in from the outside, Detective. And yes, the Meridien account may have been deleted internally and accidentally."

"So the night the woman is murdered her accounts disappear and—"

"That is none of my business. It's yours." The pink fingers clenched into fists. "For crying out loud, Officer, I didn't kill the woman. Why are you here?"

Novarro stared into the eyes. "So you still don't know what happened? But saying a janitor spilled coffee on a keyboard sounds better than getting hacked."

"I'm busy. Please show yourselves out."

Larkin returned to his meeting, shooting dark glances our way. I figured the guy had an IQ off the charts and made a million-plus a year, proving brains and money didn't buy manners.

I said: "He was trying to sell the internal screw-up line to himself as much as to you."

She nodded. "Damage control. How would it look to have security breached?"

We waited for the elevator. It opened and launched a solid and handsome woman at us, stopping just short of running into my chest.

"Excuse me," she said. "Distracted." She saw Novarro. "Oh, Detective Novarro. You're back."

"This is my, uh, current partner, Detective Carson Ryder. Carson, this is Candace Klebbin, who I suspect runs the joint."

A laugh. "More like run over by the joint. Can I help you folks?"

"We were wondering if anything new had been discovered about the Meridien breach. Kenneth was a bit elusive. Would you know?"

A grin. "I'm the office administrator, Detective. It basically means I buy pencils and check time sheets."

"Not an insider," I said.

The eyes nodded toward the meeting room, seven young guys at a table being served coffee by a pretty young woman. One of the men glanced at the girl's posterior, winking at his buddies as he made gnawing teeth behind her back.

"It's an old boy's club," Klebbin said. "Except the oldest boy is thirty-seven."

"I'm kinda surprised you're still around," Novarro said. "Last time I was here you alluded to a departure."

"I'm in this office," Klebbin said slyly. "But where are my résumés?"

The door of the meeting room opened. "Candace," the Compulsive Egotistical Osshole barked, "could you come here a moment?" He looked peeved and I figured it was because Klebbin was speaking with us.

"Busted," Klebbin said. "Gotta go."

"CANDACE!"

"Good luck with the résumés," Novarro whispered.

28

The afternoon was waning so we grabbed a couple of *tortas* and returned to HQ, Novarro having an angle she wanted to check out. A marked cruiser with a two-uniform crew was pulling away, the driver a broad-shouldered officer in his early thirties. He was staring at me from behind mirrored shades as he pulled toward the street, then studying me in the rear-view.

"That's Burton Claypool," Novarro explained. "A good buddy of Merle Castle. Or maybe acolyte. Merle's probably got Claypool feeding him information about my whereabouts."

"Castle's really got it for you."

She sighed. "Castle got bounced. It bruised his ego. Forget about it."

Fishbach was sorting through reports as he tapped his keyboard, missing the chance to trumpet Novarro's arrival. He turned his head just as we walked up, pushing the pages aside. "There she is, folks," he grinned. "The woman of the second."

"Question, Doctor Fish," Novarro said. "You know any woman around Escheverría?"

Fishbach put the heavy brogans on the desk, shaking his head. I saw that he was linked to a PPD page, more reports for Solero, I figured.

"A changing cast, Tash," Fishbach replied. "Ramon likes them young, just past eighteen. He'd like 'em younger, I'll bet, but knows we'd nail his ass on something we could prove for a change. He lures them into his nasty web with dope and restaurant trips and cheesy bling, screws them until they become boring, then tosses them out the door. They're not human to him, they're a commodity, like toilet paper."

Novarro jogged to a departmental locker and removed a long-snouted digital SLR, and we were hustling back outside. Keeping up with Novarro was like following a tornado.

"Where we going?" I asked, moving fast to keep up with her long-legged stride.

"To a photo session. If we get lucky."

We ended up on the street outside the reeking gym, slumping low in the vehicle as Novarro produced her phone.

"Is this Ortega's Gym?" she said in nasal voice. "This is Kayla Smith with the gas company. We've had a complaint about a leak on the block. Could you please vacate the premises for at least an hour while our workers locate the source of the problem? And please," she said, winking at me "whatever you do, don't light a cigarette."

Twenty seconds later the doors opened. Escheverría wasn't inside, just two of his hulking crew and both of the women from the other day. Novarro set the zoomed-in SLR on auto-fire and captured ten shots in the span of a couple breaths.

With the anxious quartet hustling away and sniffing the air, we ping-ponged back to HQ; the Juvenile Division.

Lieutenant Richard Pickett ran Juvenile, "Juvie" for shorthand. Juvie in a major metro area was a tough gig that drew cops into a world of hideous dysfunction, where the word "family" was often close to meaningless, implying only a genetic bond. I figured most of Pickett's charges were low-income kids set loose in the streets at an early age and who turned to thievery to survive.

"*I see kids who are in their mid-teens,*" a Juvenile officer in Mobile once told me, "*that have never in their lives seen an adult get up and go to work.*"

Novarro downloaded the shots to Pickett's computer and he expanded them, studying and nodding as he indicated faces with a forefinger. "I don't know this one. Looks a bit older. The young one—" He pointed to Escheverría's alibi girl. "That's Gloria Sparza. She was here a couple years back, briefly." He shook his head. "And now she's hanging with Escheverría; Jesus, what a freaking pity."

"Why?" Novarro asked.

"Gloria's actually pretty bright. Of course, maybe too much doping burned up the wires. Hard home life. Now and then you get someone who gives you a breath of hope – what you live on here. If Gloria's with that psycho, it didn't take."

"Bright, though?"

"According to several teachers she had smarts and, even better, a touch of common sense. Didn't stop her from dropping out, though. Probably thought her looks would make her the next Cindy Crawford or whatever. She got busted for shoplifting, couple joints back in high school. Went to Juvie for a couple months of rehab."

"She's damn pretty," I noted.

"Good looks are a drawback in the inner city, Detective," Pickett said. "They attract attention from pimps and people like Ramon Escheverría."

"What's she like, Rich?" Novarro asked.

"Plays the tough girl. Maybe she is by now. But there might actually be something still alive inside her. If she stays with Escheverría, it won't be there long. He'll use her up, hook her to the hard stuff and sell her off to a pimp."

"Why you think Sparza took up with Ramon, Lieutenant?" I asked.

Pickett gave me eyes that had seen it all. "Simple, Detective Ryder. Escheverría told her the lies that she wanted to believe; so she did."

It was heading onto six and Novarro wanted to scope out the gym for a bit, hoping to get lucky and see Sparza leaving, maybe follow her to her digs and strike up a conversation.

Instead, we got lucky on the way over, cruising past a tacqueria until Novarro did a double take, checking the rear-view as we passed by.

"It's Sparza! She's back at the taco stand."

"Alone?" I said, craning in the seat, too late to catch a look.

"Be still my beating heart," she said, turning around.

We parked. Gloria Sparza was sitting at a table with a single taco on the paper before her and a cup of pop at her elbow. She was taking little bird-bites, careful not to drip on the outfit: a spangly silver low-cut blouse and black designer jeans so tight they could have been a tattoo. She wore her gloss-black hair piled high and hoop earrings I could have put my fist through. We parked, walked to the counterman behind the window, ordered a pair of soft drinks.

Novarro turned when the drinks arrived, feigned surprise at seeing Sparza, who was busily ignoring us. "Yo ... how's the taco, Gloria?"

The pretty eyes went hard. "How you know my name?"

"I'm the *po*-lice, Gloria. I see all and know all."

"The tacos are *muy bueno*. Even better when you get them to go." A tough girl.

Novarro stepped closer. "You'd better load up on those tacos, Gloria. Won't be long until you're eating lots of creamed chipped beef."

"*Que?*"

"Creamed chipped beef. Learn to love it."

A frown, unsure of what Novarro was talking about. "I don't eat no creamy whatever."

185

Novarro put her foot on the bench beside Sparza. "It's prison food, girlfriend."

"What you talking about, crazy lady?"

"Slammer chow. Like grits with bugs and wet white bread."

"Why you telling me about prison food, lady?" Sparza pushed the last bite of taco between her bright red lips with a forefinger. "I ain't goin' to no prison."

The surrounding tables were empty. We sat with Sparza, Novarro at her elbow, me across the table. Sparza rolled her eyes and collected her paper.

"No, Gloria," Novarro said. "You won't go *directly* to prison. First you'll get arrested, then you'll go to court, then the *judge* sends you to prison. That's how it works." Novarro paused, studied the blue sky. "I'm thinking you'll get twenty years in the joint."

Chin-jutting defiance. But behind the flashing eyes, fear. "Yeah? How the fuck that gonna happen, lady? I ain't done nothing."

Novarro sighed, long and dramatic. "Yes, Gloria, you have done something very wrong. But it's out of my hands now." We started to stand.

"NO!" Sparza snapped. "What have I done. What … are you lying about?"

Novarro slowly re-sat and I followed her lead. She looked Sparza in the eyes, her voice set on Maximum Truth. "We both know Ramon wasn't with you last night, Gloria … no, hear me out. He was murdering a man in Tucson. Wanna know why? The dead guy said he'd lent Ramon his car for a few days."

A two-beat pause. Sparza looked shaken. "I don't know nothing about that. Ramon was with me all night." The strident voice had become a whisper.

"And there's the problem, Gloria. You're lying about Ramon's whereabouts in a murder case. You're now an accomplice. That means you share the murder. Like I said, I'm thinking a double dime … twenty years inside. You'll be out when you're forty, right?"

Novarro shot me a glance. Sparza was considering what was being said and she wanted me to spread a little more dread on the prison pastry.

I shook my head. "That's only if the dykes don't tear her apart," I said. "Some of those girls are the size of Ramon, and just as crazy."

"I hate them," Sparza said, more to herself than us. "They were always at me in Juvie."

Another glance from Novarro; we'd found something to work with.

"They run the prisons, Gloria," Novarro said. "The lesbians, the dykes. Diesel-dykes, the big ones."

Sparza shuddered.

"You're a beautiful woman, Gloria," I said. "They'll fight over you from the first day, and the winner will be the biggest, meanest, stinkingest dyke of them all, an animal."

"She'll own you your first few days in," Novarro said as Sparza began looking pale. "Every night she'll wrap you in her thick hairy thighs and make you satisfy her a dozen times."

Sparza pushed from the table and ran to a garbage pail beside the restaurant, bending her head over it and vomiting. And then Novarro and I were beside the depleted girl, Novarro shaking her head.

"What's Ramon ever done for you, Gloria … buy you food? Clothes? Jewelry? He uses your body whenever he wants. Is he so good that you'll take a twenty-year fall for him?"

"HE WAS WITH ME ALL NIGHT!" Sparza howled, her fear of Escheverría even stronger than her fear of prison. She started away, escaping what she didn't want to hear.

Novarro jogged up, took Sparza's arm and angled her to the window of a closed store beside the tacqueria. It was lightless inside and the window was a dark mirror.

187

"Look at you, Gloria," Novarro said, pointing to the reflection in the window, "you're pretty enough to be a model. But Ramon will use up your beauty and throw you away. How many women has he thrown away since you've known him? How many are selling themselves on the street?"

Sparza snapped her face away, like it would make Novarro disappear. "I ain't like the others."

"I work with a guy who says Ramon thinks his girlfriends are toilet paper. Use 'em and flush 'em. You like being toilet paper, Gloria?"

"Fuck *you*. I'm outta here."

But her feet didn't move. We'd gotten inside her head and were making her confront things she'd been avoiding. Sparza suddenly looked as deserted as the empty storefront she leaned against, her eyes shut against the horrors of her world.

"We won't say anything, Gloria," Novarro said quietly. "It goes no further, I promise. Was Ramon Escheverría with you last night?"

Gloria Sparza dropped her head. The earrings swung almost imperceptibly.

They said *No.*

Having confirmed that we weren't running down a complete wrong track, we returned to HQ where Novarro wrote and filed the daily report. The place was pretty much deserted, desktop terminals staring blankly into the overlit room.

"You up for a decent meal?" Novarro said.

My stomach had been growling as she'd worked. "What you thinking?"

"How about we grab a couple steaks and we go to my place and fire up the grill? I'll even let you turn the steaks, since that's what guys like to do, right?"

Her eyes were warm and inviting and my heart and stomach were on the same track until my mind spoke.

"I, uh … that sounds great, but I've got to call some folks back in Miami and, uh …" My mouth went dry.

She smiled softly. "The girlfriend, right?"

"That's one of the calls."

She reached to touch my arm. "That's all right. We'll get it another night, Carson. Rain check and all that."

I left the station – Novarro claiming she wanted to touch up the reports – and wandered to my car. The sky was fading past twilight and seemed to cling to the city dazzle like a shimmering, translucent vapor. My breath seemed short and twice my legs turned back to the station, but after a loose few steps aimed back at the car. It seemed to take a long time to get there.

And then, without recalling the trip, I was in my rental home, somehow not hungry after hours without a meal, pulling a chair into the backyard to sit in the night's cooling air and stare at the sky. I twice pulled my phone, but when I started to dial, put it away.

And then it called me. Harry.

"Hi, Cars," he said. "What's up? Making headway?"

I looked at my watch and realized it was midnight in Miami. "Like slogging through mud, brother," I said. "If we can keep from drowning in the muck, we might get somewhere." I paused and added: "Someday."

He cleared his throat. "Roy's got me on this case. A pharmaceutical rep moving large amounts of opioids to pain clinics, a drug dealer in Bill Blass suits. I was shadowing him to various haunts the past few days."

"Yeah?"

"He likes upscale places where he can order $15 cocktails and look legit while pedaling his wares. These aren't cheesy doper nightclubs, Carson. They're watering holes for stockbrokers and bankers. And since they're near the downtown medical complexes, lots of physicians and medical types."

"So I take it you're eating a lot of steak while on surveillance."

"First couple nights. Now I'm chomping salads. Gotta keep my girlish figure."

Like a 6'4" refrigerator was girlish. I still felt something odd in his voice. "I'm still not sure why you're telling me this," I said. "Does it have anything to do with Bowers and Warbley?"

A two-beat pause. "Twice now I've been in fancy-ass places and seen Miss Morningstar."

Vivian Morningstar, my girlfriend. The longest relationship I'd ever maintained.

A pause on my end. "Oh? And?"

"She's been with the same guy. Looks like a doctor type."

"She works with a lot of physicians," I said cautiously.

"They're having a good time, Carson. Lots of smiles and clinking of glasses. There's some touchy-feely."

"And when they left the restaurant?"

"I didn't follow them, Carson."

"Of course not. Thanks for telling me, brother. I know it was tough."

"I, uh …"

He left it there and rang off.

I went into the house and lashed together a sandwich, grabbed a beer, and returned to the backyard to watch the night as I ate, wondering what I felt, until realizing I had no idea. I didn't feel down, nor up, nor spinning unhinged in the middle.

No idea.

29

Kubiac awakened at seven. He drank a Red Bull and played a few games on the net before checking coding sites for new hacks. He'd started a game, but found himself too distracted by thoughts of his new friend and had called her.

"Uh, hello? Cat? You up?"

"*Adam?*" Catherine Maruyama had said. "*Good morning. What a wonderful surprise. What you doing?*"

"Gaming."

"*You like games, don't you?*"

A smile crossed Kubiac's face. "I love games, Cat. You do too, don't you?"

"*I do, Adam. I wish I had more time to play them.*"

"Wanna meet somewhere?" Kubiac asked, trying for nonchalance. "Like, uh Hashtag: hashbrowns?"

She'd laughed. "*You mean breakfast? Cool!*"

Zoe always slept until at least ten. He'd likely be back while she was still snoring.

Twenty-five minutes later they were at a small café down the street from Maruyama's apartment, sitting in the new morning sun and nibbling at pastry. She ordered tea, and Adam opted for the same, clearly flustered when the waiter had offered several choices: Darjeeling, Earl Grey, Chamomile, Hibiscus …

"What do I want?" he asked Maruyama.

"Tell you what," Maruyama said, "let's both get Darjeeling. It's a favorite."

"Did you tell your girlfriend about me?" Maruyama said after their orders had arrived, studying Adam over a plate of French toast and sipping her Darjeeling. "I'd love to meet her. Zoe, right?"

Kubiac studied his fork. "Uh, yeah. Zoe."

"Did you tell her about me?"

"I told Zoe I met someone who went to Meridien. But not that we were meeting now. Or, uh, yesterday. I mean like … it's kinda hard to explain. Zoe's possessive."

Maruyama waved it away with a smile. "At least tell me about her. She must mean a lot to you."

"She's almost skinny, but not quite. Dark hair that puffs out. She has big eyes, brown. She's real pretty. She likes shopping more than anything."

Maruyama sighed. "I wish I was pretty."

"You are, Cat. You're cool, too. Hashtag: coolest."

A gentle smile. "Was Zoe a patient of Dr Meridien?"

"No. Zoe's, uh, more regular. She's smart, though." He paused. "Just not like us, upgrades."

"I'll bet she's way smart and super extra pretty."

Embarrassment colored Kubiac's face. He smiled past it. "You're talking a lot better today, Cat."

Maruyama set down her tea and put her fingertips over Kubiac's wrist. "I feel comfortable around you, Adam. Safe, because I know I can trust you. I'll bet Zoe's the same way. How long have you known her?"

Kubiac stared at the soft olive-colored hand touching his and swallowed hard. "Uh, just like two weeks, maybe a little more."

Maruyama's hands rose in surprise. "You talk like you've known her forever. How'd you meet?"

"I was at a coffee shop over on Washington and she sat down beside me. She wanted me to show her how to game. Now we live together."

Maruyama clapped her hands. "Love at first sight."

Kubiac pushed back a shock of dark hair to reveal a frown. "I dunno, not really love, I guess. More like we have a thing. She's real, like, strong and is helping me through some things." He blew out a breath. "I-uh d-didn't tell you something. M-my f-father died about three weeks ago."

"Oh, Adam, I'm so sorry."

"Don't be. He was a piece of shit like I said. I just didn't tell you he died."

"Then that's what I'm sorry about, Adam. That your father was a bad person."

Kubiac leaned closer to Maruyama. "You said your father called you a freak. Mine called me a freak, too. Real fathers don't do that. He also said I was weak … like yours did."

Maruyama pushed away her plate and lowered her voice. "Mine died, too, Adam. Two years ago. A vein exploded in his brain. He was a lawyer, an important one right here in Phoenix. My father was a very good lawyer but a very bad person. You want to know what he did in his will?"

"What?"

"Left me $250,000 …"

"That's not so bad," Kubiac grunted. "Mine left—"

"… and $5,500,000 to his girlfriend," Maruyama completed. "Twenty-two times what I got."

Kubiac stared, shook his head. "So you got screwed."

A broken smile. "No, the girlfriend got screwed. About three times a day. That's probably why his will gave most of his inheritance to her."

"Jeez, it must have been awful to lose all that money, Cat."

Maruyama watched a bus glide past with something in her eyes Kubiac had never seen. Anger?

"I didn't lose the money," she whispered like Adam wasn't there. "I got every penny."

"No way."

"It was my money, Adam. Not that … bitch's, pardon me for the word. That's the only reason she was screwing Daddy."

"How did you get the money?"

A flash of fear in Maruyama's eyes; the look of someone who's gone ten words too far. "I c-can't say, Adam. I just realized I shouldn't have told you that." She looked away, then back. "I'm sorry, Adam. I lied. I didn't get any more money. I was just saying it to make myself feel important."

"You were telling me the truth. You got your money. I can tell."

Maruyama stared at her hands, clutching the edge of the table. "I'm s-sorry, Adam. I wuh-was just wishful thinking. I didn't get th-th-the money. I'm suh-sorry I m-m-misled you."

Kubiac scooted his chair to sit beside Maruyama. "You did, you did, you DID. You need to tell me what you did to get all of your money, Cat. It's important."

Maruyama stood and grabbed her purse from the table. "I'm suh-sorry, Adam. I have to g-go."

"Cat!"

But she was on her bike and moving away. Kubiac stared into his tea for ten minutes – horrible tasting stuff – then drove to Maruyama's apartment. Either she wasn't inside or not answering the door.

He went home, his mind a jumble of questions. Zoe was still in bed, snoring like a chainsaw. He tried to call Cat several more times, but all calls went to her voicemail.

"This is Cat Maruyama, please leave a message …"

*   *   *

The days in Phoenix always began with a pinkish cast to my small, neat bedroom, as if the air was slowly donning its daytime garb. Within minutes, a shimmering blue would be added, minutes later the color orange began lighting my white curtains. It always drew me from bed because I wanted to see the eastern sky, the glowing pastels sifting through wisps of purpled cloud.

I needed a bit of beauty before a day of facing horror.

Today had been no different and I had taken a run before returning to call Novarro. She had wanted to meet at HQ, to again stare at the photos and data and try to shake a sense of order from the disorder that lay in all directions.

When I arrived she was pinning a blown-up version of the last shot from Darnell Mashburn's phone to the board centered by the headshot of Leslie Meridien and Bradford Shackleton. In the lower right-hand corner I'd tacked shots of Angela Bowers and Professor Warbley.

"When'd you get the blow-up?" I asked.

"Last night. Since we couldn't have a steak dinner, I ate from the machine and pestered a night tech in forensics to enlarge and enhance the shot."

"Ate from the machine?"

"The dispenser on the first floor. Cheese-and-crackers, pretzels, a glob of sugar and chemicals masquerading as a cookie. It wasn't a steak and trimmings, but what's a busy girl to do?"

"I'm sorry."

"I'm just yanking your chain. You had to call your girlfriend, right? I hope she's fine and all that."

I changed the subject by moving to the newly added photo: an 8 x 10 of Mashburn's final photo. "It's better." I said. "I can make out more features."

"Still not gonna win the Ansel Adams award."

"So we've got the late Brad Shackleton and the woman Mashburn called Cat, plus this guy," I tapped the third face in

Meridien's backyard, "who Darnell called Leo the lion."

Novarro checked her notes. "Actually, Darnell said: 'lion lion.'"

"Whatever. He also said Leo drew him in."

"Into his *world*," Novarro said. "Whatever that means. He amended it to 'He lived in the stars. He drew me into the stars' – meaning Leo did the drawing. Darnell said he lived in the stars whenever he wanted. 'Leo draws me there' … meaning into the stars."

I ambled to the window, looking calm, but with my mind simultaneously re-playing yesterday's mad conversation with Darnell and analyzing his mental state. He had seemed a bit more lucid for the few seconds that he spoke of Leo and being drawn into the stars. I stared out the window, the sun bright across the buildings, distant mountains looming in all directions.

"*Leo draws me into his world … Leo draws me into the stars … I live I the stars whenever I want … I live in the stars when she goes away …*"

And from Novarro: "*Leo did the drawing.*"

Draws, draws, drawing …

I stared into the back of my head, feeling pieces coming together. I have dwelt in the land between the sane and the mad for so long that I sometimes make connections – no, I *feel* connections in my gut. Mostly they're wrong, but I've solved cases when they were right. I kept staring, feeling my heart begin to beat faster.

"Carson?" Novarro was saying. I turned.

"Uh, what, Tasha?"

"You've been gone so long I was about to send in the Saint Bernards."

"Sorry," I said. "Thinking."

"About?"

"A long shot. Let's go talk to Alyce Mashburn."

"Reason?"

"To see if we can get her to remove Darnell from his room for a few minutes."

30

"You want me to get Darnell out of the house?" Alyce Mashburn said, standing at the front door in a blue pantsuit, her hair in curlers. "Ain't gonna happen. He's scared to death to get in my old car, says it's a Tyrannosaurus."

A dinosaur, I thought. Was that the connection?

"Just out of his room would work, Ms Mashburn," I said. "Away far enough that he wouldn't know we were in there."

She thought a moment. "I might get him outside. He used to enjoy the sun, but now he says he lives in the stars."

"Could you try, please?" I said. "We'd really like to look through his room. If that's all right with you, that is."

She mulled it over, nodded. "You all go sit quiet in the kitchen. Darnell won't go back there, says the refrigerator is too loud. When … I mean *if*, I get him outside, I'll let the door slam behind me."

"Thank you, we apprec—"

"Don't expect much time. Darnell gets antsy after a few minutes, says the sun is eating his skin. He'll run right back inside."

Novarro and I retreated to the kitchen. We heard howling from Darnell, foot stomping. A war whoop. We winced as a thrown object thudded into the wall. Another couple of shrieks, but less fierce. More silence.

After ten minutes we heard a padding sound, like feet moving down the carpeted steps. Novarro and I held our breaths.

The door slammed.

We bolted upstairs. Darnell's room smelled of body odor and food and dead air and I wanted to open the window, to let life flow back inside, but when I peeked past the edge of the window frame I saw a pout-faced Darnell trudging across the yellowed lawn to the filtered shade of a mesquite tree. Alyce Mashburn was talking rapidly, a huge false smile on her face. Darnell looked like all he wanted was to dash back into his hidey-hole.

"We're looking for a drawing, then?" Novarro said.

I nodded. "We don't have long."

I delved into the disarray of the closet, Novarro the desk. I was still rummaging when she moved to the books on the floor, riffling pages.

"Got something, Carson," Novarro said, excitement in her voice. "Inside the pages of a graphic novel."

I jumped a pile of clothes and pizza scraps as Novarro held up three sheets of drawing paper. The one on top was a pencil drawing of Darnell Mashburn's head and shoulders. He was staring directly into the eyes of the artist, which meant he appeared to be staring into my eyes, spooky. The background was a graphic spacescape: stars, a pair of moons, Saturn, or similarly ringed planet. A comet blazed across the top of the sheet.

"Drawn into the stars," Novarro whispered in awe.

I looked at two more drawings, less detailed. I figured they were studies, the other a final version. They were simple sketches, but wrought by an amateur with a good eye and sense of line.

"Line," I said.

"Lion?"

"Leo the lion who know his lines. Leo was the line lion, I think."

"Jesus. It's like decrypting a code." She leaned close to the back of the sheet I was holding, then she took it carefully in her fingers and turned it for me to see. There, in pencil, was a tiny name:

Geraldo Trujillo

The artist's signature? Could we get that lucky?

While Novarro recorded the name in her notes, I stepped to the window to check on Darnell's progress. No one was out there.

"Darnell!" I heard his aunt yell as the door slammed.

"Out!" I said to Novarro.

Sketches in hand, we turned to the door as it burst open.

"WHAT ARE YOU DOING HERE!" Mashburn screamed.

"Uh, hi Darnell," I said, holding his precious drawings. The eyes fell to the sketches.

"THIEF!" he screamed, leaping at me with animal ferocity. I ducked back as he stripped the drawings from my hand. He leapt to his bed clutching the drawings, his eyes wild. "THIEVES! LIARS! MAKE THEM GO AWAY... I WANT THEM TO GO AWAY AND NEVER COME BACK!"

"I think that's best," Alyce Mashburn said, looking between us and her broken nephew, shaking with anger and fear, backed into the wall on his own bed in his own room, eyes blazing with a mad fire unlikely to ever be extinguished. "Surely you've taken all my poor baby has to give."

We skulked from the Mashburn residence, behind us the soft sounds of Alyce Mashburn trying to coax her nephew into a less agitated state of mind. Still, every few seconds he punctuated the air with the word "*Thieves!*"

I took the wheel, pulling away from the Mashburn address, probably for the last time. "Darnell will never talk to us again,"

I said. "We're the enemy forever."

"I'm amazed at the connections. The line lion. Drawn into the stars. What about Leo? Because of the constellation, you think?"

I gave it a few moments consideration, turning onto a main avenue and gliding into the stream of traffic. "My guess would be Leonard da Vinci. Probably a nickname for the artist."

"And it seems da Vinci may be one Geraldo Trujillo." My peripheral vision saw her stare at me, shake her head.

We arrived at PPD HQ, running up the steps to her office. "You had a crazy idea, Carson. But damn … we've got a name. I'm gonna try a bit of the Ryder wizardry and check out the name Trujillo in Sedona and the surrounding area."

"That's gotta be a hundred miles north of Phoenix, right? Why?"

"Hunch. Darnell said the kid in the pic was hiding inside a red rock. The area around Sedona is known as the 'red rock' country because of the color of the – wait for it – rocks."

"Nice."

She sat down at her computer and I jogged to the machine for coffee. When I returned she was checking out the screen.

"Four Trujillos in the area, I'm talking maybe a fifty-mile circle including Oak Creek, Cottonwood, Clarkdale, Jerome and a few one-horse hamlets."

She tried three numbers to no avail, sighed. "OK, last shot. A Hector Trujillo in Cottonwood: Verde Valley. It's between Sedona and Jerome."

She dialed, the phone on speaker.

"*H'lo?*" A female voice, mild Spanish accent.

Novarro leaned over the phone set. "Hello. Is there a Geraldo Trujillo there? And if so, may I speak with him?"

A pause. "*Who-who's calling?*"

"This is Detective Tasha Novarro with the Phoenix Police Department. There's nothing wrong."

"*Nothing wrong?*" the voice said, suddenly angry. "*There is everything wrong … Geraldo is dead. He died ten days ago.*"

The voice fell into ragged sobbing.

We drove north from Phoenix for about an hour, then went up Route 260 into the town of Cottonwood: Verde Valley. The Trujillo residence was a trailer behind a small cinder-block diner not far off the main highway, the sign saying *Tru's Restaurante Mexicano*. We were gestured inside by the father, Manuel Trujillo, a slight man with a pronounced stoop, either an early life of unforgiving labor or a deformity. He seemed slightly intoxicated, moving slow and slurring slightly, but I didn't smell alcohol.

"My *esposa*," he said, nodding toward the restaurant, "is working. The lunch rush will start soon and I have to help. She is … not doing well, but we have to work."

"Just a few questions, sir. How did your Geraldo pass away?"

The dark eyes grew darker and anger shivered in Trujillo's vocal chords. "A monster killed him. A monster with no conscience. Geraldo was coming home from work in Sedona. He worked at a Centro Médico. He had a car problem and was trying to fix it when … when someone hit him. The Sheriff said it didn't look like the car even slowed down."

A sideways glance from Novarro. We'd go from here to the Sheriff's office and check on the circumstances and any possible suspects.

A frown. "How did you know of Geraldo?" Trujillo asked, squinting like trying to keep us in focus.

Novarro took it. "I can't go into details except that we were looking at someone who used to be a patient with Dr Meridien. Geraldo was also a patient of hers, correct?"

A long pause, Trujillo wavering slightly on the couch. "Bless her. I have not been able to tell the doctor yet. About … Geraldo."

This time I shot the glance at Novarro. "When did you last see Dr Meridien?"

"Two weeks ago. It's hard for us to get to Phoenix, but we go every three weeks. It was a godsend for Geraldo, he felt so alone. Kids made fun of him because he was so smart. But there … she spoke with him. And he was in a small group with others like him. Geraldo found out he could relax inside himself."

"Do you know who else was in this group?"

A sad smile. "I was in Narcotics Anonymous years ago. The kids were like that about the group, anonymous to outsiders. I only knew Geraldo was in a small group. You could tell on group days because he'd seem extra happy after coming home." A contained sob. "He … almost made it."

"Pardon?"

"Geraldo was to move to Tempe and go to the university. A scholarship. It would have been this week. Dr Meridien said she'd see him weekly. I think it also meant more group."

"An art scholarship?"

A moment of perplexation. "Chemistry."

"Oh … we saw a couple of his drawings and assumed—"

Trujillo waved it away. "A hobby, the art thing. He was going to be a *quimíco*, a chemist. He loved to draw, especially stars and space ships. But his main love was science. Other boys wanted to do the *futbol, beisbol*, the sports, but Geraldo wanted to make the experiments in chemistry. One Christmas we saved for months to buy him a chemistry set. He set up his *laboratorio* in a tiny room in the back of our restaurant and was there for hours at a time, so much that we had to go and order him to come back to the house. As he got older, he felt strange, alone, and just wanted to live in his tiny laboratory. Our doctor recommended Dr Meridien. We went to Phoenix to beg her to look at Geraldo. We didn't have to beg, she took his case. She has a *corazón enorme* … a huge heart."

He broke down crying. It was the kind that knows no comfort and we let ourselves out.

"He was stoned on something," I said as we walked to the car.

"Pushed back into using."

"I know those people," Novarro said as we pulled away and studying the rear-view. "They work sixteen hours a day and barely make ends meet. To have a child with a chance of escaping the cycle is almost magical. Then, in the span of a few moments …"

"I know," I said, looking into beautiful, desolate mountains. "I know." It was all there was to say.

The County Sheriff was Walter Hart, a solid man in his fifties with the kind of tan that comes from living in the sun for decades. He had round glasses and big teeth and reminded me of Teddy Roosevelt.

"Geraldo was coming home from work," Hart said, shifting in the chair behind his desk. "He was employed at the Valley Verde Medical Center in Sedona. He worked in the lab, a kind of gopher-slash-intern."

Novarro nodded. "Hit and run, the Trujillos said."

"I don't think the driver even slowed down. Probably drunk or stoned."

"This was on a main road?"

"Yep. But at half past midnight. Traffic is few and far between at that hour because there's nowhere to go or be."

"And he had car trouble?"

"Trujillo drove a twelve-year-old Escort and we found a loose cable. The engine was running off the battery and not the alternator. When the battery died, so did the whole car. I figure he was looking under the hood when he got slammed. Threw him almost forty feet. Died instantly, thank god."

It was all Hart could offer.

We prepared to aim south to Phoenix, standing in the blinding sun outside the Sheriff's office and sipping the coffee Hart offered for our return trip. Novarro leaned against the bumper of her cruiser and thought, a slight but welcome breeze rippling at her skirt, the first non-slack outfit I'd seen her wear, dark-blue linen with an orange blouse. For a split-second I had a vacation from the cases.

"Four people in the photograph," she recited, pulling me back to the moment. "Shackleton, Mashburn, Trujillo and the woman called 'the Cat.' Two are dead." She looked at me. "Why not Mashburn? He'd be a simple hit. A kid in a house with his aunt."

I thought it over. "Darnell's already dead, so to speak. He's trapped in his mind, probably never leave the house again."

"He's safe because he's crazy?"

"Maybe."

"How could the killer or killers know that?"

I thought about it as fantastic mountain formations passed by, mesas and buttes and cliffs of red and pink rock. "Maybe Meridien's files weren't simply deleted, but downloaded and read. They would have described his failing mental state."

"And also give descriptions of the targeted kids' habits."

I nodded. "You better get a guard on Darnell. Just in case."

She pulled her phone and made the request, talking to someone in the uniform division. There was some pushback but she invoked the name of Solero, and that seemed that.

"It's done," she said, tucking the phone back in her purse. "Regular patrols during the day, closer surveillance at night. But there's a loose end."

I was already there. "The guy behind the camera, robot man or mechanical boy or whoever. He's in the same danger, I'd bet. He's either dead or on the way. Cat Girl's in big trouble, too. Problem is, we don't know who they are."

"I'll bet Escheverría does."

31

We were halfway between Sedona and Phoenix and lost in thought, me watching the landscape pass by, noting that rolling hills previously devoid of saguaro cacti now held hundreds of them on a single slope, like an army of green robots marching at a pace too slow for the human eye to notice, driven by a secret need.

My thoughts were interrupted by Novarro's phone, ringing from the console. She snatched it up, nodded at the caller's name, and put it to her cheek. "*Yá'át'ééh*," she said. She listened a moment, said "That was fast, Walt, considering. Thanks. We'll be there in an hour or less."

She rang off and shot me a glance. "Walter Totsonnie, a pathologist. He's just finishing the autopsy on Brad Shackleton."

"Three days to get to him. Is that quick?"

"The usual is a week or more. But Walt likes me. We're kinfolk, kind of."

The Maricopa County Medical Examiner's was in the Forensics building on West Jefferson, and we were there in forty minutes with the aid of siren and flashers.

Walter Totsonnie was a large man in his mid-forties who

recalled the Native American actor Will Sampson: prominent nose above full lips, large and piercing eyes, a brick-broad forehead.

"Sister Tasha," he said, a stone face breaking a smile at the sight of Novarro.

"Something interesting, Walt?"

"Like so much, it depends on translation."

Novarro did introductions. I expected a bone-crushing handshake, but Totsonnie's fingers barely clasped mine and released. He excused himself to retrieve the prelims of the procedure. "He's a Native American, right?"

A soft chuckle. "E-yup."

"Are you two of the same tribe?" I asked. "Pima?"

"Walt grew up in the Navaho Nation, a huge res that's mostly in Arizona, but pushes into Utah and New Mexico." She winked. "We're everywhere in the Southwest. *Aha-á tonoya etá eyutanah.*" She paused, added, "*Eyahaté yana-óhotalyana.*"

"Meaning?"

"Got you surrounded, white man." She paused, added: "Because we own all the casinos."

Totsonnie reappeared with a slender sheaf of forms. "Cause of death is indeterminate," he said, slipping on dark-framed reading glasses. "Either extensive internal bleeding or massive head trauma, a crapshoot as to which took him first. He was like porridge inside."

"So it really was a fall?" she said.

"I found some disturbing anomalies. If the deceased fell almost seventy feet onto rock, there would have been total sudden deceleration. All internal tissue and organs would – laymen's terms here – smoosh to the side of impact. Yet the liver seems to have received the largest impact from the right side, the left side ribs, and lower pulmonary lobe from the left. The pancreas seems to have suffered anterior impact, the right kidney, which is nearby, from the posterior. But like I said, it was a jumble in there."

"So he didn't fall?" Novarro said. "That's what you're saying?"

"No. A fall is possible. Especially if he dropped a couple stories, sustained an impact, fell again, spinning, sustained an impact … all the way to the bottom."

I saw Novarro mentally tracing the route from the trail to the ground. "That's not how I was reading the path of the fall. It's a straight drop."

"I know the mountains, Tasha. Looks can be deceiving. A body hits an outcropped rock, spins, catches another … all the way down."

"I'm pretty sure if I dropped a brick from the trail it would sail to the bottom as straight as da Vinci's cannonball."

Totsonnie removed the readers and walked to a small utility office at the end of the room and sat motionless at a small desk, like in a trance.

"Walt's thinking," Novarro said, taking my arm. "Let's take a walk."

We went outside and wandered down the sidewalk. It was not an area where you'd find a diner or a Starbucks. After a ten-minute stroll we returned to the morgue, Totsonnie up and pacing. "Do you have a photograph of the area where he landed, Tasha?"

"Sure, just let me … oh shit."

"What?" I asked.

"They're in Maricopa County's database. I have to call Merle."

She reluctantly made the call, not using the speaker. I heard her make the request, then say "No, Merle, not tonight. Not this weekend, either. Yes, he's still here. No, I don't know when and here's something else, it doesn't matter. Yes, I need them now. I'll wait."

She muttered *Jeee-sus*, dropped the phone in her pocket and looked back at Totsonnie and me. "Castle's out romping with his DEA buddies, but says he'll have someone send the shots ASAP."

"Which are actually here," Totsonnie said. "In the files in the forensic lab, but can only go to you with official release."

Meaning the photos were inside a computer probably a hundred feet away, but inaccessible without permission from the proper authority. It was less inane than it seemed; no law enforcement agency wanted another entity – even another official agency – scrabbling willy-nilly through its reports and case files.

But Castle was as good as his word and the scene photos arrived eleven minutes later, e-mailed to Novarro's PPD account, which she accessed with a morgue computer.

Totsonnie crouched at her side and studied the shots.

"It does look like a straight shot, Tash," he said, nodding. "But then there's this …" He tapped the screen with his forefinger, indicating a rocky ledge about thirty feet from the canyon floor. "Look over here …" He took the mouse and changed angles on the bottom of the cliff. "There's a stairstepping of rock, steep, but accessible. It goes to this small ledge about forty feet from the canyon floor."

"Meaning?" I said, seeing just stone and vegetation.

"It wouldn't be that hard to carry 140 lb human – the victim's weight – up to this lower ledge."

"And pitch him off," Novarro whispered.

Totsonnie nodded. "It's possible the victim was hauled up to the ledge and tossed to the ground. Do this two or three times and you'd replicate what I'm seeing." He slipped off the glasses and thought a moment. "It's actually pretty damn canny from a forensics point of view."

32

It was almost six p.m. when we left the morgue. Novarro wanted
to drive by Escheverría's gym, thinking she might concoct a ruse
to get Sparza loose from her companions. By tacitly admitting
that Ramon Escheverría lied about his whereabouts when Carazo
was killed, Gloria'd made a lean toward our side.

We passed the tacqueria where we'd seen Sparza yesterday, the
spicy scent priming my stomach – we hadn't eaten since breakfast
– but the hard frown in Novarro's eyes said food was not an issue.
We were headed the two blocks to the gym when I turned to
study a pitiful old woman half-hobbling down the pavement,
hunched over, a hand to her face. I saw a flash of white, like a
bandage.

My heart froze. I said: "It's Gloria."

We swung to the curb with tires squealing. Sparza's face turned
our way in terror. A hand reached up as if to ward us off as she
stumbled ahead. I saw her face: purple with bruises, a crust of
dried blood in the corner of her mouth. She tried to hobble away
but moved like a three-legged spider.

"My god," Novarro said. "What happened, Gloria?"

"G'way," Sparza said, waving us away like we carried plague.
A fat compress was over one eye, from it, pink fluid dripped

down her cheek. It had formed a crust on one bare shoulder.

"What happened?" Novarro demanded. "Who did this?"

Sparza hobbled into a storefront, banged her forehead. She probably didn't notice, loaded on drugs.

"Go way from me," she wailed. "Lemme be."

"Ramon did this, right?"

"No. NO!"

"Then how did it happen?"

Sparza hadn't figured that one out yet.

Novarro was shaking with fury. "We can get him, Gloria," she implored. "Help us take the bastard down."

But Gloria Sparza pushed between us and stumbled in the opposite direction, her hands waving like we were angry hornets buzzing her head. Novarro grabbed Sparza's arm and studied her wrist. Sparza shrieked and yanked the arm back, staggering away beneath wracking sobs that shook her hunched-over body.

Novarro quivered with fury. She spun and strode to the car, jumping into the driver's seat, the car jetting from the curb before I had my door closed.

"Where we going?" I asked.

"Gloria had a hospital wristband."

The hospital was St Luke's Medical Center, a complex on the east side of the city. We entered the emergency area, Novarro flashing the gold. I was reminded of Viv Morningstar's daily environment. I'd again neglected to call, thinking of it only after it was too late in the east. But she hadn't called either.

Three minutes later we were talking to a Dr Elian Chavez, young, slim, big eyes behind bigger glasses. He recalled Sparza perfectly. "She first went to a clinic downtown. But they weren't equipped to handle the injury."

"A beating?"

"Her right eye was punctured. She said it was an accident. That she'd been carrying a knife and had fallen."

210

"A knife in her eye?"

"Out the back of the eyeball and into the muscle cone. She was not fully coherent, drugs of some sort. I called in our ophthalmic surgeon. He was fearful of administering an anesthetic, not knowing what was already in her system. We used local, but not to great effect, I fear. She was very difficult to handle when he made repairs. He wanted her admitted, of course, but she ran off. I doubt she'll regain full sight in the eye."

"Thank you, Doctor," Novarro said, her voice wire-tight.

"If you see Ms Sparza," Chavez called as we walked away, "tell her to come back and quickly. The eye needs much more work, plus there's a terrible risk of infection."

"Ramon fucking found out," Novarro said as we climbed back into the vehicle, her voice clenched in fury. "HE FOUND OUT, CARSON. Like goddamn Carazo. The bastard has eyes in the department. It's why he's always ahead."

She pulled away with a screech, veered into a turn, throwing me into the door, then blew past a beer truck close enough that I could have reached over and offloaded a six pack.

"Let me drive," I said.

"I'm GODDAMN FINE!"

"You're not fine at all, Tasha," I said gently. "You're gonna plow us into a phone pole."

The car shrieked to the curb, the driver behind us yelling *asshole!* as he passed. Novarro was staring into nowhere, but I knew what she was seeing: Sparza's ruined eye.

"I'm hungry," I said, seizing on anything. "Is there anywhere we can go that's not here ... a place we can chill? You need it, Tasha."

She took a deep breath and pulled into a bank lot and put shaking hands over her eyes as if that would blot out the horror, then exited the car, walking to the end of the block and sitting at a bus stop, a small and symbolic break from the case. I stayed in the car, knowing what she was going through.

Ten minutes later she was back, most of the pain and tension gone from her voice. "O.H.S.O. is about ten blocks, a micro-brewery with good bar food. You're not allergic to dogs or hipsters, are you?"

A short time later we pulled into the lot of a sprawling single-story building, a mountain looming in the distance. We passed through an interior centered around brewing – huge shiny tanks, bags of malt – and to the open-air rear of the place, a central bar surrounded by dozens of booths and tables, many holding skinny men with trim beards and clothing, a mix of L.L. Bean and Salvation Army; the women svelte and pretty, and seemingly less concerned with the precision of their fashion than the males.

It was a biker joint, though not in the classic sense of ponderous genetic failures who rode Harleys, transacted in heroin and meth, and kicked the teeth out of anyone with a measurable IQ. Spandex trumped leather here, and the bikes ran the gamut from beater Schwinns to sleek Pinarellos and Cervelos. It seemed every third person had a canine companion.

We followed a giggly maître d' to a booth in back, outside, a large area centered by another bar. The ground swelled behind the restaurant, like a levee.

"What's up there?" I asked.

"The Arizona Canal, which flows from Granite Reef Dam to the New River, about fifty miles. There's a trail beside it where I hike or bike occasionally. For some reason it helps me think better."

"Maybe it's the forward motion."

She considered it for a full minute. "It's the water. Because it's so precious."

A waitress came and we ordered burgers and soft drinks.

"OK," I said. "Now we have to figure where Ramon's getting his information. How he stays ahead."

The lovely eyes darkened.

"Easy," I said. "Make it intellectual, analytical. We have to stay uninvolved."

She blew out a breath and closed her eyes, like counting in her head. After about a half a minute said, "I'm chilled. Lay it out."

I thought it through. "We have to figure out who's watching. What's your paperwork trail? It's in the paperwork. Or ..." I let it hang.

"No," she said. "No way. Not Fish."

"Everyone's under suspicion at this point, Tasha. Fish included. What's the trail?"

She leaned back and thought, her large eyes moving to follow thoughts. "I talk to Fish about the case. He's interested, obviously, hating Escheverría and not being able to take him down."

"What do you tell Fish?"

"Just the usual stuff. It's Fish, Carson ... you've told me about Harry. They're cut from the same cloth, old-school pros."

"Even if you didn't talk to Fish, he'd still have access to the case notes and whatnot, right?"

"Sure. The case reports, like everything else, go where all paperwork goes these days. All that's needed is a Phoenix PD password."

"No copies of your reports floating around?"

"All digital these days. I e-mail a copy to Castle. But I'll bet he doesn't read it. He's just pulling my chain. Plus Merle has a kind of, uh, simple clarity that would never allow him to spy for Escheverría."

"Money is a good muddler of clarity."

A long moment of reflection followed by a sigh. "Merle does like shiny things like guns and motorcycles and silver-blingy saddles on his horsey. Maybe ..."

The food arrived, massive burgers with fries and salad. I watched Tasha Novarro eat with gusto, trying not to consider my long-held observance that women who reveled in dining were better lovers than those who picked and nibbled.

"Thank you," she said, pushing her emptied plate away. "I was falling down a hole after seeing Gloria. You reached down and saved me."

I nodded. "I've been down that hole before."

She glanced around at the smiling faces, the dogs, the blue sky arching above. "This is what I needed, Carson. It's been a crappy week. I'm really glad you're here."

I held up my brew in toast. "To my vacation, then."

"Someday you're gonna have to come out here and actually have a vacation."

"I'd like that. But, unfortunately, time to get back to the real world: Where do we go from here?"

"Not yet. I'm sick of wondering who in the department is a spy for a sociopath. Right now I need to pack my head in beauty and quiet."

"Meaning?"

She nodded west, the horizon shimmering with the gold of a fading sun. "It'll be dark soon. I want to show you my favorite place in the world."

We crossed the city as twilight fell and the cityscape bloomed with dazzling artificial light that blanked out the stars. As we swept southward I saw a mountain range looming in the distance, miles long.

"South Mountain Park," Novarro said. "Sixteen thousand acres. The largest city park in the continental US."

I looked out the window as the housing grew sparse and then we were on a road climbing toward a high-jutting part of the range, our headlamps illuminating saguaros which, with their upraised branches, reminded me of ne'er-do-wells caught in an act of crime and lifting their hands.

"Come out with your hands up," Novarro chuckled, seeing the same thing.

And then we were at a gate with a small log cabin checkpoint. Novarro honked three times in quick succession. A door opened in the structure and a uniformed Phoenix cop leaned out, smile on his face,

"Time for your, uh, scheduled park reconnoitering, Detective Novarro?"

"Yep. Freddy Pence, say howdy to Detective Carson Ryder, on loan from the Florida Center for Law Enforcement."

"Go Miami Dolphins," the guy grinned. "But go Dallas Cowboys first."

"Infidel," I said, flicking a salute as Novarro gunned past the stop sign and headed up the steepening mountain. The long-fallen western sun still flung enough light to display the chiaroscuro of crags and cliffs of the mountain, rising to our right, dropping precipitously to our left. Topping the jagged peaks was a bright array of communications towers, red and white lights flashing against the cobalt sky.

As we climbed, I felt a curious sensation, as though negative energy in the vehicle was being replaced by a positive charge. Seven minutes later we came to the end of the road, an overlook and parking lot.

"We're here," she said. "Welcome to Dobbins Point." Novarro pulled into the topmost slot and exited. I followed as she sat atop a rock wall and looked out across the vast white fire of the basin. "We're about five miles from the center of town and a half mile up," she said. "Sit and watch the show."

I sat beside her and we stared into the galaxy in the center of the desert, close enough to make out individual vehicles moving down distant streets. I watched a jet drop from the sky to land at the airport which centered Phoenix. The light shimmered against the night and seemed less an assemblage of towns and cities than a single glorious entity pulsing with harmony and good intentions.

"It's beautiful up here," I said. "It's like a holy place."

"These mountains are sacred to *Akimel O'odham*, as are the Sierra Estrellas."

"The mountains where Shackleton died."

"Maybe that's why I'm eaten up by this case, Carson," she said softly. "Murders shouldn't be committed anywhere, but especially not in holy places."

We sat quietly and watched the show. After a few minutes I cleared my throat. "I've been meaning to tell you – despite the circumstances – how much I like working with you. You've been a detective for a few months, but it's like you've done the work for years. You're a natural."

Long moments passed before she blew out a breath. "Thanks, but … I nearly blew the case up a few days back. Kind of a personal thing, a mistake."

"Care to talk about it?"

"Not really. I just needed to tell someone. My confession, I guess."

She rose from the bench and walked to the end of the parking lot, staring out over the luminous plains. And then she was back beside me, her face lit by the light of cities far below.

"I think I have a genetic defect that makes me like alcohol too much, Carson. Like there's a point I shouldn't go past and when I do, the next thing I know it's the next morning. I stay on guard, but stress screws with my protection mechanism. I've been able to keep it under control, but recently I got tanked twice, something I hadn't done in years. Once was just a hangover, the other could have affected the case, maybe cost my job."

"But you got by."

"By grace and friendship. I have a younger brother, Ben. He's twenty and has the problem, too, but can't seem to find any control. It tells me a lot about how he struggles with his insecurities. And maybe influences how I handle him … I want to crash down on his head, but then I remember my own failings and …"

"You go soft because you understand."

"He has so much potential. I don't know much about geniuses, but I'm sure Ben's one. He was doing much better a couple months back and I had high hopes. but ... like always, he fell back into old ways. It's just whenever he falters, I get so damn mad, but can't bring myself to be hard on him. I wonder if I'm, if I'm ..." Words failed and she shook her head.

"You wonder if you're giving Ben permission to fail because there but for the grace of God go you?"

She didn't answer and we resumed studying the dazzling valley. Five minutes later she laughed and slapped a hand on my knee.

"You're too much in my head, I think. Let's go to my house. I need to take off my shoes."

33

Sweat poured from Ramon Escheverría, the massive barbell rising and falling with mechanical timing, *clank-one-two, clank-one-two* … The burner phone beeped and Escheverría set the weight in the holder and grabbed the device from the stained concrete floor, tight-eying the caller's name.

"You have the information, Carlos?" he grunted.

"*There is a place he went today,*" the caller replied. "*A place for sad people like him, in the basement of the Metodista Church on Sonora.*"

Escheverría hawked and spat toward an antique cuspidor, missing and hitting the floor. "I know of it. There are always sick hombres on the steps."

"*He will go back, I think, El Gila. Today or tomorrow. He will do this for days before he tires of it and goes back to old habits. It's a weakness with such people.*"

"You've got someone on this place? Eyes."

"*All the day. Are you going to … confront him?*"

The *cholos* pushed through the front door of the gym, bags of food and six-packs in hand, joking, laughing. Ramon Escheverría his finger to his lips: *shut up!* The crew fell mausoleum-silent.

"It needs the correct time," Escheverría continued as the hulking gangsters tip-toed across the floor.

"*Night is best. It hides many problems.*"

"Is he still walking or using that stupid—"

A laugh. "*Si. Like a little boy. He needs a bell.*"

"That makes for a very nice option. Quieter than gunfire. This place he frequents …"

"*He will go inside, El Gila. You might have one hour, you might have two. It depends. But he will come out and we will be waiting.*"

Ramon Escheverría returned the phone to his pocket and turned to his crew. "The last of the Meridiens has been located."

"You're sure he's the last one, El Gila?" It was an innocent question, unconsidered, the *cholo* squirting *salsa picante* onto a taco.

Escheverría crossed the dozen feet as fast and quiet as a cobra, slapping the taco from the man's hand, an explosion of meat and tortilla dappling the floor. "*Que,* Juan? You doubt my intelligence?"

Juan Mercanto was over six foot four and two hundred thirty pounds. But his eyes turned to the floor and he became a little boy. "Forgive me, El Gila," he said, swallowing hard. "I am *estupido*. I have no doubts."

"There was just the five," Escheverría spat. "Shackleton, Mashburn, Trujillo, the Maruyama woman, and this one. Shackleton and Trujillo are *muerte*, the Mashburn is loco, the Maruyama woman is no longer a problem. We have just this one and my breathing becomes easier."

"What do you ask of us, El Gila?"

Escheverría's brow furrowed in thought. "Get Vela's old van and paint it black, a soft color, not shiny. It must hide in the night. Put a five-gallon can of petrol in the back. It must be burned afterwards. It is vital that the van be burned in Phoenix. Everything must be done in Phoenix. That way I can see it."

As if commanded by Zeus, the three men hustled out the door.

Escheverría pulled a phone from a second pocket and pressed the single number on recall.

"Hola," he said. "Where are you?"

He listened, crossing the floor and opening the refrigerator in the corner to retrieve a Negro Modelo. "Working? Is that what you call it? Not much longer. Soon we will be far from this desert."

He listened for a moment, continued.

"It's tonight. We have the last Meridien in our sights. I thought you would like to hear that." He sipped from the beer, triumph lighting his face. "Now, my roving eyes … what can you tell me is the latest police report on Ramon Escheverría and his adventures?"

He listened and laughed.

Benjamin Novarro exited the AA meeting in the basement of a downtown church, the last meeting of the day, ten until eleven p.m. He'd also gone to the nine o'clock meeting, the eight, and the seven.

"Hello, my name is Ben and I'm an alcoholic …"

He stood on the street looking into traffic and blew out a breath. What he wanted was a drink; what he needed was to not drink. It was his ninth meeting in two days, but what else did he have to do … it wasn't like he had a job anymore.

And maybe not a future.

No, he corrected. That's my old way of thinking, the drinker's thinking. *Future,* he thought. Focus on the future. A future, and a good one, once he dug himself out of the shitpile he'd built. He could do it if he finally believed in his own talents. Like Tasha told him. Like his teachers had told him. Like his employers had told him. Like everyone told him, but he'd never been able to believe.

But would anyone else believe in his future, given his past? He'd promise Tasha to get clean and sober, and hold on for a month, his sister laughing and smiling and buoyed by hope. Then he'd have a simple beer, just a beer. But the beer called for an accompanying shot, a shot for a double, and pretty soon he was at the liquor store buying a bottle of grain alcohol to go with the Kool-Aid he'd just purchased. He'd fall apart. And Tasha would go back to wearing the long face.

Four months back he'd been given a great gift, a chance. He'd been embarrassed by the charity at first, but was helped to see the events as a process. There'd been setbacks, sure. He'd fallen several times, hard, like the night at his sister's when he'd danced around like an idiot and knocked over the lamp ... but he'd been given a gift and could not squander it this time. The AA meetings would help. Six weeks free of alcohol, that's all he wanted. Then he could surprise Tasha with his news.

Christ, a drink would make me feel better. No. Just a little. No. A single beer, cool, wet ... NO!

He climbed onto the Trek Liquid 10 mountain bike and pedaled toward his small, cramped apartment. Since his car had been repossessed he'd gone back to riding the bike he'd bought at age twelve when it was an abused wreck, the toy of a rich kid who simply bought another. He rebuilt it in a day with used parts and a bike manual.

With its knobby tires and mountain gearing, the Liquid was a workout on city streets, but faster than slapping shoes and better than spending money on public transportation. When you're down to two hundred eighty-three bucks in your bank account and are unemployed, every penny counts.

Ben looked ahead and saw the dancing lights in the windows of the Rio Salado Lounge, a favorite cheap dive. It was happy hour all night and a shot and a brew was four bucks.

One, just one.

KEEP PEDALING.

And then the lounge was in the past and he was cranking toward home, sweat streaming down his face and soaking his tee shirt. Traffic blew past: buses, motorcycles, cars. He angled right, cutting down his street, past a pickup truck on blocks, past houses with grated doors and windows. Past cans and bottles and fast-food bags in the gutter. Not a single vehicle on the street was newer than three years.

He wheeled to his place, one quarter of a house divided into four units, the door and windows grated against skulking burglars, the yard of sand and scruffy plants. Two of the units had *Por Rental* signs in the windows. He walked to the side porch, the door to his downstairs three-room unit, found a bright new lock on the door and a rolled piece of paper through the handle. He unrolled the note from Georgina Haluza, his eighty-year-old landlady.

I changed the lock Ben. You're two months past due on rent almost three. I need at least $400 by Wednesday or I'll put your things out on the street. I'm sorry but you said you'd be a good tenant but you don't hardly pay on time. I need another $30 for the lock.

"Shit!" Ben Novarro spat, fruitlessly turning the knob. "Shit, shit, shit!" He shook his head in despair, leaned his back against the door and let his legs collapse until he was sitting against the house.

If there was ever a reason for a drink …

He heard a rumble and looked up to see a van going past, so dark as to seem part of the shadows painted between the buildings by the flickering, failing streetlights above. It was moving unsettlingly slow and Ben felt eyes behind the smoked glass. And then there was a blast of engine and the black van blew ahead of him, like called to another dimension.

Ben returned to the bike and kept pedaling. There was only one thing to do: Throw himself on the mercy of his sister. He could get a loan maybe, his collateral being his sobriety, his promise.

Did he have anything left in that account?

Hoping against hope, Benjamin Novarro hung his head and pedaled harder, now in a darkened warehouse area as still and quiet as a corpse.

He heard the soft rumble of an engine in the alley to his right. Followed by a roar.

* * *

"It's a wonderful home," I said as Novarro handed me one of the beers I'd bought on the way over. I wandered the living room, looking through the curtains and into the night.

"In a crappy neighborhood," she said, kicking off her shoes. "But it's getting better. How about your place ... what's it like?"

Like a waterside gem appraised at four million dollars and that I rented for almost nothing, courtesy of the landlord, my brother, a long story that started when my brother killed our father decades ago.

I edited heavily. "A pretty house on Upper Matecumbe Key."

"I've only seen the sea once, in Galveston. I took my mother to visit an aunt when I was twenty. I sat on the sand and stared for hours. I'd seen pictures and movies of seas and oceans, of course, but they don't show how alive it is. You can't smell the salt water or feel how sand brushes through your toes when you walk."

"That's about how I feel about your desert," I said. "Still in awe."

"The desert is ordinary to me, as the water must be to you. That's a statement on something, I think."

"I think we are surrounded by wonder, and we grow too used to our personal wonders. We lose them."

She looked at me and nodded. The past days eddied around me like a slow flood of images, some from here, some from Miami. There was one thing I had postponed too long.

223

"I have to make a phone call," I said. "It's time."

She said nothing, though I felt her perplexed eyes follow me out the back door.

I went outside and stood beside the lime tree, fragrant in the warm evening breeze. Or maybe it was the lingering scent of Novarro's cologne, tucked in the back of my head, a gentle citrus air.

When I turned to the south I saw the flashing array of white and red lights atop the dark peaks of South Mountain Park, where we'd sat and talked a half hour ago, a brief, peaceful respite after days of frustration and horror. Less than a mile south was the glide path for the east-west runway of the airport, to the west the sky was flashing with heat lighting from far behind the jagged White Tank mountains. I watched a big jet settling in from the charged sky like a ship coming to port after time spent in dangerous seas. I hoped the passengers felt suddenly safe again, the earth stable beneath their feet.

I called Vivian. I heard a change in her voice, though she was covering hesitation with false ebullience. "Hello, Carson. I, uh, great to hear from you. How are things out there?"

"Who is he, Viv?"

A pause. "Who's who, Carson?"

"The other. Him."

"How did you hear about—" A sigh. "A doctor I work with. Just … a guy. A nice guy. We work together a lot."

"Is it serious?"

"I, um, don't know. It's just …"

"You're sleeping together, right?"

"I, I …" A muffled sob. "Yes."

I felt a long breath escape my chest. "We haven't been doing very well the past couple of months, Vivian. We're …" I couldn't get the words to come out and blinked as another jet descended from the black sky.

"It used to be so easy," she said, her voice almost a whisper. "But we got thrown into different circles, different lives. Mine has changed so much lately. I almost never see you."

"And I don't have much to talk about, do I?"

"Neither of us do. It's like what used to be a joyful space is filled with stale words and long silences."

It was the perfect description. "How do we leave it, Vivian?" I said.

"We talk when you get back, I suppose."

"Think it'll do anything but make us feel better about what went wrong?"

"Probably not."

We balanced more stale silences with ameliorative words that I'd heard myself speak before. I dropped the phone back into my pocket, helped the sky bring two more jets to the ground, then went back inside.

"How was your call?" Novarro asked, standing in the middle of the living room, her voice gentle. It was like she knew.

"Some unsettled things became settled."

A pause as her eyes studied my face "Is that good?"

"I think I want it to be."

I stepped close to her and we looked into one another's eyes as her eyes eclipsed all other eyes I knew and her lips were on mine and my hands fell to her hips and rejoiced as we moaned through our moving tongues and I felt her hands pulling desperately at my belt, as my hands went to her blouse and my jeans snapped open as I gasped the word *bedroom* and as a single entity we began stumbling down the hall.

By the time we tumbled into bed neither of us had many clothes left, me frantically trying to pull my feet through my pants with shoes on, an impossibility. "Hang on," I hissed, pulling loose my runners and kicking them away in the raw wind of lust and long-bottled needs. I forced myself to slow down, to savor

Novarro's tastes and textures and scents, and she did the same until…

BAM!

Until something hit the front door.

"What was that?" Novarro said, head up, eyes wide.

BAM!

34

We fell apart, grabbing clothes.

BAM!

Novarro, half-covered by her blouse, had her weapon in her hand. Stumbling into pants, pushing hair from my eyes, I followed her to the living room as the door exploded open. A slender young man tumbled through and fell face-down on the floor. Novarro rolled her eyes and set the gun on an end table. It seemed her brother had arrived, in his cups. Novarro looked supremely pissed, crossing the floor as she rebuttoned the top of a blouse that thankfully covered her to mid-thigh.

"Jesus, Ben. Not again."

The kid pushed up from the floor. His face was bleeding and his clothes were torn. His right arm was a bloody mess. "I'm not drunk, Tash. Someone tried to kill me."

"Don't start with your lies. You got—"

"I'M NOT LYING," the kid screamed in pain and anger. "SOMEONE TRIED TO KILL ME!" His eyes found me. "Who are you?" He didn't sound drunk to me, just scared.

"This is Detective Carson Ryder," Novarro said. "We're working on a case together."

She was in a misbuttoned blouse; I was wearing only half-zipped jeans. With a belt flapping loose. Ben Novarro seemed too agitated to notice.

"Someone just tried to kill me," he repeated. "They shot guns at me."

"Who?" Novarro asked. She didn't sound convinced.

Benjamin Novarro shook his head and tried to push from the floor, but his right arm buckled and he moaned in pain. I crouched beside him, gently palpating the arm.

"Ouch!" he wailed.

"His arm's broken," I said to Novarro. The kid was shaking and white as a sheet. "He's going into shock. We've got to get him to an emergency room."

We hastily pulled on the rest of our clothes and walked Ben to the car, setting him gingerly in the rear seat. I drove as Novarro questioned her brother.

"Who tried to hurt you, Ben?"

"I don't know," the kid said, shaky. "Someone tried to hit me with a black van. They were coming right at me, no lights. But I veered and it went by, hitting me with the side mirror. I went flying but the bike wasn't damaged so I jumped back on and kept riding."

"Where was this?"

"On Woodland where all the warehouses and stuff are. I was coming to your place, Tash. I got locked out of my apartment. I didn't want to but I had nowhere else to—"

"Forget that," Novarro said. "Tell me about this attack."

"I pulled into a church lot. They were right behind me and I heard them crash into something. They started shooting at me, Tasha. A bullet smashed a window by my head."

"Why would someone try to kill you?" Novarro held a tone of disbelief.

"I don't know. It was insane."

"Did you get messed up in something bad?"

"I got locked out of my apartment."

"Are you sure you haven't been—"

"I KEEP TELLING YOU, TASH … SOMEONE TRIED TO KILL ME!"

Minutes later a shock-woozy Benjamin Novarro was in the ER getting his shirt cut off, the attending physician a young bespectacled guy named Flores. He ushered Novarro and me out while he worked. The main ER waiting room looked like a casting call for a play titled *Down and Out and Broken*, and we found a small alcove down the hall and sat on a blue sofa.

"Jesus," Novarro said. "What if it's actually true?"

"You don't believe him?"

"Ben's made up stuff before. Almost as bizarre."

Flores appeared. "A fracture of the ulna is the worst problem. Scrapes, contusions. He'll not be moving fast for several days."

"Can I see him?" Novarro said.

"I gave him a potent painkiller. He'll not make a lot of sense for hours."

Novarro nodded and turned to me. "There's nothing to be done here, Carson. Up for a ride?"

I raised an eyebrow. "We gonna check a story?"

"Damn right. And if he's lying …"

Novarro knew the area her brother was talking about, a four-lane street in a neighborhood of light industry, warehouses, truck rental outlets and so forth. The street was two a.m. empty and the orange-yellow glow of the streetlights and the star-like brightness of nearby security lamps threw shadows in all directions.

"He said he hauled ass to a church, right?" I said.

"Keep going. There!"

We saw a Catholic Church on the left, a tall metal gate around a front yard centered by a human-size statue of Mary. It was an incongruous location and I figured the church had been there long before the area became industrialized.

229

"The gate," Novarro said, nodding toward an opening in the fence. "Ben went through the gate. The van had to go to the drive to get in."

The vehicle entrance was a hundred feet away. We parked and strode toward the church, now in the glow of its security lights.

"There's a walkway," Novarro said, pointing to a wide sidewalk that bordered the cream adobe structure on one side, leading to the church entrance fifty feet down.

"Ben said he was racing down the walkway when he heard guns popping, then a crash or something."

Four-yard-high concrete stanchions stood at the top of the parking lot, heavy chains sagging between them, delineating a line between the lot and the grassy yard. We jogged toward them when Novarro pulled up short.

"I've got a shell casing, a 9 mm."

I saw bright brass shells at my feet and checked the foremost stanchion, its surface scraped and chipped, broken glass at the base. "The vehicle hit this," I said. "Probably not hard. I figure they jumped out and started shooting."

Novarro had her phone out, calling PPD and a forensics team to the scene. When she went to slip the phone back into her pocket she missed, the phone falling to the ground. I saw her hands were shaking. She leaned against the stanchion for support, her eyes anxious and confused.

"Ben was telling the truth, Carson. Someone really tried to kill him."

35

Novarro and I stayed on the scene for an hour, answering questions from her colleagues, filing a report, then watching the techs go about their business. The final score was fourteen 9 mm shells. The church lost two plate glass windows.

"All those gunshots and no one called the cops?" I said.

"There isn't a residence within a quarter mile. And they're low-income neighborhoods, mostly Hispanic."

"Hear no evil."

She nodded.

"What next?"

A sad but speculative smile. "We could go back to my place and …" she caught herself. "No, that's gone."

I pulled her to me and kissed her lightly on the forehead. "Not gone, postponed. Let's go back to the hospital. It's important for you to be near Ben."

"You should head back to your house and get some rest."

"It's important for me to be near you."

The call came at seven in the morning, waking Novarro and I from fitful slumber in hospital chairs. Benjamin Novarro didn't stir, still under the sway of the potent painkillers. Novarro fumbled the phone to her face, the speaker still turned on.

"*You had a call from Merle, Tasha,*" said an operator from the PPD.

Novarro sighed, and dialed the phone. "What is it, Detective Castle?" she said.

"*I saw the report on the incident with your brother,*" Castle said so loudly I could have heard him with the speaker off. "*What kinda trouble Ben get his ass into now, Tash … dealing drugs?*"

"Keep it on the business side, Merle. What are you calling about?"

"*A dark van … A night patrol found one in a wash west of the Sonoran reserve an hour ago.*"

"I'll send one of our tech teams," she said. "Maybe we can get something from it."

"*You'll have another problem there, Tash. The van got torched. Ain't nothing but a pile of fried metal and drippy plastic. Hey, that Florida guy still hanging around?*"

A glance my way. "Yep."

"*Are you screwing him yet, Tash? When we worked together it took you less than five weeks to—*"

She speared her finger wildly at the phone. It went dead. "I'm sorry," she said. "I guess he figured you weren't listening."

"Yes," I said. "He knew."

We both stared at Ben Novarro, mouth open wide, drool dripping onto the sheets. Zonked. "He's got more color than last night," she said, hopefully. "I'll let him sleep and come back later. I need to ask some questions, and I'm not sure he'll like what I'm gonna ask about."

"You suspect involvement in something bad, right?"

"I don't know what to suspect. But this kind of thing …" She couldn't say the word.

"Drugs." I could.

"If he's gotten himself in debt to a dope dealer, I swear I'll kill him myself."

Adam Kubiac awakened at seven a.m. finding Isbergen already up, in a robe and staring at the television from the sofa. It was blaring, the only sound level Isbergen knew.

"Why so early, Zoe?" he said, passing through the living room to the kitchen, grabbing his morning Red Bull from the fridge.

"Just up," she said. She unfolded her legs from beneath her and padded to Kubiac, wrapping him in her arms. "How'd my baby sleep last night?"

"Hashtag: shitty. I kept dreaming about pirates. Or maybe it was lawyers."

Kubiac made a peanut butter and jelly sandwich and sat on the couch eating, and gaming on his laptop while Isbergen stared at a show about women and guys who made their own clothes. Adam thought it was the stupidest thing he'd ever seen, but it kept Zoe from talking. Zoe was cool, but sometimes she talked until his ears hurt.

At eight fifteen, Isbergen's phone rang. She checked the screen, said, "I'm gonna take it outside where it's quieter."

"Just turn the fucking TV down," Kubiac said.

But she was out the door.

Kubiac was waiting when she stepped back inside two minutes later. "Who the hell was that?" he asked.

"Cottrell. He, uh … you're not going to like it."

"What won't I like, Zoe?"

She slumped to the couch. "He says he has properties you need to buy before he changes the will."

Kubiac stared. "What properties?"

"Some real estate out west. In the desert."

Kubiac glared. "How much?"

"Uh, $5,000,000."

"WHAT?"

"Plus the, uh, other money."

233

Kubiac paced the room, hands clenching and releasing. "I know what the scumwad is doing. He's buying useless dirt for nothing, then selling it to me for FIVE FUCKING MILLION DOLLARS!"

A shrug. "Maybe. I don't know. You'll still get—"

"He wants $5,000,000 more of MY MONEY?"

A nod. "He said he's thought about how risky it is to rewrite the will. He's afraid, Adam. I can understand."

"*YOU UNDERSTAND*?"

Isbergen went to Kubiac and put her hand on his arm. "I mean … He's being a shit, but it's the only way."

Kubiac slammed the can of Red Bull into the wall. "FUCK!"

"Easy, baby," Isbergen said, wrapping him in her arms again.

He twisted free. "Maybe I should do like Cottrell told me at first, Zoe. Forget my father's money and use my brains to make my own."

"Adam, you have to take his offer."

Kubiac stared at the floor. "Maybe I don't want dear old Daddy's money. Maybe it'll make me dirty like him."

"No, Adam. You'll be the loser."

"I'll call fucking Cottrell and tell him to wrap dear old Daddy's will in barbed wire and to CRAM IT UP HIS SHYSTER ASS!"

And then Isbergen was toe to toe with Kubiac, her eyes like twin flares. "It DOESN'T MATTER, ADAM … you're still making millions. USE YOUR GODDAMN BRAIN FOR ONCE!"

Kubiac stared like he'd been slapped. "*What*?"

Zoe's voice switched to contrite. "I'm-I'm sorry, Adam. It's just … time's running out. If you don't do like Cottrell says, he won't change a thing on the will. I'm so scared that you'll get nothing."

Kubiac stood absolutely still for several seconds, absorbing the information. He screamed like a banshee and kicked over the coffee table. He grabbed up a tumbler from the table and threw it into the wall, shards of glass exploding everywhere. Isbergen's new brown boots were on the floor and he punted them across the room, shrieking with each kick.

And then the fit passed, Kubiac alone in the center of the room, shoulders slumped and on the verge of crying. "Here's the hashtag, Zoe," he whispered. "Doublefucked. Call the filthy shitwad and tell him to go ahead."

Relief flooded Isbergen's face. She pulled out her phone.

"I should waste the rotten fuck," Kubiac muttered. "Hashtag: kill; Hashtag: murder; Hashtag: dead as a fucking doornail."

"Don't think that, baby," Isbergen eyed Kubiac warily. "You'd never get away with it. Don't you ever think like that."

*　*　*

We pulled off I-10 South and followed the GPS to a road paralleling a stack of rocks resembling an exploded mountain and continued past small peaks of rock and creosote bush and the occasional saguaro. The tech team had the van taped off, two men crawling through the charred wreckage, two more walking the sand, heads down.

"Anything?"

"We pulled the Vehicle Identification Number. It's registered to Eugenio Vela." He recited a west Phoenix address.

Vela lived on a working-class street with small houses and older cars and trucks. In the drive was a blue Plymouth Voyager, some nicks in the paint, one wheel different from the others, but looking in decent shape. Vela was in his open garage and working on an ancient Harley. He walked up wiping his hand on a shop rag. Vela was maybe forty, big and big bellied and wearing a formerly white tee shirt that showed arms wrapped in tats, some pro, some prison models. "Yeah?" he said, pushing back sweaty, shoulder-length black hair and showing yellow teeth.

"Where were you last night, Mr Vela?"

"Working. I drive a forklift for Johnson Fabricators in Glendale. Night shift."

"You can document that?"

A smug smile. "Time card. Other workers. My boss. I went in at eleven, clocked out at half past seven in the morning."

Novarro began looking up and down the street, frowning, leaning out past the garage and affecting stymied, finally back up with her hand porched over her brow against the sun and looking at the roof of Vela's house.

"Are you looking for something?" Vela asked.

"The van, Mr Vela," Novarro said. "The black one registered to you. Where is it?"

A dramatic sigh. "Gone. Stolen. It was here one day, gone the next morning. I never heard it go. And it was white."

"You didn't report it?"

A big hand flicked the thought away. "It was a twelve-year-old piece of *mierde*. What would I gain but a loss of time?"

Novarro turned her eyes to the Voyager. "And there sits a nice and reasonably new van, three years old? Four?"

"*Si, tres.*"

"You're a liar, Mr Vela."

Vela's eyes flashed anger, but he chilled his face into innocence. Novarro planted herself in front of him, staring up a half a foot.

"I know how it works, Eugenio. You handed your old van over to Ramon Escheverría or one of his crew."

"Exchevario? I do not believe I know the na—"

"He gave you a better van, Eugenio. They used your beater for a crime. It wasn't stolen, it was traded for."

Vela continued the innocence project. "It disappeared one night. I know *la policía* are busy on important things and I did not want to bother you on such a meaningless matter."

Novarro returned to the car with me in her wake. "You drive. I want to check on something I already know the answer to."

I took the wheel and she spun the computer screen her way,

tapping the keypad and watching the screen. It took less than five minutes to get what she wanted.

"Vela was in prison when Ramon was there. Like prisons everywhere, they hang with their tribe, blacks with blacks, whites with whites, Hispanic with Hispanic, Presbyterians with Presbyterians."

"What was Vela in for?"

"Robbed a liquor store. Did three of five and clean since. But even though Vela's walking the line, he owes allegiance to his old prison tribe. So when Ramon comes calling for a favor – one that benefits Vela, of course – old Eugenio goes along."

I nodded. "Tribal. Blood takes care of blood. Even after prison."

Novarro stared at the distant mountains and shook her head. "Everyone has a tribe but me, and I'm a fucking Indian."

36

How did she do it? Adam Kubiac wondered, sprawling across the bed and staring at the ceiling. *How did Cat get her father's money?*

He had to find out. It was time.

Isbergen was at the door, tapping. "Adam?"

He traded wrinkled shorts for wrinkled jeans and wriggled into a green tee that said "Byte Me".

"Adam?"

He rolled his eyes. "Leave me alone, go shopping or something."

Catherine Maruyama was already at the table when he pulled to the curb of the café. Kubiac sat. Before Maruyama could say anything past "*Good morning, Adam, I'm sorry about yester—*" he was talking.

"My story is even worse than yours, Cat. My father left me one dollar. He left $20,000,000 to a bunch of stupid charities and institutions. All I've got is a little money of my own, a few thousand."

Maruyama put her hand on his forearm. "Oh Adam, that's so wrong."

Kubiac leaned close to Maruyama. "Zoe … and, uh, I came up with an idea. The lawyer's gonna make the will say that I get everything. But it's gonna cost me over half of my money. Half!"

Maruyama studied Adam. She reached out and brushed hair from his eyes. "Remember I told you my father was a lawyer, Adam? I know how they are. You have to pay the lawyer ... He's got you. It's what they do."

Kubiac slid his chair to Maruyama's side, leaning close so others couldn't eavesdrop. "I wanna know what you did to get all of your money, Cat. Please don't lie to me ... I know you got it all."

She shook her head. "I-I can't tell you, Adam. It could affect my whole life. It's that kind of se-secret."

Kubiac scrutinized the other customers sitting outside beneath large shading umbrellas. A pair of males in their thirties, gay, a tiny terrier at their feet. A suited businessman sipping coffee and reading the *Wall Street Journal*, a fortyish woman in a pantsuit with a sparkly red silk scarf around her neck and a cup of tea on the table, totally engrossed in her tablet. They were all out of earshot. He leaned closer to Maruyama. "We're *us*, Cat. Upgrades. You could never tell a Neanderthal. You can tell me."

Maruyama looked away, as if making a decision. Kubiac shot a glance at the woman in the scarf and saw her looking his way. Her eyes dropped back to her tablet. *Even older women want me*, Kubiac thought, turning back to Maruyama.

"Cat?" he prodded.

When Maruyama looked at Kubiac her eyes were both resolute and pleading. Her fingers were shaking. She put her lips to his ear.

"The lawyer had to die, Adam," she whispered.

Kubiac's mouth fell open.

Maruyama leaned away, eyes pleading. "You can't tell anyone, Adam. I'd go to jail or prison or wherever people who k-kill people go."

"You *killed* him, Cat?"

"N-no ... not me. But I p-paid a man to do it."

"How did you find someone to do that, uh, kind of thing?"

"My father got him off on a murder indictment. I knew the man was … th-that was the kind of thing he did."

"Jesus, Cat … I can't believe you …"

"My father was wrong, Adam. The lawyer who wrote the will should have paid attention to my interests, too. My future."

"That's what I told Cottrell, the bastard."

Her fingers made the money-whisk. "This is all they care about. It's all Daddy cared about. What's the name of your father's lawyer, Adam?"

Kubiac's face wrinkled in disgust. "J. T. Cottrell. Hashtag: scumball."

Maruyama sucked in a startled breath and her eyes widened to their limits. "*Jefferson Cottrell?*"

"You know him, Cat?"

"Too much. Way, way too much."

"What, *why?*"

Maruyama stared into her coffee for long moments before her eyes rose to Kubiac's eyes. "Cottrell is, was, a friend of my father. He's a scumbag, like most of Daddy's friends. He'd come to parties at our house and hit on me. It started when I was thirteen."

"The *asshole.*"

"It was sick, Adam. Cottrell's got a daughter not much older than me. Brenda was a nasty bitch, but she was his daughter and she was my age."

"Did you tell your father?"

"Daddy said it was just my imagination. That *Jeff* was just paying me a compliment and I took it the wrong way. Daddy was d-disgusting. That's why I didn't tell him about the times Cottrell … a-a-about the tuh-times th-that he …"

"Slow down, Cat. I'm your friend. You can talk to me."

"About the times he raped me, Adam, starting when I was fourteen." Tears welled in Maruyama's eyes and she pushed from the table, wobbly on her legs.

"I want to be home. I feel better there. Talking about Cottrell makes me feel sick."

Kubiac stood and grabbed Maruyama's hand. "Can I come?" he pleaded. "Can we talk more?"

"Yes, Adam. Please come with me. I don't want to be alone and you make me feel safe."

Kubiac nodded down the sidewalk. Though a block distant, the slender, whippy profile was identifiable. His eye went wide.

"It's Zoe. She's coming."

"She can join us. I've been wanting to meet her."

"If she finds out I'm hanging with someone else she'll get real bitchy. I'll make something up and see you in a few."

"If that's what you want … sure." Maruyama hustled to the small bookshop next door and ducked inside.

Kubiac returned to his seat.

"Adam!" Isbergen said, clicking up in the brown boots. He noted clothes he hadn't seen before. And a sparkly necklace. No wonder he was running out of money.

He pushed a smile to his face and finger-waved. "Yo Zo."

"What are you doing?"

"Hanging. Playing a couple games."

"You were so angry when you left. I got worried."

"I'm chill with it, Zoe. Nothing to do but pay the man, right?"

"I'm sorry Cottrell's doing this to you, Adam. You're sure you're going to go through with—"

He waved it away. "It's over, Zoe. Hashtag: donedeal. I'll be home in a couple hours."

"What you gonna do?"

He held up the tablet. "Some fool in Brunei thinks he can take me in *Combat Zone*. I'm gonna fry his Arab ass. Can you go to the store, Zo? I'm almost out of Bull."

"Sure."

"And get some Hot Pockets and Tostitos, would ya?"

241

Isbergen bent over Kubiac and kissed his forehead. "It's good to see you back. Being the Adam I love."

"Yeah. See ya. Don't forget the Tostitos."

When Isbergen turned the corner, Kubiac went into the bookstore. Maruyama was nowhere to be seen. He saw an elderly clerk putting books on a shelf.

"That girl who was here a few minutes ago, black hair, white dress. You see her?"

"She was looking at the magazines by the window. Then she seemed to see something that made her upset and she ran out. She went that way …" The clerk pointed to the direction of Maruyama's apartment.

Adam Kubiac knocked and rang the doorbell simultaneously. Maruyama opened the door seconds later, looking up and down the pavement. "Is she with you?"

"Zoe? No … she went out to get some food stuff. Why?"

Maruyama went to the door and stood on the stoop, looking down the street.

"She didn't follow you? You're sure?"

"What's going on, Cat? You're scaring me."

"Her name's not Zoe, Adam," Maruyama said, closing the door, her voice tense. "It's Brenda."

"*What*?"

"I haven't seen her in years. But I'm sure it's her."

"Who is she?"

"Cottrell's daughter. Remember I said her name was Brenda and she was about my age? That's her."

"Wh-what's going on, Cat?"

"Sit down, Adam. Tell me about Zoe … everything."

*   *   *

242

When we returned to the hospital Benjamin Novarro was looking much better, color returned, eyes bright. Flores said there was nothing more to be done at the hospital, Ben needing only rest and food and hydration. Ben sat in back as Novarro drove us to her house.

"We went to the church last night, Ben," Novarro said, looking into the rear-view. "Do you have any idea why it happened?"

"No. None. Maybe I was just there. Maybe it was someone crazy."

I turned in the seat. "You're on someone's shit list. We have to figure out who and why."

"Where were you last night?" Novarro said. "Before you found you were locked out of your apartment?"

"At, uh, that little Methodist church over on Belmont."

"Church?"

He reddened and looked at his shoes. "There's like these meetings there. Uh, AA."

"Jeez, Ben," Novarro said, "don't be ashamed. That's great."

The kid swallowed hard and turned away.

And then we were at Novarro's home. Ben leaned on me as I walked him into the house and set him on the couch. His arm was in an inflatable cast and his face and side were bandaged. Novarro made coffee and brought her brother a bean and bacon taco that he ate greedily. Novarro sat on the couch and looked at me. "Ready for another day of Meridien, Carson? God forgive me, but I am so tired of that name."

Ben looked up from his taco. "Meridien?"

"A case," Novarro said.

He frowned. "It wouldn't be Leslie Meridien, would it? The shrink?"

37

Adam confessed every aspect of his brief period with Isbergen to Maruyama: Meeting her at the café, moving from the sprawling Scottsdale home he hated – his father's commanding presence in every room, crack and crevice – to her apartment two days later, how she'd been instrumental in arranging the deal with Cottrell. Maruyama listened intently, now and then asking a question, mostly about timing.

"You said Zoe showed up not long after your father died?"

"She sat next to me at the café. I went there every day."

"She approached you?"

"She came to my table and sat down. Said I looked deep in thought. She made me laugh."

"They're working some angle, Adam."

"You know this law shit, Cat," Kubiac pleaded. "Hashtag: Help."

Maruyama thought. "I'll bet Cottrell's going to hit you up for more money. He'll say he's reconsidered the risks he's taking and needs more. It'll probably be a sob story."

Kubiac's mouth dropped open. "He did that yesterday!"

A sigh. "I knew it. Pay him, because it's the only way you're going to get any money. He's in control, Adam. *They're* in control. You're stuck."

"They're trying to steal *my* money." Kubiac stood and began pacing, his face growing from anger to determination with each succeeding pass around the room. He stopped in front of Maruyama. "I can do it, Cat," Kubiac said, pounding a fist into his palm. "Cottrell raped you, and he and his daughter are trying to screw me. I can kill him."

Maruyama shook her head. "It might be justice, but it's too dangerous."

"My uncle used to take me hunting in Utah. Sheep and stuff. I'm a good shot."

"No, Adam. It scares me to have you in danger."

Kubiac paced another two turns around the room. "We'll hire the guy you used to kill your father."

"He's in prison. He got caught for robbery not long after he … did what I needed. D-don't think this way, Adam. It scares me."

"I'll kill Cottrell, Cat. You won't have to think about him ever again, and I'll get all my money. Hashtag: justice."

"It doesn't just happen like that, Adam. Think about it."

Kubiac leaned back and thought, a frown settling over his features. "Shit. If I shoot his scumbag ass, the will still says I get nothing. He's not going to change it to me getting the money until I sign some papers that give him half my money. Now he's raping *me*."

"You have to sign, Adam. It's the only way." Maruyama paused, stood, went to the window and looked out with arms crossed. "Unless …"

"Unless what, Cat?"

"Unless you signed the paper and we could get into his office. We could destroy the paper. If the will has already been changed, everything will work."

"I can hack into Cottrell's security system. The sign outside says what kind it is. I've done that kind of system before. It's easy."

"Where?"

"I opened Meridien's gate by getting between her system and its central core. I've done other hacks. Code is what I do." He paused, his eyes pleading. "Will you help me?"

*　*　*

Ben Novarro had no idea Leslie Meridien had been killed, but like many of his generation, Novarro's little brother wasn't big on watching the news or reading papers. He shook his head in disbelief. "Horrible. Unreal."

"How did you know Dr Meridien, Ben?" his sister asked.

"It was after I quit school last year. I felt completely lost and drifting. Remember?"

"It's in the past, Ben. Keep going."

"Two of my former instructors kept calling, trying to get me to come back. It went on for weeks. Then one of them, Professor Evelyn Galen, showed up at my door and handed me Dr Meridien's business card. Professor Galen said that she'd talked to Dr Meridien about me and wanted me to contact the doctor. It took about three weeks and more prodding from Dr Galen, but I finally made an appointment and showed up. Dr Meridien and I talked for over an hour and she took me on."

Novarro looked stunned. "Wait. You were one of Dr Meridien's patients?"

"Dr Meridien worked with a few people like me. Pro-pro—"

"Pro bono. For good. Free. How long did you see her?"

"I went to like two dozen personal sessions and four or five group sessions over four to five months." A sad smile. "Guess I didn't learn much."

"For crying out loud, Ben," Novarro said, not hiding the exasperation in her voice, "why didn't you tell me you were seeing a therapist? Were you ashamed for some reason?"

Ben swallowed hard. "I wasn't ashamed, Tash. I just didn't want to disappoint you."

Confusion. "Disappoint me? How in the world does your getting help disappoint me?"

"I know how bad you feel when I … fall down. I figured if I told you I was seeing a psychologist, you'd get your hopes up high like you always do. Higher even. And if – or when – I failed again, you'd feel worse than ever. I didn't want to do that to you, Tash, hurt you again. I wanted to make sure I was truly clean and sober before telling you about Dr Meridien. And the AA meetings."

Novarro hugged her brother tightly. "Oh Ben Ben Ben … my beautiful Ben." She leaned back and looked him in the eyes. "What was it like with Dr Meridien?"

Ben's voice dropped low. I had to lean in to hear him. "She was super smart and super nice. She told me there was no difference between me and anyone else there." He paused and swallowed hard. "It was nice of her to lie like that."

"Lie?"

Ben looked at his hands. "Most of the others in the groups I was in were rich kids or smart. Super smart, like geniuses. I didn't belong with people who studied medicine and computers and science. They were all Einsteins."

"You're a genius in your own right," Novarro scolded. "You can stand with them any day. Stop doubting yourself."

He wiggled his fingers. "I fix simple shit with my hands."

"You're brilliant with mechanical systems, Ben. You always have been."

"Mechanical systems?" I said.

Novarro nodded at me. "Ben *is* truly a genius with anything mechanical. It's like an extra sense."

"The mechanical boy," I whispered to myself.

Novarro frowned. "What?"

"Mashburn's mechanical boy. It's Ben … It has to be." I

247

popped open my briefcase and fished out the photo taken in Meridien's backyard. "You know these people, Ben?" I said, holding it to his eyes.

"Sure. Brad Shackleton, Geraldo Trujillo, Darnell Mashburn, Catherine Maruyama. I took the picture."

"That was *your* group?" I said.

He nodded, entranced by the photo. "I think Dr Meridien wanted us to talk out our problems. To relax. And get used to—"

"Wait ..." Novarro interrupted. "Darnell said the mechanical boy was hiding from a big blue sissy. Was that ..."

Ben cleared his throat. "I, uh, maybe told Darnell that I had a cop sister and I didn't want her to know I was seeing a shrink. I expect I told Geraldo Trujillo, too."

"Ben, Trujillo is dead. He was killed in a hit and run."

It took a moment to sink in. "Jesus. Geraldo was a nice guy. Jumpy and a little odd, but I guess that's why he was there."

I pulled Novarro aside. "Two of the four are dead and someone just tried to kill your brother."

"I gotta make a call." She stepped quickly to the kitchen.

"So ..." Ben said, looking at me. "You guys serious?"

"Uh, I like your sister a lot, Ben. We've gotten close." I paused, recalling our deshabille when he'd tumbled into the living room. "Uh, that was probably a poor choice of words."

"Tash doesn't do anything but work and worry. She needs someone to make her smile. She used to smile a lot more." He frowned. "But most of that's on me. I haven't given her much to smile about lately."

"Going to a twelve-step is the best way to get her smiling again, Ben. Getting clean. And seeing Dr Meridien, though you probably should have told your sister. She'd have been overjoyed."

He thought a moment, leaned close. "Don't tell Tash, Detective Ryder, but I think I'm gonna get clean for good this time." He paused. "Something in me feels hopeful."

I winked. "Our secret."

We bumped fists just as Novarro returned. "I upped the security on Mashburn's house. OK, Ben, tell me about this Catherine Maruyama. We've got to find her." She didn't add *if Maruyama's still alive.*

"Her nickname was Cat. Everyone liked her. She was funny and smart and was nice to everyone. But she's gone."

"Where?"

"Her father had a temporary job in Phoenix. She flew back to Japan a few months ago."

I turned to Novarro. "Darnell said Maruyama flew into a red sun. The Japanese flag is a red sun."

"Jesus," she whispered. "It makes perfect sense when you know the language."

"Mashburn, Ben. Tell me about him."

"Brad and he were buddies back before Darnell started to weird out. He started seeing things, hearing things."

"Darnell liked Catherine Maruyama a lot, right?"

"Darnell had a crush on Cat. But one day he started screaming at her to, uh, fellate him. We never saw him again."

Novarro said: "We've got to keep you safe, Ben. You're now staying with me, little brother."

Ben looked between his sister and me. "You think I'm part of this ... this plot? That's why someone tried to kill me?"

Novarro looked at me for my thoughts.

"Ben's a target," I said. "Maybe the last one."

"We better track down Maruyama as well."

I winced at the hours it could take to find the flight Maruyama flew out on, then the tracking job in Japan. I blew out a breath. "We're gonna have to do it ourselves, Tasha. It can't go through a system Escheverría seems to be watching."

"No Fish? He's great at that stuff."

"Can't risk it." I thought a moment. The Meridien case was tied to the Bowers case. I pressed number one on my speed dial.

"Yo, Cars," Harry said. "What's up?"

"Things are breaking slow here, brother. But they're breaking. Got a minute to talk?"

38

It took ten minutes for a PPD cruiser to pull across the street and park. Novarro let them in on the details and showed mugshots of Escheverría and his core crew. Ben fell asleep on the couch.

Novarro's phone trilled and she studied the screen. "Park Service," she said, putting the phone on speaker. "Detective Tasha Novarro."

"*Hello, Detective Novarro?*" said a tentative male voice. "*This is Mike Warman with the Park Rangers at Estrella.*"

"Of course. What can I do for you, Mr Warman?"

"*I'm not sure if this means anything, Detective, but there was a fire in the canyon yesterday; the call came in about six thirty in the morning. It burned almost a third of a mile toward the mouth before we cut a firebreak and stopped the damn thing.*"

"A fire? Where?"

"*At the far end, where the body was found. The Shackleton fellow.*"

Novarro shot me a look. "How did the fire start?"

"*Well, I'm not an expert on these things, but I smelled something at the head of the canyon, something pungent. Not gasoline, but more like motor oil. A heavy petroleum smell.*"

"How's the area look?"

"*Burned over. Black. It hurts to look at.*"

"Thanks for the call, Ranger Warman. Much appreciated."

She rang off and stared out the kitchen window. "It could only be Ramon. He found out we're poking around the Shackleton death scene and got antsy, thinking maybe someone left something incriminating at the scene – a handprint on a rock, a cigarette butt, who knows. So he calls for the place to be torched, just in case. The *cholos* go up there, splash some accelerant ..." She caught herself and frowned. "Hmmmm, not working."

"Sounds good to me. What's wrong?"

"The upper canyon is a bowl and no wind gets down that far, not that there's any breeze this time of year. They slop gasoline all over, the fumes accumulate in the bowl. The minute they light a match ..."

"An explosion," I said, again impressed by Novarro's analytical prowess. "They're toast."

"Even if they don't incinerate themselves, there's smoke rolling into the sky, visible for miles. Bad news when you have to get back to the canyon mouth and disappear. Something's missing."

"And why the day and not the night?"

"That's easy. Too hard to get back there in the dark. Plus they'd need lights on the ATVs. Too easy to see and report to the Park Service."

She had me. "So the muffled ATVs come in at first light, splash accelerant. That still brings up your point: Even with the wheels they're twenty minutes from the canyon mouth. And that's where fire teams will go in when the blaze is spotted. It's chancy, and Ramon doesn't do chancy."

Novarro's nails clicked a rhythm on the tabletop as she thought. "Oh Ramon," she said to herself, "you are one smart little psycho."

"What?"

"Try this out: the *cholos* make their way to the top of the canyon and soak the area with a mixture not as volatile as

252

gasoline or kerosene or whatever. They use, like Warman suggested, motor oil mixed with charcoal lighter, something like that. Fuels that burn readily, but don't evaporate in minutes. They douse the canyon and haul ass." She gave me a lifted eyebrow. "Got it yet?"

I though it through. "You're thinking when they're nearly out of the canyon they make a phone call."

"And the guy standing on the trail high above makes sure no eyes are on him, and tosses a highway flare into the canyon. Whoosh."

"Ramon had his eyes on us again," I said. "When did you file the report that mentioned going to the canyon?"

"The next morning. Usually I write up my notes and whatnot as the last thing I do. Sometimes I go home, write them up, and send them in from there. But that was the day we drove to Tucson to brace Carazo and I was too worn to type."

"I think it's time I had a little tête-à-tête with Mr Castle. Just kind of feel him out."

She grabbed her jacket. "Let's go."

"This one's mine," I said. "Don't worry. I'll be suave and diplomatic."

It was half past six and I figured that Castle might be at his home. He lived in a subdivision in West Tempe and as I approached I saw his vehicle in the driveway, a Dodge Ram pickup, and what wasn't jet black was shiny chrome. I rang the doorbell and Castle answered a minute later, dressed in jeans and a strap tee and holding a can of Budweiser. His puzzlement at seeing me turned into amusement and he stepped out on the stoop.

"Hey there, boy, you still in Phoenix? Don't Florida need you?"

"It's a tough case, Officer Castle." I paused for effect. "But you probably know that."

"I'd a thought ol' Three-Point would have nailed it by now. There a reason you're standing on my doorstep?"

"I thought I'd turn to you for a little help."

Surprise. "Do what I can, Florida."

"See, there's a problem, Officer Castle. Ramon Escheverría knows our every move. He's wired in to the PPD."

A frown. "You saying he's bought somebody?"

"It's the only way, amigo."

"Who you thinking?"

I crossed my arms and pretended to think. "Could be anyone who has an active password to the PPD record-keeping system. Or maybe it's someone without PPD access."

"Hunh-unh. They couldn't log into the system. Plus it has safeguards."

"I'm thinking maybe it's someone who doesn't need to log in."

Confusion. "What … like a hacker?"

"Not necessary. There are some folks outside the department who get copied on all materials. One seems to be you."

"Yeah, cuz Meridien was in MCSD's jurisdiction. We passed the case over to PPD, but I wanted to see all of Tasha's …" My inference finally sank in and the concentration turned to bunker eyes. "Wait, what the fuck you saying?"

"It seems strange that you wanted Detective Novarro to send you her reports in the first place … you don't have enough illegals to deport?"

Not only were Castle's eyes tightening, the muscles were, too. Including biceps like skin-upholstered cannonballs. "You better goddamn watch your mouth …"

"Not an answer, Merle. Why did you specifically request Detective Novarro send you copies of her reports on a case involving Ramon Escheverría?"

"Mister, you don't know how close you are to …"

"Again, Merle, not an answer. Tell me about the reports. Detective Novarro thinks you wanted them to keep tied to her. I know y'all used to rock the mattress, and I also know that it ended, you being the only one clueless enough to miss the message. But maybe you wanted the reports so you could pass information on to —"

He lasted longer than I'd expected, the punch thrown hard and fast and at my mouth. He was an iron-pounder and even blocked I felt the damn thing down to the soles of my feet. He was fast, too, and the second shot went for my belly and blew the wind from my lungs. I grabbed for the clinch, and we grunted and grabbled like a pair of wrestlers, him with a 20 lb advantage. He pushed me backwards into the truck and rocked my spine before pulling away and throwing a haymaker right that would have taken my head off if I hadn't ducked. The momentum opened his right side to me and I laid everything into a low rib punch. He grunted and tried to wheel around to me, but I was slowed by pain.

My next shot was a spear hand into the solar plexus. Castle gasped, staggered, grabbed at the shiny extended mirror of his truck, then went down.

"The reports to you are over," I said.

"You're ... a stupid ... fuck," he said, trying to simultaneously talk and regain his breath.

I bent over his semi-fetal form. "Here's how it is with Novarro, Merle: Over. She's truly not enamored of you."

"This ain't ... done," he grunted as I walked away. "Not even ... close."

39

A tentative knock at the door.

"Mmph?" I mumbled into Novarro's hair, smelling of soap and lavender.

Ben's lowered voice: "You asked me to keep thinking about people I met at Meridien's … people I met in groups?"

I turned to the clock: 7.23 a.m., sun streaming golden through the curtains. My side ached from my fight with Castle. Novarro and I had discussed the incident when I returned, me thinking Castle's flashpoint anger was over perceived insult and not the discovery of a dirty alliance. I doubted the Meat Cowboy was the leak.

I roused Novarro for what was likely to be another long day.

Fifteen minutes later we were in the living room with Ben, me just into khakis, sky-blue tee and cream jacket, Novarro in tight, low jeans with a black leather belt embellished with conchos and a rough-woven sleeveless linen blouse. I looked Miami, she pure Southwest. She checked the security patrol, still in place.

"You remembered something else?" Novarro said to Ben, sucking down coffee after running cups out to the guys in the cruiser.

Ben wore battered brown cargo shorts and a tee shirt advertising a local brewery, the comfort-with-an-arm-cast look. "There was this dude I met. He was in our group for a couple sessions, guy named Adam, I think. I didn't care for him, he had issues." Ben smiled. "But I guess we all did."

Novarro said: "Tell me about him."

"Skinny, regular height. Shaggy black hair. I think his eyes were brown. He was always strutting around like superior to everyone else – the *Neanderthals* as he called, well, about anyone not him. I took it that he was a computer whiz. But hearing anything he didn't want to hear set him off on a tirade, or maybe a tantrum since he seemed stuck at age thirteen. Either he quit the group or Meridien didn't think he fit. Like I said, I just saw him one or two times."

"Last name?"

"I'm not sure I ever heard a last name."

"Think there's anything there?" Novarro asked me.

I pondered. "This is the first time we've heard the name. And he wasn't in Darnell's photo. Let's stay on present track."

She wasn't convinced. "I dunno, maybe we should—"

Her cell rang and she pulled it from her pocket, hit speaker. "Larkin, our friendly CEO from DataSĀF."

"Could you come over here to our offices, Detective?" Larkin paused and added, "Please?"

"Does it have to do with the Meridien files?"

"I, uh, am wary of speaking on an unsecured line."

She shot me a raised-eyebrow look. "Sure, Mr Larkin. We're on our way."

"What do you think this is about?" I said when she rang off.

"*Oho'no't'odonho wa t'ndaho.*"

"Which is?"

"Your guess is as good as mine, Kemo Sabe."

We were in the DataSĀF offices within fifteen minutes. Larkin was pacing the lobby, whispering to a dark-suited and fiftyish man with penetrating black eyes that seemed out of place in a gentle and avuncular face, his gray hair a fringe around a balded dome and longish, giving him a friarly air. Larkin looked anxious, but was polite. "Come back to my office, please."

We followed him to an expansive corner office, pleasantly sterile, with a wide view of Camelback Mountain in the distance. Above Camelback the sky was an aching blue. Larkin cleared his throat. "I want to apologize for my behavior on your previous visits. Sometimes I'm not good with—"

Novarro waved his words away. "What's happened, Mr Larkin?"

"We know where the Meridien files went. We just don't know why." He nodded to the dark-suited man. "This is Malcolm Kent, a computer-security consultant and a specialist in finding breaches in systems. We flew Malcolm in from Palo Alto yesterday. He worked all night and struck gold an hour ago."

"Who swiped the Meridien account, Mr Kent?" Novarro asked, cutting to the chase. "Who broke in?"

A twinkle in the green eyes. "No one did."

"How about you explain that?"

Kent crossed the room and took a moment to study the distant Camelback Mountain. "Think of a castle behind four burning moats, detectives," he said, his hands clasped behind his back. "Add a guard of fire-breathing dragons. And a phalanx of archers behind the battlements. The castle is impenetrable." He turned. "Yet one day the king is found dead. How did the killer get in?"

Novarro didn't miss a beat. "He was already in. It was an inside job."

Kent shot a thumb-up. "I got deep into the software and discovered the Meridien files had been reviewed by a specific computer inside DataSĀF."

"Reviewed?" I asked.

"Studied before destruction. DataSĀF uses a potent program to obliterate files of clients who go out of business or move to another storage facility, and that's what was employed here. After the files were removed and the correct command given, the safe-guards erased Meridien's files from the server; the cloud."

"Whose computer was used to access the goods?" Novarro asked.

"Follow me, if you will."

We jumped into Kent's wake and he led us two dozen feet down the hall to another office. "That one right there," Larkin said, pointing to a monitor and keyboard on a desk. We'd stood in this office before.

"Candace Klebbin," Novarro said. "The office administrator."

Kent nodded. "Ms Klebbin was accessing the Meridien data. Over months, it seems."

"It was against all rules," Larkin growled, standing up for his company.

"Where's Klebbin now?" Novarro asked.

"She hasn't shown up since Mr Kent arrived," Larkin said. "I wonder why."

"So the Meridien files are smoke," Novarro sighed, not hiding her disappointment. "Patient names, appointment times, every-thing's gone ... including Klebbin."

A smile from Kent. "Gone from the main server. But let's go back to my earlier analogy of the castle. Let's say it has two hundred rooms. Most are orderly and much the same, arrayed down halls. Each holds thousands of file cabinets. But several rooms are willy-nilly, random. In high towers or low dungeons. Under stairways. Out in the stables."

I raised an eyebrow. "Uh ..." Our Mr Kent had a thing for metaphor.

"Sorry. The main rooms hold the data of DataSĀF's clients, large storage arenas accessible by those with a key. In this case, a password."

"And the other rooms?"

"They hold the materials helpful in the day-to-day operations of the castle. Servants quarters, guardhouses, broom closets."

"The operating system?" I ventured.

"Precisely. Candance Klebbin simply copied the files to a broom closet. In this case, a program used for security. Then she completely erased the original files, leaving nothing behind but a digital void. Thus hidden, the files didn't reside on her office computer, should anyone look. A very bright and cautious woman."

"A psycho," Larkin corrected.

"How long will it take you to pull Dr Meridien's files out?" Novarro asked.

Kent reached into his pocket. When he held out his palm we beheld a tiny oblong egg, a memory stick. "Already done," he said. "A bit under a half a gigabyte: the entirety of Dr Leslie Meridien's files."

"Did you check them?"

Larkin stepped in. "We can't open them for legal reasons. They're private."

I nodded. "A court order is necessary." I turned to the security pro. "Can we borrow you, Mr Kent?"

"Go, Malcolm," Larkin said. "Five hours or five days. I'll pay for it." He turned to Novarro and me. "Get Candace," he said. "Nail that lying bitch."

40

Catherine Maruyama slumped in Adam Kubiac's car, fifty feet from the door of Hunters Supply and Range. Adam had been inside for forty minutes. He emerged a minute later, his arms full. He put packages in the trunk and slipped into the passenger's seat.

"Did you get, uh … what you wanted?" she asked.

"An Ambush 300 Blackout rifle, ammo, an ATN Arrow 6—"

"Arrow?"

"A night-vision rifle sight. So I can shoot in the dark. Plus I got a suppressor—"

"What's that?"

"It reduces the sound of the shot a whole lot. It's more like a loud cough. It's expensive stuff; I'm almost out of money."

"You were in there so long I got afraid."

"I used the range to try out the equipment. I saw Cottrell's lying face on every target."

"Adam, are you really going to—"

Kubiac spun to Maruyama, his features a rictus of anger. "All my life people have been screwing me over like I'm some little bitch. It's gonna end. Hashtag: hadenough." Kubiac pulled his cellphone from the pocket of his black jeans. "Time to sign the papers. You're sure you can destroy them if I get you inside Cottrell's office?"

Maruyama made the motion of flicking a lighter. "No biggie. I just take them somewhere and burn them."

Kubiac phoned and Cottrell's receptionist answered. "He's on another line. I can have him call you back later today."

"Tell him it's Adam."

Ten seconds later Cottrell was on the line. "Adam, it's good to hear from you."

"I'm on my way."

"Excellent."

Kubiac entered the lawyer's office fifteen minutes later, Cottrell ushering him through the door like they were old friends. The receptionist was absent. They went to Cottrell's office, papers centering the desk. Cottrell sat as Kubiac forced a fake yawn.

"Didn't my father say you had a daughter, Jeffrey?"

A nod. "Sure. She's not much older than you. She's in Spokane studying to be a teacher."

Kubiac made a show of looking across Cottrell's desk and credenza.

"Cool. Got a picture of her?"

"Uh, no. I have one, but the cleaning lady knocked it over. Glass broke. I'm having it reframed."

Kubiac kept his face even. "Oh. Too bad."

Cottrell changed the subject. "Where's your girlfriend, Adam?"

"We're doing this one alone, Jeff. Just you and me. Why do you want to know?"

The lawyer shrugged and turned the documents to face Kubiac. "You want a few minutes to read the revised will and the, um, other instruments?"

"I trust you, Jeff," Kubiac said sardonically. "Where's this land I'm buying?"

"A few miles below the San Carlos Reservation, a great speculative deal."

"It's a shitload of sand in the middle of nowhere, Jeffrey. What'd you pay per acre? And what am I paying per acre?"

A tight eye from Cottrell. "I suggest you get used to our deal, Adam. Anger's not going to help either of us." Cottrell pushed the pages toward Kubiac and held out a pen.

Twenty minutes later Adam Kubiac was back at Maruyama's apartment. "Cottrell rewrote the will?" she asked.

"I get everything. Greed-boy just has to file it with the probate court to make it official, and he says he's doing that now." He paused. "What if he fucks something up?"

"He won't. He thinks he's gonna get rich."

Adam spun his car keys around his finger. "Jeff lives north of Scottsdale. The houses are far apart. I want to go look at the asshole's place."

"I better drive in case he goes home. He's seen your car."

Maruyama drove the pair in her blue Miata.

Adam turned from the window. "I was thinking … what happens when Cottrell's dead, Cat? Like, what happens to Zoe? I mean Brenda. What if she goes to the police? She hasn't seen me in a day. She texted for a while, then just stopped."

"Why would she go to the cops? She'd have to implicate herself in a scheme to steal your money. Plus if we do it right, there's no way you can be a suspect. And don't text or call Zoe. She's bad news. She and that rapist were trying to steal your inheritance."

"I'm never talking to that lying bitch again." He paused, the worried look returning. "You're sure about the cops? They scare me."

Maruyama laughed. "Cops don't like lawyers, Adam. Especially not ones like Cottrell. They'll be happy someone whacked the bastard."

"Whacked?"

A smile. "You need to watch more television."

They came to Cottrell's address, his house a one-story adobe with a tile roof, the yard landscaped with desert fauna. Set on five acres, it was raw desert on both sides. Adam had Maruyama twice drive slowly past as he slumped in the seat and studied the terrain through oversize sunglasses with a Phoenix Suns cap pulled low over the shades.

"Okay," he said. "I know what I'm going to do."

They returned to Maruyama's apartment. Kubiac said: "You're coming along, right, Cat? It would help me, like, if I get nervous or something."

Maruyama shook her head. "I have to stay here and send e-mails and tweets and play games."

"Why?"

"Our computers, phones and tablets will show us using them all night, like we never left here. You have to leave me your phone so I can pretend to be you."

His face filled with panic. "No! I need to be able to talk to you when I'm—"

Maruyama reached in her purse and produced a pair of cheap burner phones, handing him one.

"They'll keep us close, Adam. It'll be like I'm standing right beside you. We'll throw them away afterwards." She kissed him on the cheek. "You won't get nervous, Adam. You're the strongest man I know."

41

We sat in Novarro's cubicle and shot the breeze with Kent for twenty minutes, Fishbach listening at the edge of the conversation. Then Solero's door opened and he yelled, "You've got the court order, detectives. You can crack the Meridien files connected to the primary cases."

Novarro shooed a cleaning woman out of a conference room and gestured for Kent to take a seat. The security expert removed his jacket and carefully hung it over the chairback. He sat, opened his brown briefcase and removed a laptop the size of portable computers in the nineties. He saw me looking.

"Big memory, big power. And fast like you wouldn't believe."

"About time things started moving fast around here," Novarro said.

Kent plugged in the flash drive and began tapping keys. The screen showed ranks of symbols and numbers. "Still with a layer of encryption," he said. "I'll have to access the DataSĀF security system to remove it."

"You'll need my password to get on the net," Novarro said. "Protection for our files, also in the cloud."

Kent nodded. "DataSĀF stores the Phoenix Police Department files as part of their JurisFile division. I saw them when I was analyzing the DataSĀF systems."

Novarro's mouth fell open. "Wait … every time I put a report in the PPD system it went to DataSĀF?"

"At nearly the speed of light." Kent said. "Don't worry. They're encrypted." Kent started keyboarding.

"Hold on, Mr Kent," Novarro said. "You're saying Klebbin could have looked at the PPD files?"

A beat of consideration followed by a nod. "If Klebbin had the expertise and passwords to get into Dr Meridien's files, she could likely go anywhere."

"There was no mole in PPD," Novarro hissed to me. "It was Klebbin. She was *in* the damned cloud and watching our every move. That means she's in league with Escheverría."

Kent wasn't buying it. "That would be a huge amount of information to monitor, Detective. Even an hour's worth of data from the PPD would be overwhelming: reports filed, images from the CCTVs in cruisers, prisoner intake, administrative data, accounting data, all constantly streaming in. It's unlikely, unless …" his eyes turned inward as his voice trailed off.

"Unless what?"

"Can you tell me the name of a person that might appear in the files on your special case? Someone pivotal?"

"Everything revolves around a monster named Escheverría," Novarro said. "Ramon Escheverría." She spelled it out.

"Let me look at a few things," Kent said, his fingers picking up speed on the keyboard. "You may want to get some coffee," he said. "This might take a while."

42

Harry Nautilus stared out his window at the gleaming, strident Miami skyline.

Maruyama ... Maruyama ...

It had taken two calls to Sky Harbor International Airport, one to the TSA, and one to an airline, to discover that a Hisao Maruyama and a Catherine Maruyama had boarded a flight from Phoenix to Tokyo six weeks ago. That was the easy part. But Carson wanted to know where they might have gone from there. And did Catherine Maruyama return to the States?

Jeez ... how many Maruyamas are in Japan?

Nautilus took one more look at a blue sky dappled with cumulus, then returned to sit at his desk and stare at the ceiling. Roy McDermott passed the door, stopped, looked inside.

"You look deep in thought, Harry."

"Trying to think through a tracking problem, Roy."

McDermott laced his big fingers together and spun his thumbs around one another. "Try twiddling your thumbs, Harry. Always works for me."

McDermott grinned and scooted away. Nautilus thought a moment, then put his hands together and started twiddling.

* * *

Kubiac grinned and held the tattered paper target to Maruyama. Twenty-seven shots had echoed across the barren landscape, three finding the center ring of the target, seven in the secondary ring, the others clustered nearby.

"My god," she said, hands clapping together, "you're incredible, Adam."

Kubiac tacked another target to the saguaro and they walked back toward his shooting position a hundred yards distant. There was nothing but wide and raw desert for a mile in any direction, the nearest highway on the other side of a jagged rise. The sky was cloudless, an opalescent bowl from horizon to horizon.

"I told you I knew how to shoot," Kubiac said. "Hashtag: sharpshooter."

"But where'd you ever learn to shoot so good? Just the hunting trips with your uncle?"

Kubiac's face darkened and he punted a stone down the path. "Plus my old man yanked me outta junior high and put me in a military academy. Said it would make a man out of me." He paused, thought a moment, and smiled. 'I got kicked out after four months. The only thing I liked was marksmanship."

Kubiac reached his shooting position, marked by boxes of ammunition and a small cooler with water, Red Bull, and egg-salad sandwiches from a convenience market. He steadied the rifle atop a boulder and flicked off the safety.

"Why are you shooting from the rock?" Maruyama asked.

"To steady the rifle. There's a boulder just about this size on the east side of Cottrell's property. And his front door is just about as far from here as the cactus is."

"You think of everything," Maruyama said, laying her forehead against Kubiac's back and smiling with contentment.

Harry Nautilus was still twiddling his thumbs. He'd had to visit the DA to give a brief deposition in a case, but was now back and again pondering the problem. What might link Phoenix and Japan?

What do I do when I travel?

His thumbs ceased whirling. A widening smile on his face, he pulled a business card from his wallet and grabbed his phone.

"This is Sonya," said a rich voice. "How may I help you?"

Nautilus pictured the ripe-bodied lawyer with the big eyes and rolling saunter. "Ms Burroughs, this is Harry—"

"Nautilus," she completed. "How wonderful to hear from you."

"I've been wanting to call, Ms Burroughs. Not on police business, but more of, uh, a personal nature."

"Call anytime, Harry. And it's Sonya."

"I've been beating my head against a wall, Sonya. A case that's got me bamboozled. As soon as I get it behind me, we can enjoy a drink, or a quiet meal."

Her voice dropped to a purr. "How soon do you think you'll be free?"

"It depends on how fast I can track down a person in Japan. Someone who was in Phoenix, but flew to Tokyo some weeks back."

"I hope it goes quickly, *real* quickly …"

"I was thinking that generally, before I fly somewhere, business or pleasure, there's phone calls between me and my destination … setting up lodging, car rental perhaps, or telling friends or family when I'll arrive. That sort of thing."

"Sure. I do that, too."

"I was wondering, Sonya, given your inside ties …" he let it hang.

The woman was fast. "If I can speak to a counterpart in Phoenix and get phone records? I expect so, as long as I have the exchange of the person in Phoenix who made the calls."

"They'll do that? I mean, without me having to get a subpoena or court order?"

"I'll do it through the billing department, mostly women."
She laughed, a throaty sound. "I call it the sister system."

"How, uh, fast might that be done?"

"It's four thirty here – three hours difference this time of year, so one thirty out there. I'll find someone to help me, I mean you."

"Us," he said. "You and me. We're partners on this."

"Oh my, Harry. There's a thought."

When Kent called us back to his hacker's lair, we were on our second cups of coffee. Outside the window a rare summer shower was blowing through, overhanging clouds dappling the valley with raindrops. I took it as a good sign.

"You were right, Detective," Kent said to Novarro as we sat across from him. "You did have a mole in your system. Or a spybot, rather. A hidden piece of code that sent Candace Klebbin select data triggered by the name Escheverría. She received only what pertained to her specific needs and interests. No megabytes of material to review."

Novarro shook her head. "So every time a report mentioned Ramon Escheverría …"

"The bot sent it to Ms Klebbin."

"Which she passed on. Shit. No wonder Ramon stayed ahead. He must have been laughing his ass off."

Kent re-perched his fingers on the keyboard. "Are we ready to open Dr Meridien's files?"

I looked at our security expert. "Can you find what she wrote the last night of her life?"

Kent leaned forward and tapped keys. Instead of techno-gibberish, the screen filled with a dozen boxes with titles like Patient Files, Financial, Contact Info, Writings, Articles, and so forth. I sat beside Kent while Novarro, too nervous to sit, looked over his shoulder. Kent highlighted a line and double tapped Return. It opened to a secondary file named "Session Notes/

Observations."

"It was uploaded the night of her death," said Novarro, almost breathless. I leaned over and saw the title of Meridien's final entry:

The Kubiac Conundrum

Kent opened the file. It was small, just a few hundred words. "Read it, Tasha," I said. She leaned forward and began her recitation.

"Adam Kubiac arrived at 9.30 p.m. tonight in an agitated state, angry, accusatory, and in the company of a young woman named Zoe. He somehow used his software expertise to open my gate and door. I expected his anger was somehow connected to the recent death of his father, and was proven correct, but not in a fashion I could have predicted …

"Two months ago Adam's father (Elijah Kubiac) came to me with a misguided plan to gain a modicum of control over Adam. I tried to talk him out of it but was rebuffed. The father was adamant that the best way to control his son was the threat of disinheritance. He went so far as to have a false will drafted, one purporting to leave his son the sum of one dollar. To my understanding, the false will was only meant as a last-ditch threat if all other efforts at gaining at least some compliance failed. Elijah Kubiac repeated this several times.

"Then Adam told me things that made the entire scenario suspect. I think it's possible Adam's lawyer may be involved in some form of subterfuge. Or not. That's the problem. I am (or perhaps was) Adam's therapist, not his lawyer. I know nothing of the law and have not been privy to the actions of Elijah Kubiac and his legal representation. They had their own confidences.

"Should I call the police and explain my fears? To convey the matter to the authorities will necessitate offering insights into the relationship between the Kubiacs, as well as explaining how Adam's almost infantile naiveté makes him particularly vulnerable to

271

manipulation. Is that a violation of D/P privilege and a breach of ethics? And is it beyond my boundary? Should I just keep my nose out of things—?"

"There it is," I said, "in the last paragraph. The ethical quandary. Keep going."

"Thought: Call Angela Bowers in Miami and see what she thinks, and have her run the situation past her professor friend who studies these things (Warbler? Warbley?) I'll call tonight and proceed from knowledge gained. I have some time to figure this out."

"Meridien didn't have time," Novarro said quietly. "She had about six hours."

"Klebbin was monitoring Meridien's account, maybe even as the information was uploaded to DataSĀF. Klebbin had to work fast in case Meridien decided to go to the police. So someone killed her eight hours later. Odds are 99.9 percent that it was Escheverría."

"And Bowers and Warbley had two more days."

"They had to die. Though Klebbin knew everything the doctor put in the cloud, she couldn't listen in on phone conversations. She had no idea what they knew."

"So Klebbin took out insurance," I said. "Sending Escheverría to Miami to deliver the policy."

"Cold. But it's still cryptic. Nothing tells us why."

"It's somehow about keeping information secret. And that always comes back to money. Could you check Dr Meridien's patient contact list, Mr Kent? There should be information on Adam Kubiac."

Kent tapped for a few seconds. "Here's a folder called Patient Information. Opening and ... bingo! Address is in North Scottsdale. Phone numbers, home and cell."

Novarro rang the home number and got a recording. *"This is Eli Kubiac,"* a smooth and self-assured older voice crooned. *"I'm not in right now but ..."*

"The recently dead father," I said, "Try the kid's number."

She dialed. I heard one ring, then the sound of an exchange switching. A recorded voice said, "*this number is no longer in service.*"

"Damn," Novarro whispered.

Kent was hunched over the keyboard like a twenty-year-old hacker. He leaned forward and studied some symbols. "Well, this is interesting. I searched the doctor's file for Candace Klebbin's name, wondering if there was an indication how she and Dr Meridien might have crossed paths."

"Good question," I said because it was. "And?"

"I found not a Candace Klebbin, but a Rosa Klebbin, age eighteen. It appears she was a patient for over two years, last visit, uh …" he held his reading glasses up. "Three weeks ago."

"Open her file," Novarro said.

Kent worked, then looked to us. "I've got over a hundred pages of session notes."

"Anything like a summary, or bottom line or whatever?" Novarro asked.

"Uh …" Kent scrolled through what appeared to be a list of headers. "Here's something called 'History and Etiology.'"

"Open it and read it to us, sir," Novarro said.

"*Rosa Klebbin, nee Rosa Blankenship,*" Kent started, "*spent her early years in a mute, semi-catatonic state, diagnosed as retarded. Her father was a nuclear engineer who ran off with another woman when Rosa was seven. Her mother gave the child up for adoption, no takers because of her supposed mental incapacity. Rosa was institutionalized for two years before workers noted food disappearing from locked kitchen stores two floors below the dormitory. Thinking a thieving employee, management had cameras discreetly placed throughout the floor, and were amazed to see eight-year-old Rosa taking the food. It seems Rosa had seen workers entering the lock and elevator codes all the way to the kitchen and memorized them.*"

"Getting food," I said. "It probably meant comfort. And a goal her limited landscape allowed her to pursue. A challenge, a puzzle."

"But somehow creepy," Kent said, continuing to read.

"*At eleven, Klebbin was placed in a foster home where she, experimentally at first, was placed in a school for exceptional children. Rosa thrived and continued to amaze with her perceptual and intellectual prowess. There were emotional and anger issues, and Rosa went through three foster settings before being adopted by a single forty-year-old woman, Candace Klebbin, at the age of fourteen, a relationship that perplexes me, but has somehow endured, though the mother also had difficulties with Rosa and sought my help.*" Kent paused.

Novarro said, "Keep going."

"*I've administered two IQ tests, one reading 161, the other 168. Yet Rosa expresses no desire to train for a field or advance in standard fashion. Still, all seems fodder for her relentless, searching brain. Lazy? Unchallenged? I don't have a clue. She's currently expressing an interest in psychology, haphazardly absorbing every book she can find on the subjec—*"

"Observation," I said. "And acquisition."

"*Although I suspect this is typical: In whatever setting Rosa occupies, physical or psychic, she absorbs information relentlessly—*"

"Data," Novarro said. "Like Candace."

"*… which is of compelling interest until the next setting arrives, at which time the interest in the previous setting is abandoned.*"

"Rosa plays the game," I said. "Gathers what she needs and moves on."

Kent had been reading ahead. "It just gets stranger," he said.

"Don't keep us in suspense," Novarro said.

Kent took a breath.

"*I've never seen a patient like Rosa Klebbin. She seems a traveler from another dimension, and perhaps a very frightening one. I'm wondering if I'm seeing a sociopath so enmeshed in experiential data that she's able to totally disguise her true nature, assuming

274

any shape needs to inhabit. It's a frightening thought. And if so, what does her future hold?"

*   *   *

Harry Nautilus was polishing his cufflinks when his cellphone rang. He glanced at the screen. "Come on, baby," he whispered. Then pressed Talk: "Hello Sonya.

"Hi, Harry," Sonya Burroughs said, her voice sweet cream and honey. "I think I have the information you wanted."

Nautilus sat at his desk, leaning forward, mentally crossing his fingers. "Damn, girl, that was fast."

"It was finding someone to punch a few keys in Arizona, simple."

"One of your sisters?"

"Us ladies got to stick together, Harry. There were forty-seven calls from the Maruyama in Phoenix to Japan in the last three months. Thirty-two were to one number in Osaka. You want me to fax you the readout?"

"Is that, uh, copasetic?"

"You didn't get it from me, right?"

"Who?"

The throaty laugh again. "Think this'll put you closer to escaping your case? Maybe drinks, dinner, like you said."

Nautilus smiled. "I'm already building up an appetite, Sonya."

"Call me when it's unbearable, Harry Nautilus. Soon, I hope."

Nautilus rang off and called Phoenix, hoping the Maruyama he'd tracked down was the one Carson was seeking.

43

Our first priority was finding Adam Kubiac, hoping A) he was alive, and B) he would able to tell us something.

The Kubiac home was in east Scottsdale, a ritzy neighborhood with large lots and pastel walls. "The garages here cost more than my house," Novarro said as we wound toward the address. "And they're bigger."

We pulled into the drive of a sprawling two-story adobe and glass structure with elaborate tiered landscaping. There was a black Mercedes 500 series in the driveway. We rang the doorbell, knocked at windows. The place seemed unoccupied.

There was only one other home near the Kubiac residence, a lovely but more modest – if modesty was a term for multimillion-dollar homes in Scottsdale – dwelling, smaller, but with wilder landscaping. Unlike the Kubiac plantings, which were obviously professionally tended, the flora next door looked less attended than managed, an untamed look in tune with the Sonoran surroundings.

The door was answered by a handsome woman in her early sixties, slight and slender and with an honest tan and long salt-and-pepper hair untouched by dye. Her eyes shone with intelligence and her smile alone gestured us into the great room of mountain-facing windows and a cathedral ceiling. Her name was Darlene Landsmere, and she wore loose blue denim jeans and a Western-style shirt embroidered with yellow roses.

"Terrible thing," she said.

"What's terrible, Ms Landsmere?" Novarro asked.

"Eli's death. I didn't care for him as a person, but—"

"When exactly did he die?"

"About a month ago, I suppose. I feel so sorry for Adam."

"Do you know how Eli Kubiac died, Ms Landsmere?" Novarro said. That was of interest as well.

"Wasn't much detail in the newspaper or television, just that Eli was found dead in the Redstone Motel …" she let it hang.

"You're not saying something," I said.

A half smile, not happy nor sad, but knowing. "I was married for eighteen years to a dentist who claimed he worked all the time, but now and then I could smell things on his clothes. Perfume and other womanly potions. I hired a private eye. Turns out the bastard was doing as much drilling at the Redstone as he was in his office. I expect old Eli was the same. Probably blew out his ticker; the guy was a heart attack waiting to happen."

"You knew Eli Kubiac well?"

"They moved here five–six years back. I'd wave, maybe wander over to the drive and talk if someone was out. At least until a couple months ago."

"What happened?"

"I was taking a stroll through the neighborhood – it was near noon – and I hear 'Hey Dar,' from behind me. I turn and see old Eli at the mailbox, a big-ass grin on his face and a weird sparkle in his eyes. I was ten feet away and could smell liquor. 'How you doing, Eli?' I said. He wavered on his feet and grabbed his crotch and asked if I was feeling lonely. I told him I'd never get that lonely. It was sad."

"You know the kid, Adam?"

Ms Landsmere blew out a long breath. "I always felt sorry for

Adam … eyes like a lost puppy. I'd see him outside sometimes on the back patio. I don't think I ever saw that kid when he didn't have one of those e-whatevers in his hands, phone, tablet, computer. He'd sit there for hours and peck at them like a zombie chicken."

"Eli Kubiac ever talk about Adam with you?"

A shrug. "It was usually a sigh, like 'What'll I do with this kid?' But last year I saw Eli out and he was all charged up, smiling. I said, 'You're looking merry today, Eli.' He told me Adam had just gotten a scholarship. The man was floating in the clouds, he was so proud." She paused. "I remember seeing Adam driving off to school that fall, his old car piled with suitcases and stuff. Then, about two months later, Adam was back on the patio and staring at e-things. And I never saw Eli grin again. At least until the day he hit on me."

"Do you know where Adam Kubiac might be today?"

"I haven't seen anyone over there since Eli passed. I figured Adam is staying with friends. It's maybe not so nice a thing to say, but perhaps with Eli gone, it's finally Adam's time to shine."

Novarro asked if we could use Ms Landsmere's Wi-Fi, and the woman gave us her password and graciously went outside, saying the stones needed watering. We sat in the cool of the lovely home as Novarro tapped her tablet. After a minute she leaned back.

"I just ran a general localized search on the name Kubiac, not too common, right?" She clicked the screen with her nails. "Check this out."

I moved close and read …

WELL-KNOW LOCAL AUTO DEALER DIES
A cleaning woman entering a room at the Redstone Motel on the eastern edge of Scottsdale was dismayed to find the body of Elijah Kubiac, 58, whose regional chain of automotive dealerships numbered as many as eight a

decade ago. Police are investigating the death, but find no evidence of foul play. His appearance was a familiar one on television, Mr Kubiac often a spokesman for his dealerships. He was known for his generosity and charitable giving, and was a member of several clubs and foundations in both Scottsdale, where he made his home, and throughout Arizona. He leaves one son, Adam T. Kubiac. Services will be at …

"Brief freakin' article," Novarro said. "And why no follow-up stories? I remember the guy's face from commercials some years back, big fake grin, fluffy toupee, 'Come to my dealership and I'll sell you a car for less than it cost to make it' … that kind of spiel. Why nothing after this little blurb?"

"Scottsdale," I said. "That's where big money hangs out, right?"

"*Ho'odona't dineha. A-hao'te.*"

"Which means?"

"Ritzy and glitzy and white as snow."

The head honcho at the Scottsdale Investigative Division was a trim, neat, imperially mustached man named Diego Ibarra. He and Novarro knew one another, and I figured with so many municipalities jammed together in one valley, local law enforcement entities had to keep close contact.

"Ahhh," Ibarra said, studying the article Novarro had copied. He looked uncomfortable. "Mister Kubiac."

"Seems strange nothing else was ever noted, Diego. The news coverage just died. Like Kubiac."

Ibarra sat back in his desk, sighed. "You know these type of moments, Detective Novarro. A prominent citizen passes away. There was no reason for suspicion of foul play. Publicity of additional facts serves no one but the gossip mongers."

"There were tawdry aspects is what you're saying."

"He gave to the community, Detective Novarro. A big donor

to civic organizations."

"Come on, Diego," Novarro prompted. "What really went down?"

Ibarra stood and crossed the room to a filing cabinet, reached deep, returned with a file folder. He pulled out some photos. "The Redstone has individual units clustered around a parking lot and courtyard. It's expensive, and well known as a place where the errant spouses of Scottsdale go to, well ... be errant. Maid went in to do cleaning at ten, found this ..."

Novarro and I leaned close and flipped through a dozen shots. It was a familiar scene to a homicide detective: a naked body on the floor beside a bed, dried froth dribbled from the mouth and across the chest, eyes open to a cold nothingness. The room was dressed for a party, several tumbled bottles of top-shelf liquor on a dresser, another on the TV, flanked by a baggie of what I took to be weed. Several hashmarks of white powder were atop the desk.

"Coke?" I asked, holding up the photo.

"Heroin. Almost pure and laced with fentanyl. A nasty mix and given its strength and the amount of alcohol in Kubiac's system – plus some Oxy – he simply OD'd."

"His record ... was this unexpected?"

Ibarra let out a long breath. "Mr Kubiac had loads of money and perhaps too little to do once he sold his franchises. He liked women and parties. He had been pulled over twice with women in the car – a Jag – and maybe too much to drink."

"No bust, though. He received a warning. Or was driven home."

"He was a big contributor to the police fund."

I studied the photos. "There's too much hooch here for one person."

"A witness at the motel heard a commotion, a broken bottle around four a.m., looked out the window. She saw a woman scurrying away from the unit, almost running. The witness was an elderly lady and said the woman looked like a cheap whore, her words. We never found her."

"Anything say robbery?"

"Kubiac had over three grand in his wallet and a Rolex on his wrist, a twenty-grand model."

"Does kind of rule out robbery," Novarro noted. "Lotta money."

"Chump change to Eli Kubiac," Ibarra said. "Rumor had it Eli was worth around twenty million bucks."

Novarro and I shot each other a glance.

We returned to Phoenix, Novarro driving as we batted around ideas. "You think someone switched him up to death-strength heroin?" she said.

"In this case I'm believing the worst. We've *got* to find Adam Kubiac."

"How many reasons do we have to talk to him?" Novarro said, feeding me the line.

"Twenty million," I answered, not missing a beat.

44

We returned to HQ and the conference room, me staring out the window in thought, she googling the name Kubiac, fishing for background.

"It's all stuff relative to the father," she said, scrolling down the screen. "Automotive dealerships. Several still bear his name, so—"

My phone rang from the table.

"Carson, Harry."

My heart skipped a beat. "You've got something?"

"Unless there are other Maruyamas out there. I'll send it now."

"Hang on." I turned to Novarro. "You have a personal e-mail account?" I didn't want Harry to send it via the PPD system, which seemed to have been compromised.

"Of course." She called out her addy.

"Pressing send," Harry said. "I hope we nailed it."

"We?"

A low chuckle. "Me and the sisters. Don't ask."

The numbers were on Novarro's computer screen a minute later, and she relayed the information: thirty-one calls from a Maruyama in Phoenix to a number in Osaka. Novarro tapped up the international calling sheet from her desk, first entering the US exit code, then the country code for Japan, 81. She handed me the handset.

"Your buddy got the info. You win the call." She turned on the intercom as I put the receiver to my face and heard a clicking of distant connections.

Seven thousand miles away, a phone rang.

"*Konnichiwa*," a female voice said. In my haste I'd stupidly forgotten the language barrier.

"Uh, yes," I ventured, "is a Catherine Maruyama there?"

A pause, then heavily accented English. "Who is call?" I heard suspicion.

"Carson Ryder, I'm working with the Phoenix Police Department."

An intake of breath. "Is trouble?"

"I need to speak with Ms Maruyama, please. There's nothing wrong." I kept my voice light and friendly, hoping amiability translated into Japanese.

The sound of a receiver being covered, a brief muffled exchange. A male voice came on the line.

"Hello? This is Saito Maruyama. Can I help you?" Mildly accented English, the voice refined with Brit undertones.

"I'm with the Phoenix Police Department, Mr Maruyama. It's kind of a long story but—"

"Phoenix? I was in Phoenix two months ago. What is wrong?"

"Nothing, Mr Maruyama. Like I said, it's a long story. Is Catherine Maruyama there?"

"My daughter. She is right here."

Maruyama was alive. I looked at Novarro, miming wiping her brow and whispering *Whew*.

"May I speak to Ms Maruyama, please?"

Another covering of the phone, replaced by a youthful female voice, perplexed. "This is Catherine Maruyama."

I gave my particulars, only adding to her perplexation. Then into the darker details. "We're investigating several murders Ms

Maruyama. Dr Leslie Meridien, among them."

A startled pause. "Oh, my god. That's terrible."

"You were a patient of hers, were you not?"

"For seven months. Dr Meridien was a wonderful person and helped me with some difficulties I was having at the time." Intellect covers distance and I heard it in her voice and diction.

"May I ask if you knew Bradley Shackleton and Geraldo Trujillo?"

A pause. "They were in one of my groups."

"Darnell Mashburn?"

Another pause. "In the same group. We didn't meet on any schedule, just kinda whenever we were all in the same area. We'd meet at Dr Meridien's, then maybe go to a park or coffee shop or that kind of thing. Very informal."

"Darnell had a kind of crush on you, didn't he?"

"He was sweet. Then, a while back, he … changed. It was sad."

"How about Ben Novarro? Did you know him?"

A pause for recollection. "A Native American?"

"Yes."

"I heard someone mention the name. The groups were loose and sometimes people were in a couple of them. I think he was in another one …" She paused in recollection. "There was a girl, Rosa, or something, who was briefly in a group of mine and talked about a Native American she'd met at another group session. She said he was dreamy and real smart, that's all I remember. The girl was kinda of weird, but we all were, basically, in our own ways. It's why we were there."

"So you haven't been in Phoenix for two months?"

"My father's an engineer. He was consulting with a company in Glendale. I traveled with him – my life needed a change – and was going to take university classes, but I had, uh, anxiety attacks and Dr Meridien was suggested." A pause. "You said murders, plural, but only mentioned Dr Meridien."

I blew out a breath and told her about Shackleton and Trujillo.

Catherine Maruyama was a third of a world away but I swear I heard her hang her head.

A whispered "Why?" was all she could say.

"We hope to know soon," was all I could reply. Night was nearing and we felt closer to a reason for the madness but, outside of $20,000,00, no idea what or why. Novarro instituted a BOLO for Adam Kubiac, and tomorrow's task would be tracking him down.

We hoped he was still breathing.

45

The stars wheeled overhead as Adam Kubiac steadied the rifle on a rock. Headlights flashed in the distance. He wore a wireless Bluetooth headset, Catherine Maruyama on the other end of the line. He needed her there, if not in person, in voice.

"Car coming," Kubiac whispered.

"Make sure it's Cottrell," she said. "You've got to be sure."

"I'm looking through the night sight. The car's pulling into his driveway. Door opening. It's him. He's going to his mailbox by the street. He just got his mail. He's … heading toward the house."

"You have to do it now, Adam."

The world was spectral green through the telescopic night-vision scope; powerful enough to make it appear the lawyer was a dozen feet from the crosshairs. Cottrell was in slacks and a dress shirt, his jacket in one hand with a few envelopes in the other. The lawyer paused as if taking in the night air, his eyes looking toward Kubiac's hiding place in the dark. *He can't see me,* Kubiac thought, hair prickling on the back of his neck. *He just sees darkness.* Kubiac took a deep breath and placed the crosshairs over Cottrell's chest. The lawyer's face was in view. He looked small and human and vulnerable.

"Adam?" Maruyama said. "I don't hear anything."

The crosshairs were quivering. Kubiac took another deep breath and re-trained the sights.

"Adam … what's going on?"

"I-I'm wuh-wuh-waiting f-f-for it to be pur-perfect."

"Adam! He raped me when I was fourteen!"

"May-maybe you c-can still tuh-tell the police, C-Cat."

"Shoot the bastard, Adam," Maruyama hissed. "Fire the fucking gun! Kill him!"

Kubiac squinted through the sight at Cottrell, leaning against his hood and checking his watch. The crosshairs had drifted, but again found the center of Cottrell's chest. Wavered.

"Adam … what's going on? SHOOT!"

A chuffing sound, like spitting. "What?" Maruyama said. "*What*?"

Silence.

"Adam, talk to me! What happened?"

"Cottrell's … he's on the ground. He's not moving."

"Shoot him again, Adam!"

"I … Jesus, I'm-I'm getting out of here."

Twenty minutes later Adam Kubiac exited his car on unsteady legs. Maruyama grabbed his arm and pulled him inside, wrapping him in an embrace. "Adam, you did it … you're incredi—"

He shrank away, face glistening with sweat. "I-I couldn't do it, Cat. I started sh-haking … so bad … I shot over to the side. I tried to m-miss him. I don't understand …"

"You didn't miss, Adam. You said he went down, right?"

"I-I don't know how."

Maruyama thought for two beats and snapped her fingers. "A ricochet. It happens a lot. A friend of my nephew's got killed by a ricochet while some gangs were fighting. The bullet hit a building ten feet away and ricocheted. It doesn't matter … You did it. Adam. You killed the bastard!"

Kubiac stared past Maruyama, terror on his face. "I killed him," he whispered. "I did." He grabbed his stomach, dry heaving. "I'm gonna be sick."

Kubiac ran to the bathroom, fell to his knees, and began vomiting into the toilet. Maruyama followed like a shadow.

"The rifle, Adam. It's the only evidence. Where's the rifle?"

Kubiac upchucked again.

"The *gun*, Adam. You didn't leave it there, did you? Tell me you didn't leave it!"

Kubiac pointing a shaking finger toward the street. "In th-the trunk."

Relief flooded Maruyama's face. "I'll take care of it. You can open the door to Cottrell's office, right? With the code?"

"Y-yes."

"Wait fifteen minutes and unlock his office. Adam …?"

"What?"

Her eyes flashed. "'GET OFF YOUR KNEES AND DO IT!"

Maruyama dashed away. Kubiac stood on rubbery legs and staggered to the couch. He sat and opened his computer, weeping like his soul had been ripped apart.

Ramon Escheverría stared at his phone as it rang. He'd been waiting.

"Tell me," he said. "Say what I need to hear."

He listened and nodded. "That was a fear of mine, and why I sent you. No … not a problem. You moved away to somewhere safe? *Bueno*. You have indeed earned your money this night."

He listened again. "We are almost done, *amigo*. There is only the matter of the two Novarros and the Miami detective. When they are gone, we will have a party, no? A good way to savor a big payday."

Another string of questions from the other end. Escheverría thought a moment. "We will need a truck. I know of one used to transport various substances across the border and through the region. Let me give you the number to call. Tell the man El Gila would like to rent his special vehicle. No … no gasoline cans needed. We will be returning this one."

46

Novarro awakened me before seven a.m. We had a big day ahead, convinced that if we could track down Adam Kubiac, we'd be close to a solve.

If the kid was still alive, that is.

"Helluva day yesterday," I said as we stood in the kitchen eating stand-up *tortillas con huevos y frijoles*. "We're getting close."

"To me the best thing about yesterday was finding out that Fish wasn't snitching to Escheverría." She thought for a moment and sighed. "Shit."

"What?"

She sighed. "I'd better call Merle and apologize for thinking he might have been Ramon's source. It's the right thing to do." She pulled her phone and pressed in numbers. I heard his overblown voice.

"Yeah, Tash? What is it?" There was the sound of a siren in the background.

"Merle, I wanted to apologize for thinking you might be leaking to Escheverría."

"It wasn't you that thought that. It was that Florida A hole. Gotta go, Tash. Busy here."

"What's going on?"

"*I'm just north of Scottsdale. Got a lawyer shot dead in his front yard. No big loss, it's Jeff Cottrell. Call me later so I can yell at you, OK?*"

"What's a Cottrell?" I asked after she rang off.

Novarro wrinkled her nose like a rotting mackerel had entered the cubicle. "Some scumbag who combines ambulance chasing with criminal defense, a sneaky, snaky type. Think Saul on *Breaking Bad*, just with nicer clothes and fewer scruples."

*　*　*

Adam Kubiac was face-down on her couch when Maruyama entered the room. It was how she had left him last night, unable to coax him into bed. She scowled down, then assumed a smile and shook a bony shoulder.

"Time to wake up, Adam. We need to buy you a suit."

"A suit?" he moaned into a cushion. "WTF?"

"To wear to the probate hearing tomorrow." Maruyama sat beside Kubiac and put a hand on the small of his back. "You have to pull it tighter, Adam. You're in control, again. You put yourself in control."

"I … I killed a man, Cat."

"You killed an animal … a rapist and a thief trying to steal millions of dollars of your money. He backed you into a corner and you did what a man has to do." Maruyama ran a finger down his spine. "You're afraid of the police finding out, right, Adam?"

"I'll go to prison … I hated the guy, but I didn't expect—"

"It had to be done. Adam. You did it for me as much as for you. And there's no way anyone will ever find out."

Kubiac rolled over, his hair disheveled, eyes red. "You got in his office after I unlocked it?"

"The agreements you signed are gone. We both did what we needed to do. We're a team."

"What about the, uh, gun?"

A mysterious smile. "Long gone."

"Where?"

She ignored the question and pulled him to his feet. "We need to get you ready for tomorrow. That means nicer clothes, conservative."

Kubiac hung his head. "I don't wanna go to a store. I hate shopping."

Maruyama's jaw tensed. "How about in Scottsdale?"

"My old man made me buy a couple suits. He picked them out, like dressing a baby."

"Come on. We'll go there and get one."

"I don't want to see that place again, Cat. I never want to go back."

Maruyama wrapped Adam Kubiac in her arms, nuzzling his neck. "For me, Adam. Just one more day and it's all over. Please, baby?"

Twenty minutes later Catherine Maruyama stood in the open great room of the Kubiac house and stared at every wall in turn.

"My god, Adam, what a fantastic place."

Kubiac scowled. "See that couch? When I was twelve I was staying overnight at a friend's but forgot my game controller. When his mom drove me back to get it I found my old man on that couch with two women." He took Maruyama's hand and pulled her to his bedroom. "Let's get the shit and get out."

"You'll need a dress shirt. And shoes."

He pointed to black canvas Vans. "I got shoes."

"Leather ones, Adam. To go with the suit."

Adam Kubiac rolled his eyes, crossed to his closet, and opened the door. "Is this crap necessary?"

Maruyama smiled. "Just once, Adam. Tomorrow. Your big day."

Novarro's phone rang and she grabbed it up. "Now?" she said, tensing. "Adam's there now?" She hung up.

"What?"

"Darlene Landsmere, the Kubiacs' neighbor. She just saw Adam and a woman going into the house." She began tapping at her phone. "I'll see if I can't get the locals over there to hold him for us."

We rolled up in front of the Kubiac house fifteen minutes later, a Scottsdale patrol car out front. We exited simultaneously with two officers from the marked vehicle, the driver shaking his head.

"Sorry, Detective. Gone when we got here."

Novarro muttered a brief strand of expletives and thanked the men. She turned to me. "Well, that's a chance blown."

"Let's check with Ms Landsmere."

Darlene Landsmere's door opened as we approached. "I'm so sorry. I know you wanted to talk to Adam."

Novarro was in the lead. "He was here with a woman, you said?"

"She was twenty or thereabouts, kinda pretty, a bit chunky. They didn't have much to say."

"You spoke to them?"

"When I saw them going inside I figured I'd wander over and maybe find out what Adam's going to do with the house … sell it, live there, whatever. I knocked. When the door opened it was Adam with clothes on a hanger. A suit, I think."

"How'd he look?" I asked.

"Frazzled. He looked even sadder than usual."

"The woman?"

"She stayed inside and hidden, maybe on purpose."

Novarro frowned. "What makes you think that?"

"After I pecked on the door I heard whispering and footsteps like maybe she was ducking out of sight. It had – I don't know – a furtive sense."

"What'd you say to Adam, Ms Landsmere?" Novarro asked.

"Just small talk, how you doing, hope you'll be back soon, that kind of thing. I told him detectives were looking for him, thought I might be doing him a favor."

Novarro shot me a glance. "What happened?"

"That boy turned white as a sheet and almost slammed the door in my face. That's when I called Detective Novarro. But a minute later I saw them hustling out the door. They weren't gone but three minutes when the Scottsdale police showed up."

Adam Kubiac had driven an erratic three miles before Maruyama made him pull over. "You're going to hit something, Adam. You went through two stop signs."

"The cops know I killed Cottrell," Kubiac wailed, pulling into the lot of an Ecuadorian restaurant. "They're after me."

"They're not after you. There's no reason to be. If they knew you killed Cottrell, you'd already be on your way to jail."

"I didn't want to kuh-kill him. Not at th-the end."

"But you did," she affirmed. "You killed him as dead as a doornail."

"Why are d-detectives looking for me?"

"It's a rich person's house, Adam. That's what cops do in rich places like Scottsdale: they check on empty houses. They went to make sure everything was safe. LISTEN TO ME!"

"What?"

"That lady who came over … a busybody, right?"

"Maybe, kind of. She's nuh-nice."

"There you go. She's the one who called the police and asked them to watch the house. They were looking for you so they could make sure the place was safe and secure."

"But she said a couple of d-detectives were asking about

muh-me. Not *cops*, d-detectives."

"It's the way old people talk. All cops are detectives. It's just a general word they use. Here, let's switch places. I'll drive and you can relax."

Kubiac seemed frozen in place, hands tight on the wheel. "I'm s-scared, Cat."

"Of what?"

"What if I show up at the w-will reading and get suh-surrounded by cops? They'll arrest me and throw me in p-p-prison. I can't go to p-prison, Catherine … do you know what happens to smaller guys like m-me?"

Maruyama's hand cut through the air and whipped into Kubiac's cheek. He drew back, eyes wide, hand on his face.

"Jesus, Cat!"

She pulled him close. "You've got to calm down and hold it all together, Adam. Everything's going to be all right. Have I been right so far?"

"Y-yes," he sniffled across her shoulder. "Always."

"You've been my strength, Adam. Let me be yours. We'll get through this, I promise. Now get out and I'll drive us home."

* * *

We spent the rest of the day interviewing everyone we could find who had gone to school with Kubiac, including several teachers.

"*I dunno, he was kind of a loner,*" said a kid who'd been in Kubiac's homeroom. "*Plus he could be a real asshole, y'know?*"

Another student: "*We used to hang out back in middle school, he was OK. A big nerd, but OK. But all he wanted to talk about was gaming and code. It was, like, his world and if you didn't speak its language, you were like dumb or something. But I think it was how he, like, protected himself somehow. He almost never looked like he was having fun.*"

"*Girlfriend? Kubiac?*" Laughter from a kid he gamed against at arcades.

"*He took my advanced math class when he was in the ninth grade,*" a teacher commented. "*A college-level course. He was a standout, incredible mind. No, let me qualify that, an incredible mind when he chose to use it. When he didn't feel sufficiently engaged or motivated, he'd put on a whining voice and complain that he was too smart for 'all this shit.'*"

"*I dunno, dude,*" said a kid who'd been in five of Kubiac's classes. "*I don't think anyone knew him real well. He was too ... like we're right here, but he'd be way over there. In another world. I think he liked it that way.*"

A girl who had sat behind him in a math class: "*His old man used to be on the tube in Phoenix, some kind of car dealer. I remember one time someone asked, 'Hey Adam, you gonna grow up and sell cars?' Just kidding around, y'know? And fucking Kubiac just went ballistic, screaming and swinging on the other guy like an out-of-control monkey. It was nuts.*"

Adam Kubiac had a lonely life, it seemed, but maybe his life was on the Internet, though it wasn't Facebook. He had an account, but his last entry had been over a year ago. There were four photos, three of Kubiac with some kind of electronic device in hand, one of his battered white Subaru. The post said

"*Got this today and parked it behind my father's M-Benz. Ha! Major fucking meltdown!*"

Not one of the twenty-one "friends" had responded.

Eight hours passed and the sun turned to twilight, the dusk to dark. We had BOLOS out in all jurisdictions in the valley. Wherever Kubiac's car was, it wasn't on the road, or hadn't crossed the path of the correct eyes.

Ben was on the couch and watching TV when Novarro and I arrived. He left a few minutes later and returned with cartons of Thai food. We ate and, knowing tomorrow would be a full, and hopefully productive, day, we were in bed by ten p.m.

47

I heard the sound before I realized what it was: the slight squeak I'd learned to associate with the opening of Novarro's bedroom door. My eyes opened to the darkness of the room and the distant whine of a jet arriving at the airport.

Was that it? I wondered, ears searching the room. *Just an incoming plane?*

Rhythmic breathing, deep and regular; Novarro beside me, her warmth and scent in the furrows of the sheets. I blinked at the digital clock and watched 4.25 a.m. turn to 4.26.

Another sound. Human. Was Ben up and moving around … maybe in the bathroom? No. I heard one person *shush*ing another, less a sound than an exhalation. My hand moved toward my piece on the nightstand. It was inches away when I felt cold steel press against my ribs.

"No, amigo," a voice said. "Not a choice that you have."

The light snapped on, Novarro sat up. She too was facing a wicked-looking and suppressed machine pistol. We knew the two men by sight …

Escheverría's gangster puppets.

"You will be so kind as rise and dress," one said, killer eyes defying the curling grin. "Be fast. And be sure that if you make one wrong move, it is not only the last for you, but for baby boy in the other room."

As if on cue, a moan from down the hall: Ben's room. The third member of the crew was in there. Novarro's eyes flashed. "If you hurt him I will fucking—"

"Again," the *cholo* said into the air. Another moan. "If you speak again, I will hurt him again."

"What do you want?" I said.

"It's simple. You will rise and dress and we will go out the back as quiet as *ratóns*, no? Do not think to call for the ones out front or you will all be dead and we will be gone."

I knew that Novarro, like me, had already considered that as an option. Give the firepower in the crew's hands, it would be slaughter.

"Where?" I asked, already knowing the answer.

"You have a meeting scheduled, *hombre*. Hurry, El Gila does not like guests who are tardy."

There was no choice. My weapon was whisked away, and we dressed with the grinning gangbangers making what I assumed were foul comments in Spanish as we pulled on yesterday's clothes: tan chinos and a wrinkled blue dress shirt for me, blue jeans and a pink blouse for Novarro. Eyes blazing at our captors, she began stepping into her shoes.

"No," the one I knew as Pablo said, waving us to the door with the muzzle of his gun. "You will not need *los zapatos*. You will not be going far."

Ben was in the hall, the third thug holding a knife to his throat.

"Have him put away the blade," Novarro said. "We're going quietly."

Pablo nodded to the blade man, who let the knife drop a couple inches from Ben's throat and spun him toward the kitchen. The door was open wide.

They herded us into the backyard, Pablo tapping the door frame. "It was a very good lock, *chica*. But we have a specialist for such occasions. He's very expensive, but I am assured you are worth it."

A locksmith, I figured, pushed past the lime tree. Escheverría would have someone like that on the payroll.

And then we were in the alley, the *cholos* working a dark and practiced choreography, binding our wrists and ankles with cable ties and lifting us into the back of a step van. Two sat up front, the third sat in back, keeping a flashlight beam and Glock 9 trained on us as we moved out and onto the highway.

48

The morning sun sifted through the veil of curtains. The woman who called herself Catherine Maruyama dressed in a demure blue skirt with a ruffly white blouse and dark hose ending in simple cobalt pumps. Adam Kubiac was in the shower; he'd been in the shower for twenty minutes, standing motionless under the water.

"Adam!" she called over the spray. "The reading of the will is in a half hour. Come on."

After five minutes Kubiac slumped into the room, wet hair hanging to his cheeks, but wearing a fitted gray suit and blue Oxford shirt.

"You need a tie, Adam. We brought back a tie. Go grab your tie."

"You sound like my father," he pouted.

"Get the fucking tie."

He slumped into the bedroom, back seconds later with a blue tie, handing it to Maruyama. She threaded it through the collar, knotted it, then combed his hair.

"This isn't going to work," he whispered. "It's a set-up."

Maruyama put her hands on Adam's shoulder and pulled him closer. "Study my eyes, Adam. Do you trust me that all will work out, Adam?"

"I think … Yes, Cat. I trust you."

They drove to Government District in downtown Phoenix, pulling into a subterranean parking lot and riding an elevator to ground level. The pair emerged into the sunlight and rush of traffic on Washington Street. Car horns blasted, buses rumbled, motorcycles roared. A woman in a blue dress and huge sunglasses walked past. Adam turned to watch her retreating back, thinking he'd seen her somewhere before.

They continued down the street. Maruyama was walking three paces ahead and checking her watch when she heard a gasp and turned to find Kubiac leaning against a lamp post, clutching his chest, his face so pale it looked blue.

She jumped at his side. "Adam? What's wrong?"

"A cop car just went by. I c-can't, I can't breathe … A heart attack, can't—"

"Get over here and sit," Maruyama commanded, pulling him toward a shaded bus-stop kiosk.

"I c-c-can't breathe … my heart …"

"You're hyperventilating," Maruyama said. "Relax."

"I'm g-g-g-gonna duh-die. It's because I k-ki-killed …"

"Relax, Adam. Breathe slowly." They sat in the shade, her hand on the back of his neck. "In …" Maruyama instructed, "now out. Go slow and easy."

The color returned to Kubiac's face. "I-I think I'm better."

"It's going to be fine, Adam. Don't panic." She kissed his cheek and tousled his hair. "Trust, remember?"

"I, uh … sh-sh-sure."

Maruyama took his hand and led him step-by-step into the municipal building and upstairs to the probate court offices. She announced him to the receptionist and one minute later the pair were led into the office of retired Judge Elmer Craine, in his late sixties, bald and pink-faced, with small brown eyes behind owlish glasses. Craine was behind a dark wood desk centered by three slim sheaves of papers.

"This is Mr Adam Kubiac, Judge," the receptionist said. "He's here because—"

"Ah, yes. The former client of Mr Cottrell," Craine said, pursing slender lips. "And perhaps the less said about that the better, *de mortuis nil nisi bonum,* and so forth. Pull a couple of those chairs close, folks. We won't be long."

Kubiac and Maruyama sat, Kubiac's anxious eyes searching the room as if fearful of snipers. Craine studied the pair, his gaze holding on Adam. "Did you know Jefferson Cottrell well, Mr Kubiac?"

Kubiac swallowed hard and forced a quivering smile to his lips. "He, uh, was my father's lawyer," he said, the lines rehearsed. "I saw him a few times is all."

Craine shook his head. "Bad business with Cottrell. Sad business. I see Mr Cottrell filed this instrument with this office two weeks ago."

"*What?*" Kubiac said, turning white.

"Shhh," Maruyama whispered, discreetly patting Kubiac's forearm. "Relax."

"Pardon?" Craine said.

Maruyama looked at the jurist. "Sorry. Adam is feeling a bit light-headed."

"I need a drink of w-water," Adam said, standing unsteadily.

"There's a fountain right around the corner. Perhaps you should go with your friend, Ms ...?"

"Maruyama, sir. Catherine Maruyama."

Craine nodded politely. "You'd best accompany Mr Kubiac to the water fountain, Ms Maruyama. He looks a bit pale."

Adam pulled Maruyama to the hall and closed the door. "Cottrell filed the will before he said he changed it," he hissed between clenched teeth, his face as pale as chalk. "I'm fucked. Let's go."

"Craine's an old guy, Adam. He's confused. Or maybe Cottrell somehow backdated the filing. Come on ... we've come this far."

"It's not going to work," Kubiac wailed, stepping away, "I'm getting out of here."

Maruyama grabbed his sleeve, pulling him toward the office. "Just trust me, Adam. Come on, you can do this. You're strong."

They returned to the office. The judge's eyes studied Adam Kubiac with a hint of sadness. "I'm sorry about your distress, Mr Kubiac. I was informed yesterday that Mr Cottrell was the executor of your father's estate, and the news of his ... Would you like the courts to secure other representation of the estate before we continue? You have that right."

Adam shot a look at Maruyama: *What was this?* Her head shifted almost imperceptibly. *Say no, Adam.*

"I'm f-fine with whu-whatever, Judge."

Craine hit a button on his intercom. "Alice, send him in now."

"He's alerted," the receptionist said.

"Who's alerted?" Kubiac said, eyes wide with fear and jumping halfway to his feet before Maruyama's hand stopped him.

"Are you sure you're all right, Mr Kubiac?" Craine asked, honestly interested.

"Y-Yes," Adam stuttered as he lowered to the chair with Maruyama's hand on his wrist. "What ... what's going on?"

Craine leaned back. "I brought in a special administrator to assure that all details are covered. It's *pro forma*, Mr Kubiac, when an executor is deceased without naming a second executor. All protocols must be observed."

The door opened and a dark-suited man entered. Though in his eighties, his carriage was erect and, using a simple wooden cane for stability, he moved with slow purpose. His hair was full and gray and echoed eyebrows like tufts of cumulus.

"This is Judge Harold Jensen," Craine said. "Judge Jensen previously held this position. He's sitting in to assure the interests of the estate are maintained."

Jensen took a small leather sofa against the wall, and Craine rose to bring him one of the sheaves of paper. Jensen turned his gaze to Adam Kubiac, his water-blue eyes scanning Adam from head to foot. "These are difficult times," he said, putting half-glasses over a long and aquiline nose. "And all aspects of legality must be observed, especially in something as important as the transfer of an estate. Is that not right, Mr Kubiac?"

"Uh, y-yes s-s-sir."

"That said, the terms are quite, uh, straightforward. You're sure you're fine without your own representation, Mr Kubiac? Another legal adviser, perhaps?" The blue eyes bored into Kubiac.

Kubiac waved the suggestion away with a shaky hand. Jensen opened his file and retrieved the slender sheaf of pages comprising the last will and testament of Elijah Kubiac. He studied the contents briefly, shaking his head. His eyes lifted to Kubiac.

"Tell me, Mr Kubiac … Did your father ever share with you the contents of this instrument?"

"*If you keep acting like this Adam, I swear I'll change my will,*" Eli Kubiac screamed in Adam's head. "*You'll get what you've contributed to this family … a fucking dollar. I'll send the rest to institutions that won't squander it like you're squandering your life … Think about it, Adam. I could change my will in minutes. Think about the consequences of continuing this kind of behavior, Adam. And then, please, please, please grow up …*"

Kubiac closed his eyes and swallowed hard. "Nossir."

"I guess there's nothing more to say," Jensen sighed. "I'm going to skip all the wherefores and whereases. That all right, son?"

"Yessir," Kubiac said, his words the weight of vapor.

Jensen stared at Adam Kubiac, then removed his glasses and re-tucked them in his pocket. He stood and walked to Adam, extending his hand.

"Happy Birthday, Mr Kubiac. You now own monies and properties totalling over twenty million dollars. I hope it helps assuage your grief to know your father put such faith in you."

49

We were in a shadowy warehouse, tires piled against the concrete walls, wooden boxes spread willy-nilly. It smelled of dust and oil. We added the reek of fear. We had been roughly sat on the floor against a wall. Though our hands and feet had been bound, we hadn't been gagged, which told me we were far from the range of ears. Escheverría appeared in a doorway across the wide room. He wore jeans and a sleeveless tee shirt, his shoulders like beef roasts.

"What's going on, Ramon?" I said.

Escheverría spit on the floor. His gaze moved between the three of us and held on mine. "You can consider that while we wait for the truck that will take you to the desert. You can wonder that while my crew digs your graves. You can guess right up until the moment my bullet splits your forehead."

He turned and disappeared through the port. We heard an outer door open and the click of entering shoes crossing the floor. Escheverría laughed, like pleased with something. A throaty chuckle followed. A woman's voice.

"The three of them?" the female voice said.

"Wrapped tight and ready to visit the desert." Escheverría.

"The vehicle?"

"A fruit truck often seen on the roads, but with a double purpose. It should be here in minutes."

"There can be no mistakes," the female voice said, strong and assured. "It must all be over today."

Footsteps approached the door and a woman entered the room, tall and striking and wearing a cream pantsuit with quasi-masculine tailoring. She wore a sparkly silk scarf around her long neck.

Candace Klebbin, the administrative director of DataSĀF. She crossed her arms and smiled at Novarro.

"How does it feel," she said, "to have lost?"

"How does it feel," Novarro countered, "to be nuts?"

Klebbin's eyes were cold brown dots as dead as the lens of a camera. I realized that all Klebbin had presented to us, to everyone around her, was false. She was likely a full-blown sociopath, perhaps brilliant, as dedicated and driven as a typhoon.

And maybe as unstoppable.

"The truck's almost here," Escheverría called. "Time to boogie."

Klebbin showed no sign of leaving and I figured it was cat-and-mouse time, a need of many sociopaths when they feel they've won. Something within that vast emptiness needs to crow. I countered with a derisive laugh.

"What?" she said, walking to me and looking down.

"I've been in this business long enough to know you and Ramon are operating mid-range minds in a big-mind world. The problem with mid-range minds is they always think they're bigger than they are. Whatever you're doing will fall apart."

The one thing all sociopaths share is extreme narcissism, megalomania. Anything or anyone diminishing their claim to total control and genius thinking insults their being. I was challenging her superiority, pushing buttons.

The eyes tightened. "You're a worm wriggling on my floor, Ryder. You know nothing."

I managed a chuckle. "I know fifteen years of dealing with common crooks. I know how card houses fall apart in a breeze."

She lowered to a crouch and held thumb and forefinger a half inch apart. "Really? I know where $20,000,000 is, and I'm this far from getting it."

I did perplexed. It could keep her talking. Klebbin needed to wallow in triumph, to explain her genius to the lowly vanquished. "Twenty-million ..."

"American dollars," she finished. "Ours."

"How?"

"Candace," Escheverría called from the front. "The truck is pulling in. We must leave."

"*Momentito*, Ramon," Klebbin called. She turned the eyes to us. "DataSĀF started as three units, one for legal firms, one for business, one for municipal organizations, but there was no reason for specialization: it all goes to the cloud, and DataSĀF is the biggest cloud-storage facility in the Southwest."

"Right," Novarro said. "I read your stinking brochure: a bazillion gigawigs."

"We stored information for Dr Meridien. We also stored information for the Phoenix Police Department. It turned out that we even stored information for a lawyer named T. Jefferson Cottrell."

"Make sense," I said, pretending it was all new to us and needing to hear what we'd missed.

"I'm making excellent sense, Detective Ryder. Maybe your mid-level brain isn't capable of understanding."

"Enlighten poor dumb me."

"Until very recently, my daughter, Rosa, was one of Meridien's patients. I wanted to track Rosa's progress. Doctor–patient confidentiality kept Meridien from telling me much, so I opened Meridien's DataSĀF account and looked at Rosa's records. The subject and detail were quite interesting, so I read other patient files, including a particularly fascinating one, detailing sessions with a little lost boy with daddy issues and a $20,000,000 inheritance that he often bragged about to Meridien. The amount took my breath away. So I kept track of each of little Adam's sessions."

"Twenty million is a lot of reasons to keep track," I said.

"When Daddy died, the money would go to Adam. But Daddy might have lived another twenty or thirty years."

Novarro said: "To hurry things up you sent Escheverría."

The robotic eyes swiveled to Novarro. "I didn't know Ramon then. Our partnership was yet to come. This was hands-on."

Novarro said: "You were the woman in the motel room with Eli Kubiac."

Klebbin clapped her hands in slow applause. "He was a horny old goat. I fucked him senseless while pouring liquor into his slobbering mouth."

"Then the H," I said. "High-powered and mixed with fentanyl."

Klebbin laughed. "It was like he'd been hit with a hammer: His eyes rolled back and he became a foam dispenser. I scattered drugs about and retreated, just loudly enough to draw eyes."

"Candace!" Escheverría called. "Time to *vamos*."

"*Momentito*, Ramon!" Klebbin yelled, high on her story, regaling in victory.

"Back to the kid," I said.

"I was prepared to wait until Adam came into the money on his eighteenth birthday, then separate the two. I was thinking of something appealing to greed … an incredible investment opportunity, double his money in a year, that sort of thing."

I nodded. "It worked for Bernie Madoff."

"Then, three weeks ago, Adam went to Meridien's howling about how he had been screwed out of his money. How he was only going to get a dollar. Naturally, that caught my attention."

"No doubt."

"I looked up the lawyer's name and – surprise! – found Jefferson Cottrell had kept his files with our JuriSĀF division for seven years. But over a third of the law offices in the Southwest use our data-storage services. Still a nice bit of luck."

"You found much of interest in Cottrell's files, I expect."

"I entered Cottrell's files on Eli Kubiac's account and found two wills: one leaving Adam everything Eli owned, basically twenty-million-plus in cash, stocks and bonds and property, another leaving squat to kiddy-boy, everything to various charities and foundations. But number two was fake, with only one use, according to Cottrell's notes. He kept excellent notes."

Novarro saw it immediately. "To hold over the son."

"Adam was hard to handle. Lazy. Angry. Self-absorbed. Deliberately disruptive. Eli Kubiac had planned to use the will as a threat of last resort: 'Act like an adult, Adam, or end up with a dollar.'"

"Looking through Cottrell's files I quickly figured out lawyer-boy had actually printed out the will and employed Daddy's ruse. Cottrell obviously planned to extort a good portion of the money by saying he'd change the instrument if paid enough. Cottrell used a spicy little con artist to keep watch on Kubiac and keep him in line: Terri Isfording, temporarily named Zoe Isbergen. They'd met when Cottrell had handled her extortion case three years back."

"And then you inserted yourself into the scheme. Easy, from your position in the cloud."

"Like I said, I saw the real will, and I saw the false will Eli Kubiac had drawn up, but never actually used. A change of heart perhaps. The fake could never have been entered in probate. It had intentional mistakes to avoid that possibility. But Adam believed it when Cottrell showed it to him. And Daddy died before he could have the fake destroyed."

"All Cottrell needed to con Adam Kubiac."

"Cottrell and his little vixen were trying to slice off half the money." Klebbin shook her head. "Imagine leaving ten mill on the table. Such small-time thinking."

"You obviously had bigger ideas," I said. *Keep her crowing.*

"Oh, goodness yes, Detective. I armed Rosa with facts about Kubiac's pathetic little life and, using tidbits I'd gleaned from

Adam's sessions, she gained his trust in a day. When he trusted Rosa, I sent Ramon to scare little Zoe away. We improvised as we went, finally settling on a course of action that eliminated Cottrell, and an attendant idea that will make it easy to get money from Adam. He's going to hand it over." She looked at her watch. "Which is set to happen just a few of hours from now."

Novarro came to the bottom line. "So in the end, Adam Kubiac was always going to get the money."

Klebbin looked down in smug affirmation. "Kubiac never *wasn't* the sole beneficiary of Daddy's will. Of course, with Daddy dead and Cottrell working his con, Adam never knew that."

Escheverría was at the door. "The truck is outside, Candace. My men will take it from here."

"Why the killing?" Novarro said. "Why kill Meridien's patients?"

"They were the only ones who knew my daughter wasn't Catherine Maruyama. A chance meeting, a communication between people in the group, a casual text with photo, it could have been all over. I didn't want my $20,000,000 to evaporate."

"The kids didn't communicate," I said angrily. "They weren't that tight."

An amused shrug, death meaningless to a machine like Klebbin. "Maybe the chance of being discovered was one in fifty. But I wasn't about to jeopardize $20,000,000, no matter what the odds."

"You're a monster," Novarro said to the retreating back.

Klebbin angled her head back toward Novarro, her smile as hard and cold as the reaper's blade.

"And you're a hide-bound little rodent condemned to scurry across the floor waving your badge and gun and pretending you mean something to someone." She wiggled her fingertips. "Adios, people. Enjoy your trip to the desert."

We were marched into the rear of a box truck with a twenty-four-foot trailer, shoved roughly to the front. The outside of the trailer was emblazoned with the words *Southwestern Produce Co-op,* the subscript saying, *Better produce for Less*! A cornucopia spilling out tomatoes, green beans and melons was below that. As trucks go, it was innocent, one more working vehicle on the road.

We were shoved to the front. One of the gangbangers ran his hand to the side of the steel panel and pulled. The seeming front wall of the trailer swung open to reveal a foot-deep space, a hidden repository for smuggling drugs and humans. The inside was padded with acoustic fabric. I doubted any yells would be heard above the sound of the diesel engine.

"Inside," the *cholo* grunted, pushing us against the true front of the trailer. He knocked on the panel. "The cab is right there. If we hear any sound we will pull over and kill you." His eyes said he meant it.

The false panel swung shut and we were standing shoulder to shoulder in darkness. We stood and listened to a flurry of footsteps and activity on the other side of the panel, and I realized crates of vegetables were being stacked against the panel, dressing for the subterfuge. Anyone opening the rear door would see a cargo bay loaded with veggies.

Escheverría had thought of everything.

"Are you all right?" I said as the engine fired up and we felt motion. I struggled against my bindings but no mistakes had been made there, the ties tight and unyielding. Novarro tried the same, but her slumping shoulders told me she'd come to the same conclusion: no escape.

"I'm so sorry, Carson," she whispered and we struggled to stay standing through stops and starts and turns.

"It was my case, Tasha," I said into the rocking dark as the truck gained speed. "You had Meridien, I had Bowers and Warbley. When Dr Meridien heard Adam Kubiac ranting about being cut out of the will, she suspected something had gone awry. Eli Kubiac had told Dr Meridien he was having a fake will drafted.

But she was under the impression that it was a last-ditch effort to effect change in Adam. And she was also under the impression that Eli Kubiac hadn't reached the point of using the false will to threaten his son. But she couldn't be sure; Eli Kubiac was volatile. He could easily have gotten fed up and shown Adam the fake will.

"So going to the authorities—"

"Going to the authorities presented an ethical problem, a violation of doctor–patient privilege. And what would she tell them? 'I think a crime may be being committed, but then again, not necessarily.' Was a suspicion worth violating a sacred oath? So she confided in Bowers, who spoke to Warbley."

"No loose ends for Klebbin," Novarro said.

"And Escheverría as well. He was the perfect partner in an enterprise demanding cold and brutal executions. She probably found him in PPD investigative files and made a proposition, a big cut for the killer."

"You all right, Ben?" Novarro said to her brother. The kid grunted an affirmative sound. He was stronger than he seemed, and I was sad that his life was almost over. The truck veered around a corner and the ride became bumpier, and I knew we'd left the pavement for a desert road, one leading to a lonely place in the center of sandy nowhere.

* * *

Adam Kubiac was lying in bed playing *World of Warcraft* with a geek from the Ukraine. He wore spongy blue flip-flops, ragged cargo shorts and a stained tee shirt emblazoned with the words *Proud Nerd*. A knock came at the door. Kubiac sighed, quit the game, and slapped to the floor.

He opened the door to see a woman taller than he was, and old, like maybe forty. Something about her was familiar, but he didn't know why.

"Yeah?"

"May I come in, Mr Kubiac?"

"Why? Who are you? You look famili—"

She walked past him, closed the door and set the lock.

"What the fuck are you do—?"

She spun to him. "I want your complete attention, Adam. I have a job for you."

"Look, lady, I don't know you and I don't—"

"You're now in possession of $27,000,000, Mr Kubiac. And a house worth another $3,000,000."

"How the hell do you know that?"

She ignored the question. "Adam, I need you to transfer your money to another account."

Kubiac stared. "What the fuck are you talking about, bitch?"

"Do it, Adam," said a voice behind Kubiac. He spun to see Catherine Maruyama entering from the door to the adjoining suite.

"Cat?" Kubiac said, eyes wide. "What?"

Her face was impassive. "You have to do what she says, Adam. There's no alternative. Mommy knows best."

"Mommy?" he echoed. "*Mommy?* What is GOING ON?"

The tall woman pressed a slip of paper into Kubiac's hand. "Transfer the money to this account, Mr Kubiac. It's that simple."

He yanked his hand away, the slip falling to the carpet. "NO FUCKING WAY! YOU CAN'T MAKE ME DO IT!" He pulled out his phone. "I'M CALLING THE POLICE!"

The woman calmly held up an 8 x 10 photograph of a weapon with a box beside it. "You recognize this, of course, Mr Kubiac. An Ambush 300 Blackout rifle equipped with a scope. A Silencer. And a carton of bullets."

Kubiac froze at the sight of the rifle. "Wh-what is this?"

Maruyama stepped close, a half smile on her lips. "We have the gun, Adam. It has your fingerprints all over it. You bought the rifle, scope, and ammunition at a gun store that not only has a receipt of the transaction, but video footage. Need I explain that within 24 hours of you buying that gun, T. Jefferson Cottrell was shot dead in the desert."

There's something wrong with her eyes, Kubiac's mind said. *They look like ice feels.*

"You … it was your idea! You encouraged me. You told me to—"

A smile. "Actually, Adam, it was your idea. I kept trying to talk you out of it, remember?"

Kubiac stared, mouth open, hands shaking.

"You're a murderer, Adam," she continued. "A simple ballistics test will match your gun with the bullet removed from T. Jefferson Cottrell. Arizona has the death penalty. You may not be put to death, but you'll be in prison the rest of your life. Twenty million dollars will be meaningless to you."

Kubiac's eyes bounced from one woman to the other. "You're … you're stealing my money."

"You get to keep the house, Adam," Maruyama said. "That's worth plenty."

"You wuh-won't do it … the rifle."

The woman took Kubiac's chin and turned his face to hers. "If we're not going to get the money, Adam, we're going to make sure you don't get the money either. The rifle and everything else goes to the police immediately. If you fuck this up, life as you know it is over."

"I-I n-n-n-need time to—"

A head-shake. "Time's up, Adam. You need to go to the bank and get this done. Rosa will go with you."

Kubiac spun to Maruyama. "Rosa? Is that your real name, Rosa? P-p-people talked about a R-Rosa who was in one of Muh-Meridien's groups. She wuh-was a psycho."

Rosa Klebbin's hand slashed out and cracked Kubiac's chin, spinning him into the wall. "Don't be a moron, Adam," the former Catherine Maruyama said. "Go put on your big-boy clothes and let's get this over with."

50

A half hour passed in the shaking, quivering truck. The heat in the enclosed space was withering. Our mouths were too dry to talk. Sweat rolled down my face. We had been off-road for the last fifteen minutes judging by the sounds from the tires and the rough terrain.

The truck's brakes squealed and we stopped. The engine rattled off. The cab doors opened at our backs.

"Easy," I whispered to my companions. "Tasha, look for any opening. Any chance to grab a gun. Take it, no matter how slim."

I heard her breath. "You got it."

We heard the rear gate of the truck creak open. Footsteps crossed the slatted floor moving aside produce boxes as they went. After a minute the false front of the trailer was pulled away. The light hurt my eyes.

"Out," a hulking thug spat, pulling first Ben from the compartment, then Novarro, and finally me. He and the two others roughhoused us to the ground and pushed us against the side of the trailer in the same order as inside: Novarro beside me, Ben beside her.

The terrain was barren save for desert vegetation. Piles of broken rock and low hummocks lay in all directions, effectively putting us in a low bowl perhaps a quarter mile in circumference. I saw mountains to the north. The three thugs smoked by the cab a few paces away, looking down the trace of road that had brought us here.

"Are we in Mexico?" I whispered.

A bark of ironic laugher from Novarro. "Those mountains? The Sierra Estrella. We're still in Maricopa County, southern end, just above Pima County. We're maybe thirty miles from downtown Phoenix."

"Shut up," one of the gangbangers snarled. "No talking."

Novarro looked at me. She started talking louder. 'What a shit thing, only forty miles from Phoenix and our only company a trio of stinking—"

One of the thugs stepped over and backhanded her. I dove at him from one side as Ben howled in from the other. But with our hands bound and feet hobbled all we did was end up on the ground with the thugs kicking at us.

"He's coming," one of the thugs said, pausing just before punting my head. "El Gila."

They pulled us back to our feet as a black SUV drove up with a trail of dust in its wake. Escheverría stepped from the passenger side, a triumphant grin on his face, a wicked black pistol in his hand. He crunched across the sand to within a dozen paces and aimed the muzzle at me like a pointer.

"Him," he said. "He goes first. Then the brother." He looked into my eyes and laughed. "We'll have a quick party with the woman." He looked at Novarro, held up between two of the thugs. She spat.

"Spirit," he said. "I like that."

Two of the thugs stood me up then stepped to the side. "Any last words?" Escheverría said, enjoying his moment. "You need to pray? Or cry for Mommy?"

I stared into the reptilian eyes. "Just gimme an answer, Ramon. How did Klebbin find you … an arrest record with the Phoenix cops, right?"

He shook his head. "Cottrell was my lawyer. Candace read Cottrell's confidential file on me and discovered my business of making people either pay or disappear. She came to me with an offer: do some jobs for her and I'd make $3,000,000." The teeth bared in a rictus of smile. "An offer I couldn't refuse."

"I'll give you four to let us go, Ramon. You can walk away."

"You don't have such money and we both know it."

Escheverría racked the slide on the weapon to put a round in the chamber. Oddly, I felt no fear. Only sadness. And sickness pooling in my stomach because my life would end on a dusty patch of sand at the hands of a psycho coated with gang and prison tattoos.

Escheverría raised the pistol. "Get on your knees," he commanded.

"Go fuck yourself," I said.

One of the gangsters kicked the back of my knee and I went down.

"Look at me," Escheverría said as he sighted down the barrel. He needed to be the last thing I saw on earth. I looked away.

"I said LOOK AT ME."

I calmed my face as if I were standing in a gentle breeze on some faraway island and my eyes looked everywhere but at him: I saw cirrus clouds drifting at the edge of the sky; heat rippling from the desert floor; a hawk in the air above a pair of saguaros; the low rocky rise in the near distance, on it a rippling mirage shaped like a man on a horse …

"Suit yourself." Escheverría laughed. "Adios, lawman."

I heard the shot and a single echo as the bullet slammed into me. All was whitehot pain and, an eye-blink later, the world collapsed into black.

* * *

318

Carrying a suitcase, Rosa Klebbin stepped over the body on the floor, wrinkling her nose at the thought of getting sticky blood on her new shoes. Blood seemed to be everywhere, like a paint can had exploded. She threw the suitcase on the sofa and checked again, making sure she had everything. Not that it mattered all that much; she could would soon be able to buy anything she needed, but that was a couple of days away, and she wanted to be comfortable on the trip.

Though she had packed the suitcase days earlier, it seemed she'd anticipated well and nothing needed to be added. Satisfied with her planning, she zipped it shut and walked to the door, again having to negotiate the blood on the floor. She looked down at the body and smiled.

"Nice meeting you," she said.

And was gone.

51

The void was a sucking, liquid darkness and I swam with it, going deeper until I found a place to hide, to sleep, to cover myself with shadows. And then, a hundred years later, someone lifted the edge of a shadow and peered underneath.

"I think he's finally coming around."

I blinked and noticed it had snowed, the whiteness blanketing everything. The white melted into shadow and form and became white blankets, the folds of a white pillow beside my head. I blinked again and saw an IV rack floating above me, tubes like clear fingers reaching to my body. I started, shifted, felt searing pain in my chest and shoulder. The pain was beautiful because it told me I was alive.

"Don't move, Carson. Just lay easy, buddy." Harry's voice.

I wrenched sideways and felt my chest scream in agony. Wonderful.

"I'll get the doctor." Tasha Novarro.

A man in a blue jacket entered and looked at the machines surrounding me. He was in his fifties with eyes blanked out white until I realized they were glasses reflecting sun through the wide window. He leaned low and the reflections became solicitous brown eyes.

"How are you feeling?"

"I hurt. What happened?"

"You took a round just below the clavicle. It punctured the lung, but missed important pulmonary plumbing by millimeters. You're lucky to be here." He turned to Harry and Novarro. "You can talk for a bit, but he needs a lot of rest." The doc disappeared.

I looked at Harry. Things were starting to make sense. "How bad?" I whispered.

"You're gonna get some fine vacation. And a couple months of rehab."

"Pour some ice water on my face." Water was my restorative.

I felt a splashing of cold water followed by a wiping with a towel. "Thanks," I said. "How? … what?"

Novarro leaned over me like a cloud radiating light. "Merle was just over the rise, Carson. He shot Escheverría from six hundred feet away and atop a horse. But Ramon pulled the trigger when he got hit."

I closed my eyes and saw again what I had thought would be the last thing I saw: a tiny and faraway cowboy on a horse.

I said: "It wasn't a mirage."

"Mirage? What?"

I waved it away. "Nothing. Escheverría … is he, is he—?" My mouth was too parched to continue. Novarro handed me the water.

A wry smile. "The infamous El Gila didn't wait until nightfall to release his grip on life, Carson. He kicked the bucket on the way to the hospital. A good day for the gene pool."

"Is Candace Klebbin in custody?"

"Candace is in the morgue."

My head jerked up to face her. "*What?*"

"Easy, pardner," She eased me back to the pillow. "When we got to her apartment she'd been shot in the head at very close range. Ballistics has already determined that the slug is from the same rifle used to kill Jeffrey Cottrell."

"Who killed Klebbin? Do you know?"

"It could only have been her daughter, Rosa."

My mouth drooped open. It was beyond words.

Novarro continued. "After killing Mama, little Rosa phoned an anonymous message to Maricopa County SD informing them that one Ramon Escheverría was in the south county desert whacking people. Rosa even gave map coordinates."

It didn't make sense. "Why the hell would Rosa send in the cavalry?"

"Money, of course, Carson. Rosa figured the cops would run into Escheverría on his way out of the desert and Mr Macho would go down fighting."

Ah. "Leaving the full $20,000,000 to Rosa," I said.

Novarro winked. "What Rosa didn't know was that Merle and four DEA agents were already in the south county looking for smugglers. They got there a lot faster than little Rosa planned. Merle rode over the ridge, pulled up the binocs, and realized Escheverría was two eyeblinks from executing you."

I'd been there before, having to make a snap decision followed by a snap gunshot, and suddenly realized there was more to Merle Castle than I had thought.

"I owe your former boyfriend my life," I said.

"Yep ... *former* boyfriend, which I think he's starting to realize. Maybe you thumped some sense into him. Anyway, just buy Merle a steak dinner and a case of beer and he'll consider it even."

"I will," I said, meaning it. My mind returned to the case, to Rosa Klebbin. "Killed her own mother?" I said, disbelief in my voice. "Cold as it gets."

"Remember Dr Meridien's last words regarding Rosa, 'what does Rosa's future hold?'"

I nodded. "She became a wind-up toy for Mommy. One even Mommy could no longer control. Where's Rosa now?"

"In the lockup. We nabbed her on her way to the Cayman

Islands. It's a long story and it'll wait. I want you to meet someone." She turned toward the door. "Adam?"

I canted my head to see a skinny kid in a white tee with an Apple logo, grubby brown cargo shorts and blue skateboarder shoes, one untied. He looked as goofy and awkward as a hobbled flamingo.

"So you're the mysterious Adam Kubiac?" I said.

He hemmed and hawed toward me. "I uh, want to thank you for what you did to save my money. Did they tell you the Feds got it back?"

"Not yet. But good. I'm glad."

"I got suckered," he said, having a hard time meeting my eyes. "Twice. Especially with Cat – I mean Rosa. It was like she was me. I felt … I felt …"

Novarro nodded. "Like I explained yesterday, Adam, she and her mother studied all of your sessions with Dr Meridien. Rosa Klebbin knew how to press all your buttons. She created a fake father to mimic your father, a way to gain your empathy and your trust. In a way, she became you."

The kid kicked at the floor. "Well, yeah, y'know … like, thanks again." He flicked a quick wave, turned and was gone.

I looked at Novarro who sighed and shook her head.

"The kid's about twelve emotionally. Another reason Cottrell and the Klebbins were able to yank him around like a puppet."

"I've met toasters with more charm," I said, hearing the kid's retreating shoes squeak down the hall. "Where from here?"

Harry moved closer. "I'm heading back to Miami directly. You're here until you get released from rehab, when Roy demands you take a minimum six weeks of vacation. Real vacation this time."

"Do I have any choice?"

"No," Novarro said, standing above me like a beaming sun. "When you leave here you're coming to my place. Ben's re-registered in school, but he'll be home for several hours each day and able to care for you until you can." She winked. "And, of course, I'll be there at night."

"Settled." Harry clapped the huge hands. "I'll be heading back to Miami this after—"

We heard a fierce whining sound from outside, then a scream of tires on asphalt.

"Jesus," I said, looking toward the window. "What the hell is that?"

Harry went to the window and looked down on the parking lot two stories below. "It seems Adam Kubiac is taking his leave in what looks to be a brand-new Ferrari."

Novarro went to the window and watched. When the engine whine and screeching tires faded in the distance, she turned to me. "*Te'aho'u'nona' odango*," she said, the dark hair flowing as she shook her head.

I thought a moment and translated. "The world is one screwy place?"

She patted my hand and leaned to kiss my forehead.

"You're getting good at this."

KILLER
READS

DISCOVER THE BEST
IN CRIME AND THRILLER

Follow us on social media to
get to know the team behind
the books, enter exclusive
giveaways, learn about the
latest competitions, hear from
our authors, and lots more:

/KillerReads  /KillerReads